# Bolan grabbed the H&K P-7 from the nightstand

Aiming at the door, he waited for the kick. Instead, a key scratched into the lock. The warrior rolled from the bed and slipped through the door onto the balcony.

Bolan frowned. Keys weren't given out lightly by Russian hotel clerks, which meant that the three men filing into his room had connections. The insignia on their caps pegged them as local police. But that made no sense. Only a few people knew he was in Russia, and he'd done nothing to attract the attention of the authorities.

Two of the intruders held Makarov pistols, and the third toted a Colt AR-15. The presence of the American weapon sent a caution light flashing through the Executioner's brain. Then one of the men turned to his companions and said in perfect English, ''Where the hell is he?''

Those words sealed the man's fate. Bolan triggered the H&K as he stepped in front of the glass door. His first round drilled the closest gunner in the temple. A double punch took out the survivors before they could bring their weapons into play.

In the sudden silence, Bolan realized there was a leak somewhere, and not just within Russian Intelligence. This one could be laid at the President's door.

DON PENDLETON's

# MACK BOLAN.

# ONSLAUGHT

A GOLD EAGLE BOOK FROM

# WORLDWIDE.

TORONTO • NEW YORK • LONDON
AMSTERDAM • PARIS • SYDNEY • HAMBURG
STOCKHOLM • ATHENS • TOKYO • MILAN
MADRID • WARSAW • BUDAPEST • AUCKLAND

First edition May 1993

ISBN 0-373-61431-4

Special thanks and acknowledgment to
Jerry VanCook for his contribution to this work.

ONSLAUGHT

None can love freedom heartily but good men; the rest love not freedom, but licence.
                                    —John Milton, 1649


Courage isn't the absence of fear—it's the ability to push through it, the fortitude to do what has to be done in spite of the odds.
                                    —Mack Bolan

# PROLOGUE

Maniacal laughter drifted up from the lagoon.

Harmon Pinder glanced through the screen into the darkness. The loon was nowhere to be seen, hidden somewhere among the swaying palm trees that dotted the banks of the remote Bahamian island.

Pinder turned back to the dining room, where ten men sat around the table. He circled them, pouring wine into their crystal glasses. His thick shoulders fought against the white steward's jacket that Mario Hernandez had given him. The coat was too tight, and he longed for the loose cotton tunic he had worn as a Bahamian police officer until his retirement three weeks earlier.

Pinder felt a twinge of guilt shoot through his chest as he bent to fill the glass of the man Hernandez had called "Don Joseph." The title, and the man's thick New York accent, could mean only one thing: he was Don Joseph Esposito, the head of the most powerful Mafia Family in America.

Other faces seated around the table recalled police intelligence photos to Pinder's mind—Kurt Kaufman of Argentina, Luis Carranza of Bolivia and, of course, Hernandez himself, from Colombia. All were familiar to the ex-cop as the leaders of mighty South American drug cartels.

Pinder emptied the bottle. He eyed the rest of the men clandestinely as he twirled the corkscrew into a new cork. He recognized none of the other faces, but he knew the men just the same. They had the same sharkish look in their eyes as Esposito and Hernandez. Whoever they were, they led powerful criminal organizations.

A sudden rush of shame enveloped the ex-cop.

He'd served thirty years, Pinder reminded himself as he resumed pouring. He'd done his part, and it was over. He didn't sell out by going to work for Hernandez.

Pinder filled the last glass. He draped the towel over his arm and took up a position in front of the hall door that led to the kitchen.

Mario Hernandez stood and raised his glass in salute. "We have come to terms, then, gentlemen?" he asked the others. "We will all share equally in both expenses and profits. But Don Joseph and I shall oversee the operation."

Kaufman spoke in a thick German-South American accent. "Who is the Russian agent you have recruited?"

Hernandez smiled. "Our new relationship, Señor Kaufman, must be built on trust. In order to ensure the man's identity remains confidential, I feel that is best kept between Don Joseph and myself."

Kaufman's face reddened. "But—"

Hernandez set his glass down. "My silence is not meant to be taken as an insult. Let us leave the subject with the fact that our contact is in a position high enough to be of value."

Murmurs of consent filled the room as the rest of the men nodded agreement. Kaufman dropped his gaze to the table.

Hernandez smiled, lifting his glass once more. "Let us drink to our new alliance. To the New Brotherhood."

Halfway through the meal, Hernandez's right-hand man, Jake Pool, burst through the dining room door. Pinder watched curiously as the tall, slender American in the black cowboy hat bent to whisper in his master's ear.

Hernandez's eyes fell briefly on Pinder. The drug lord whispered back to Pool, then returned to his food. Pinder wondered briefly what had happened, then forced the curiosity from his mind. He was no longer a police officer and whatever it was didn't concern him.

Erich, the German waiter, brought out a flaming tray of Bananas Foster as Pinder resumed his duties, changing the wineglasses for brandy snifters and pouring two inches of Rémy Martin VSOP cognac into each vessel.

When the meal was over, Hernandez stood and rang the small bell next to his plate.

Pool returned to the room.

"We have had an unexpected development," Hernandez said, smiling. "But it will provide us with a small bit of entertainment." He turned to Pinder, and all eyes in the room followed his. "I am afraid, Señor Pinder, that you were not completely honest with me when I hired you a few days ago."

Pinder felt the blood rush to his cheeks. He hadn't told Hernandez he was a retired police officer, knowing it might prejudice the man against hiring him. Now, he realized what a serious mistake he had made.

Hernandez turned to Pool. "Most of you have met my personal bodyguard, Señor Pool. But none of you has witnessed his abilities. Señor Pool is a student of America's Old West, of a man known as Wild Bill Hickock in particular. It is my suspicion, however, that Jake Pool's abilities have probably surpassed that of the legendary American gunfighter."

Pool shoved his black frock coat back over the hand-tooled Western gun belt on his hips. The gleam of nickeled steel seemed to fill the room. Pool's tiny black pupils were devoid of emotion, but his handlebar mustache twisted up into a grin as he stared at Harmon Pinder.

"It appears, gentlemen," Hernandez went on, "that my new wine steward is a Bahamian police officer."

Twenty eyes glared toward Pinder, who dropped the towel. "Señor Hernandez," the ex-cop said, "I *retired*. I came to you only because I needed a supplemental income for—"

"So *you* say," Hernandez said. "But we cannot afford to take chances." He turned toward Pool. "Señor Pool, if you please."

The ex-Bahamian cop saw a blur of shiny silver as Pool's nickel-plated revolvers leaped from their holsters. Then the silver turned to sparkles of red, orange and blue.

Then all color faded from Harmon Pinder's brain, and he saw only black.

ROTISLAV PUGACHEV heard what sounded like cannons on the other side of the window. He watched in horror as blood splashed through the crack between the frame and the door, splattering his face and jacket. In the dining room he heard Hernandez say, "Jake, please tell Erich to come and clean up this mess."

Pugachev pivoted toward the kitchen, pulling the microcassette recorder from the side pocket of his jacket and dropping it into his trousers. The bloody coat came off as he ran.

The loud bangs of pots hitting pans met his ears as Pugachev entered the kitchen. The cook ignored him as Pugachev dropped his soiled jacket in the trash, bent hurriedly over the sink and scrubbed the blood from his eyes with tap water. He was drying his face when Jake Pool stuck his head through the door.

"Some janitor work in the chow hall for you, Erich. Get your ass in there and get it done."

"*Ja.*"

Pugachev slipped into a clean jacket. He glanced quickly at the cook, made sure the man was still preoccupied, then transferred the recorder to the new jacket.

A sudden thought struck Pugachev as he walked back down the hall to the dining room. Sweat broke on his forehead, and his chest fluttered with fear.

Hernandez had said the New Brotherhood had a contact within Russian Intelligence. A *high* contact. But he hadn't named any names. The traitor could be any of several dozen men.

Pugachev sighed quietly. Thank God that due to the sensitivity of the mission, he was reporting directly to the Russian president himself. At least, for the time being, he was still safe.

# CHAPTER ONE

Niklai Tachek had a frightful thought as he stood to address the men seated around the conference table in his Kremlin office.

He suddenly realized he was about to preside over a meeting not so different from the one their enemy had had the night before.

Tachek raised the water glass to his lips and drank slowly, watching the hard faces, using the water more as a stall for time than to moisten his dry throat.

He had no idea what kind of reception he'd get for the plan he was about to propose. He worried about their response, because without their cooperation, his nation—all of their nations—were doomed.

On the surface the men seated around him looked as if they had little in common. The Slavs—the new presidents of Ukraine and Belorussia—wore conservative gray suits like himself. The leaders of the Muslim nations had returned to the formal robes and headdress of their ancestors, looking to Tachek like men on their way to a cast party of *Lawrence of Arabia*. And President Kodzhor of Georgia had split the difference, wearing a navy suit but adding a colorful red and black *keffiyeh*.

They looked different, Tachek thought, perhaps *were* different in many ways. But the Russian president knew that the men seated before him had at least one thing in common.

They were tough. They had been through hell, and they hadn't escaped that hell by being foolish, naive or easily led. They landed on their feet to lead the countries that now made up the new Commonwealth of Independent States by being shrewd and hard to fool.

No, these men wouldn't be easily duped. But then, for the first time in many years, the Russian wasn't trying to dupe them.

Tachek set the glass back on the table. "Gentlemen," he said. "Thank you for coming at such short notice. I know it was not easy to fit this meeting into your busy schedules."

Gennady Zorobulis, the new president of Belorussia, spoke up immediately. "You are correct, President Tachek. It was difficult to leave the *coordinating center* in Minsk with so many new duties to perform."

The Russian suppressed a sarcastic smile at Zorobulis's emphasis on "coordinating center." In their excitement to erase the memory of forty-five years of Soviet totalitarianism, the founders of the Commonwealth had made a hasty and premature decision to move the seat of power from Moscow to Minsk, a city in Belorussia that could boast only two major hotels. Minsk was simply too small, not to mention less centrally located than Moscow, and for those two reasons business usually still took place at the Kremlin.

Minsk had become the "coordinating center" in name only. True power remained in Moscow, and always would, regardless of what form the government took.

Tachek allowed the smile to show through, but made sure it was the warm smile of one ally to another. "I appreciate your inconvenience, President Zorobulis," he said, then looked up to address the table as a whole. "Gentlemen, the United States is no longer our enemy. But we now face a threat from America that is far more real than what we once feared from the U.S." He cleared his throat. "I am telling you nothing new when I say that organized crime has already taken a foothold in our nations during these times of readjustment. But what we have seen so far has been nothing compared to what is coming. And what is coming threatens to destroy all that we have worked so hard to build." He paused for effect, then went on in a low voice. "Last night, leaders of the top Mafia Families in North America met with representatives of South American drug cartels. They have formed an alliance known as the New Brotherhood, and intend to move into our nations with a vengeance."

A man in a black-and-white-checked *keffiyeh* snorted. He stood at the other end of the table. "And how can you be so sure?" the President of Uzbekistan asked.

Tachek hesitated. Now came the sensitive part. He cleared his throat again. "A former KGB mole, now in the employment of Russian Intelligence, has infiltrated the coalition."

Murmurs and grumbles echoed through the office, and Tachek knew he had said the "black" magic word. Or letters, really. Russia had always been the stronghold of the oppressive KGB, and the very thought of the now-defunct secret police might be enough to put the new leaders off the project. But he had sworn to himself he'd be honest and tell these men all he could without risking the security of the plan he had in mind.

Before the discontent could get out of hand, he said, "I assure you, the mole is loyal to Russia, and in turn, to the Commonwealth."

President Poltava of Ukraine now took his turn. "Please, President Tachek. We are all busy men. And we are aware that the Mafia and other similar organizations have been anxious to steal what little we do have during these times of famine and unrest. You have obviously thought this out, or you would not have called us here. Please, tell us what you want from us, then let us decide."

Tachek took a deep breath. "Cooperation," he said. "We are forced to deal with an enemy much different than those we have prepared for in the past. Simply put, I do not think we know how to handle it ourselves. I have taken the liberty of already calling Washington, and the American President has suggested a plan of action. He has agreed to attempt to enlist a man who is an expert at dealing with both the Mafia and cartels. I ask that you allow me to coordinate the mission, and—"

"Who is this man?" Zorobulis demanded.

Tachek hesitated. "I cannot say."

More grumbles sounded around the table.

Finally Poltava said, "President Tachek, what you ask is most unusual. There is unrest in all of our countries, and *all* of our political positions are on shaky grounds. Do you expect us to allow this man into our countries without knowing his identity? How do you know he is not a member of this Mafia himself?"

"I know," Tachek said, "because I know this man. At least, I know who he is, what he has done and what he is capable of doing. True, he was once a strong enemy, but I firmly believe that now he might be our only chance. More than that, I cannot say. I ask that you trust me." He stopped talking momentarily, then said, "I know you will want to discuss this among yourselves, for what I ask of you is great. In the spirit of democracy, for which we have all fought so long and hard, I will leave the room." Before anyone could say more, he walked briskly to the door and stepped into the hall.

Tachek hurried down the hall to the coffee machine, sweat breaking out on his forehead. What he had presented to the other leaders of the Commonwealth was the only possible way to stop the New Brotherhood.

But would they understand that? Everything he had told them was the truth.

But after seventy years of lies, treachery and deceit, would any of them now recognize the truth when they heard it?

Tachek drank his coffee, the heat and caffeine causing him to sweat even more. He gave them fifteen minutes, then walked back down the hall to the door, opened it and returned to the head of the table.

"Gentlemen?" he said.

There was a long pause, then Poltava said, "Go ahead."

The rest of the heads nodded.

"But God help you," Zorobulis interjected, "God help us all if this is a mistake."

Tachek was suddenly taken aback. In his forty years as a Soviet leader he had never heard God referred to at a meeting such as this, let alone asked for help.

"Then I will begin immediately," he said. "And I believe you are correct, President Zorobulis. I believe that God may indeed finally be willing to help us."

President Farhad nodded. The narrow eyes, set deep in his dark features, flashed over his long nose as he spoke. "God *will* be with us," he said. "But we will put our faith in this mysterious American of yours, as well."

THE FOOTSTEPS IN THE HALL outside Room 288 of Moscow's Metropole Hotel were soft, made by men not wanting to be heard.

Mack Bolan closed the Russian Intelligence file and slipped it between the mattress and box springs. He reached across the bed to the nightstand for the Heckler & Koch P-7. The weapon had been issued to him less than an hour earlier at the Kremlin, by Russian president Niklai Tachek himself.

Aiming at the door, the man known as the Executioner waited for the kick. Instead he heard whispers, then a key scratched into the lock.

A key.

Bolan rolled from the bed and slipped through the sliding glass door to the balcony. Keys weren't given out lightly by Russian hotel clerks, which meant whoever was about to enter the room had influence and connections. Most likely it would be the local police, the *militsya*.

Staying to the side of the glass, the Executioner peered back around the corner as the door to the hall opened.

The tall rangy man who burst into the room wasn't *militsya*. As the intruder hurried toward the bed, Bolan saw three thin stripes on the shoulders of his uniform. The stripes, and the letters BB on his cap, denoted him as a sergeant of the Russian Ministry of State Security.

The Makarov pistol in the sergeant's hand tracked back and forth as he scanned the empty room.

Bolan frowned as he watched a captain join the sergeant next to the bed. It made no sense. Only five other people in the world knew the Executioner was in Moscow—Tachek, his top aide, Alexandr Solomentsev, Russian Military Intelligence Colonel Katerina Kerensky, the President of the United States and Hal Brognola. The warrior had done nothing to attract the attention of authorities since arriving. Why were Russian police entering his room?

The third uniformed man who stepped through the door answered the Executioner's questions. He wore the rank of lieutenant, and the uniform looked as authentic as those of the sergeant and captain. But the lieutenant didn't carry a Makarov. He wielded a Colt AR-15.

The American weapon sent an amber caution light flashing through Bolan's brain. The lights turned red as the sergeant turned back to the door and said, "Where the fuck is he?"

In English.

With those words the man sealed his doom. Bolan depressed the H&K's squeeze cocker as he stepped in front of the glass, and flame burst from the short stubby barrel. The sliding door shattered into thousands of shards as the Executioner's first round drilled through the glass to hit the sergeant's russet hatband.

The man with the AR-15 jumped to the side as Bolan fired again. A 9 mm bullet ripped through the rifleman's knuckles, and his weapon fell to the floor. As his bloody fingers scrambled under his coat for some unseen weapon, the warrior squeezed the trigger twice more, sending a double-tap of 9 mm rounds into the gunner's chest.

The "captain" turned to the balcony door, firing his Makarov. The round sailed over the Executioner's shoulder as Bolan dived back through the broken glass and rolled behind the bed. Counting a quick one-two, he rose from cover, the squeeze cocker gripped in both hands.

The odor of cordite burned the warrior's nostrils as he drilled three raging hollowpoints into the phony policeman's head, throat and chest.

Sudden silence returned to the room.

Bolan moved quickly to the hall door, the H&K leading the way. The corridor was clear.

Hurrying back to the dead man on the bed, the Executioner dug through the pockets of the uniform for identification. Nothing. He came up just as empty with the other two men. But the captain's wrist sported a gold Rolex watch.

A thousand-dollar timepiece for a Russian military man?

Bolan didn't think so. He had no idea who the three men were, but he knew who they *weren't*. Russian Ministry of State Security officers didn't carry American-made assault rifles, and they didn't wear Rolexes.

And if they ever used the expression "Where the fuck is he?" they said it in Russian.

Bolan returned to the bed. Lifting the mattress, he slid the H&K on top of the Russian Intelligence file. Then, pulling from his pocket a scrap of paper Tachek had given him, he hurried to the black rotary phone on the desk against the wall.

The Executioner knew he had only minutes. Someone on the floor would have already called the cops. This time, it *would* be the *militsya* that arrived.

And if he didn't reach Solomentsev or Kerensky before that happened . . .

Bolan lifted the receiver. There was a leak somewhere, all right. And not just from within the Russian Intelligence. The leak that had brought the phony police to his door had to have come from the president's office.

The Executioner had started to dial when the first Moscow *militsya* officer burst into the room.

"Halt! Do not move!" screamed the Russian cop, his pistol locked on the Executioner.

This time, the words were in Russian.

ALEXANDR SOLOMENTSEV squinted his eyes against the bright streetlights as he crossed Red Square. The area was still crowded with government officials tarrying at the many local after-work bars.

He passed the Hotel Moskva and continued down the street. He watched three men engaged in the time-honored Russian tradition known as "three-on-a-bottle." The earflaps of their rabbit-pelt *shrapki* dangling over their ears, the men guzzled vodka, resting between drinks only long enough to allow their comrades a turn. Solomentsev stared at the bottle as it floated between hands.

After the long grueling day with the president, and then the American, he was ready for a drink or two himself.

Solomentsev's mind flew back to the whirlwind events of the past few hours. He and RMI Colonel Katerina Kerensky had met the American, Michael Belasko, at Sheremetyevo airport and escorted him to the Kremlin. There, they had reviewed the plan of action both the leaders of America and Russia had agreed upon the day before.

With the dissolution of the Soviet empire had come freedom. And the door had been opened to crime. Now, an undercover Russian Intelligence mole had learned of a combined effort by North American Mafia and South American drug cartels to take advantage of that freedom. Tachek wanted it stopped.

The President of the United States did, too. He feared a sudden crime wave in the former USSR might shift the balance of power away from Tachek and his progressive ways, and return it to the hands of old-line authoritarians. He had readily volunteered to send a man he claimed had single-handedly come close to destroying the Mafia in America.

Solomentsev watched a drunk fall on the sidewalk as he hurried on along the street. Only a few short months before, alcoholism had been President Tachek's first priority. He had restricted the hours during which alcohol could be sold, but his actions had had little effect on consumption. It had simply increased the sales of black-market profiteers.

Alcohol was still high on Tachek's list. But now, he had bigger problems.

Solomentsev opened the glass door to the Ukrainian Café and entered. He paused to remove his hat and allow his eyes to adjust to the darkness. In the booth farthest from the door, he saw the familiar silhouette. Unbuttoning his coat, he crossed the room and caught himself smiling.

Colonel Pyotr Leskov of Russian Intelligence wore a wrinkled brown suit and a mashed and scarred fedora. During their ten-year friendship, Solomentsev had never seen him in any other clothes. The former KGB major had no need to look beneath the table to know that Leskov's feet would be covered by the heavy, scuffed, black brogans.

Solomentsev dropped into the booth across from his friend. Leskov had begun service under Stalin. He was a true believer in Communism, the Russian president's aide-de-camp knew.

Both of Leskov's hands were curled around a glass of chilled vodka. *"Dobryi den,"* he said, smiling up at Solomentsev.

"Good day," the younger man replied in Russian.

Without being told, the waiter appeared and set another glass in front of the new arrival.

"You are looking well, my young friend," Leskov grinned. "It appears that your new position agrees with you."

Solomentsev sighed wearily and raised his glass. "Looks can be deceiving," he said.

Leskov laughed. "Let us drink to your continued good health," he said, and both men drained their glasses.

Solomentsev felt the vodka burn its way down his throat and warm his stomach. Slowly the tension in his neck and shoulders began to disappear. "As usual these days, all hell has broken loose in the Kremlin." He caught himself and stopped abruptly, wishing he could bite back the words.

"Ah?" Leskov said, leaning forward. "And what is the president's concern these days? Has he discovered a family somewhere in Moscow that does not own a color TV? Perhaps the new McDonald's has run out of sesame-seed buns and our American hamburgers will not be genuine." Leskov spit to his side in disgust. "I am assuming you do not mean the usual petty problems—like ongoing treason in the Baltics."

Solomentsev chuckled nervously. "I meant nothing, actually. It is just that the daily pressure wears one down." He watched Leskov closely for a reaction.

Pyotr Leskov's eyes fell to the table. His face drew tight. "I have spent my life in the Committee for State Security, Alexandr," he said quietly. "I am familiar with matters that cannot be discussed with those not directly involved." The aging Russian Intelligence colonel's eyes flickered up, and Solomentsev saw the pain in the man's face. "You have been like a son to me," Leskov murmured. "Simply tell me that it is classified and you cannot speak of it. Do not shame an old man by lying to him."

Solomentsev felt his own shame as he stared back into the faded blue eyes. It was true. Pyotr Leskov had been like a second father to him. Indeed, had it not been for Leskov's influence, he wouldn't have risen so quickly through the ranks of what had been the KGB. Certainly he would never have been appointed to his present position as Tachek's chief aide.

"I am sorry, Pyotr," Solomentsev said. "You are right. I have been sworn to secrecy. And it was wrong of me to lie."

Leskov smiled wearily, then shrugged. "My days grow short," he said. "In many ways I look forward to retirement. But I cannot help missing my younger days. Days when *I* was trusted to carry out matters of importance, instead of merely shuffling papers."

"You have served your country well," Solomentsev protested. "You are an example to all who have come after you."

"Yes, perhaps." Leskov sighed. "But I long for the days of excitement. Can you simply tell me what..." He paused, looked away, then turned back. "No, now it is I who am sorry. It is wrong to ask you to divulge things you have sworn to keep secret."

Solomentsev felt his shame turn to pity. "It is not that you are not trusted, Pyotr," he said. "You—"

Leskov raised his hand, cutting Solomentsev off. He nodded sadly. "I know." He signaled the waiter and the man hurried over to the booth. "Two more," the colonel said. "Doubles."

The two men waited in strained silence as the waiter left with their glasses, returning a few seconds later with fresh drinks. Solomentsev watched the languid face of the man who had done so much for him. Leskov was nearing seventy. At the same time Solomentsev's career had skyrocketed, Leskov's had begun to fizzle. For the past several years younger administrators had attempted to force Leskov's retirement. Finally they had been successful, and the fateful date was now only months away.

Solomentsev lifted the vodka to his lips as he watched the sad eyes across from him. What would become of Leskov then? The colonel had never married. He had no hobbies; no outside interests, no life, other than his work.

Without his career he would slowly wither away. Or stick his Makarov in his mouth some lonely night and end it quickly.

"So how is Natalya?" Leskov asked, abruptly changing the topic.

"Natalya is fine. She has been promoted, and now supervises all canning at the factory."

Leskov's face brightened. "Wonderful!" He held up his glass. "Let us drink to your wife, a lovely woman and faithful daughter of Russia." He tipped back the glass, draining the vodka.

Solomentsev followed suit, feeling the double shot of vodka hit him harder than the first. His eyes watered slightly as he caught his breath.

On Leskov's signal the waiter appeared with a bottle of Stolychnaya in an ice bucket and left it on the table.

Solomentsev looked at the bucket. "Really, Pyotr, I must be getting home. Natalya and the boys—"

"Yes!" Leskov said. "The boys!" He hefted the bottle, pouring vodka over the ice still in their glasses. "Tell me of the boys. What have they done lately?"

The younger man grinned. His head felt light as he relaxed in the warm atmosphere of the bar. Through the window he could see the sun setting, casting dark, friendly shadows over the snow-covered sidewalks that ran along Kalinin Prospekt. He turned back to Leskov. "Igor is captain of his hockey team. Fyodor has just won the Tolstoy award for writing the best short story in grammar school."

"Excellent!" Leskov almost shouted. Raising his glass once more, he said, "To Igor and Fyodor—the future of Mother Russia."

Solomentsev felt the room begin to sway as he gulped his drink. He didn't wish to offend his old friend, but he knew he must get home. The pressures of his new position had found him drinking more lately, and he had no desire to face Natalya's wrath if he showed up drunk again.

Setting the empty glass on the table, he looked into Leskov's beaming face, then rose to his feet. "I must go."

Pure and utter dejection replaced Leskov's smile. His eyes fell again to the table. "Thank you for coming," he murmured.

Solomentsev sat back down. "One more. But one more *only,* Pyotr."

Leskov's eyes widened in delight. "Yes," he said, as he refilled their glasses. "One more only. And we will toast no one."

Solomentsev nodded through the vodka haze.

"Tell me of your new position," Leskov said, and Solomentsev was astonished at the clarity of his voice. It was a talent of the older man's he had long admired. Leskov seemed capable of drinking dry a river of spirits without showing the effects.

"It is hectic," the younger man replied, slurring his words. "I know you do not agree, but President Tachek is a good man. Of that I am convinced. He wants nothing but the betterment of our country." He sighed. "But the work is never done."

Leskov nodded as he sipped at his drink. "I can imagine." His eyes turned sad once more. "I miss it, Alexandr. I miss it all. When one is behind the scenes, privileged to information that can determine the course of mankind, he feels...*alive.* When that is over, well..." The colonel's voice trailed off.

Solomentsev stared across the table and felt his heart break. He thought of the many favors Leskov had done for him over the years, never asking anything in return. He had never, and would never, be able to repay the man.

Then suddenly, as the alcohol hit his brain full-force, Alexandr Solomentsev saw his chance. He saw instantly at least one small favor he could do for his former mentor.

He could give Pyotr Leskov a reason to live.

Solomentsev looked over his shoulder, then leaned across the table. "I could use some advice from a man of your experience," he whispered. "Advice on how to handle a rather delicate situation."

New life blossomed in the tired eyes across the table.

"There is a man presently staying at the Metropole," Solomentsev began, "an American who I am told has great experience fighting organized crime. He calls himself Belasko...."

Leskov poured another round of drinks as Solomentsev began his story. At first the younger man felt pleasure as he watched his old friend's spirits rise. Then, as the bottle emptied and another appeared to take its place, he began to feel nothing.

And when Pyotr Leskov excused himself to use the rest room, Alexandr Solomentsev hardly noticed.

THE DULL THUMP of the heavy bolt being unlocked echoed through the cell. Bolan's eyes opened, squinting as morning light shot through the door. He swung his legs over the side of the stone sleeping platform and sat up.

A *militsya* prison guard entered, carrying a bundle of clothes. "Get dressed," he ordered as he dropped the bundle next to the Executioner.

Bolan stood, stripping off the coarse prison garb and reaching for the gray suit beside him.

"What's going on?"

The guard shrugged. "I know only that we have received orders to turn you over to Russian Military Intelligence. They will transfer you to another facility until trial. I would not want to be in your shoes, American.''

Bolan nodded as he draped the suit coat over his arm. The guard followed him out of the cell.

Colonel Katerina Kerensky stood in the waiting room at the end of the cell run. She had traded the dark blue suit she had worn to pick him up the day before at the airport for a Russian Military Intelligence uniform. Bolan studied the woman as they walked down the run. Her eyes held a hard stare, but the skin around those eyes was smooth; soft. Kerensky wore no makeup, and her straight, dark brown hair was of medium length—short enough to be easily dealt with, yet long enough to be feminine.

Katerina Kerensky was a choice example of a woman who could have been attractive had she made the effort. But she had sacrificed beauty so as to take no chances on anyone misinterpreting her professionalism.

"Be very careful with this one, Colonel," the guard said. "He was responsible for the deaths of three men last night."

Kerensky looked at him in agitation. "We are aware of how dangerous he is, thank you," she barked, and the guard shrank from her. "Why do you think we are taking charge of him ourselves?" She turned to Bolan. "What do you have to say for yourself?"

Bolan said nothing.

Kerensky's lip curled into a snarl. "Ah, you Americans. You want the right to remain silent, eh?" Her hand shot out suddenly, cracking the Executioner across the face. She turned back to the guard, shrugging in disgust. She produced a set of handcuffs and secured the Executioner's wrists. "You will follow me," she said and turned on her heel.

Bolan followed her down the steps and out of the building toward the parking lot. The colonel glanced around to make sure there were no curious ears, then raised her voice over the sounds of the downtown Moscow traffic. "I am sorry. Particularly about the slap. But it had to look realistic. We do not wish the *militsya* to be aware of your identity."

"No problem," the Executioner replied as they neared a black ZIL parked alone near the edge of the lot. "I've been hit harder."

Kerensky pulled a key ring from her uniform. She had inserted it into the door when suddenly a small, round hole appeared in the window on the driver's side. Through the window Bolan saw the car seat jump, then yellow stuffing popped out of the upholstery.

The colonel froze, staring at the hole uncertainly.

His hands still cuffed behind his back, the Executioner lunged forward as a second hole appeared in the glass next to the first. He struck Kerensky in the side with his shoulder, driving her to the ground. "Get down!" he whispered.

More holes suddenly appeared in the body of the ZIL. "Get under the car!" the Executioner shouted.

Bolan and Kerensky squirmed beneath the ZIL, and the shooting stopped.

The warrior looked out from under the car. Traffic, both vehicular and pedestrian, was proceeding undisturbed. The quiet coughs of the suppressed weapon had attracted no attention. He rolled to his side, away from Kerensky. "The cuffs!" he barked. He heard the rustle of clothing as Kerensky worked her hand into her uniform in the cramped quarters.

"The key's on my key ring—in the door."

Bolan rolled back to his stomach, scooting forward to the edge of the car's underbelly.

A vehicle backfired in the distance. Then concrete flew into his face as a heavy rifle round chipped the pavement two inches in front of him.

Jerking back, he rolled to face Kerensky. "No way to make the shooter's position in this noise," he said, "but we know he's on that side. And we can't stay here. Sooner or later, whoever it is will go for the gas tank."

Kerensky nodded toward the side of the ZIL away from the firing. "There is a narrow alley between buildings. Perhaps a hundred feet from here. Can you make it with your hands cuffed?"

The Executioner nodded. "Getting out from under here and onto my feet is the only problem. But I can do that and stay behind the car. Whoever this is won't see us until we get away from the vehicle. Yeah, I'll make it. Just lead the way."

Bolan and the colonel inched toward the far edge of the ZIL. The Executioner rolled from under the vehicle to his knees beneath the passenger's window.

Suddenly a hole appeared in the glass above his head.

The warrior jumped to his feet. "There's two of them!" he yelled down to Kerensky. "One this side! Let's go!"

He turned and cut a zigzag path toward where he hoped the alley Kerensky had spoken of lay. He heard the colonel's feet pounding the pavement behind him as more silenced rounds chipped away at the parking lot, both in front and from the rear. As they neared the buildings, the Executioner's eyes scanned the area. He saw no sign of cover other than a thin sycamore spruce recently planted in an island of grass near the edge of the lot.

Diving forward, Bolan hit the concrete in a shoulder roll as two more shots chipped into the ground on both sides of him. The delay gave Kerensky a chance to take the lead, and she cut sharply to the left toward the sapling.

Bolan followed. A second later, he saw the alley, half-hidden by an outcropped corner in the ancient architecture. Kerensky disappeared around the corner to safety.

His running hampered without the use of his hands, the Executioner followed. There was a brief lull in the quiet shooting. Then a volley of unsuppressed fire boomed above the sounds of the city as the snipers switched weapons in a last-ditch effort. Full-auto 7.62 mm rounds ricocheted off the walls of the buildings, buzzing like bees past Bolan's head.

The warrior dived forward again, hit the grass next to the tree and rolled around the corner.

The shots in the distance stopped.

MARIO HERNANDEZ tied the sash around his red silk robe as he lowered himself into the chair beneath the umbrella. He stretched his arm to his side. As if by magic, Erich appeared to place a steaming mug of coffee in his hand.

Hernandez sipped the coffee. Still low on the horizon, the morning sun had risen far enough to predict another day of idyllic weather. The cartel man watched the tide roll lazily onto the beach, turning the sand a deep dusty beige. Then, from the lagoon to his left, the loon suddenly cackled.

The drug lord frowned, turning toward the noise. God, how he hated that sound. The bird's irritating laughter reminded him of the classmates who had ridiculed his dreams of power when he'd been a child. He wished they could see him now.

Hernandez turned to Erich, who stood waiting at attention. Since Pool had killed Harmon Pinder, Erich had taken over many of the undercover cop's responsibilities. The German was a fine servant, attentive to the needs of his master. And Erich, he could trust. He had been careless with the Bahamian cop, thinking the man could be no more than what he appeared—a harmless middle-aged man needing work. But since the incident, he had had the backgrounds of Erich and all other employees reinvestigated. Erich's past had stood the test. He *was* what he claimed to be.

"Erich, get me the phone and morning paper," Hernandez ordered.

From behind his back Erich produced both.

Hernandez grinned. Damn, the man was good. He deserved a raise. Maybe a promotion.

Hernandez tapped numbers into the cellular phone. A few minutes later, he heard the irritating, choppy accent on the other end. The loon cackled again in the distance as the woman said, "Esposito Construction

Company, how may I help you?" in thick Brook-
lynese.

"By letting me speak to your boss."

"Oh, Mr. Hernandez. Hold one moment, please."

A second later, Esposito was on the line. "So where
do we stand?" he asked without formalities.

"The guns and dope are both scheduled for this
week," Hernandez said. "Coke first, near Vladivostok. The guns go through the next day, farther
west."

"Good God," Esposito said. "You're taking them
in through fuckin' China?"

Hernandez suppressed a laugh. Esposito had grown
old. His *cojones* had shrunk to the size of peas.
"Mongolia is not Beijing, Don Joseph," he said
calmly. "It is the frontier. It might as well be another
country from Red China."

"But those Chink cops aren't—"

"China doesn't have anything to do with the dope,
Don Esposito. It's on its way to Vladivostok by sea.
And as far as the weapons are concerned, I've cut a
deal with one of the Triads. They've been running their
own small-time smuggling ops into the former Soviet
Union for years, and they've got the border guards in
their back pockets. We won't be bothered."

"Dammit, Hernandez, I know I agreed to let you
run the guns and dope, but the *Triads?* How much is
their cut?"

"Substantial," Hernandez admitted. "But their in-
volvement is only temporary. As soon as we get a regular route set up, we'll make our own arrangements
with the authorities and cut them out."

"Yeah? What's to keep the slant-eyes from just ripping the shipment off?"

Hernandez sighed. As an aging fat cat, Don Joseph had forgotten that there was never profit without risk. "They have been promised more money down the line," the drug lord said. "Besides, Pool will be with them."

"That worries me even more. That crazy-ass cowboy doesn't impress me worth shit. Where in the hell did you find him, anyway?"

"Jake is eccentric, I grant you," he said. "But dependable. He's not the raving maniac you make him out to be."

"Oh, yeah? Well, just make sure he doesn't get out of your sight without his Thorazine," Esposito said. "Tell me more."

"Pool goes from Vladivostok to Darchan where he'll meet the Triad. They'll take him north as far as the border. The guns cross at K'achta."

There was a long silence on the other end, then Esposito said, "I hope the fuck you know what you're doing."

"I do. Where is Furelli?"

"His plane ought to be hitting Moscow right now."

"Good. He will be in Vladivostok, then K'achta in time?"

"He'll be there," Esposito said. "But I'm warning you, Hernandez, this sounds risky as hell to me. And Furelli's my best man, not to mention my son-in-law. If I lose him over some hare-brained—"

From the lagoon, Hernandez heard the exasperating staccato call of the loon again. He didn't know which annoyed him more—the bird, or the powerful Mafia boss who worried like an old woman.

"Sorry, Don Joseph. Your voice is fading out. I'll have to call you back." Hernandez hung up.

Setting the phone on the table, the Colombian drug lord lifted his coffee cup once more. He smiled at the ocean, feeling suddenly like a twentieth-century Napoleon.

He was about to invade Russia.

Everything was working out perfectly. While he set up the pipelines into the former Soviet Union, Don Esposito's men were already establishing loan-sharking, gambling and prostitution bases. He hadn't bothered to ask the old man about progress in that arena. The Esposito Family had run such safe criminal enterprises for more than a century. They would have no problems.

Hernandez turned to Erich. "I feel like celebrating," he said. "Bring me a gimlet." As the servant hurried off, he settled back to watch the sea. Yes, soon he and Esposito would control all organized crime in the New Commonwealth.

As if mocking his plans, the loon chuckled in the distance.

Hernandez turned toward his invisible persecutor as Erich returned with a stemmed glass. Damn, the drug lord thought. The German *was* efficient. Perhaps Erich could be put to better use in some other section of the operation.

Hernandez raised the glass to his lips as the loon snickered again. He turned to Erich. "Are you familiar with firearms?'' he asked as he swirled the sweet lime juice and gin over his tongue.

The German smiled. "*Ja*, Señor Hernandez," he grunted. "I was a corporal in the Panzer Grenadier Brigade. I thought surely you knew."

Hernandez nodded as the loon continued to laugh. He had forgotten. The background investigation had revealed that. "You want to be my waiter all your life?" the drug lord asked. "Or are you interested in some *real* money?"

Erich's smile widened. "I am always interested in improving myself."

"Good." Hernandez pointed toward the house. "In my closet you will find several shotguns. Pick one. Then hunt down that maddening bird and kill it." He stuck his tongue into the glass and licked sugar from the rim. "Kill it quickly. Efficiently. Show me that you are capable, and we will see what else you can do."

Erich bowed, turned and left.

Mario Hernandez checked his watch: 9:47 a.m. He finished the gimlet, then leaned back in the sun as drowsiness overtook him.

A few minutes later, the maddening sound of the loon jolted him from a half sleep. A second later, he heard a loud boom in the distance.

The drug lord grinned as his eyes returned to his watch. Not bad, he thought. It was 9:59.

Mario Hernandez smiled. Yes, he would give anything if those children who had laughed at his dreams were here right now. They would never mock him again.

And now, neither would the loon.

# CHAPTER TWO

Kerensky opened the door of the ZIL, shoved Bolan roughly into the back seat, then turned to the multitude of *militsya* officers who had appeared when the assault rifles had replaced the silencers in the parking lot. "Thank you for the quick response," she said. "Perhaps you can now see why we have taken charge of this prisoner ourselves."

"Do you need officers to escort you, Colonel?" a police captain asked. "There could be yet another attempt to free him."

The woman shook her head. "It will not be necessary. If another attempt comes, it will not be now." She opened the driver's door.

"But Colonel—"

Kerensky whirled. "I said *no*, Captain," she spit angrily. "Take my word for it. We know things about this case that you do not." She slid behind the wheel, closed the door and started the engine.

She guided the vehicle through the parking lot and turned onto the street. As soon as they were out of sight of the police station, she handed the handcuff key over the seat to Bolan, then nodded to an overcoat and fur hat next to him. "Please put them on. We must meet again with the president, and there will be far more curious eyes around the Kremlin today than there were last night." Keeping one hand on the steering wheel, she dug into her purse with the other.

Bolan removed the cuffs and shrugged into the coat. Kerensky's arm stretched once more over the seat, holding a small black box. "If you please," she said.

The warrior opened the box, which contained a slim tube of spirit gum and a bushy mustache the same color as his hair.

Kerensky reached across the front seat, pulling down the visor on the passenger's side to reveal a mirror. "You can see?"

Bolan nodded. He ran the tube of cosmetic glue across the rough backing of the mustache. "So," he said as he pressed the hair to his upper lip, "only you, Solomentsev and the president know I'm here. But so far, there've been two attempts on my life. Got any ideas?" He watched Kerensky's face in the rearview mirror.

The ZIL passed Sobakina Tower and neared the Kremlin. Kerensky looked tired, her face a road map of worried lines as she said, "I have my suspicions."

"Who, Solomentsev?"

"It is better if the president himself expresses my fears to you."

"I understand Solomentsev passed a polygraph test," Bolan said.

"I will say no more."

The Executioner settled back as they drove slowly though the streets of the Kremlin. Alexandr Solomentsev had been chosen by the president to be an aide, but he was still a former major in the old KGB. That association, combined with the news of the RI traitor from the mole in the Bahamas, had prompted Tachek to bring in Russian Intelligence as Bolan's backup. It had also prompted the Russian leader to require his top aide to take a polygraph exam before being trusted with the knowledge that Bolan would arrive in Moscow.

According to Tachek, the young aide had passed with flying colors.

The Executioner knew the polygraph—or "lie detector" as it was commonly called—was an accurate tool. It was a cold, calculating instrument that registered responses. But Bolan also knew that the people who administered the tests were of flesh and blood. Human. They could be influenced and misled. Therefore, while he had always looked on such tests as helpful, he had never considered them definitive.

As Kerensky parked the automobile and they started up the steps to the president's office, an old police expression crossed the Executioner's mind: "You can't beat the machine—but you can damn sure beat the guy manning it."

The president of Russia looked worried as Kerensky ushered Bolan into the office. Taking the same seat he'd had the night before, the Executioner glanced briefly to Solomentsev in the chair across from him.

Tachek shook his head, staring down at his desk. "First, Mr. Belasko," he said, "I am embarrassed. Please accept my apology for what happened last night and just now. Had I had any idea—"

"Your apology is accepted, Mr. President. What concerns me is the leak. It's obvious that one of two things has happened. Either others besides Solomentsev and Kerensky are aware of this operation, or..."

He let his voice trail off, but the implied meaning was obvious.

Tachek nodded. Lifting a piece of paper from his desk, he addressed Solomentsev and Kerensky. "If you please," he said, nodding toward one of the room's side doors, "I would like to speak to Mr. Belasko privately."

The colonel and aide rose and left the office.

As soon as they'd gone, Tachek took the seat next to Bolan. Crossing his legs, he looked down at the page in his hands. "Mr. Belasko," he said, "according to the hotel guests on your floor, the first shots were heard between 2315 and 2320 hours last night."

"That'd be about right. I didn't have a lot of time to look at the clock."

Tachek grunted. "I can imagine." He squinted at the paper. "The *militsya* received what your American police would call a disturbance report from an anonymous caller at 2307."

Bolan frowned. That was eight minutes before the men entered his room. "That explains the quick response. The cops knew it had happened before it happened. Did the *militsya* trace the call?" he asked.

The president nodded. "A phone booth in the lobby of the hotel."

"So the three phony policemen made the call, then came up to my room figuring they'd be long gone before the real cops arrived."

"It appears that way."

"We're back to square one. How did they know I was here, and where I'd be staying."

The president folded the page into his breast pocket. He looked the Executioner squarely in the eyes, then with a nod indicated the door through which Solomentsev and Kerensky had left. "I can think of no other explanation."

"So what do you intend to do?"

"I have had the polygraph set up again," Tachek said. He glanced toward an open door to a side room.

Bolan turned and saw the instrument sitting on a table.

"I will require Colonel Kerensky to submit to the same test as Solomentsev did."

"Fine," the Executioner said. "But you won't learn anything."

Tachek cocked his head to the side. "You think not?"

"No. Call it a hunch. A gut-level reaction if you want, but I don't think Kerensky's our problem."

"You believe it is Solomentsev?"

Bolan shrugged. "I don't know."

"He showed no signs of deception on the polygraph."

"With all due respect, Mr. Tachek, I put a lot more faith in hard evidence than I do machines."

The president shifted uneasily. "But from where else could the leak have sprung? I have taken the utmost precautions to assure your anonymity."

"There's a thousand possibilities," he said. "Someone may know bits and pieces of secondhand information that they were able to piece together. Someone who knew Kerensky or Solomentsev by sight may have been at the airport when they picked me up—the only fly in that ointment being that if this was a random assemblage of accidentally gained info, it got assembled awfully fast.'' He paused. ''How about your polygraph examiner?''

Tachek smiled. ''I was once with the KGB, Mr. Belasko. I am trained, and administered the test myself to avoid including anyone else.''

Bolan nodded. ''My guess is that somebody you've never dreamed of is somehow getting secondhand information. Solomentsev or Kerensky, or with all due respect even *you,* Mr. President, may be giving us up without even being aware of it.''

Tachek frowned and nodded. ''It is possible. Colonel Kerensky believes that Solomentsev is behind the leak.''

''I know. And Solomentsev probably thinks it's Kerensky.''

''Yes.'' The president shook his head. ''As with your various intelligence departments in the United States, Mr. Belasko, there is great jealousy between Russian Intelligence and Russian Military Intelligence. Solomentsev was not happy with my decision to bring in RMI on this. But with the knowledge we have gained from our man in the Bahamas, I had no choice.''

Bolan nodded. ''Anything is still possible at this point. Okay. I'd say go ahead with the polygraph. It can't hurt anything, and we may pick up a lead that eventually takes us where we want to go.''

Tachek stood. ''Your weapons and other equipment have arrived.'' He walked to the filing cabinet, slid open a drawer and pulled out a Beretta 93-R and a Desert Eagle .44 Magnum. Setting the two automatics on the desk, the Russian leader pulled two billfolds from another drawer.

Bolan picked them up. The passport and travel orders within the first identified him as Dwight McNeil, an agricultural expert from Stillwater, Oklahoma, who would be inspecting various farming sites. The second billfold held a Czechoslovakian air force card and listed him as Colonel Frank Hlupnik. Both sets of ID bore pictures of the Executioner that had been taken the night before, upon his arrival.

"You will have the best of both worlds," Tachek said. "As Colonel Hlupnik, you have permission to inspect military installations. And you will be respected. But as a Czech, your accent and poor command of Russian will not be questioned." He pointed to the second billfold. "The McNeil papers are for situations in which you find it more convenient to pose as a civilian." He paused and cleared his throat. "There is an official vehicle in the parking lot registered to Colonel Hlupnik. You will find an AK-74 in the trunk. The plane you requested is waiting at the airport."

"McNeil could also use an open letter of introduction from the president," Bolan said.

The Russian leader nodded. "I'll see to it." He knelt, sliding open the bottom drawer of the filing cabinet. Then rising to his feet, he turned and set a long plastic case on the desk. Several boxes of shotgun shells went next to it.

Bolan flipped the hinges on the case and lifted the lid. The mission he had undertaken would require heavy personal firepower. But within the strict firearms policy of the Russian government, concealment was an equal necessity.

In the foam rubber cutout, he saw the short full-auto shotgun he'd requested. Roughly twice as long as the Desert Eagle, it was still capable of firing up to a dozen 12-gauge shells or slugs in 2.6 seconds.

Bolan lifted the weapon from the case and began loading the magazine from a box of double-aught buck. The South African-made scattergun had an appropriate name for the Executioner—*The Striker,* which was also Bolan's code name.

The president pressed an intercom button. "Alexandr, Katerina, you may return." Then, turning to Bolan, he said, "The rest of the equipment you requested is in the car. Will you need storage space?"

Bolan hesitated as Kerensky and Solomentsev returned to the room. "Yes," he finally said. "But under the circumstances, I'll take care of it myself. We've still got the leak to consider."

Tachek turned to Kerensky. "Colonel, I must require you to submit to the same test that Alexandr underwent."

Without hesitation the woman turned on her heel and disappeared into the side room with the polygraph.

The president turned to Solomentsev. "Go across the square to the GUM store," he ordered. "Get Mr. Belasko a variety of appropriate clothing, shaving equipment, luggage and the like."

"Pick up some wrapping paper, ribbons and bows, too," Bolan added.

Solomentsev looked at him curiously. Before he could question the request, Tachek shrugged and said, "Do as he asks."

The aide nodded and left the room. Tachek disappeared into the polygraph room and closed the door behind him.

Alone now, the Executioner opened the Russian Intelligence file that Solomentsev had rescued from his room at the Metropole. The reports from the mole in the Bahamas had been translated from Cyrillic to English, and Bolan continued the studies he'd begun the night before.

The New Brotherhood. An alliance of Mafia and cartel that could spell doom for a free Russia. The New Brotherhood intended to take the Commonwealth by storm during the countries' initial months of chaotic freedom, moving in like vultures over a dying man. The President of the United States had voiced his fears when Bolan had met with him two days earlier.

"As you know, Striker, Tachek's position is already shaky. All it would take at this point is an outburst of crime to oust him. The government could fall back into the hands of the Communists overnight."

Skimming the reports submitted by the mole, Bolan learned that cartel boss Mario Hernandez and Don Joseph Esposito of the New York Esposito Family were the kingpins in the operation. The cartel would handle drugs and gunrunning, while the mob took care of gambling, prostitution and other such illegal activities. The New Brotherhood intended to flood the Commonwealth with crime, setting up before the police had time to adjust to the new leniency in the formerly oppressive society.

The Executioner paused. It was inevitable. Emancipation was always a two-way street—it worked for the criminal as well as the law-abiding. Oppressive governments always had less crime than democracies.

Such was the price of freedom.

Bolan returned to the reports. Already a casino and loan-sharking business had been set up in Saint Petersburg. Shipments of cocaine and automatic weapons were scheduled over the next few days, and the mole had heard rumors of an elaborate prostitution ring being set up along the Black Sea coast. The Executioner turned to personality profiles the mole had put together on Esposito's and Hernandez's two top men—the men who would be running the show in Russia.

Ray Furelli of the Esposito Family appeared to be a typical "wise guy" who'd risen through the ranks through both a talent for mayhem and knowing the right people—he'd married Esposito's daughter. But Jake Pool, Hernandez's personal bodyguard and chief enforcer, was cut from a different bolt of cloth. Pool had been in and out of both prisons and mental institutions since his tenth birthday. A homicidal psychopath, Pool believed himself to be the reincarnation of Wild Bill Hickok.

Bolan continued to study the profiles. Throughout his career he had dealt with men like Esposito, Hernandez and Furelli on almost a daily basis. He understood how they thought and what motivated them. They were cold, calculating and out for two things: money and power.

And the Executioner had come across his share of crazies like Pool, men who lived in an unfathomable netherworld somewhere between fantasy and reality. The Pools of the world were harder to predict. Their actions were determined by rules that existed only in the secret universes within their brains. They followed a logic that made sense only to themselves.

Bolan closed the file and leaned back as Solomentsev returned, set two suitcases on the floor and silently took a seat next to the Executioner. A moment later, the door to the polygraph room opened.

Kerensky's face showed no emotion when the president led her back into the office. "I have mixed emotions," Tachek said. "I am pleased to announce that I do not believe Colonel Kerensky is involved in any traitorous activity whatsoever. On the other hand, that fact leaves us with the same problem."

Bolan nodded. "Exactly why I've decided to change my plan of attack."

All eyes turned to the Executioner.

"I don't intend to work through Solomentsev, or Kerensky, or *anyone*. I'll call this office periodically, in case your mole comes up with new intel. Other than that, I'm on my own."

A silence fell over the room. Tachek stared at Bolan. Finally he shook his head. "I am sorry, Mr. Belasko. This, I cannot allow. I have already given you far more freedom than even my own operatives are permitted."

Bolan shrugged. "I can appreciate your hesitancy, Mr. President, but this is the only chance of success we have."

Tachek dropped into the chair behind his desk. He lifted a calendar, toying with it as he said, "Last night, you were mistakenly jailed here in Moscow. Consider the consequences if that happens in some remote part of the country. I might very well never even learn of it. You could spend the rest of your life in prison."

"I'm willing to take that chance," Bolan said bluntly.

The president rose from his seat and walked to the far side of the room. He clasped his hands behind his back and stared at the wall. "So what you are saying then, Mr. Belasko, could be summed up in one of your popular American adages. 'Your way or the highway'?"

"I'm no diplomat, Mr. Tachek, but there's no need to put it like that, either. Believe me when I say, I *want* to help you. But yes, I've got to do it my way—the only way it will work."

The president turned back around. "I may very well regret this," he said, "but so be it." He paused and wiped a thin line of sweat from his brow. "I suppose there is no need to tell you what will happen to me if my political opponents learn that I have given an American agent false ID and free run of the country?"

"No, sir." Bolan rose and walked to the door, stooping to pick up the suitcases. "I'll check in when I can," he said, as he opened the door and stepped into the hall.

The Executioner pressed the call button and waited as the elevator climbed the shaft. As always, he was on his own.

No reinforcement. No backup. No support of any kind.

Just the way he liked it.

THE BLACK ZIL Tachek had provided looked identical to the one Kerensky had driven.

Except this one had no bullet holes.

Bolan slid behind the wheel, catching sight of a Czech colonel's uniform hanging from a clothes rod in the back seat.

Pulling out of Red Square onto Gorky Street, the Executioner crossed Moskvoretsky Bridge. On the other side of the Moscow River, he cut down several side streets, his eyes glued to the rearview mirror for signs of a tail. Satisfied he wasn't being followed, he took Krymskaya along the edge of Gorky Park, to the Crimea Bridge, then cut back across the river and turned left on Kosmolsky Prospekt.

It had been some time since Bolan had been to Moscow, but he still remembered the city's general layout. The central core was built around several concentric rings that bordered the main boulevards.

From somewhere in the back of his brain, the Executioner pulled the memory of a line of rental storage garages on Frunze Nab, the street paralleling the north side of the river. If he remembered right, it sat across the street from a recreational paddleboat area on the riverbank.

Spotting a modern supermarket near the Church of Saint Nicholas, Bolan pulled into the parking lot and entered the store. He had no idea what hardships this mission would throw at him, so it made sense to stock up on provisions now, while he had the opportunity. He'd be temporarily ditching the ZIL as soon as he found the garages, and the hidden car could serve as both storage and "safehouse" should the need arise later.

Bolan filled a shopping basket with what food was available—a few fruits and vegetables and three cans of tuna—and tossed the grocery bag into the trunk of the ZIL when he returned to the lot.

Ten minutes later, the Executioner pulled into the parking lot in front of a line of overhead doors. Throwing the parking brake on, he exited the ZIL and pushed through a glass door into the office.

A thin layer of dust covered everything in the room. Six feet from the wall, opposite the door, was a cracked linoleum counter. Behind the counter, a fat, balding man in a soiled undershirt sat asleep in a straight-backed chair, his hands clasped across a massive girth of belly as his feet balanced precariously on the counter.

A half-empty bottle of lemon-flavored vodka stood next to the man's crossed feet, and loud, irregular snores came from deep within his nose and throat.

Bolan tapped the bell on the counter and the man's head jerked up. First his right, then his left eye opened as he struggled to focus on the Executioner. *"Da?"* he asked.

"I need a stall," Bolan said in Russian. "Large enough for a car."

The man behind the counter laughed, burped and laughed again. Then his expression changed to one of distrust. "You are not Russian."

"No," Bolan told him. "Czech."

The laughter returned. "There are *Russians* who have waited six years for a garage." He chuckled. "But if you wish, I will put your name on the list." He stood slowly and pulled a drawer out behind the counter. "Who knows? Perhaps someday, like in the next century..."

Bolan reached inside his jacket, produced the Hlupnik credentials and laid them on the counter. "Do not let the civilian clothing fool you, Comrade," he said with the voice of authority. He paused, watching the fat man's eyes struggle to focus on the card. "Now. I was told by my associates in the Kremlin that I would have no trouble with you. But perhaps you would like to call and verify my identity for yourself." He stared hard at the man, letting the implication set in.

"No, no," the man in the undershirt said quickly. "I am sorry. I was mistaken. We have one garage left. Number 10, at the far end. You are certainly welcome to it." He reached under the counter, came up with a key and extended it to the Executioner. "My most humble apologies for the mistake."

Bolan nodded curtly, took the key and returned to the automobile. He didn't like intimidating innocent men; contributing to the paranoia that seventy years of Communist rule had instilled in the average Russian citizen. But he wouldn't have a choice during this mission. He'd be working under severe limitations imposed by language and cultural differences, and would have to use whatever worked for the greater good.

Like the fat man had said, Garage Number 10 sat at the far end of the row. The Executioner pulled to a halt in front of the door, stepped out of the car and inserted the key into the heavy Swiss-made padlock. A moment later, the hinges and pulleys screamed for oil as he pushed the door up.

When the car was safely inside, the Executioner turned on the interior light, rolled the door back down and opened the trunk. Inside he found a variety of boxes, including a case of ammunition each for the Beretta, Desert Eagle and Striker. Two longer boxes rested at the bottom of the trunk. Bolan flipped the lids and saw the standard army AK-74 and the Heckler & Koch MP-5 H-3 submachine gun he'd requested.

The Executioner paused. It was impossible to know what weapons he'd need in the upcoming phases of his offensive. But assault rifles and subguns should be easy enough to come by if he needed them. No, better to leave these two boxes where they were. He'd have enough trouble getting the Striker through checkpoints without detection.

Bolan transferred several boxes of ammo to his luggage, then smiled as he began unrolling the tube of wrapping paper Solomentsev had purchased. The request had piqued the man's curiosity, but Tachek hadn't blinked an eye. The Executioner had enjoyed watching the president's mind work as he realized what the paper and ribbons were for.

Bolan drew a Cold Steel Mini Tanto combat knife from the sheath hanging under his arm opposite the Beretta. Slicing down the paper, he wrapped the case containing the Striker, then added ribbons and a bow.

The Executioner changed into the Czech colonel's uniform and grabbed his suitcases and the "present."

Locking the garage behind him, he walked to the edge of the street.

The next cab that came by screeched to a halt when the driver spotted the uniform. Bolan slid into the back seat and gave the man the address of the small private airport reserved for visiting dignitaries.

The driver glanced over his shoulder and raised his hand to his forehead. "I was a senior sergeant—border guard, Colonel," he said. "I salute you."

Bolan returned the salute.

"I then served in Afghanist—"

The Executioner glanced impatiently to his watch. "I do not mean to insult you, soldier," he said, "but I am in a hurry."

The former sergeant threw the taxi into gear and took off.

Bolan settled back into his seat. He had fought Communism and other evils all his life. He would continue to do so until his death. It bred corruption and imposed hardship on those who suffered under it. In fact, the Executioner thought as the taxi driver skirted toward the airport, he had just witnessed the only possible advantage that the fear Communist rule inspired *might* have.

Occasionally it saved time.

THE MIKOYAN/GUREVICH 27 shot through an opening in the clouds, and the naval base suddenly appeared in the distance. Farther yet, Bolan saw the waters of the Pacific, and the separate docks housing both commercial vessels and the ships of the Russian Pacific Fleet. Then the waters of Golden Horn Bay disappeared below the horizon as the plane dropped toward the runway.

The Executioner rode the soft bump as the wheels hit the tarmac. He pulled back on the controls and the MiG-27 slowed to a crawl as he neared the hangars.

Bolan had been surprised at the choice of aircraft the Russian president had left at his disposal. He had requested a fast plane, since he'd be crossing the largest country in the modern world. With a maximum speed of Mach 1.1, the 27 certainly fit the bill. But the MiG was a ground attack plane, and the Executioner had never dreamed that Tachek would trust such a weapon to a former enemy.

It was yet another indication that, at least under the present circumstances, the Russian leader could be trusted.

And trusted Bolan—to a certain extent.

Bolan grinned as he ground the MiG to a halt. A quick inspection during a refueling stop near Krasnojarsk had revealed that the MiG carried no bomb load, and the six-barrel, 23 mm centerline gun had been removed as well.

A military jeep pulled onto the tarmac as the Executioner dropped from the cockpit. The vehicle stopped next to the plane. A naval infantryman, wearing the black beret with a red triangular flash, got out and walked forward.

"Colonel Hlupnik," the infantryman said. "Welcome to Primorsky Territory. I am Lieutenant Brodsky. It is my honor to greet you."

Bolan returned the salute. "It is my pleasure to be here, and I hope you will excuse my lack of command over the language."

Brodsky smiled. "Your Russian is excellent, Colonel. It is much better than my Czech." He climbed into the cockpit, grabbing the Executioner's luggage. He hesitated, looking at the package wrapped with ribbons and bows. "Should this gift come with us, Colonel?"

Bolan grinned. "It certainly should, Sergeant. It is for an old friend. Who knows? She may still be here in Vladivostok."

"Ah," Brodsky said. His eyebrows rose knowingly. "Then you are one of the lucky ones, Colonel. Female companionship is a rare commodity on the frontier." He lifted the suitcases and package over the side of the jeep, then slid in behind the wheel.

Bolan took the passenger's seat. As the jeep pulled out, a Sukhoi Su-7 took off from an adjacent runway. Brodsky shouted over the roar. "Your tour of the base is not scheduled until morning, Colonel. I hope that is to your liking."

The warrior turned toward him, yelling into the wind. "Fine. Right now, all I want is a shower, dinner and to find my friend. You don't realize how vast the Commonwealth is until you try to cross it—even by MiG."

Brodsky laughed and nodded as they pulled to a halt at the terminal. Bolan followed him into an outer office.

A secretary wearing a brown military uniform rose and saluted from behind her desk. Her name tag identified her as Sergeant Mirkien. She smiled and reached for the intercom as Brodsky led the way into a larger office.

An aging major jumped hurriedly to his feet, his hand flashing to his forehead. "Greetings, Colonel. And welcome. I am Major Lissitsky."

Bolan nodded.

The major's voice quavered slightly as he spoke. The Executioner had no problem figuring out why. One of the former KGB's favorite means of internal investigation was to masquerade as allied officers, running undercover checks on military operations. Evidently Russian Intelligence, as well, was suspected of the same tactic.

"We have prepared a room for you in the officers' quarters," Lissitsky said.

Bolan shook his head. "Major, I have seen base after base within your country." He waved a hand in front of his face. "Officers' quarters are all the same. Nice, but the same. If you please, I would prefer to stay in town this evening. I have not been in this area for some time, and I'd like to see it on my own."

Brodsky caught his eye and winked.

The major nodded quickly. He lifted the phone, tapped several numbers, then spoke into the receiver. "Melaniya," he said, then glanced nervously back to the Executioner and cleared his throat. "Sergeant Mirkien, Colonel Hlupnik prefers to stay off base this evening. Please reserve a room at the Tolstoy."

When Lissitsky hung up, he turned to Brodsky. "Drive Colonel Hlupnik to the hotel. Stay with him in case he needs anything."

Bolan followed the man out of the building. "So, Lieutenant," the warrior said as the jeep started toward the gate, "your major appears nervous. Is he afraid I will report that he is having an affair with his secretary?"

Brodsky stiffened. Winking and smiling were evidently one thing. Actually saying the words was something different. "The major does not confide his private life with me."

Bolan laughed, watching the man's reaction. Establishing the trust of this man was imperative to the cover he had planned for his actions. "Loosen up," he told Brodsky. "I am not RI or RMI." He shrugged. "If I was stranded away from home in the outskirts of my country, and had a secretary like your Sergeant Mirkien..." He paused, then added, "Who knows?"

Brodsky laughed self-consciously as the guard at the gate passed them through. "We have a name for men like you in the army, Colonel," he said. "You are what we call a soldier's officer—a man who cares for his troops and understands we must have some...recreation."

Bolan smiled. Brodsky continued to relax as they passed several stores and bars at the edge of the base that were obviously designed to provide such recreation.

"Major Lissitsky is a good man and a fine commander," the infantryman went on. "But his philandering is well-known in Moscow." He turned toward the Executioner and smiled. "Which is why he is in Siberia to begin with."

Bolan chuckled. "We all have our weaknesses, Lieutenant."

Leaving the base area, the jeep pulled into the downtown district. Vladivostok was the Commonwealth's only fair-weather port, but the term "fair" was relative. The men and women walking the streets still wore heavy sweaters or jackets. The Executioner studied the storefronts that lined the street, seeing both department stores and more exclusive shops that specialized in bone carvings, jasper ornaments and furs. They passed a sign announcing The Polar Bare Club and through the open door, Bolan saw a scantily clad woman dancing on the stage. A wry smile curled his lips as they passed another sign that read Chubbie's American Café, and the odor of frying hamburgers and onions wafted to the jeep.

Things *were* changing in Russia.

The two-story Hotel Tolstoy sat on the corner of Mir and Gagarin Prospekt next to the Children's Puppet Theater. Obviously dating back to the days of the czars, it wouldn't have looked out of place in old Saint Petersburg. The only change in the thick stone face of the building was the many inlaid plaques commemorating battles of the Russo-Japanese War.

The Executioner turned to Brodsky as the jeep halted in a no-parking space in front of the hotel. "I know the major ordered you to stay with me," he said. "May I assume that means you follow my orders?"

"Certainly."

"Then get lost, Brodsky," the Executioner said. "My friend and I will not need a chaperon." He nodded toward the Polar Bare. "And it appears there are plenty of amusements to keep you busy."

Brodsky's eyes flickered with indecision, and Bolan realized the lieutenant's orders had been twofold. Brodsky was not only to remain at the Executioner's beck and call, he was to report back to the major if Bolan appeared to be investigating the base commander.

"I have one request before you go, though," the Executioner said. "Just in case my friend doesn't live here anymore, or got married or something...where does a man go to find a little quick female companionship?"

Brodsky's smile spread from ear to ear. "The Georgian Bath House." He nodded down the street. "Three blocks east. Not quite to the docks. Do you have civilian clothes?"

Bolan nodded.

"Wear them. And tell Andreas that you are a friend of mine."

"Thanks." Bolan stepped out of the jeep.

"I will get your luggage," Brodsky said.

"You'll do nothing of the kind, soldier." The Executioner smiled and grabbed the suitcases and package. "You'll go have some fun yourself—and that's an order."

Brodsky shook his head in dismay at the good luck. "I was correct, Colonel Hlupnik. You *are* a soldier's officer." The young lieutenant cut a U-turn and headed back up the street.

Hefting the suitcases and the gift-wrapped Striker, the Executioner walked up the steps of the Hotel Tolstoy.

## CHAPTER THREE

The half-moon glowed dully through the coastal fog, and a cold chill bit the midnight air. A dog barked from a side alley as the Executioner neared the docks.

In the khaki work pants, black turtleneck sweater and navy watch cap Solomentsev had purchased for him at the government-owned GUM store in Moscow, the Executioner looked no different than other merchant sailors who were staggering back to their ships after a night in port. The half-empty quart of vodka that hung from Bolan's right arm was hardly out of place, either, as many of the men had picked up "one for the road" before leaving the downtown area.

In the sheath under his right arm, the Executioner carried the Cold Steel Mini Tanto. The knife wasn't out of place, either. While the returning sailors might not carry American steel, Bolan knew seamen, and most would have a blade of some sort.

The differences really began with what else lay beneath Bolan's three-quarter-length navy pea coat. The silenced Beretta hung under his other arm in a ballistic nylon shoulder rig. The Desert Eagle rode snugly in the same material on his hip. The differences between the Executioner and the rest of the sailors continued with the deadly Striker, which dangled from his right side on a sling, the coat pulling it close to his body.

Bolan also carried a number of other items the sailors wouldn't be likely to have, among them several light C-4 plastique charges and a remote-control detonator.

The warrior walked on, tipping the bottle in his hands to his lips with every few steps. He had purchased the vodka from a black market vendor in an alley near the Tolstoy, sprinkled his pea coat with the spirits, then dumped the contents into a trash can. The bottle, now half-filled with water, not only aided the drunken-sailor image he was promoting, it would fill a more vital role as the night progressed.

As he neared the docks, the Executioner saw two erect figures suddenly turn a corner and start toward him. Round-crowned, short-billed uniform caps were silhouetted against the sky. A dark, shadowy lump was clear on each man's hip, and as they walked forward, Bolan saw a flash of stainless-steel buckle on a Sam Browne belt.

Cops. The local *militsya* had seen him.

The Executioner continued forward. At the next corner he turned onto a side street in front of a closed dry-goods store. The *militsya* men were too close to avoid, but with any luck, they'd mistake him for just another sailor in search of another bar on his way back to the ship.

Luck was not with the Executioner.

Bolan heard the voice as he turned the corner under a dim streetlight. "Stop!"

The Executioner walked on, stepping up his pace, hoping against hope that he'd spot a darkened alley or an open bar to duck into before the cops rounded the corner. Instead he saw a deserted commercial area, the stores all closed for the night. The nearest alley was a block away.

The sound of running footsteps echoed through the night behind him. The two Siberian cops raced around the corner and ground to a halt.

Bolan turned to face two drawn Makarovs.

The nearer man was as tall as the Executioner. He wore a heavy blond beard that seemed to bounce as he broke out in a long stream of Russian Bolan couldn't follow.

The Executioner shrugged, holding his hands out, palms up.

The tall police officer blew air between his teeth in disgust, then tried English. "What nationality are you?" he asked.

Bolan smiled. "American."

The cop's eyes narrowed.

"You are on a ship?" he asked, the Makarov still aimed at the Executioner's abdomen.

Bolan hesitated. If he said yes, the next question would be, "Where are your papers?" The McNeil papers wouldn't hold water with him dressed as a sailor. The Hlupnik ID would be equally out of line. But they were going to ask him for his papers eventually anyway.

Stalling, the Executioner nodded.

"Your papers," the tall cop demanded predictably.

"I'm sorry. I left them on the ship."

The lips within the bushy blond beard tightened. "Which ship?"

Bolan had no idea what craft were in port. "The *San Juan,*" he said off the top of his head.

"There is no ship by that name anchored in Vladivostok."

The Executioner nodded. "Sure there is. We docked maybe a half hour ago. Out of Costa Rica."

The cop's eyes narrowed. He said something to his partner in Russian, then holstered his weapon.

The shorter man kept his Makarov aimed at the Executioner's stomach.

"Drop the bottle," the cop with the beard ordered, "and get up against the wall."

Bolan let the bottle fall from his fingers. The thick glass hit the sidewalk and bounced, miraculously not breaking. He moved slowly to the nearest wall in front of a floral shop, his hands held at his shoulders.

Now would come the search. And with the discovery of three guns and enough C-4 to blow half of Vladivostok into oblivion, would come the arrest. Then, as Tachek had predicted, Bolan would spend the rest of his life in prison while the president of the Russia wondered what had become of him.

The Executioner didn't intend to let that happen.

Bolan leaned forward against the wall and spread his legs. He felt the tall cop's hands rip the watch cap from his head, run through his hair, then fall to his shoulders. As one of the hands struck the Beretta under his arm, the Executioner pivoted suddenly, turning to drive an elbow up and out into the blond beard.

A sharp crack echoed through the night. The tall cop slumped forward into the Executioner's arms.

Bolan kept the limp form between him and the other officer as he drew the Beretta. The shorter cop was darting hastily back and forth, jockeying for a position from which he could fire without hitting his partner. Using the blond man as a shield, the Executioner pressed the Beretta's suppressor into the unconscious head and said, "Drop it, or I'll kill him."

The shorter cop stopped in his tracks, hesitating.

"You speak English?" Bolan asked.

At the man's nod, he said, "You've got three seconds. Then I blow your buddy away."

Fear filled the shorter cop's eyes as the Makarov fell to the sidewalk and rolled next to the bottle.

Bolan let the limp man fall from his arms. He glanced up and down the side street. It was still deserted. "Turn around," he ordered.

The cop stood, frozen. His voice quavered when he spoke. "You will kill us both?"

"I will if you don't do what I just told you."

The man closed his eyes tightly, his lips moving silently in prayer as he turned.

Bolan brought the Beretta down on the back of his neck and the cop fell next to his partner.

Quickly the Executioner lifted the blond man into his arms and hurried toward the alley at the far end of the block. Halfway there, he spotted a five-foot gap between the closed retail stores. Large, sturdy water pipes shot out of the walls connecting the two buildings. Bolan dropped his burden beneath the pipes and hurried back for his partner.

The Siberian cops were both conscious by the time the Executioner had handcuffed them to the pipes. He ripped the men's shirts, fashioned gags, then shoved the Beretta into the blond man's face. "You're going to be cold by morning," he said, "but you'll live. *If* you keep this in mind—I'll be checking on you every few minutes throughout the night. If somebody comes by before daybreak and you call out to them, you're dead. You got it?''

The blond beard bobbed again.

Bolan turned the Beretta on the shorter man. He nodded, too.

Without another word the Executioner turned and disappeared into the night.

Moments later he reached the docks and turned down the long line of ships. He walked slowly along the quayside, breathing in the damp, salty sea air as he passed frigates from a variety of countries. Voices echoed down from the decks as the Executioner stared straight ahead, furtively noting the registration of each vessel.

He had no idea who the Russian mole was, but the man was doing his job. He had learned that the first cocaine shipment of the New Brotherhood would come to port in a pair of South America cargo ships. But like most undercover agents, the mole had gotten only part of the story. He didn't know which ships or even from which country they had sailed. Bolan's jaw set in determination as he neared a vessel flying the colors of Ecuador.

Specific target identification, and destruction, would be up to the Executioner.

Two hard-looking sailors stood watch as he passed the vessel from Ecuador. In the dim port lights Bolan saw pistol shapes breaking the lines of their tight sweaters. He took note of the ship's name—*Boyaca*—and made a mental note of its position on the dock.

Continuing along the quay, the Executioner raised the vodka bottle to his lips. He had retrieved it, and stashed the Siberian cops' Makarovs in a mailbox outside a floral shop.

Bolan had passed several Russian fishing vessels and a Japanese whaler when he noted the Colombian flag atop another ship. The three men covering the gangplank looked like carbon copies of the guards from the Ecuadorian ship. The Executioner moved on.

Near the end of the docks, Bolan came to a three-hundred-foot cargo ship under Peruvian registration. Both gangplank and decks appeared deserted, and he quickly discounted the craft.

Hundreds of thousands, maybe millions of dollars' worth of cocaine didn't go unguarded. No, the dope was in the Colombian and Ecuadorian ships.

The Executioner took a seat on a cold concrete bench facing the sea. He swigged water from the bottle again as he planned his infiltration and attack. Somewhere in the holds of the two vessels lay untold amounts of cocaine. In days not so long ago, with the information they had, the KGB would have simply boarded both crafts—maybe all ships in port—and conducted a search. Now, those days were in the past. Russian drug agents were learning something their American counterparts had known for years.

Simple knowledge that a crime had been committed didn't constitute probable cause to search.

Bolan rose from his seat. Exaggerating his stagger, he moved back toward the Colombian ship. As it came into view, he saw the letters on the hull—*Valdez*.

The same three guards still stood at the top of the brow. One wore a khaki seaman's cap with a black visor. Another, a blue chambray shirt beneath a leather vest. The third man wore a light poplin jacket over a sweater similar to Bolan's.

Making sure the men's eyes were on him, the Executioner tipped the bottle to the sky and guzzled water. With short, weaving footfalls, he started up the gangplank, casually shifting his grip to the bottle's neck.

Laughter rolled down from the ship. "Look, Felipe," the man in a khaki cap roared in Spanish. "Even *you* have never been that drunk."

Bolan reached the top of the gangplank and stared bleary-eyed at the men. "What . . . shhhip is this?" he mumbled.

The man in the khaki cap placed his hands on the Executioner's shoulders and shoved roughly. "The *wrong* ship, hombre," he said.

In one swift movement Bolan twisted back and swung the bottle across the bridge of the man's nose.

Blood spurted from the fractured bone as the man in the cap slumped to the deck.

The other two guards froze, but only for a second. As the man in the vest reached for him, Bolan swung the bottle horizontally. The blow caught the man solidly on the jaw, and the bottle shattered. Blood, water and glass fragments rained over the leather vest.

By the time the Executioner turned to the third guard, the man had recovered from shock. His left hand lifted his jacket, the right fumbling for the pistol in his belt.

Bolan caught the man's hand as it found the gun, pinning it to his belt. The Executioner drove the ugly, jagged bottle stump into the man's throat, severing the carotid artery.

Suddenly all was still on the deck of the ship.

The Executioner dragged the men across the deck to the canvas-covered anchor windlass. He looped plastic Flex-Cuffs around the wrists and ankles of the men in the cap and vest. Fashioning gags from strips of their shirts, he stowed them out of sight under the canvas.

The third man needed no gag or restraints. Bolan shoved him in after the others.

Footsteps sounded across the deck as the Executioner pulled the canvas back over the anchor windlass. Lifting a corner of the flap, he dived in on top of the three men.

Voices in Spanish rose as the steps neared. "But why haven't we gotten our money, Efren? That is what I want to know."

"I don't know. I assume the cowboy has not received payment yet."

Bolan lifted the canvas high enough to see two pairs of shoes nearing the anchor windlass.

"I do not trust the crazy bastard with his long coat and shining guns," the first voice said. "We haven't been paid, and we are taking a great risk just to—"

The two men suddenly halted three feet from where Bolan lay. He could see them only to the knees. Both wore OD green work pants and black brogans that faced away from him.

"Where is the watch?" the second voice asked.

Without warning the Executioner climbed out from under the canvas. He wrapped his arms around both sets of ankles and jerked back. The two men shot face forward to the deck.

The head of the man to Bolan's left cracked the deck with a hollow thump. The second man turned as he fell, landing on his side, his wild eyes staring into the Executioner's as Bolan crawled over him.

The warrior twisted the Mini Tanto into an ice-pick grip as he raised it overhead. The armor-piercing tip plunged down through the drug runner's ribs and into his heart. Moving swiftly to the man who'd cracked his head on deck, Bolan checked his pulse.

Zero.

The Executioner withdrew the Tanto, wiped it on the man's jacket and returned the weapon to its sheath. Rising quickly, he scanned the deck. Clear. He squeezed one of the men under the canvas where he himself had hidden moments before. But the body count was rising. The other man wasn't going to fit.

Spotting a heavy line coiled on the deck to dry, the Executioner knotted a loop and slipped it under the arms of the man he'd stabbed. He dragged the body to the rail, heaved it over and lowered the man silently into the water.

A hatch was just aft of the anchor windlass. The Executioner lifted the cover and cautiously descended a ladder that led into the bowels of the ship. A moment later, he found himself in the forward cargo hold.

Down the hatchway, he heard the constant hum of the ship's engines and generators. Pulling a Mini-Mag flashlight from his pants pocket, the Executioner surveyed the hold.

Huge refrigerators lined the walls. Opening the first, Bolan found sides of beef hanging in the cold compartment. Employing the Tanto once more, he poked and prodded through the meat until he was satisfied it contained nothing more deadly than bone.

The rest of the beef proved equally harmless.

Above the noise from the engine room, the Executioner heard footsteps. Moving to the door, he backed against the wall and drew the silenced Beretta. He knelt and risked a quick glance around the corner.

Two men, one Hispanic, the other Oriental, stood near a row of machine spaces.

"You will be paid as soon as we are," the Hispanic told his companion in an irritated tone. "Not before. I cannot give you what I don't have."

The Oriental's voice was equally agitated as he answered in the same language, but with a heavy Manchurian accent. "My men are restless," he said. "We have fulfilled our end of the bargain, but we have seen no sign that you intend to hold up yours."

The warrior pulled his head back, taking a deep breath. It didn't take a Rhodes scholar to figure out what was going on. As the "new kid on the block," the New Brotherhood would need help setting up a pipeline into the Commonwealth of Independent States. So they had gone to the logical source of aid: the infamous Manchurian Triads.

The sound of heavy heels echoed into the engine room. Bolan peered around the edge once more. A tall, lanky man who looked like he'd just stepped out of

Buffalo Bill's Wild West Show stood next to the Manchurian. A thick handlebar mustache flared up his cheeks, and a flat-brimmed gunslinger's hat sat atop the long brown hair that fell to his shoulders.

Bolan recalled the intelligence reports. Jake Pool. Hernandez's right-hand man. Wild Bill Hickok's psychotic clone.

"What's wrong, Gomez?" Pool demanded.

"Mr. Hong wishes to be paid immediately."

Pool grabbed the Manchurian by the collar of his shirt. With lightninglike swiftness, a nickel-plated Colt Single Action Army .45 leaped into his hand. He shoved the revolver's stubby four-and-a-half-inch barrel into the man's open mouth. "You just relax, there, Hop Sing," Pool drawled. "You're gonna get what's coming to you. Just make sure what's coming to you's the money—and not a .45 Long Colt."

Bolan pulled back again, thumbing the Beretta's safety to 3-round burst. He'd have to deal with Pool sooner or later.

And sooner would be better.

The Executioner turned back in time to see the tail of Jake Pool's black frock coat disappear up the ladder.

The opportunity missed, Bolan shifted the safety of the 93-R to semiauto. He dropped the sights on the back of Hong's head and squeezed the trigger.

The Manchurian fell to the deck. Gomez stared down at him in surprise. Then, as the Executioner pulled the trigger again, he saw the South American's face light up in sudden fear and understanding.

Gomez turned toward Bolan just in time to catch the Executioner's next silenced round in his face.

Bolan rose and hurried down the hatchway. A quick inspection of the engine room revealed several machine spaces against the wall. He slid the bodies under a lathe.

He moved quickly now, hurrying down the hatchway to the after hold, conscious of the fine line between speed and silence. He had taken out seven of the crew so far. Sooner or later, they'd be missed. He had hidden the bodies, but there'd been no time to mop up the trail of blood he was leaving in his wake. When that was spotted, a major search and destroy would be launched by the rest of the crew.

The Executioner switched on the Mini-Mag flashlight as he entered the hold, spotting a long row of 55-gallon cardboard drums, marked Cafe. Jabbing the knife just under the vacuum-sealed lids, the rich odor of fresh coffee filled his nostrils.

Bolan sliced through the cardboard as the coffee began to fall to the floor like sand in an hourglass. The blade snagged suddenly. Scooping out more grounds with his hands, he saw the clear plastic bags.

And the white powder they contained.

Excited voices reached Bolan's ears from the deck above. He pulled a small, precut charge of C-4 from his coat, fixed an electronically detonated primer to the claylike substance and buried it inside the drum. Moving along the line, he cut smaller holes through the cardboard of the rest of the barrels and planted the charges.

Sounds of men descending the ladder reached the Executioner. He turned to see two brown-skinned seamen burst into the cargo area toting Uzis.

A 3-round burst of hushed 9 mm slugs sent both men crashing to the ground.

Bolan hurried up the ladder, the Beretta hidden beneath his pea coat. A dozen men stood on the deck scanning the area, shotguns and automatic weapons in their hands.

"Below!" the Executioner shouted in Spanish, pointing back down the ladder. "Two guys. They're armed!"

He stepped to the side as the men hurried past him toward the hole.

The Executioner sprinted down the gangplank, turned toward the Ecuadorian ship and raced along the docks. The two vessels were bound to have radio communication, and in a matter of seconds, the guards on the *Valdez* would figure out what had happened and alert their sister ship. Reaching the *Boyaca,* he raced up the gangplank, waving his arms.

Two men stood guard on deck. One wore a navy watch cap. The other was bareheaded, his short, curly blond hair glistening under the ship's lights. Both drew Government Model .45s and aimed at Bolan's chest.

The Executioner stopped and raised his hands. "Take me to the captain," he demanded.

The man in the watch cap cocked the hammer of his side arm.

"Look, dammit," the Executioner said. "We don't have time for this. Pool sent me to warn you. The

Chinamen tried to rip off the dope. They're planning to do the same down here. If we don't hurry—''

"Oh, yeah?'' the curly-haired man said. "How come he didn't just radio?''

Bolan's voice rose, anxious. "Because the Triad knocked out communications,'' he said. "Look, you want Pool to hold *you* responsible when the same thing happens down here?''

Indecision ruled the eyes of the two guards. Then the man in the cap said, "I'm not taking *you* anywhere.'' He turned to his partner. "Matty, bring the captain here.''

The man with the curly hair hurried away.

Bolan waited, planning and counterplanning as the seconds ticked by and turned to minutes. He wondered briefly if Pool had already contacted the captain of the *Boyaca.* If he had, the story about the radio being knocked out had him burned, and every gunner on the Colombian ship would soon converge on him, weapons firing.

The Executioner pushed the thoughts from his mind. He would deal with whatever came his way.

After what seemed like an eternity, the curly-haired guard led a man with an immense belly across the deck. Wiry gray hairs jutted at uncontrollable angles from the captain's head. "What did Pool say? Why didn't he radio?'' the captain asked.

"He sent a note,'' the Executioner said. Slowly his hand moved under his jacket. He saw the guard's hands tense around their weapons.

In one smooth, lightning move, the Executioner drew the Beretta and pumped one shot between the eyes of each guard. The man in the cap fell over the rail into the water. The bareheaded man slumped to the deck.

The captain stared in disbelief as the Executioner mounted the gangplank and shoved the suppressor under his chin. "What—"

"Keep your voice down," he ordered. "Do exactly what I tell you and you might see the sun come up tomorrow." He moved close to the captain, shoving the Beretta into the man's side and cloaking it from view with his pea coat.

Half a dozen men, both South Americans and Chinese, raced across the deck toward them. "Tell them it's a false alarm," the Executioner whispered. "Tell them to get ready to shove off."

The captain turned toward the men, a nervous grin making his jowls shake. "No problem, mates. False alarm," he said. "Make all preparations to sail."

Slowly the men turned and disappeared throughout the ship.

Bolan shoved the captain toward the superstructure amidship, then up the ladder to the radio room off the flying bridge. The radioman turned toward them as they entered.

The warrior heard Jake Pool's excited drawl over the airwaves. "Goddammit, get ready. Some son of a bitch, I don't know who he was, he just—"

Bolan aimed the Beretta at the radioman, grabbed the mike and keyed the transmitter. "And you won't find out who I am for a while," the Executioner said into the mike. "But don't worry, we'll meet eventu-

ally. Just remember this, Pool. I know who *you* are."
He set the mike back on the table.

As the ship began to move, the radioman lunged
suddenly for a drawer in the control station. Bolan
watched his fingers curl around a Colt Government
Model .380.

The man had the gun halfway out of the drawer
when a hollowpoint from Bolan's Beretta sent him
sprawling to the deck.

The warrior turned to the captain. The man's fat
belly and jowls were shimmying in time to the ship engines' vibrations as the vessel began to leave port. "If
you want to try something like that, let's get it out of
the way right now."

The captain shook his head.

Bolan pulled the remote-control detonator from his
pocket and tapped a series of buttons. Through the
glass windows he heard a dull thud and felt the con-
cussion from the other end of the docks.

As the *Boyaca* pulled out to sea, smoke began to rise
from the bowels of the *Valdez*.

## CHAPTER FOUR

Except for the waiter and the young man by the front window, the Ukrainian Café was deserted. Of course it usually was. Which was exactly why Pyotr Leskov had chosen it for his meetings with Alexandr Solomentsev.

Leskov scanned the empty tables. He wondered briefly how the café stayed in business, then his eyes fell on the young man again. The kid wore American blue jeans and a sweatshirt that proclaimed he was a member of the U.S. Drinking Team. On top of his head was a New York Yankees baseball cap.

The old man watched from the corner of his eye as the youth's foot tapped in time to the music over the loud speaker. The lyrics were in Russian, but Leskov recognized the music for what it was. Rock and roll. American rock and roll.

Another great leap backward for Russia.

The door opened and Solomentsev walked in. He scanned the darkened bar as he removed his gloves. His eyes met Leskov's and he nodded, slipping out of his overcoat as he slid into a chair. "Hello."

"Good evening, Alexandr," Leskov replied. "I have taken the liberty of ordering for us."

Solomentsev folded his coat and laid it in the chair next to him. "I can stay only a moment," he said. "Natalya is expecting me—"

The waiter appeared with a tray and set glasses of dark brown liquid in front of them. "If you please," Leskov said, "we'll have the food now. And bring the black beluga, not the red."

"Really, Pyotr," Solomentsev protested. "I do not have time for—"

Leskov let his gaze fall to the table. "Yes, I have forgotten. You are a very important man. Far too important to waste your time with a stumbling old oaf like myself."

"Pyotr, I did not mean to sound—"

Leskov looked up and reached for his glass. "Forget it," he said brusquely. "It is I who am sorry. I value the time you find for me, Alexandr. It is the only social life I have." Lifting his glass, he said, "To your health," and tossed back the dark vodka in one gulp.

"And to your health, Pyotr," Solomentsev echoed, and did the same.

Leskov felt the aged vodka warm his stomach. He watched the strain in Solomentsev's face fade as the smooth, dark liquid began to work its magic. He snapped his fingers and the waiter returned. "Another drink for my friend and myself," he ordered.

This time, Solomentsev didn't protest.

"So tell me what is new at the Kremlin," Leskov said. He watched Solomentsev's tired eyes flicker uncertainly, then relax again. "There is a leak somewhere. Last night an attempt was made on the American's life."

Leskov's brow furrowed deeply. "How is that possible, my young friend? Besides yourself, the president, and Colonel Kerensky, no one knows of his presence."

The waiter returned and set a large plate of pancakelike rolls on the table. Inside the heavy appetizers Leskov could see the tiny black grains of caviar covered with sour cream. He ignored the food, immediately picking up the glass of vodka as the waiter set it down. Solomentsev followed suit, then both men chased the liquor with a gulp of black-bread beer known as kvass.

"It seems obvious," Leskov said, reaching for one of the pancakes. "Colonel Kerensky is a traitor."

Solomentsev took another gulp of his kvass and stared across the table. His eyes had already begun to redden, and Leskov fought the chuckle that threatened to rise from his chest. Alexandr Solomentsev was so easy to mold. He made Leskov think of the ridiculous American children's toy called Silly Putty.

"Impossible," the young man replied. "She took the same test I took."

"There are ways to deceive one who runs the polygraph," Leskov said, swatting a fly from his face.

"The president administered the test himself," Solomentsev countered, his words beginning to slur.

"My point exactly, Alexandr. Polygraph exams are art, not science. In order to be effective one must practice; stay current with the technique. I doubt very much that the leader of Russia has had time to do so."

Solomentsev drained his glass. The waiter came from nowhere and set more beer and vodka on the table. "It is possible you are correct," he said, reaching for a pancake. "You believe that Kerensky is behind the leak?"

Leskov shrugged. "Agents of RMI are tricky bastards. Untrustworthy. And no one else is aware of the American's presence." He paused, then added, "Except one other person we have not mentioned. Perhaps I should take the polygraph exam myself."

The younger man's bloodshot gaze shot up from the plate. Again, Leskov suppressed the laugh. Solomentsev could hardly allow that—Tachek would learn that his aide had spoken out of school.

"Don't be ridiculous. I trust you implicitly, Pyotr."

Leskov nodded. Solomentsev nervously threw back the new shot of vodka and ate another appetizer.

"I have thought long and hard about this American of yours," Leskov said, breaking the uneasy silence. "He intrigues me. Can you tell me more about him?"

Solomentsev paused in midbite, his eyes reflecting a last moment of caution through the alcohol haze.

"I ask only because there is yet another possibility that we have not discussed. The leak could be the American himself."

Solomentsev laughed, tiny granules of caviar falling from the corners of his lips. "He was almost *killed*, Pyotr. Would he do that?"

Leskov shrugged. "The operative word is 'almost,' my young friend. Doesn't it seem odd that one man could so easily defeat three? Three who had surprise on their side as well as numbers?" The old colonel caught his mistake even as he spoke, cursing himself, wishing he could bite back the words.

Solomentsev's mouth dropped open. "How did you know there were three men, Pyotr? I said nothing of it."

Leskov smiled. "I am afraid that you did, Alexandr. But we had certainly had a few drinks first. I am not surprised you do not remember."

The confusion returned to Solomentsev's eyes, this time mixed with fear. Leskov could almost read the younger man's thoughts:

What else have I said that I am unaware of?

Leskov passed his hand in front of his face to dismiss the issue. "Relax, Alexandr. The information is safe with me. Now, tell me of the American. The power in my arms has left me, and these legs no longer run." He tapped his temple with his fingers. "But the brain still functions."

Solomentsev guzzled the rest of his beer. In a slow, slurry voice, he described the American.

Pyotr Leskov felt the chill run through him as the younger man's words stirred a half memory locked somewhere in the back of his mind. Big. Fast. Deadly. Leskov remembered an American like that. A man who single-handedly had nearly destroyed the KGB. But he couldn't remember the details, couldn't raise the thought to his conscious mind and identify it, analyze it, put a name with it.

Leskov knew only that the memory brought terror.

"Where is the American now?" he asked.

Solomentsev looked over both shoulders, then leaned in close, his voice a conspiratorial whisper. "We have learned of a shipment of cocaine coming to Vladivostok," he said.

Leskov watched the young drunk's face relax again as Solomentsev threw caution to the wind. "We have a mole within the group known as the New Brotherhood."

BOLAN KEPT THE BERETTA hidden under his jacket as he escorted the captain from the radio room across the deck to the superstructure.

"What's going on, Skipper?" asked a crewman wearing a red bandanna tied over his head.

Bolan spoke with authority. "I've just come from the *Boyoca*," he said. "Nothing to be alarmed about. Stand by."

The man glanced curiously to the captain, who nodded and the sailor walked off.

When they'd descended the ladder, Bolan shoved his prisoner forward. "Your cabin," he ordered. He followed the gray-haired man down the hatchway, then pushed him through the door.

"We need to have a little talk," he said. "What's your name?"

The captain's eyes crossed as he stared down at the gun. He hesitated, then said, "Ortez," in a soft, shaking voice.

The Executioner heard the powerful diesel engines roar as the ship made ready to sail. "Okay, Ortez. I'll make this short and sweet. You've got a chance to stay alive. Do everything I say, and you might get lucky. You with me so far?"

Ortez continued to stare at the Beretta as he nodded.

"Where's the coke hidden?" Bolan demanded.

"Several places."

Bolan pressed the 93-R into the captain's windpipe.

"Well, let's go take a peek."

The ship began to roll beneath their feet as Ortez led the Executioner out of the cabin, down the hatchway to the rear hold. Large cardboard boxes, stacked to the ceiling, covered the deck. Bolan used his combat knife to slice into one of the cases and found that it contained smaller cartons—shoe boxes. The foot size, and Genuine Ecuadorian Leather had been stamped on the ends of each box.

"Which ones?"

"Size ten."

The Executioner slashed through the cardboard until he came to a box marked "10." Ripping the lid off, he found the same freezer bags of white powder he'd seen in the coffee on the other ship. "All the tens?" he asked.

The captain nodded.

"Any other sizes?"

Ortez shook his head.

"Where else?"

The captain pointed to the other side of the room. Metal containers lined the wall. Brass plates fixed to the sides read Pharmaceuticals.

"The cocaine's mixed in with all the legitimate drugs," Ortez explained. "It'll take you a week to locate it all."

The Executioner didn't have a week.

But he didn't need one.

The deck rolled suddenly beneath their feet as the ship left the harbor for open water. Bolan caught his balance and hurried to a porthole. Outside, the lights of the harbor were dimming. They were already a good mile from shore.

Shoving the captain down the hatchway to the engine room, Bolan saw a tall, swarthy man wearing a custom-made cross-draw holster. The man's hand fell on the grip of a single-action revolver when he saw the Beretta.

The warrior dropped him in his tracks with a single hushed 9 mm round.

"Stand still," the Executioner ordered Ortez. He kept one eye on the captain as he pulled more of the C-4 from his pocket.

"What are you doing?" Ortez asked, his voice an octave higher than it had been.

Bolan began assembling two separate bombs. "You don't own this ship, do you?"

The captain shook his head. "It belongs to—" He caught himself in midsentence.

"The New Brotherhood."

The captain nodded slowly.

"Then relax," Bolan said as he hooked the primer to the clay. "Collecting the insurance won't be your problem."

The Executioner pressed plastique against the ship's boiler and the engine valve. Then he turned to Ortez. "You need to come up with a good reason for us to take a ride in the captain's gig."

Ortez took a deep breath. His eyes shot nervously around the engine room, as if the answer to his problem might be found among the machinery. Finally he said, "I'll tell the crew it's a maintenance check."

"That's pretty thin, Ortez. Think they'll buy it?"

The captain's face tightened, and what little blood still remained drained from his face. "Maybe. I don't know. But I can't think of anything better."

"Then you better hope it works," Bolan said bluntly, then prodded the captain up the ladder to the deck.

Ortez led the way around the superstructure to the large motorized lifeboat known as the captain's gig. A crewman, wearing a heavy leather jacket and jeans, stood near the davits by the rail. The round butt of a Smith & Wesson Chiefs Special .38 jutted from his back pocket.

"Maintenance check," Ortez told the man. "Lower the lifeboat as soon as we're in."

Bolan and Ortez climbed over the rail.

The crewman stood still, his face a mask of disbelief. "You, er, checking her out yourself, Skipper?"

"That's right.

Suddenly four more seamen rounded the superstructure. A man with a bright, orange-red beard led the others across the deck. The man's face, as well as those of his followers, reflected the same confusion as the crewman in the leather jacket.

By now, the crew knew that there had been some kind of trouble on the *Boyoca*. They also knew both ships were transporting cocaine, and it hadn't been unloaded yet.

So why had the *Valdez* suddenly shoved off?

"Skipper?" the red-bearded man asked as he approached the gig. "What the hell is going—"

What little courage the captain possessed had been used up. "Lower the *fuckin'* boat!" he screamed suddenly.

The terror in his voice drove the last shred of indecision from the crewmen. They might not know *what* was wrong, but something was. Pistols suddenly appeared in their hands, pulled from under their shirts.

Bolan drew the Beretta from beneath his pea coat and fired as the man in the leather jacket drew the .38 from his back pocket. A 3-round burst of subsonic 9 mm bullets swooshed through the air, leaving star-shaped crimson caves in the gunman's forehead.

Two of the other four men dived for cover behind a deck housing. A third drew a Taurus PT-58 from his belt as a Colt Python snubbie appeared in the hand of Red Beard.

The mighty roar of the .357 Magnum pierced the night. Bolan felt the round whiz past his ear. He twisted toward Red Beard and cut loose with another trio of hushed Parabellum rounds. The revolver fell to the deck of the ship, followed by the gunner.

The Executioner leaped back on deck and grabbed the davit wheel, breaking it loose as two more rounds boomed out. Metal screeched against metal as the wheel spun out of control and the captain's gig descended. Bolan squeezed the trigger as he pivoted back toward the superstructure. Another burst of hushed 9 mm rounds punched through the man bracing the Taurus.

Bolan glanced over the rail. The gig was now twenty feet below, nearing the water. With a final burst of cover fire toward the deck housing, the Executioner jumped over the rail, landing feet first on the deck of the descending lifeboat. He switched the Beretta to his left hand as the gig hit the water. He aimed high overhead, sending more rounds toward the heads popping over the rail. With his right hand he swung the Striker out to the end of the sling.

A hand holding a Detonics .45 Scoremaster eased over the rail.

The Executioner's first burst of automatic 12-gauge buck cut through the gunner's forearm, a shrill scream letting the warrior know he was dead-on. The hand, still gripping the Detonics, fell over the side of the ship and landed on the deck of the gig.

Bolan disconnected the retaining lines, and the gig drifted away from the hull. He turned toward Ortez, who stood next to him, frozen like a statue. "You'd better get this thing going."

Ortez didn't have to be told twice. He waddled into the cabin, and Bolan heard the engine start.

More shots rained down into the lifeboat as the vessel broke away. Small holes cracked the deck on both sides of the Executioner's feet. He swung up the Striker again and tapped the trigger. Empty plastic shotgun shells flew from the automatic scattergun to litter the deck as hundreds of tiny pellets sprayed the rails of the *Valdez*.

Bolan dived to the deck as a volley of automatic rounds showered the gig. He looked up to see a man leaning over the rail, an Uzi gripped in his fists. More of the crew, armed with subguns, joined him at the rail.

Bolan drew the Desert Eagle as the boat raced out of the Striker's range. Sighting down the barrel, he squeezed the trigger twice.

At least one of the massive .44 rounds hit its mark. The Uzi fell from the gunman's lifeless hands and splashed into the sea.

The Executioner rose from cover and glanced into the cabin. Ortez faced away from him, shaking as he guided the boat.

Bolan pulled the remote transmitter from his jacket as the assault faded then quieted altogether. He tapped the buttons and heard the explosion. Fire leaped from the bowels of the ship, illuminating the dark sea as the captain's gig continued to race away.

A wheezing gasp echoed across the deck as the Executioner pocketed the transmitter. He turned to see Ortez stumble from the cabin, his gaze locked on the Detonics.

With a roar of anger he lunged for the pistol.

The blast of the Desert Eagle drowned out the man's war cry as Bolan pumped a Magnum round into Ortez's heart.

JAKE POOL FELT like tiny daggers had invaded his bloodstream, spread throughout his body, then pierced each capillary and embedded themselves in his flesh.

Pool was mad. And when he got mad, he wanted to kill.

He glanced to the pilot next to him. The weasely little man smiled, then turned back to the sky. Pool closed his eyes.

By now the cocaine should have been halfway across Siberia to Moscow. He and Furelli should be ready to do the gun deal at K'achta.

But was it? No. And were they? No.

Why? Because some son of a bitch had blown up the dope.

Pool wanted to kill someone. Preferably the bastard who'd blown up Hernandez's ships.

The hired gun felt the pressure on his bladder and opened his eyes. He rose from his seat, left the cabin and walked through the plane's empty cargo area toward the rest room. Originally he'd planned to pick up a load of "ice," the smokeable Oriental amphetamine, before flying back. But that wouldn't happen now.

There'd be no money to buy it with.

Pool ripped open the rest-room door and stepped inside. Moving into the crowded stall, he unzipped his pants and pulled out his "carrot." The word brought a smile to his face as he remembered the book where he'd learned the term. *Lonesome Dove.* That's what the cowboys and Texas Rangers in the book had called their dicks—carrots. Pool didn't know whether the word was genuine Old West terminology, but it had the ring of authenticity, so he'd incorporated it into his own vocabulary.

He suddenly grimaced as a halting stream of urine jerked into the toilet. He steadied himself. The pain in his bladder didn't bother him, really. It was part of his very being—his roots. He'd picked up the "blood disease" in Deadwood, South Dakota, back in the 1870s—probably from that dirty wench Calamity

Jane—and suffered from it right up until the end. Right up until the day that coward Jack McCall caught him with his back to the door in Saloon Number 10 and put a bullet through his head.

Pool bit the ends of his mustache as fire shot through his groin. Funny how some things stayed with your soul and followed you into the next life. Things like the ability to draw and shoot. And blood diseases. Well, the clap was one of the things he could have done without in this life, but he'd have to live with it.

The pain began to fade as Pool washed his hands. He squinted into the tiny metal mirror bolted above the sink. Lowering his left eyebrow, he twisted his lips into the lopsided grin. The death grin, he called it. He liked the grin; liked showing it to men just before he blew their brains out.

Straightening the black string tie and smoothing the lapels of his black frock coat, Pool tilted the hat down slightly over his right eye. He grinned again and casually brushed an imaginary speck of dust from his sleeve. "Now wait a minute, partner," he whispered out loud into the mirror. "Fightin' ain't the answer. Why don't you and me just—"

In a sudden blur of speed Jake Pool whisked the frock coat back. His grin faded and was replaced with a dead, emotionless gaze as the fishing sinkers sewn into the hem of the coat sent the tails past his hips. The nickel-plated Colts flashed in the overhead light as they leaped into his hands. The hammers clicked back and a microsecond later Pool was staring down the bores in the mirror.

The grin returned. Twirling the revolvers twice around his trigger fingers, the gunfighter slid them smoothly back into their holsters.

Pool left the rest room and returned to his seat. He stared through the windshield into the clouds. The Chinese behind the controls glanced at him, smiled, then turned back.

The gunslinger wondered briefly who the yellow man had been in his former lives. Ghengis Khan, maybe? No, hell, no. Nobody important. Reincarnation didn't work that way. Your soul was either big-time, or it wasn't, and the hell with what the Hindus said about coming back as a king or a cow or a fuckin' door-knob. You came back each time pretty much the same way you went out.

Suddenly, and as always without warning, Pool heard the buzz in his ears. His hands shot to his temples as the buzz became a roar. Minuscule sparkles of light danced before his eyes. Jake Pool gave a low, guttural moan.

Slowly the sharp shooting pains subsided and the familiar dull throb set in. Pool's eyes opened into tiny slits, and the sun through the windshield blinded him like a 1000-watt floodlight.

The pilot turned, smiling. The bastard was laughing inside, reveling in his pain. Pool knew it.

He fished the prescription bottle out of his vest pocket and palmed four of the Talwin capsules. He tipped his head back, feeling the back of his skull split as if he'd been hit with an ax. He washed the pills down with whiskey from his tin flask and closed his eyes again.

The blood disease. The fuckin' blood disease. It had reached his head a few months ago.

As the alcohol and Talwin raced through his system, Pool wondered just how much time he had left in this life. If the blood disease didn't do him in first, the Talwin and whiskey were bound to eat away at his reflexes. He'd die of a bullet again—just like he had in Deadwood.

Pool took another swig from the flask. His head continued to throb, but now the pain seemed dull, far away. He wiped the sweat from his forehead with his sleeve.

As the DC-10 began its descent, Pool pocketed the flask. He opened his eyes and caught the pilot staring at him.

"Land the fuckin' plane," Pool gritted, and his eyelids dropped again. He squinted hard, trying to concentrate. He didn't need the pilot anymore. In fact, he'd planned to pay the man off at this point and send him away.

But the fucker had laughed at his pain.

Suddenly the Talwin sank in, full-force. The throbbing in his head disappeared, and Pool began to feel good. Not as good as he would have if he'd have been able to kill the bastard who'd blown up the ships, but better than before. He turned back to the pilot and returned the man's smile.

The wheels of the DC-10 hit the tarmac. Pool watched the hilly terrain on both sides of the runway race past. "Okay, cowboy," he murmured to himself, "you know what to do now."

Pool waited until the plane had stopped completely, then turned in his seat. The big .45 Long Colts might burst his eardrums inside the cabin. He didn't need noise like that.

Reaching into his vest pocket, he drew the Butler .22 Short Derringer. His face twisted into a disarming grin, and he saw the pilot's eyes brighten in anticipation.

The asshole thought it was a gift.

Pool extended the tiny weapon in his open hand. "You want it, Ghengis?" he asked.

The pilot nodded and reached for the gun.

Pool twisted his wrist, cocking the Butler's hammer and angling the barrel up under the man's chin.

The little .22 sounded no louder than a firecracker in the cabin of the DC-10, but it did its job, drilling up through the pilot's soft palate and into his brain.

Pool pulled the sun visor down, staring into the mirror on the back. He liked what he saw. The handlebar mustache fell just right over his lips.

He stepped down from the plane to the landing strip as two uniformed Chinese soldiers walked forward. Just beyond the terminal, he saw the trucks and the waiting Triad escort.

Pool reached into his pocket, pulled out his bankroll and started counting. He handed the money to a soldier wearing a black eye patch.

"Let's hightail it, boys," he said.

The soldier stared in bewilderment at the words.

"Don't you speak English?" Pool asked.

The soldier's lone eye squinted. "Yes, I speak English."

"Then let's vamoose," Pool said. Dumb fucks, he thought as he walked past the man to the trucks.

HARSH RUSSIAN SCRATCHED over the radio as the MiG-23 climbed above the clouds over Vladivostok. As soon as he'd set course for K'achta, Bolan switched the control to automatic pilot and pulled a Leatherman Pocket Multi-Tool from his pocket. Flipping out a small screwdriver blade, he went to work on the panel in front of him. A few seconds later, the radio went dead.

The Executioner pulled a map of Russia from the breast pocket of the Czech uniform. On the map, K'achta lay only a few inches from Vladivostok. But on the wide open frontier of the largest country on earth, the distance was considerably farther—almost fourteen hundred miles. Refolding the map, Bolan found the topical atlas and briefly studied the terrain around K'achta.

The gun transfer would go down somewhere nearby. He wanted to know what obstacles he'd be facing, as well as the ground advantages that would be provided.

Bolan turned sideways in his seat, leaning forward with his elbows on his knees. The long flight would give him time to think—iron out the details for the next phase of the war.

The Executioner's mind returned briefly to the night before. He had set the captain's gig adrift in the Sea of Japan. Then, still in his sailor's clothing, he had hitched a ride back to the docks with a carload of drunken Japanese whalers. The whalers had stolen a car, gone for a joyride and gotten lost. Bolan had guided them back. They hadn't asked what the Executioner was doing so far from port, being far more concerned with returning the car before they found themselves in a Siberian prison.

Back at the Hotel Tolstoy, he had taken the back stairs to his room, showered, shaved and become Colonel Frank Hlupnik once more.

Before he checked out, a quick call from the lobby to Solomentsev in Moscow had provided several new details. The gun shipment was being escorted by a Mongolian Triad that evening. Several truckloads of Chinese Kalashnikovs were already on their way north, accompanied by Pool. Furelli and a band of New Brotherhood gunners planned to take possession somewhere along the border.

The Executioner's eyes burned from lack of sleep. He rubbed one, then the other, forcing his mind to clear. His first thought had been to simply locate Furelli, take him out, then step into the Mafia lieutenant's shoes and take the shipment off the Triad's hands himself. But Pool accompanying the Triad had ruled that out. Pool had met Furelli in the Bahamas.

Bolan leaned forward, resting his face on his arms. If he'd known the terrain around the meet site, there might have been a way to set up an ambush. The problem was, he'd never seen this part of Russia.

No, he'd have to find another approach. If he didn't stop this shipment of illegal weapons, every street punk in Moscow would be lighting up the night with automatic fire. It wouldn't take Tachek's political opponents long to have the Russian army patrolling the streets.

The MiG raced on through the sky as the Executioner forced himself to relax. He cleared his conscious mind, letting his instincts take over. Then suddenly, in a flash of precision, the plan came to him. Not just the idea, but every step that he had to take in order to thwart the shipment of ChiCom AKs on their way to the streets of Moscow.

Bolan spread out the map again, then opened his suitcase, digging through it until he found the travel guide. He would need to know all he could about the Russian-Chinese border if his plan was to be successful. He skimmed briefly a section about Lake Baikal, just to the north, where scientists had discovered thousands of life-forms unique to the area, then turned to the terrain along the border—heavy forest broken by natural valleys.

The Executioner grinned. Where there were valleys, there had to be the high ground that formed them.

An hour later, the Executioner returned to the controls and dropped the MiG down through the clouds. Soon, a tiny airstrip appeared in a clearing of the thick coniferous forest. A moment later, he pulled back hard on the stick and the wheels hit the runway. The K'achta airfield hadn't been designed to land fighters, and the MiG screeched to a halt three feet from the trees lining the end of the tarmac.

Bolan stepped down from the cockpit. Several figures, led by a large man dressed in the distinctive green hat, shoulder boards and collar tabs of the Russian Intelligence border guard, raced from the small office building to the plane.

His hand on the pistol grip of an AK-74 slung over his shoulder, the border guard stopped a foot in front of the American. The broad gold bar depicted him as a sergeant. He eyed Bolan's uniform suspiciously, then warily removed his hand from the rifle and gave the Executioner a stiff salute. "Good afternoon, Colonel."

Bolan returned the salute. The man was obviously nervous. Like the officers in Vladivostok, he wondered if the Czech colonel might actually be an RI spy.

The warrior's eyes lingered a moment at the name-plate over the man's left breast pocket. "My apologies, sergeant, for not notifying your tower of my arrival. But as you will soon see, that is the reason I landed. My radio is out."

The sergeant snapped his fingers and one of the other men, wearing oil-stained brown coveralls and a matching cap, vaulted up into the cockpit.

Bolan looked back to the sergeant's name plate. It read Khrushchev. "Sergeant, I must ask the obvious question. Any relation?"

The soldier's chest puffed out in pride. "The former general secretary was my grandfather's brother."

The man in the cockpit stuck his head back out before Bolan could comment further. "I can't tell what it is," he said. "It might take time."

The Executioner glanced at his watch in disgust and blew air between his closed lips. Then he shrugged, finally smiling. "Then I will make the most of the inconvenience," he said. Pulling the Hlupnik ID and the letter from Tachek from his uniform, he handed them to Khrushchev. "I have never had the pleasure of visiting this southern border of Russia.'' He faced the sergeant, noting that they were the same height. ''Sergeant,'' Bolan said, ''my most urgent need is your closest rest-room facility. Do you mind?''

Khrushchev nodded as he returned the Executioner's papers.

''Certainly, Colonel,'' he said. ''Please follow me.''

The warrior grabbed his bags and followed Khrushchev into the small office building. ''Through there, Colonel,'' the border guard said, pointing to a set of swing doors. ''At the far end, on your right.''

Bolan passed through the doors into a dressing room. A large, open shower stall sat to one side of the room. A row of green metal lockers lined the wall on the other. The Executioner eyed the name plates on each locker as he passed.

Khrushchev, V., was second from the end.

Glancing quickly over his shoulder, Bolan set his luggage on the floor and pulled the Leatherman from his pocket. Inserting the knife blade into the crack between the door and frame, he jimmied the lock and the door sprang open. A brown-and-green uniform, identical to the one the sergeant wore, hung from hooks on the sides of the locker.

The Executioner knelt in front of the locker, opening one of his suitcases. He glanced again toward the swinging doors as he stuffed the pants and tunic into the bag, closing the locker door quietly with his knee at the same time. As he fastened the latches of the suitcase, the doors to the hall swung open.

''Trouble, Colonel?'' the sergeant asked.

Bolan looked up, pointing down at the bag. He tightened his abdominal muscles, forcing blood to his face as if embarrassed. "Even a colonel is sometimes clumsy, Sergeant Khrushchev. I am afraid I dropped my suitcase." He grinned. "The latches must have been made in Germany."

The border guard laughed nervously at the joke, then hurried forward. "Please," he said. "Allow me to take it for you. And my deepest apologies. I should have done so from the beginning."

Bolan watched the man lift his bag and walk back to the hall.

The Executioner moved on to the rest room, closing the door behind him. He waited a few moments, flushed the toilet, then ran his hands under the faucet in the sink and dried them on a paper towel.

"Would you like a tour of the area?" Khrushchev asked when he returned to the hall.

Bolan shook his head. "I prefer to wander about on my own. It is a freedom we have not always had."

Khrushchev nodded vigorously. "I understand fully."

"But I could use a ride into town. And the name of a good hotel."

The sergeant glanced down at his feet. Looking back up, he said, "I am sorry, Colonel Hlupnik, there are no hotels in K'achta. But there are two private homes that rent rooms. The better of the two, I regret to say, has been occupied for the past two days by an American." He drew in a deep breath, looking down at his boots once more. "My quarters are humble, but if you would like—"

Bolan cut him off. "I would not wish to impose," he said. "The other rooming house will be fine. Please, if you would..." He held out his hand toward the door.

Khrushchev escorted him to the parking lot. Bolan slid into the passenger seat of a car bearing the state seal, and the sergeant climbed behind the wheel.

A few minutes later they entered a small village. Khrushchev pulled to a halt in front of a private home surrounded by a paint-flecked picket fence. Bolan got out and reached over the seat for his bags.

"I feel I have done very little for you, Colonel Hlupnik," the sergeant said, giving him a final salute. "If there is anything else that you need..."

Bolan lifted his bag and smiled. "You have done a great deal already, Sergeant Khrushchev."

## CHAPTER FIVE

"God bless *the hell* out of America," Ray Furelli muttered to himself. He pulled the heavy quilt comforter tighter around his neck. It was as cold as hell in his tiny rectangular ten-by-six-foot room, and the gas heater in the corner was about as effective as lighting a match in a snowstorm. It hissed away, doing nothing but adding its stench to the odor of old Mrs. Komosev's boiled cabbage.

The smell made him want to puke.

Sometimes being the son-in-law of Joseph Esposito helped. Sometimes it didn't.

Furelli stared up at the photograph on the wall. One of those old brown and white jobs, whatever you called them. Tintypes? No, he didn't think so. Whatever it was, it looked fifty years old and showed some old fool with a heavy beard, wearing furs and holding up a fish the size of a ten-year-old boy. Furelli studied it for the thousandth time. The old man's eyes were bright, twinkling. They made Furelli think of his grandmother, a superstitious old woman who had emigrated from Sicily in the 1920s. His grandmother had claimed she could read life and death in a man's eyes. Not the life or death of the man himself, but the destiny of whomever he was looking at.

Furelli grinned. He didn't know what the old fisherman in the picture was looking at, but he guessed Grandma Sardini would have given it a lengthy life.

The Mafia enforcer shivered again. And this is the *good* rooming house in this godforsaken Russian end-of-the-earth hellhole, he thought. What poor bastard might be staying down the street in the bad one?

Furelli's teeth continued to chatter. Damn, he'd have been just as well off camping in the forest with the rest of the men. At least he wouldn't have had any false expectations of comfort.

Forcing himself out of bed, Furelli stood. He crossed his arms and slapped his shoulders as he looked down at his watch: four-thirty. At least in another few hours he'd meet with the Chinese, pay them for the guns and get the caravan started toward Moscow. Then one more night in this frozen hell and he'd be on his way back to civilization. Home to his wife and kids, and a life in the twentieth century instead of the Middle Ages. He'd be smelling Jenny's perfume instead of boiled cabbage. His youngest son, Casey, would be four next week, and he'd rather watch *him* dance around the room than Mrs. Komosev's cockroaches.

Furelli reached down, lifting his coat off the top of his suitcase. He had left his clothes packed, not because he expected to have to leave in a hurry, but because there was nowhere else in the room to put them. Besides the bed, the only other items of furniture were the unpainted wooden table and chair against the wall. Slipping into the coat, he hooked the chair back with his foot and sat down.

The New York hitter stared at the unopened bottle of vodka in the center of the table. Would a drink warm him up? Maybe. But more than warmth, he wanted his wits about him when he went after the guns. There was no telling what the Triad men might try. If they got through this deal, established trust with the Chinese, *then* he might think about relaxing a little. Or he might just give it to that psycho Pool. The eccentric cowboy could use it to wash down his pills.

Jake Pool, in full costume, flashed through Furelli's mind. The thought made him shudder. What the hell was Hernandez's problem, trusting a nut-case like that with anything important? Furelli shook his head. He blew air through his chattering teeth and watched the condensation rise from his lips in the frigid air. The cartel men were just flat . . . well, crazy. Pool, Hernandez—all of them. They took chances nobody in their right mind would take. It was as if the adrenaline charge was the important thing, and the money just a way of keeping score.

Furelli shook his head again and reached for a deck of cards in his coat pocket. He couldn't argue with the millions, *billions,* actually, of bucks they made each year. But for what? What good was that much bread if you weren't around to spend it? Taking the deck from the box, the Mafia man began to shuffle. Above the hiss of the heater came the brisk whir as the plastic cards slapped onto the table.

Ray Furelli played his own brand of solitaire. He called it two-hand stud. Dealing a hole card and one up to himself and an imaginary player across the table, he set the deck down. His opponent showed the four of hearts. He wouldn't look at the invisible man's hole card until the end of the hand.

Checking his own hand, Furelli found the ace of diamonds. He had the queen of spades showing.

Down the hall, Furelli heard the front door open and glanced again to his watch. Mrs. Komosev. The woman had taken the trash out at the same time the past three days, as if it were some law or something. He dealt another card. Then the woman's heavy footsteps echoed down the hall. Furelli dropped the cards on the table. Oh, boy—cabbage time. In a moment the old hag would stick her head through the door and say the three words she knew in English: "You eat now."

Furelli had turned to the door when the knock sounded. He froze.

Whoever it was, it wasn't Mrs. Komosev. She never bothered to knock.

Moving silently, the Mafia lieutenent crossed the room to the bed, lifted the pillow, and reached for the butt of the Llama .380.

The sound of splintering wood reverberated through the room, and the bedroom door burst open.

Furelli's hand froze an inch from the weapon. He turned to see a tall man wearing the uniform of the border guard. The man held a Russian automatic in his right hand, pointed at Furelli's heart.

Behind the big man stood Mrs. Komosev, her pudgy fingers covering her mouth in fear.

"Hey, uh, I can explain about the piece, Officer," Furelli said, trying to keep his voice from shaking.

The big man didn't speak. He turned and dismissed Mrs. Komosev with a hand, entered the room and closed the door behind him.

The man in the uniform slid the gun under his tunic and stared at Furelli.

Furelli stared back, and suddenly it felt as if Mrs. Komosev's cabbage had stuck in his throat. He thought of his grandmother again.

For in the big man's eyes, Ray Furelli could see his own death.

THE SUBURU bearing the Intourist sticker sat just to the side of the house. Bolan opened the gate and walked up the sidewalk to the door.

The ''good'' rooming house, Khrushchev had called this one, the place where the American was staying.

The Executioner glanced over his shoulder, wondering what made the room in this house better than the one he'd rented down the street. Both houses, in fact the entire border town of K'achta, appeared to have been overlooked by the ''people's revolution.'' He didn't know how poorly the villagers had lived during the times of the czars, but it couldn't have been any worse than this.

Bolan raised his fist and rapped smartly on the door. A few seconds later he heard the bolt thrown back and then the thick smell of boiling cabbage wafted through the opening. A short, squatty woman clutching a dishrag in both hands looked up at him. The rag shook with fear as she studied his uniform.

The warrior stared down, carefully studying her reaction. His uniform bore minor discrepancies. A

Makarov pistol and belt gear had come with his Hlupnik identity, but the leather differed slightly from that issued to the border guards.

The landlady would be his sounding board; if she didn't note the divergence, there was very little chance that Furelli would.

"I must speak to your guest," Bolan said in a cold, firm voice. He watched the fear heighten within the poor peasant woman. As much as he'd have liked to quell her terror, he knew such consolation would be out of character for an intelligence officer. No, better to get in, do his business and get out again. His actions would speak louder than words anyway.

The old woman stepped back, opening the door wider.

Bolan followed her through a small living room, into the kitchen and down the hall. She nodded at a door and he knocked.

Inside the room, he heard feet hurrying across the floor. The Executioner raised a leg and kicked. He recognized Furelli from the file pictures. Medium height, medium build, quickly becoming medium bald. The hitter was reaching for a small automatic under his pillow.

"I can explain about the piece," the mafioso said, his voice quavering.

Bolan drew the Makarov. He waved the landlady away, crossed the room to the bed and lifted the Llama .380. Dropping it into his pocket, he turned back to Furelli. "There's no need to explain," he said, using short, halting, accented English. "I understand what is happening, Mr. Furelli. Perhaps I should explain it to *you*."

Furelli's face became a mixture of fear and confusion. He started to speak, then stopped.

"Your contacts on the other side of the border have received certain gifts for looking the other way," Bolan began. "In short my feelings are hurt. I feel left out." He gave the enforcer a hard-edged smile.

Furelli's face relaxed instantly. He blew air between his teeth in relief. "Thank God," he said, shaking his head. "If that's all it is..." He burst out in nervous laughter. "Oh, shit, I could already see myself in some prison camp eating rats and getting chased by polar bears." He indicated the chair at the table with his hand. "Have a seat, Mr...."

"Sergeant." Bolan dropped into the chair.

"Yeah, right. We can work this out, Sergeant." Furelli sat on the edge of the bed, facing the Executioner. "I don't know what went wrong," he said. "There were, er, gifts you were supposed to get from us. I talked to another of your crew. You telling me he didn't cut the money up with you?"

"That's exactly what I'm telling you."

"Well, hell. Maybe there was some confusion. Tell you what, to save any more..." Furelli knelt in front of a suitcase on the floor.

Bolan cocked the Makarov. Sharp metallic clicks echoed through the room as the hammer passed the notches. He leveled the weapon on Furelli's chest.

"Hey, come on," Furelli said. "I'm just gettin' the money, okay?"

Bolan nodded. But the Soviet 7.62 mm automatic didn't move.

Furelli unzipped his bag and pulled a thick yellow envelope from an inside pocket. He opened the flap and withdrew a wad of bills. Counting several off the top, he handed them to the Executioner. "Here you go," he said. "That's 62,000 rubles. About a thousand U.S. A little more than Khrushchev got, but what the hell, I had to deliver his. You picked yours up, right?" He smiled tensely from his position on the floor.

Bolan stuffed the money in his tunic. He kept the Makarov trained on Furelli and didn't speak.

"Is there, uh, something else?" the mafioso asked, his gaze glued to the bore in the end of the gun.

"I am concerned with what you are bringing into my country," the Executioner said. "If I am correct, it is guns."

Furelli's face froze. "Hey, listen, Sergeant—"

Bolan held up his hand, silencing the man. "You are more than welcome to add to our new capitalist system," he said. "But you must realize it is a very serious offense if you are caught smuggling guns. Not only for you, but for anyone who might have aided you." He paused, then went on. "I want to make sure that Sergant Khrushchev and myself are not underpaid for the risk we are taking."

"Well, listen. I'll tell you what. I might be able to get you a little more. But it'd mean more protection. You'd have to... I mean, well, how would you feel about going with us? Then if there was any trouble we'd have your uniform. The whole deal would look legit."

Bolan squinted up at the cracks in the ceiling as if in deep thought. He scratched his chin. Finally he returned his eyes to the man on the floor.

Nodding slowly, the Executioner said, "That is an idea we should consider, Mr. Furelli. It may very well have merit."

THE SUN HAD BEEN DOWN for half an hour when Mrs. Komosev stuck her head into the room. "You eat now," she told Furelli. Then, looking fearfully at Bolan, she switched to Russian. "Please," she begged. "It would be an honor if you would join us."

The Russian landlady smiled nervously throughout the meal. She offered Bolan more cabbage and potatoes than an army of hungry border guards could have downed. She insisted that he and Furrelli divide the pitiful amount of mutton on hand, claiming unconvincingly that she had no taste for it.

Bolan knew better. When they left the table after the meal, he waited until Furelli had headed down the hall, then turned back to the woman. Mrs. Komosev's eyes were wide with terror, wondering what crime, real or imagined, she might have committed.

"I apologize for the inconvenience this has caused you, Mrs. Komosev," the Executioner said. He watched her fear change to puzzlement. "The door I kicked in will need to be fixed. And food is not cheap in Siberia." Reaching into his tunic, he withdrew the ruble notes Furelli had given him and set them on the table. "This should cover the damage and the meal. But for reasons left best undiscussed, for the security of the country, I must insist that you tell no one about your reimbursement—even Mr. Furelli."

Bolan turned on his heel, but not before he saw Mrs. Komosev's expression change once more—this time, to shock.

The full moon had risen high in the Siberian sky, illuminating the town and making the dark forest surrounding it appear even darker, as Bolan and Furelli left the house. The hitter slid behind the wheel of the Subaru as the Executioner opened the door on the passenger's side.

"Where has your party camped?" Bolan asked in his hesitant, Russian-accented English.

"About five miles to the east," Furelli replied as he twisted the key in the ignition.

"The Chinese will meet us there?"

Furelli pulled onto the street. "Hell, no. They got no idea where the camp is. I don't trust those sons of bitches not to ambush us. I imagine they'd love to have the guns and money both."

Bolan nodded. "Will we cross into China, or will the Triad bring the rifles to us?"

Furelli turned onto a path leading into the woods. Suddenly the heavy overhead limbs of the firs and cedars shielded them from the moon. The only light in the car came from the dim reflection of the headlights off the tree trunks.

"There's a little stream runs along the border due south of the camp. We're going to do the deal right there. Anybody steps over the border, it won't be more than a foot or two."

Bolan settled back. The evident distrust the two groups held for each other was good. They would play right into his hands.

The Executioner's mind returned to the topographical map he had studied during the flight from Vladivostok. He remembered the stream. It flowed along the border in a low valley surrounded by steep cliffs on the Russian side.

Bolan smiled in the darkness as the Subaru continued through the trees. Originally he had planned to tail Furelli to the exchange site. But the plan had flaws. The chances of following the mafioso down the winding forest roads without being spotted were almost nil.

Bumping into a border guard who wore the Executioner's size, and had an extra uniform in his locker, had cut the odds considerably.

Furelli steered the Subaru around a bend. They emerged in the mouth of a clearing. The Executioner squinted into the darkness. Six panel trucks, their sides lettered in the Cyrillic alphabet, stood in the center of the clearing. Loosely translated, the signs read Russian Marine Life Reseach Center—Lake Baikal.

The cover was perfect. Esposito and Hernandez planned to transport the ChiCom AKs to Moscow disguised as animal specimens from the lake just to the north. Officials along the route would hardly care to invoke the wrath of Moscow's powerful scientific community by delaying the caravan.

Furelli stopped the Subaru as two armed men walked forward. The lead man wore a heavy green parka. The moon glistened off the slick black finish of the Valmet

M-71 assault rifles in his hands. Recognizing the Subaru, he stepped to the side and let Furelli through.

The Subaru jerked forward to the center of the clearing next to the panel trucks. Furelli rolled down the window as a man strolled up wearing a SIG-Sauer automatic on his hip. "Everything ready, Vinnie?" Furrelli asked.

The man nodded. "You going to lead the way?"

"Yeah. But keep your eyes open. No telling what surprises those Triad bastards might have in store."

Vinnie nodded again and turned away. Furelli backed out of the clearing and turned onto the road. The panel trucks fell in behind.

Bolan rode silently as the Mafia enforcer led the caravan through several twists and turns through the trees. The next step of his plan was critical. The idea he was about to introduce had to look spontaneous, and his timing would have to be perfect if he expected Furelli to fall for it.

The Executioner turned toward the man. "You sound like you really are expecting trouble. From the Triad, the Chinese military, or both?"

Furelli shrugged. "The Triad, maybe. The border guards have been paid to stay clear of the area."

Bolan waited a moment, then said, "So was I. But we changed our minds. What if they did the same on the other side? What conclusion would you come to if we arrive to see Chinese uniforms?"

This time, it was Furelli who hesitated. "I see your point," he finally said. "Hell, yes. My first reaction would be that it was a setup. The Triad will think the same when they see you."

"My thoughts exactly."

Furelli hesitated again, then said, "Damn, they'll go apeshit when they see you. Why didn't I think of that?"

Bolan shrugged. "I didn't think of it, either. Until now. Drive me as close as you can, then let me out. You can pick me up on the way back." He turned in his seat to face the mafioso and let his voice grow more menacing. "But don't think you can just leave me out here, Mr. Furelli. I can get to a phone faster than you can get the rifles to Moscow. One phone call, and your convoy won't even make it out of K'achta." He watched the enforcer's shadow as the man drove on.

The Executioner could almost hear the mafioso's thoughts. The arrival of the greedy border guard had been an unwanted thorn in Furelli's side. But so far he'd seen no opportunity to pull it out. Now the guard himself was unwittingly providing him with the chance. Furelli could do the deal, then his men could cut the Executioner down when he tried to get back in the car.

Furelli turned to Bolan in the darkness. "Man, I'm glad as hell I hired you, Sarge. This thing could have turned into a battlefield if you hadn't thought of that. In fact, I'm going to give you a raise on these deals from now on. You like that idea?"

"Yes, I do."

The hitter turned back to the road. "We're maybe a quarter mile from the creek right now. Why don't you hop out here? Just wait in the woods. We should be back in a half hour or so." He slowed the Subaru to a stop. Without another word Bolan got out.

Furelli opened the door and leaned into the darkness. "Hey, Vinnie," he called out. "Come on up and ride the rest of the way with me."

The caravan moved on through the night as the Executioner disappeared into the trees.

BOLAN RACED through the forest like a running back seeking open ground. He dodged trees and heavy boulders as he gradually climbed the slight but steady grade overlooking the stream. When he reached the edge of the cliff, he dropped to his belly and looked down into the valley.

A hundred yards away and fifty feet below, the bright half-moon reflected off the water that separated China and Russia.

Just beyond the stream, on the Chinese side of the border, stood two semi rigs and half a dozen cars. Groups of armed men dressed in rough woolen garments and heavy fur vests stood around the vehicles. The red tips of cigarettes moved back and forth from hands to mouths, the embers looking like fireflies gliding through the night in the distance.

In the midst of one of the groups stood Jake Pool. The schizoid cowboy had covered his Wild Bill Hickok garb with a calf-length sheepskin overcoat.

Bolan drew the suppressed Beretta from under his jacket and steadied his elbows on the rock in front of him. He watched as the headlights from the Subaru and panel trucks appeared through the trees to his side. A moment later, the convoy left the forest and entered the clearing. Passing the Executioner's vantage point, they parked by the stream.

Pool and three of the fur-clad Mongolians walked toward the stream as Furelli and Vinnie stepped out of the Subaru. There was a moment's hesitation when the parties reached the water, then one of the Mongolians, wearing a scraggly mustache and a curved sword, stopped and stubbornly crossed his arms.

Furelli said something to Vinnie, then both men leaped across the water to the opposite bank. Unintelligible voices drifted up to the Executioner on the breeze.

Cupping the Beretta in both hands, Bolan steadied his arms on the rock in front of him. He thought briefly of the .460 Weatherby Magnum he preferred for sniping, then pushed such thoughts from his mind. It would do no good to dwell on what weapon he wished he had with him. He would have to make do with what he had.

Besides, the Executioner thought as he flipped the safety to semiauto and thumbed the hammer back to single-action, a kill shot wasn't necessary to his strategy. All he needed to do was make it appear that one of the criminal organizations, either the New Brotherhood or the Triad, was attempting to rip off the other side.

Then all hell would break loose and the rest could take care of itself.

The Desert Eagle, with its .44 Magnum round leaving the barrel at over 1600 feet per second would suffer less bullet drop at this range than the Beretta. But its roar would pinpoint his location. The hushed Beretta would make no sound at all from this distance, adding to the confusion when the first man dropped.

Bolan aimed the front sight of the 93-R at a tree limb, half an inch above Pool's head. Taking a deep breath, he squeezed the trigger.

A soft whoosh exited the Beretta. Then a dull thump sounded across the valley. Pool, Furelli and the other men glanced curiously in the direction of the trees, then turned back to their conversation.

Bolan lowered the sights. He squeezed again. This time, he saw soft movement in a clump of leaves just over Pool's shoulder.

The Executioner dropped the sights a hair more. As he was about to pull the trigger again, Pool stepped behind the Mongolian with the sword.

Taking another deep breath, Bolan let half of it out, held his aim and squeezed. A loud clang sounded as his 9 mm round struck the blade of the Triad man's sword.

The warrior didn't wait. He raised the barrel and fired again. A split second later a thin line of blood dripped from the Mongolian's temple. The guy fell to his knees, then sprawled forward on his face.

Instantly gunners from both sides of the stream opened fire. Furelli, Pool and Vinnie jumped back across the water and sprinted for the panel trucks.

Pool, a Colt Single Action Army .45 in both hands, paused every few steps, firing blindly over his shoulder before running on.

The Executioner holstered the Beretta and drew the Desert Eagle. Now that chaos had taken over, no one would make his position in the rocks. Even if they did, this was hardly the time for them to think things through and figure out what had happened.

The Executioner sighted over Pool's head and fired at the fleeing figure, knowing the chances he'd hit a moving target at this distance were a million to one. The round fell harmlessly, somewhere on the death field below.

Vinnie had almost reached the trucks when he stopped in his tracks. His back arched like an Olympic diver leaving the springboard, then the gunner lunged forward in a belly flop.

The battle continued to rage as men fell on both sides of the border. Bolan rose to his feet and moved across the rocks, his eyes searching the outcropping for a pathway down to the action. The Executioner was a soldier—a fighter, not an observer—and he needed to get within pistol range to snipe at both sides. With luck he might even get a decent shot at Furelli or Pool.

The chance never came.

Truck engines roared across the valley as both the New Brotherhood and Triad vehicles began their retreats. Sporadic gunfire continued to ring through the night, but gradually declined as both parties headed back in the directions they'd come from.

Bolan stood on the ledge as the panel trucks disappeared into the trees on their way back to camp. He watched as the semis and cars faded out of sight on the Chinese side of the border.

The Executioner shoved the Desert Eagle back under his tunic. The shipment of illegal Kalashnikovs was still intact, and for a moment he was tempted to follow the Triad into China and destroy it. But that was another battle. He would file the knowledge away for future reference, but for the time being he had signed on to destroy the New Brotherhood.

And that war was far from over.

Bolan hurried back through the forest toward the road. Dropping behind a tree, he watched the New Brotherhood convoy pass. When the taillights of the last truck disappeared in the distance, he rose and broke into double-time.

Furelli and the others would return to camp to regroup. The Mafia enforcer wouldn't know exactly what had happened, but if he had any brains at all, it wouldn't take him long to realize the man in the border-guard uniform had been somehow involved in the mix-up.

But Furelli would also figure that he'd seen the last of Bolan for the night.

And that's where Furelli would be wrong.

THE WINDOW IN THE DEN of Colonel Pyotr Leskov's holiday home faced the Moscow River. Through it, Leskov watched the snow trickle down through the porch light to melt on the water.

Leskov set his book facedown on the arm of the stuffed easy chair and rose to his feet, his hands moving automatically to his lower back. The ache was a constant reminder that he was no longer a young man.

Shuffling across the carpet to the fireplace, the colonel picked up the poker with one hand and slid the chain curtain to the side with the other. Slowly, methodically, he poked at the glowing embers as he stared into the charred wood.

Who was this American?

One hand on his knee to support his back, Leskov bent and reached for a log next to the fireplace. Struggling, he worked the log to the top of the embers and watched as new flames began to dance around the edges.

Leskov moved back to his chair and lifted his book. He stared blankly at the page, then set it down again and reached for the meerschaum pipe on the table next to him. The pipe brought a smile to his face. He had purchased it in a Tangier bazaar years ago while on assignment in Morocco. The pipe had a large yellow bowl and a bent black stem. Inlaid in the stem was a tiny ivory elephant—so small he hadn't even noticed it before the purchase.

The memory caused Leskov's smile to grow. He remembered the first time he had seen the elephant. After buying the pipe, he had gone to a nearby café for lunch. He had ordered, then decided to inspect his new purchase.

In the dim lighting the tiny fleck of white had looked like a piece of the gummed paper in which the pipe had been wrapped. When his thumbnail failed to remove it, Leskov had become convinced it was a blemish.

Dropping the book into his lap, the colonel stared back out the window. His smile became a chuckle, then the chuckle grew to a laugh. The blemish had made him so angry he had stormed back to the kiosk and demanded that the proprietor return his money. The pipe seller had smiled and produced a jeweler's glass.

It was only then that Leskov had seen that what he thought to be a defect was in actuality a remarkable, intricate work of art.

Leskov studied the pipe. The tiny elephant had been a valuable lesson to an impulsive young man—things weren't always what they seemed. One had to look closely, sometimes under the magnifying glass.

So who was this American?

The colonel set the pipe back in its stand and stared into the fire. His eyes grew heavy and threatened to close. He forced them open and turned back to the window.

Leskov loved this house on the banks of the river just outside Moscow. The state had treated him well, granting him the vacation home almost twenty years earlier. Stalin, Khrushchev, even Brezhnev had realized that KGB officers needed a break from the constant stress they endured.

Leskov stared at the knotty-pine walls, the oak beams spanning the ceiling, the beautiful hardwood floor. He needed only to drive thirty minutes from his small, depressing, downtown Moscow apartment to feel refreshed.

A surge of fear shot suddenly through his body. Mandatory retirement was approaching. Under the current policies, he had less than six months, and already they were easing him out of things. Besides his job, what else would he lose? The house. Definitely the house. And with it would go his self-respect.

And most likely his sanity. And his reason for living.

Leskov nodded, as if agreeing with himself. He might possibly keep from putting his own Makarov in his mouth if he was allowed to keep this house. God, if there was a God, knew there were enough things that interested him. He could spend his final days in this chair reading, getting up only to eat, sleep and relieve himself. But he had never been able to do that in the two-room flat in the city. The atmosphere was simply not the same.

Could he convince the higher-ups that he was still useful?

No, not unless policies changed. And for policies to change, leadership would have to change.

And to change the leadership of Russia, it would have to be proved beyond a shadow of a doubt that Tachek was incompetent.

A wave of guilt rushed over Leskov, but he fought it back. What he was doing wasn't treason. He wasn't being selfish. Sure, he wanted to keep his house. He *needed* to keep his house. And the money Hernandez and Esposito paid him could always be put to good use. As some wise man, undoubtedly a Russian, had once said, "A young man's luxuries become necessities as he grows older."

But that wasn't his only reason for cooperating with the New Brotherhood. If Tachek continued along this course of Americanization, Russia would eventually be a country of anarchists. No, better the president be revealed as an idealistic dreamer before he took Russia down with him.

A new calm replaced Leskov's anxiety. He lifted the pipe again and reached for the leather pouch of Turkish tobacco on the lamp stand next to it. Thoughtfully he began to fill the bowl and was about to light the pipe when the shrill sound of the telephone broke the silence of the room.

Leskov shook the match out. As the thin stream of smoke rose to the beams, he pried the receiver from the cradle and held it to his ear. "Yes?" he said.

"Colonel," came the voice over the crackling line, "it is Sergeant Khrushchev. We have encountered a problem."

"Is your line clean?" Leskov asked immediately.

"Yes. I am at a public phone."

"One moment." Leskov leaned over the table and pushed a button on the strange-looking instrument hooked to the telephone. An electrical-output dial sat on the face of the instrument. The needle rose swiftly into the red zone of the dial, then fluttered back to settle in the green.

Satisfied that his own line wasn't tapped, Leskov said, "Go on."

Khrushchev spoke fearfully. "Colonel, the shipment from the south was interrupted. At first my contact believed that the Triad had attempted to simply steal the money and keep the weapons." He paused, and Leskov heard the excited breaths on the other end of the line. The border guard returned to tell Leskov about his stolen uniform, and Furelli's mysterious visit from the unknown guard.

Leskov reached for a pen and notepad. "You encountered this impostor yourself?"

"I believe so," Khrushchev replied. "He was posing as a Czechoslovakian colonel. Frank Hlupnik. But what confuses me is the papers he carried—they included a letter from the president himself. They appeared authentic."

Leskov pressed the end of his pen with his thumb and the point shot out. "Give me a description of the man, Sergeant."

"Big," came the reply. "Tall. Perhaps six-two, six-three. Well over two hundred pounds, but no fat. He was the type of officer who would have obtained his colonel's bars the hard way, coming up through the ranks." Khrushchev paused.

Leskov wrote furiously on the notepad. "Can you give me more?" he asked.

"The man has seen battle, Colonel. You could read that much on his face."

"Anything else?"

"No."

Without formalities, Leskov said, "Carry on," and hung up.

The colonel's legs took on new life as he hurried across the den to the computer hutch in the corner of the room. Punching the On button, he waited impatiently for the machine to boot up.

Who was this American? He didn't know. But he was getting closer to finding out.

The computer stopped, showing the time and date in glowing yellow letters. Leskov punched the Return button again. Then, linking into the main RI system in Moscow, he punched in his ID number, several codes and waited.

Whoever this American was, the odds were good that the Committee for State Security had dealt with him in the past. With any luck at all, there would be a file.

As soon as he'd cleared security, Leskov began typing in the details Khrushchev had given him. Nationality, approximate height, weight, hair color. He punched for Scan Files, and forty-three possible file numbers shot out on the screen.

Leskov racked his mind for other details that might narrow the search. He had forgotten to ask Khrushchev for an approximate age, but a man capable of the things this American had done could be no rookie. On a hunch he entered *Vietnam veteran*.

Thirty-one numbers disappeared from the list.

Somewhere in the back of his brain, independent of the computer, a memory tried to scream its way to the surface of his brain. Leskov closed his eyes, trying to clear his mind; doing his best to let the unconscious thought rise. Then, opening his eyes again, he typed *Currently wanted by Russian Intelligence*.

The list fell to three.

Leskov took a deep breath as the chills flowed through his body. Goose bumps rose on his shoulders as the memory began to take shape. Suddenly, like a door opening, it came to him.

The American's name flashed in Pyotr Leskov's mind even before he started to type again: *Open contract: RI and CIA.* He saw the yellow words appear on the screen and held his breath as he hit the the Enter button.

KGB file #JF44056 339 flashed onto the screen.

Leskov let out his breath. He typed in the number and hit Enter.

As the computer clicked and hummed, searching for the file, Leskov thought back to the man who had

almost single-handedly destroyed the elite branch of
the KGB known as Directorate 13. The man who had
killed both Leskov's best friend, Greb Strakov, and
Strakov's son as well.

It was no surprise to Leskov when this time the
words MACK BOLAN A/K/A COLONEL JOHN
PHOENIX flashed in front of him.

Nor was he surprised that the yellow letters on the
screen had changed to red.

## CHAPTER SIX

Coveys of birds flew from the trees, their winged silhouettes gliding across the night-time sky as the dark figure jogged along the tree line.

Bolan reached the curve leading to the New Brotherhood camp and slowed to a walk. Leaving the road, he threaded his way through the forest, angling toward where the trucks had been parked earlier. Through the thick limbs and needles of the evergreens, he saw glimmers from the headlights. The faint growl of idling engines hovered in the air.

When he'd reached the edge of the clearing, the Executioner parted two cedar boughs and peered out. Squinting, he could make out the shadowy forms of the men. They stood huddled in groups outside the vehicles. Some spoke in high, frightened voices. Other voices, angry and excited, floated toward the trees.

The men's outlines were unclear in the darkness, mingling with the shadows of the trucks, and the trees on the other side of the clearing. The net result was an indistinct mass of moving, gray-black shapes.

One head, several inches taller than the others, broke the outline. It wore a flat-brimmed gunslinger's hat.

The Executioner drew the Beretta and thumbed the safety to semiauto. But as he lowered the sights on the hat, Jake Pool stepped behind a truck. Bolan dropped the 93-R back to his side. Once again, the fates had graced the demented gunner.

Bolan returned his attention to the mass of men in front of the trucks. He was close enough now to employ the strategy he'd have used with a long-range weapon at the border. He could snipe quietly away in the darkness, dropping as many men as possible before the inevitable happened and his position was located by muzzle-flash.

Then he'd have to move, and move fast. Which meant he needed some idea of where he'd be going before it all started.

Of the various conifer trees and shrubs that surrounded him, most grew low to the ground. But here and there, deep sawtooth scars in the limbs showed where beaver had come up from the stream to chew into the wood. In those areas he might be able to rise to a kneeling position, or even crouch. But the bulk of the battle would have to be waged from a prone position.

Mentally outlining a zigzag path, Bolan turned back to the clearing. He pulled an extra 15-round magazine from under his tunic, clenched it in his teeth, then flipped the Beretta to 3-round burst. Holding the 93-R "point-shoulder," he took a deep breath. Precision sighting within the dark body of New Brotherhood personnel was impossible.

Aiming the Beretta at center mass, the Executioner pulled the trigger.

The 93-R jumped three times in his hand. A faint shriek of surprise came from somewhere within the group. The Executioner squeezed again, and another trio of hushed coughs leaped from the suppressor. More screams broke the stillness in the clearing. The mass of shadows parted, hurrying in two dusky divisions toward the sides of the trucks.

Bolan continued to fire half-blind, spraying a carpet of 3-round bursts after the dark splotches. More cries of panic echoed through the night as men fell to the ground, their bodies regaining distinction as the moon shone down to clarify the silhouettes.

The 93-R locked open, empty. Bolan thumbed the magazine release, and the empty box hit the grass at his feet. His left hand ripped the full mag from his teeth and shoved it up the grips of the Beretta.

As the Executioner worked the slide release chambering a round, return fire crashed through the branches above his head. Rolling to the right, he came to a halt on his stomach under the low boughs of a spruce and tapped another burst of 9 mm slugs through the low vegetation.

One, two, maybe all three rounds hit a New Brotherhood gunman kneeling foolishly next to the headlights of a panel truck. The Uzi in his hands cartwheeled to the side as the man fell screaming after it.

More fire sailed into the trees. The strong odors of spruce and pine filled Bolan's nostrils as the rounds ripped through the branches, and needles and twigs rained down over his head and shoulders.

Bolan rolled on. He heard a truck grind into gear as he rose to a kneeling position under the boughs of a fir. He pressed the trigger again, firing to the right end of the caravan. Another shadowy figure sprawled to the ground.

In the corner of his eye the Executioner saw dark forms race through the night toward the Subaru. One of the shadows, of average height and build, slid behind the wheel.

The other still wore the flat-brimmed Western hat. A flicker of light reflected off the Subaru's metal trim, then danced across the yellow sheepskin coat as the passenger's door opened.

Bolan twisted, firing a second too late. The Subaru skidded into a 360-degree turn toward the road.

Another burst of rounds sailed over the Executioner's head. He rolled away from the attack and came up firing again.

Until now, the New Brotherhood men had shot high—a mistake common to men with little night-fighting experience. But as Bolan swung the Beretta back toward the fleeing Subaru, the gunners realized their error.

A dozen rounds suddenly splintered a tree trunk two inches to the Executioner's right.

Bolan pushed away from the assault. When he came up, the Subaru had vanished onto the road. Turning back to the trucks, the Beretta jumped again in his hand. Glass splintered as the deadly Parabellum rounds took out windows in the panel trucks. A dull moan sounded, then a vehicle horn screamed as a dead man fell forward into the steering wheel.

Amid the howl of the horn and the screams of fear and pain, Bolan saw a muzzle-flash under one of the trucks. He emptied the Beretta toward the light. The

flashes stopped, and a lonely wail of death came from under the truck.

The Executioner shoved a fresh mag up the butt of the Beretta as one by one, the remaining men broke cover and sprinted across the clearing toward the trees.

One by one, he dropped them in their tracks.

Bolan waited a full five minutes as the horn shrieked on through the night. Then, staying low, he crept cautiously from the forest, the Beretta leading the way. Bodies lay strewn across the clearing, all dead.

Except one.

A man wearing a heavy gray greatcoat and muskrat hat lay whimpering on the ground ten feet from the nearest truck. He stared up in terror as the Executioner moved over him, his eyes wet with a mixture of blood and tears.

Bolan studied the man's wounds. He'd caught rounds in both knees. Another had grazed his forehead. None of the wounds were life-threatening, and unless he bled to death here in the Siberian wilds, he'd walk again someday.

An East German MPiKM lay next to the man on the ground. The Executioner hooked his foot under the carriage and flipped it end over end out of reach before hurrying toward the screaming truck horn. Gripping the body draped over the wheel by the collar he pulled it from the truck. The horn quieted, and the only sound in the clearing came from the quietly idling panel trucks.

Bolan returned to the man with the injured knees. "You speak English?" Bolan asked.

The man nodded slowly. "A little."

"What's your name?"

"Yuri." The man grimaced as new pain shot through his legs.

"If I was you, Yuri, I'd consider this my lucky day," Bolan said. Quickly he knelt and patted the man down. Finding no more weapons, he returned the Beretta to his shoulder rig, then ripped strips from the shirt of a nearby body. Tying Yuri's hands behind his back, he dressed the man's knees and head with crude field bandages.

Yuri watched, puzzled. He didn't speak.

When he'd finished, the Executioner left Yuri face-down on the ground. Searching through the nearest truck, he found a heavy, black-and-tan briefcase. Inside were carefully wrapped packs of rubles.

Close to half a million dollars' worth.

The New Brotherhood could finance the rest of Bolan's mission themselves. And he had an idea of what could be done with what was left over.

The warrior lifted Yuri in his arms, carried him back to the truck and climbed behind the wheel.

"Why... why you have not killed me?" Yuri asked as the Executioner pulled out of the clearing.

"Because you're going to deliver a message for me."

Dawn broke as the Executioner started back along the winding path toward K'achta. The sun peeked over the horizon, and the new day began. Neither the Executioner nor his prisoner spoke until the small village finally appeared in the distance.

Still a mile from town, Bolan pulled to a halt on the side of the road. He got out, walked around the truck and opened the passenger door. Pulling the wounded man from the cab, the Executioner laid him on the grass.

Fear covered Yuri's face. "I will bleed to death out here."

"Do you know what the English term *hitchhike* means, Yuri?"

Yuri shook his head. "No."

"I imagine you can figure it out."

The Russian looked up at him, stammering, searching frantically for a reason he should be taken along. "You said I would deliver a message," he reminded Bolan.

The Executioner nodded, and untied the prisoner's hands. Then he reached in his pocket, withdrew a small metal object and flipped it through the air.

Yuri's hand shot up automatically and caught it.

"You just give Furelli that," he said and turned back to the truck.

The Executioner threw the vehicle in gear and drove slowly away. He had debated whether to let the New Brotherhood know who it was they now faced. Anonymity had advantages. But knowing who they were up against would produce fear and disorder, too. He'd finally opted to wait until after the first strike, then let his identity be known. Hernandez and Esposito would get scanty descriptions of him here and there from their men, anyway. And with the leak from within the president's office, and the high-ranking RI officer on the take, it would only be a matter of time until the New Brotherhood put two and two together on their own.

In the rearview mirror, the Executioner saw Yuri at the side of the road. The Russian gunman held the glittering piece of metal in front of his eyes for inspection.

Bolan grinned. Yuri might not recognize it as the trademark of the man who had fought and destroyed half the world's organized crime over the years. But Furelli would. Anyone associated with the Mafia should.

And Esposito, in particular, would know it.

Bolan wondered about the Mafia leader's reaction when he heard about the marksman's medal—the mark of the Executioner.

HERNANDEZ HUMMED A TUNE quietly in the back seat of the limousine, ". . . the lullaby of Broadway."

Through the smoked-glass window, the Colombian drug lord watched people hurry down the sidewalks of the theater district toward restaurants and coffee shops. He lifted his wrist to his face, staring at his watch. Yes, they still had time to grab a bite before the curtain rose.

The South American sighed as the limo cruised on through the theater district. He would have preferred to have been attending a show tonight himself. Instead he would spend the evening listening to the fears of a Mafia don who had begun to worry like an old lady.

Hernandez glanced to Erich, seated next to him. As always, the German stared straight ahead in silence. It was one of the qualities Hernandez had grown to appreciate in his former waiter. Erich didn't speak unless spoken to. He didn't volunteer opinions without being asked.

He certainly didn't brag without end, or lecture on the Old West as Jake Pool did. Of course he wasn't as good with a gun as Pool, either, but he was good enough.

The limousine turned off Broadway, cruised down a side street lined with skyscrapers, then pulled to a halt at the curb. Hernandez waited as Erich walked around the vehicle to open the door. He watched the catlike grace of the German's pace. It bespoke the quiet self-confidence within the man.

Hernandez stepped onto the sidewalk. Erich hurried ahead to open the glass door into the building. The drug lord smiled to himself as he walked through, removing his gloves. Erich had rid him of the insufferable loon outside his house within minutes of being given the order. One lone shot and his tormentor had been silenced forever. On a hunch, as well as out of boredom, the cartel man had then instructed one of his top gunmen to drive Erich and himself to the firing range a short distance from the house.

There, he had learned that the shotgun wasn't Erich's only talent. He had the eye of a marksman with pistol, rifle and machine gun as well.

Hernandez walked to the elevator and pressed the up button. With Pool away he had needed a personal bodyguard—especially now that trouble had arisen and he'd been forced to fly to New York. He glanced at Erich out of the corner of his eye as the elevator descended. The German had waited his last table. From now on, his talents would be put to better use.

The forty-seventh floor was dark. Hernandez's heels clicked along the tile as he led the way to a door at the end of the hall. A dim light glowed inside the office, illuminating the words Esposito Construction in the smoked glass. Hernandez let Erich pass him just before the end of the hall. Once again, the German got the door.

The girl behind the reception desk snapped her bubble gum as they entered the outer office. She wore a long black coat dress, and metal-studded leather wristbands and collar. A leather cartridge belt bearing plastic bullets, such as a child might play with, cinched the coat at her waist, and her hair looked as if she had just gotten caught in the vacuum of a passing subway train.

"Mr. Hernandez?" the girl said between gum snaps.

Hernandez recognized the irritating Brooklyn accent from his phone conversations. Unconsciously his eyes swept the desktop for the manicure set he had known would be there.

It sat open next to a bottle of fingernail polish.

"Your voice is as lovely in person as on the phone," he said, forcing a smile.

The girl giggled and pushed a button on the telephone. "Mr. Esposito is waiting."

A moment later Hernandez was standing ankle-deep in the shag carpet that covered Esposito's office. He glanced around the room as the don rose to his feet behind a massive oak desk. Framed photographs of the Mafia godfather shaking hands with celebrities and politicians lined the walls. The chairs, lamps, end tables—all antiques. Bookshelves ran the length of one wall, and a leather easy chair sat next to it.

Hernandez stared at the top of the desk as he extended his hand to Esposito. It was bare of paper-

work. Only photographs of the mafioso's grandchildren, and a Rubik's Cube, sat on the desk.

The drug lord made sure the scorn he felt didn't
show on his face. The room was more "den" than office. The workroom of a man who didn't work anymore.

The scorn turned to inner amusement. When the
time came to ease the mafioso out of the picture, it
would be easy. Esposito would want no trouble; certainly not a gangland war. At the first sign of trouble
within the ranks of the New Brotherhood, this man
would cut his losses and run, happy to depart with
what he had already acquired.

"I guess Pool's filled you in on what happened?"
Esposito said, his face deadpan. But in the eyes, Hernandez could see fear—the fear of a man who has
made a fortune, and now worried he might lose it.

Hernandez waved a hand in front of his face. "It's
nothing we can't handle, Don Joseph," he said. "According to our Russian source, it is one man we are
talking about."

Esposito dropped behind his desk as Hernandez and
Erich took seats in front. "Hernandez, you're good at
what you do, but in some ways you're nothing but a
young fool."

Instead of anger, the words brought laughter to
Hernandez's soul. "In what way do you mean, Don
Joseph?" he said, careful not to smile.

Esposito pulled open a desk drawer and spoke as he
rifled through it. "You're right. We're talking only one
man. But this is a very special man." He found what he

was looking for, closed the drawer, and flipped a small metal object through the air.

Hernandez caught it. Looking down, he saw it was a marksman's metal. He shrugged. "So the man is a good shot," he said. He indicated Erich with an elbow. "So is Erich. And no one is better than Jake Pool. Your men can shoot as well, Don Joseph."

Esposito shook his head. Rising, he moved to a file cabinet across the room and slid open the top drawer. Returning to his seat, he shoved a leather-bound book across the desk to the younger man. "Take a look."

Hernandez opened the cover. A scrap book. How nice. Yellowed newspaper clippings had been inserted behind the sticky transparent plastic covers on each page. He glanced hurriedly through the collection. Each article was about Mack Bolan, the man known as the Executioner.

Hernandez closed the book and rested it on his lap. "I have heard of him."

Esposito nodded. "And what have you heard of him?"

The tolerance and condescension in the Mafia boss's voice wasn't lost on Hernandez. Ignoring it, he said, "He's made trouble for you in the past. And he's hit a few of the South American cartels. I understand that. But—"

Esposito's fist crashed down onto the empty desktop. The sudden change in demeanor caused Hernandez to freeze.

The don took a deep breath, regaining control of himself. "You've just made the understatement of the century, Hernandez," he said in a quiet, carefully regulated tone. "This 'one' man, as you call him, has caused more damage to our Families than all the world's cops, prosecutors and judges combined."

He rose from his seat and began to pace across the room. "It had something to do with Bolan's family, years ago," he went on. "They couldn't repay a debt and got snuffed or something. I can't even remember now." He turned back to Hernandez. "But that's not what's important, my young friend. What *is,* is that Bolan never lets up. Once he's latched on to you, he's like a pit bull after a bone. He's gonna get it or die trying." Esposito stared at the ceiling, looking for the right simile. "He's like...no, he's worse than fucking Sylvester Stallone in a *Rocky* movie. He might go down for a second or two, but you can be damn sure he won't stay down."

Hernandez smiled tolerantly. "He will stay down if he is dead, Don Esposito."

This time, Esposito's laughter didn't try to hide his contempt. "Don't think that hasn't been tried. The problem is, it's never worked."

Hernandez stared down at his feet. He would have to try a different tack with the old man. Esposito reminded him of many latinos who romanticized their enemies to build up their own standing. If a man's enemies were powerful, then the man must be even more powerful to have remained unharmed by them. Looking up at the Mafia man, he said, "How did Bolan know of the shipments? Their time and place?"

"Who the hell knows?" Esposito walked back to his desk. With shaking hands he opened a wooden humidor and pulled out a long thin cigar. "Who the hell knows how he does *any* of the shit he does?"

"Have you checked with our Russian contact?" Hernandez asked.

"Yes." Esposito lighted the cigar with a marble table lighter and set it back on the desk. "He came up with Bolan's name about the same time we did. He knows Bolan's getting advance notification, but he doesn't know how, yet. He's working on it."

Hernandez felt his chest suddenly tighten. "So Pinder was not the only leak within the New Brotherhood?"

Esposito puffed nervously on the cigar. "You figure it out."

Hernandez remained silent for a moment. "I will make a suggestion, Don Esposito," he finally said. "Pick your five best men. I will pick mine. We will send the team to join Furelli and Pool. But they will not assist in the new operations. Their only assignment will be to locate this Bolan and kill him."

The mafioso snorted. He stared across the desk, his eyes strangely vacant as the blue smoke from his cigar rose slowly toward the ceiling. "There's another solution," he said.

"And that *is*, Don Joseph?"

"To disband the Brotherhood. Call Russia, pack up and go home. We both go back to the business we do the best."

Hernandez felt his patience coming to an end. There was a limit to how much respect he could show this old fart who so desperately wanted to avoid conflict. Gathering his self-control, he gritted his teeth as he said, "Don Joseph, word is already out that we have launched the largest new enterprise since your Families came to America. It would have been acceptable to all if we had chosen never to attempt it. But to begin, then quit... and because of *one* man. We could never again show our faces." He paused, then stared the old man directly in the eye. "We would not only lose respect, we would lose what we've already obtained."

Esposito's expression never changed, but Hernandez could see he'd hit home.

Slowly, like a man who'd just placed last in a marathon, Esposito rose from his desk and walked to the door. Opening it, he turned back. "I'll pick my five men, but *you're* in charge of this action. I don't want to hear any more until it's over."

Hernandez nodded. He had just climbed another rung. He might not be in charge of the whole operation yet, but he was closer. With the old man's weak stomach, he might even accomplish a bloodless coup.

The drug lord stood and walked to the door, extending his hand to Esposito. "This is a wise decision, Don Joseph," he said. "Don't worry. When you hear from me next, it will be to learn that Mack Bolan is dead."

A thin grin curled Esposito's lips. "We've got an old saying in this country, Hernandez," he said wearily.

"What is that, Don Joseph?"

"I won't hold my breath."

THE SMALL CORNER ROOM in the Hotel Rachmaninoff was ornate by Russian standards. Scroll-design Finnish wallpaper ran the length of the walls, dropping even with the door tops from the ceiling. Below the paper, icons of the Blessed Mother and Christ Child had been hung. Oriental rugs covered the center of the floor, but highly polished wooden tiles could be seen around the edges.

Bolan awoke to the soft sound of snow pattering against the windows. He threw both legs over the side of the bed and stared out toward the Neva River. It had been almost 0600 by the time he'd arrived in Saint Petersburg. Landing at the Russian navy base on the Baltic coast, he had stored the MiG in a hangar with a dozen naval fighters. As had happened in K'achta, a few eyebrows had risen when he landed without formal notice. But the authoritarian repression that had kept the Russian people in line for seventy years was a two-edged sword. Paranoia remained. The Executioner had been passed through. Quickly.

Bolan grabbed his watch from the nightstand. Almost noon. Outside, the sun stood high in the sky. But that was hardly unusual for this time of year. Along the same latitude as southern Greenland and parts of Alaska, Saint Petersburg was one of the world's northernmost cities. It enjoyed almost perpetual light part of the year, culminating in the "white nights" when the only darkness was a half hour of eerie, mystic twilight.

Bolan turned, opening the draperies of the other window. Two floors down, he saw the famous Peter and Paul Fortress, which had been built as a fort, renovated into a torture dungeon for enemies of the czar, and now served as a state-run museum.

Bolan walked into the bathroom, twisted the shower knobs and adjusted the water. He stepped into the cubicle and closed the curtain around him, feeling the hot spray wash the slumber from his mind. The Rachmaninoff was the top hotel in the city. The Executioner hadn't chosen it for comfort, but because it fit the images of both an American businessman and a touring Czech colonel.

Finishing his shower, the warrior stepped onto the tile and pulled a towel from the rack, drying off as he walked back to the bedroom. He dug through the suitcase, finding the gray suit, a white-on-white shirt and the shaving kit Solomentsev had purchased for him at GUM. He hung the suit and shirt from the bathroom's overhead light fixture and closed the door, watching the steam from the hot water build and the wrinkles in the suit disappear.

The Hlupnik ID wouldn't be appropriate for what he had in mind today, so it was time to start thinking like an American agricultural expert.

Bolan turned the tap in the sink and covered his face with shaving cream. As he lifted the razor, he thought back to his last communiqué with Solomentsev. He had called Tachek's young protégé from a refueling stop in Omsk. Solomentsev had just heard from the mole.

Hernandez had let it slip that several of Esposito's men were in Saint Petersburg, setting up a dual operation of gambling and loan-sharking. The mole didn't know the exact location, but it had to be somewhere near the downtown area to cater to the widest clientele.

The mole had other news, as well. Hernandez had promoted him to the position of personal bodyguard, which meant he was in almost constant contact with the drug lord.

The Executioner's jaw set firmly as he dragged the razor across it. His thoughts returned to the New Brotherhood's casino and loan-shark business. Many people looked at gambling as a victimless crime. The same people cried that anyone crazy enough to do business with a loan shark who charged one hundred percent a week deserved what he got.

The Executioner didn't hate those people. He pitied and envied them at the same time. Pitied their naïveté. And envied the fact that they hadn't suffered from such "victimless" crimes as he had.

Bolan rinsed his face, as he fought the sorrow in his heart that time seemed never to heal. The Executioner's mother, father and sister flashed through his brain—all lying dead in pools of blood on their living room carpet.

Dropping the razor into the sink, the warrior returned to his suitcase in the bedroom. You could forget about the fact that compulsive gambling ruined marriages and families if you wanted to, he thought as he began to dress. And you could forget about the fact that people lost their homes and businesses to loan sharks.

All you had to do was take a look at some of the dead bodies littering the ground when the Mob didn't get paid on time.

"Then tell me it's victimless," the Executioner muttered.

Bolan buttoned his shirt, added the burgundy tie and slipped into the shoulder rig carrying the Beretta. He slid the hip holster through his belt and added the Desert Eagle. Shrugging into the London Fog trench coat, he studied himself in the mirror. He looked too American. He needed something to show he was sight-seeing, vacationing, out to combine business with pleasure and have a good time.

Descending the stairs, Bolan entered the foreign currency shop. He walked along the aisles until he spotted a row of fur hats hanging from the wall. Picking one with earflaps made of the traditional Russian hare, he paid a humorless woman in dollars and put the hat on his head.

On the way out the door, the Executioner caught his reflection in the window. He looked like a tourist who'd have bought a beret if he'd been in Paris, or a cowboy hat in Dodge City. All he needed was a camera around his neck.

In the lobby Bolan spotted a short skinny bellboy. Catching the little man's eye, he nodded him to the side of the room. Glancing clandestinely both ways as if they might be overheard, he pressed ten rubles into the bellboy's hand and whispered, "You speak English?"

The bellboy pocketed the money and gave Bolan a knowing grin. "Impeccably."

Bolan reacted with feigned shock. "Hey, that's *good*. Listen, pal. I got some spare time on my hands. You got any idea where I might find a little action?"

The bellboy's smile widened. "You came to the right man," he said. "Domestic or foreign? Blonde or brunette?"

Bolan played dumb. "Huh?"

"The woman, my American friend. You don't look like the kind who'd want a boy."

"No, no," Bolan said. "Well, maybe a woman later. First I want a little card action. Maybe some roulette and dice. You know any place around here like that?"

The bellboy stared up, studying the Executioner. Finally deciding Bolan must be what he appeared, he said, "I can direct you to a place. But I don't run it, and that means I don't make any money for the service."

Bolan reached in his pocket again. He pulled out another twenty rubles and handed them to the man.

The bellboy took the money. "It's a *very* fine establishment," he said. "You'll have a *very* fine time there."

Bolan laughed as his hand came out with more money. The bellboy gave him directions to a spot on Nevsky Prospekt. "Be sure to tell them Anton sent you."

The warrior nodded as Anton pocketed his money. "You guys caught on to capitalism pretty fast."

The bellboy smiled. "It's the American way."

Bolan caught a cab outside the hotel and gave the driver the same directions he'd gotten from Anton. Ten minutes later, they passed the October Concert Hall and pulled to a halt near the metro station at the corner of Nevsky and Vosstaniya. The Executioner paid the driver and got out.

As Anton had predicted, the windows of the art gallery were dark. Bolan took the cracked concrete steps leading down under the building and knocked on a splintered wooden door.

A small trap opened at eye level, and a bearded face stared through the hole like the doorman in a Prohibition speakeasy. "The gallery is closed," he said gruffly.

"Anton sent me."

The door opened and the man in the beard ushered Bolan inside.

A roulette table surrounded by men and women, laughing or cursing their luck in a variety of languages, sat against the far wall. A green felt covered blackjack table faced the side. Next to it were long dice tables. People stood at the slot positioned at various points throughout the casino, jerking the steel arms down and letting them float back upward as oranges, cherries and bells flashed past the tiny windows.

Bolan moved across the room to a bar along the side wall, where a tall man wearing a Princeton University sweatshirt poured drinks. A small bulge broke the outline of the sweatshirt just above the belt line. When the Executioner's turn came, the man paused for breath, then studied Bolan momentarily. "American?" he asked with a heavy Lithuanian accent.

Bolan nodded.

The bartender smiled. "What'll you have... pardner?"

"Beer."

The bartender whipped a bottle from under the counter, set it on top and moved on.

Bolan swiveled on his stool, sipping his beer and watching the games. A man he hadn't noticed before, wearing a dark blue American-cut suit, circulated through the crowd, patting people on the shoulders, congratulating winners and consoling losers. He wore a pencil-thin mustache, and his thick black hair, carefully slicked back, had gone gray at the temples.

The New Brotherhood's gambling establishment couldn't have been more than a week old, but word of mouth had traveled fast. It was still early evening but men and women—some locals, others tourists—crowded the smoke-filled room. By nine o'clock the place would overflow.

Which meant the Executioner needed to get started.

Bolan rose from the stool. Taking his beer with him, he walked to a barred window next to the roulette wheel. Behind the barriers sat a young man in his early twenties.

The warrior pulled a wad of bills from his pocket. Counting off thirty thousand rubles, he pushed them under the bars. The man stared boredly at the Executioner as he traded the money for chips.

Moving back to the roulette table, Bolan dropped a hundred-dollar chip on red. The man at the wheel turned the crossbar and the wheel began to spin. A moment later, the wheel slowed and the white ivory ball fell on fifteen.

The wheel man shoved another hundred-dollar chip toward Bolan. The Executioner let it ride. A moment later, the ball fell on thirty-two and the wheel man whisked both chips away.

"Not my game anyway," Bolan said loud enough for the people nearby to hear. He moved on to the blackjack table. A young woman dressed in a short slit skirt, and who looked like she'd have been at home in Reno or Las Vegas, dealt behind the table. She glanced at Bolan as he slid onto a stool.

The Executioner pulled five hundred-dollar chips from his pocket and placed them on the table.

"Feeling lucky?" the woman asked as she dealt.

Bolan returned the grin. He took a swig of beer as the girl dropped the ten of spades before him. Lifting his hole card, he saw the six of clubs. "Hit me," he said without hesitation.

The girl dealt him another six, then swept the cards and his chips away.

Bolan continued to play, betting heavily and losing at a rapid rate. He flexed his legs, arms and abdominal muscles in silent isometric exercises until the sweat broke on his face. When the chips were gone, he hesitated, then looked up at the girl. "Save my place," he said. "I'll be right back."

The Executioner returned from the window a moment later with a fresh load of chips. Still sweating, he continued to lose. He watched furtively as the man in the dark blue suit began to take interest in him.

Bolan repeated his trips to the window until he'd gone through more than eight thousand dollars at the current rate of exchange.

When the last chip was gone, the Executioner rose from the stool and returned to the bar. He was digging through his pockets, trying to find enough cash for a final beer, when he felt the hand on his shoulder.

Bolan turned to see the man in the blue suit. The pencil mustache rose in a friendly grin. "Bad night, huh, my friend?" he said.

"No kidding. You American?"

The man laughed. "As American as you can get when you're born in Queens. Citta's the name. Ralph Citta." He looked up at the bartender. "Hey, Feo. Bring my buddy here a drink. On the house."

Bolan wiped the sweat from his forehead as Feo handed him another bottle of beer. "Thanks."

"Don't mention it," Citta said. "You looked like you could use a good deed. Besides, we Yanks got to stick together over here, right?"

Bolan raised his bottle. "Right." He waited, letting Citta take the conversation in the direction he knew it would go.

"Bring me a gin and tonic, Feo." Citta turned back to Bolan. "I didn't catch your name?"

"Dwight McNeil."

"You look like you're here on business, McNeil."

"*Was* here on business," the Executioner answered. He indicated the blackjack table with his head. "I'm afraid you put a crimp in my cash flow."

"Ah," Citta said. "Business is over for now?"

"Business is over *period*. Like the man said, 'I got some good news and some bad news.' The good news is it wasn't me who lost money tonight. The bad news is twofold. It belonged to the company... and I don't own the company."

"Oh, shit." Citta arched his brows high on his forehead. In the dark, shifty eyes, Bolan saw greed rather than the concern the casino manager was affecting. "Like we say back home, you're up Shit Creek without a paddle."

Bolan stared down at his feet. "I'd say this is my last trip to Russia. My last trip anywhere—at least with this company."

"What was the money for?" Citta asked as his drink came.

Bolan shrugged. "We're in agricultural research. I was buying samples to take back. We're setting up a training program for Russian farmers. We've got . . . well, this is pretty boring stuff really. You sure you want to hear it?"

"Naw," Citta said. "No point in making yourself feel worse." Bolan could see the wheels turning in his head. "What'll your boss do? Send you more money for the samples, then fire you?"

Bolan nodded.

The bartender returned. Without being told he set another beer on the counter.

The Executioner lifted the bottle and turned back to Citta. "Yeah, they'll fire me, all right. But not before I get back. They need those samples, and they won't want to take the chance I might tell them to shove it and come back empty."

He watched Citta as he drank his beer. The New Brotherhood's casino manager saw his opportunity now, the axis to spin the con around that would make the whole deal work.

Finally Citta raised a hand to his temple, gently massaging the gray hair over his ear. "I got an idea," he said. "How'd you like to keep your job and come out of this smelling like a rose?"

Bolan laughed. "You a magician, or what?"

"No, but I think I can help." Citta indicated the rear of the room with his head. "Come on."

The Executioner followed him through the throng of gamblers. Citta opened a door at the back and led him down a short hall and up two flights of stairs. They passed through the art gallery to an office on the top floor.

The office was all business. A gray metal desk sat against the wall, a short safe of similar color next to it. Two men sat on folding chairs next to the desk. One of the men, dressed similarly to Citta, was in his late forties. The other, considerably younger, wore jeans and a plain black T-shirt. A Colt Diamondback .38 jutted openly from his belt.

"Take a seat," Citta said.

Bolan dropped onto a ragged couch facing the men.

Citta stood before him. "Dwight McNeil, meet Mr. Baker." He hooked a thumb at the kid with the .38. "And Mr. Carella. They're in the business of bailing out guys who get in your predicament." He grinned over his shoulder at the two men. "Here's what we do, McNeil. We lend you the money, then when you get back to the States, you pay our associates back. Simple enough?"

Bolan frowned. "Yeah, fine. But I don't have eight grand in cash at home, either."

Citta smiled. "Surely a man like you's got something he can turn for a quick sixteen grand. Cars, house..." His voice trailed off.

"Sixteen?" Bolan said. "But I only need eight."

Citta's smile widened. He looked like a cartoon cat eyeing a captured mouse as he sharpened his knife and fork. "This is a high-risk deal, McNeil. Interest has to be high, as well. Hell, you're a businessman—you can understand that." He leaned in close, grasping Bolan by the shoulders. "Besides, what's a lousy eight grand more when you consider how much you'll lose while you're hunting another job?"

Bolan slumped dejectedly in his chair. "Yeah... maybe."

"So, let's get it done and over with. Give me your passport."

Bolan pulled the document from his coat pocket. Citta handed it to Carella who began copying the information into a journal.

The man in the T-shirt knelt in front of the safe, twisted the dial and swung open the door. He pulled several stacks of notes from inside and handed them to the Executioner.

All pretense of friendliness had left Citta's face when he spoke again. "Now, just in case you're sitting there thinking you'll go home and forget this whole thing, McNeil, let me remind you we've got your address and social-security number." He paused, letting it sink in. "You got a wife, Dwight? Kids, maybe?"

Bolan nodded.

"Be a shame if they got hurt, wouldn't it?"

Citta, Carella and Baker laughed in unison.

The warrior pocketed the money, stood and walked toward the door.

"Hey," Citta called.

The Executioner turned back.

"I'm not sure you're taking this seriously. We don't like to get tough, McNeil, but we will if we have to. You ever dealt with anybody in this kind of loan business before?''

For the second time that day, the faces of his mother, father and sister flashed through Bolan's mind. Then he saw the bodies of the loan sharks who'd been responsible for their deaths, as clearly as if he had killed them only yesterday.

The Executioner stared back at Ralph Citta. "Yeah," he said. "I've dealt with you before."

heard the soft rumble of the gamblers. From the office above came muffled voices.

Staying close to the wall, the warrior mounted the steps. When he reached the landing, he unbuttoned the trench coat. The Beretta held at ready, he glanced around the corner.

The scene inside the office looked like a rerun of that afternoon. Carella sat behind the desk. Baker, still wearing the black T-shirt and Diamondback .38 on his belt, stood to the side. Citta had resumed his place in the center of the room and stared down at the couch.

In fact, the only thing that had changed was the frightened face of the man seated below him. Instead of the Executioner, a balding man in an electric-blue sport coat leaned forward, his arms on his knees and his pudgy face hidden in his hands. He whimpered softly as Citta went through his well-rehearsed monologue of threats.

Bolan hid the Beretta behind his back and stepped into the room. Three sets of eyes turned toward him.

"McNeil?" Citta said. "What the hell are you doing back here? You can't come up here without—"

Bolan ignored him. He turned toward the man on the couch. "You too, huh?" he said. "How much did they get to *you* for?"

The man looked up, his face white, his eyes red with tears. "Almost ten grand," he said. "That's without interest."

Bolan nodded. Suddenly he whisked the Beretta from behind his back and leveled it on Citta.

The man on the couch screamed, convinced he was about to die in a robbery. Carella froze where he sat, seasoned enough to know better than to draw on a cocked gun. Slowly his hands rose above his head. But Baker was young. He didn't hesitate. His hand shot for the Diamondback on his belt.

Bolan turned toward him, the Beretta coughing three near-silent rounds of death. The 9 mm slugs hit the black T-shirt in a triangle pattern. Baker looked down at his chest in disbelief as the black shirt began to shine wetly. The Diamondback fell from his hands. He dropped to his knees, then toppled forward on his face.

The Executioner swung the gun on Citta. "Open the safe," he ordered.

The man on the couch buried his face in his hands again. "Oh, God... Oh, God..." he chanted as he rocked back and forth.

Citta didn't argue. He squatted quickly next to the combination and spun the dial.

Bolan waited for what he knew would come next. Citta hadn't argued—hadn't even tried a threat. He'd been far too willing to cooperate, and that could mean only one thing.

The Executioner squeezed the trigger as the casino manager spun back from the safe. The nickel-plated .45 fell from Citta's hands as a new trio of Parabellum rounds drilled his face. Blood streaked down the casino manager's cheeks. The gray hair at his temples soaked to his scalp, turning a slippery black as he slid to the floor.

Bolan turned toward Carella. "Reach inside and pull out the money." With the 93-R he indicated the two men on the floor. "Do I need to warn you?"

## CHAPTER SEVEN

Bolan's combat blacksuit was constructed of tough elastic fabric, and it clung to the warrior's body as if painted on with a brush, eliminating the fear of bulky folds that could snag in rough terrain. The suit featured pockets of varying shapes and sizes, accommodating whatever specific equipment a particular mission required.

The Executioner donned the suit, then fixed the matching black Kevlar shoulder rig around his back. Next he shoved the Beretta under his left arm. Under his right, at the other end of the rig and balancing the suppressed 93-R, hung a pouch holding two extra 9 mm magazines. An upside down, quick-release knife sheath had been attached behind the pouch with Velcro, and in it could be found the razor-edged Mini Tanto fighting knife.

He snapped the modular buckle of the black utility belt around his waist. Hanging from the ballistic nylon was the Desert Eagle and two double magazine caddies filled with .44 box Mags. The padded sling of the short, deadly Striker went over his right shoulder.

Bolan covered the arsenal with his trench coat.

Untying the earflaps of the rabbit fur *shrapki,* the Executioner let them drop over his ears. The temperature outside had fallen below freezing, but the flaps would do more than keep his ears warm on the way to the casino. They'd help camouflage his face, making him difficult to identify later, in the unlikely event that anyone else lived through what was about to happen at the casino.

The warrior moved across the room to the full-length mirror attached to the closet door. The blacksuit hugged his calves between the tail of the trench coat and the top of his combat boots. What could be seen of his legs looked strange, but odd clothing combinations were hardly unusual in this land of constant shortages and shipping problems. People wore what they had, and no one was likely to give him a second glance.

The Executioner locked the door behind him as he left the room. Ignoring the elevator that might contain curious eyes, he descended the stairs to the ground floor, then hurried down a side hall away from the lobby. Approaching a servants' entrance, he saw a rubber door-stopper on the carpet next to the door, and a sudden, minor modification to his battle plan flashed through his mind.

Pocketing the stopper, he left the Rachmaninoff and strolled casually up Kirovsky Prospekt, away from the river. On the other side of the Peter and Paul Fortress, a cab sat idling in front of Lenin Park.

Bolan gave the driver the address of the October Concert Hall and sat back as the man navigated the bridge across the Neva, then took side streets to the ancient music hall.

The thunderous chords of Tchaikovsky's *1812 Overture* blared through the building's front door as

Bolan paid the driver. Cymbals crashed shrilly as he mounted the steps and bought a ticket.

Inside, a lanky usher in white tie and tails tore the ticket in half.

"Where's the men's room?" the Executioner asked in Russian.

The man nodded toward the side of the lobby.

Bolan made his way down the hall. The only other occupant was an old man swaying drunkenly to the music in front of the urinal. A lone smoked-glass window led from the room to what the Executioner realized had to be the alley.

Walking past the old man, Bolan entered one of the toilet stalls. He watched through the crack between the door and frame until the drunk zipped his pants and left. Then, hurrying to the lobby door, Bolan shoved the door stopper under the threshold and turned back to the window.

The wood squeaked in protest as Bolan raised the sash, pulled himself up over the sill and dropped to the ground.

Following a winding path of dark alleys, the Executioner made his way toward the casino. Coming to a corner, he saw the art-gallery sign in the window. He ducked back into the shadows as two middle-aged couples passed and descended the steps.

Bolan looked both ways, then darted across the street into the alley behind the gallery. He moved silently through the darkness to a door leading inside. Pulling a roll of adhesive tape from a pocket, he tore off several long strips and covered the window in the top half of the door. Then, using the butt of the Desert Eagle, he rapped softly until the glass cracked and the tape caved inward.

Pulling the tape and broken glass out of the opening, he reached inside and flipped the bolt.

A moment later, the Executioner found himself in a storage room piled floor to ceiling with boxes and empty picture frames. He traded the Desert Eagle for the silenced Beretta and moved through the semidarkness to a doorway. Back against the wall, he peered around the edge.

Venetian blinds covered the windows facing the street. Thin slivers of light knifed between the cracks of the slats to illuminate the paintings resting on easels around the walls. The Executioner moved to the closest picture—a scene from the Russian Revolution. Pulling the Mini-Mag flashlight from his suit, he squinted at the canvas.

The artist's signature was in the bottom right-hand corner—I. I. Brodsky.

Bolan reached up, gently rubbing the paint around the signature with his thumb. It smeared.

The painting had been finished less than a week before.

The Executioner grinned into the darkness. The New Brotherhood had entered more fields of criminal activity in Saint Petersburg than just gambling and loansharking. Unless I. I. Brodsky had learned to wield his brush from the grave, the painting was a counterfeit.

Bolan killed the light and moved to a door at the far side of the room. In the hallway he saw the steps he'd mounted to the office a few hours before. He paused, listening. Down the stairwell, through the steel door, he heard the soft rumble of the gamblers. From the office above came muffled voices.

Staying close to the wall, the warrior mounted the steps. When he reached the landing, he unbuttoned the trench coat. The Beretta held at ready, he glanced around the corner.

The scene inside the office looked like a rerun of that afternoon. Carella sat behind the desk. Baker, still wearing the black T-shirt and Diamondback .38 on his belt, stood to the side. Citta had resumed his place in the center of the room and stared down at the couch.

In fact, the only thing that had changed was the frightened face of the man seated below him. Instead of the Executioner, a balding man in an electric-blue sport coat leaned forward, his arms on his knees and his pudgy face hidden in his hands. He whimpered softly as Citta went through his well-rehearsed monologue of threats.

Bolan hid the Beretta behind his back and stepped into the room. Three sets of eyes turned toward him.

"McNeil?" Citta said. "What the hell are you doing back here? You can't come up here without—"

Bolan ignored him. He turned toward the man on the couch. "You too, huh?" he said. "How much did they get to *you* for?"

The man looked up, his face white, his eyes red with tears. "Almost ten grand," he said. "That's without interest."

Bolan nodded. Suddenly he whisked the Beretta from behind his back and leveled it on Citta.

The man on the couch screamed, convinced he was about to die in a robbery. Carella froze where he sat, seasoned enough to know better than to draw on a cocked gun. Slowly his hands rose above his head. But Baker was young. He didn't hesitate. His hand shot for the Diamondback on his belt.

Bolan turned toward him, the Beretta coughing three near-silent rounds of death. The 9 mm slugs hit the black T-shirt in a triangle pattern. Baker looked down at his chest in disbelief as the black shirt began to shine wetly. The Diamondback fell from his hands. He dropped to his knees, then toppled forward on his face.

The Executioner swung the gun on Citta. "Open the safe," he ordered.

The man on the couch buried his face in his hands again. "Oh, God... Oh, God..." he chanted as he rocked back and forth.

Citta didn't argue. He squatted quickly next to the combination and spun the dial.

Bolan waited for what he knew would come next. Citta hadn't argued—hadn't even tried a threat. He'd been far too willing to cooperate, and that could mean only one thing.

The Executioner squeezed the trigger as the casino manager spun back from the safe. The nickel-plated .45 fell from Citta's hands as a new trio of Parabellum rounds drilled his face. Blood streaked down the casino manager's cheeks. The gray hair at his temples soaked to his scalp, turning a slippery black as he slid to the floor.

Bolan turned toward Carella. "Reach inside and pull out the money." With the 93-R he indicated the two men on the floor. "Do I need to warn you?"

Carella shook his head. Slowly he began stacking packets of ruble notes on the desk.

"Count out ten thousand," Bolan ordered.

The hardman complied.

"Now give it to this gentleman."

The man on the couch looked up. He reached out, taking the money from Carella, then glanced at the rest of the piled stacks on the desk. With new confidence and greed in his eyes, he looked back to Bolan. "You think I should get anything for... say, punitive damages? Stress, emotional—"

Bolan gave him a piercing look. "What I think is that you should take what you got and go home."

The bald man rose quickly from the couch, scampered out of the room and down the stairs.

Carella had risen to his feet, his hands still over his head. "You're the guy they been talking about, aren't you?"

"Who's been talking about?" Bolan asked.

"Furelli and Pool."

"Tell me more."

Carella caught himself. "I ain't sayin' nothin'." Without warning the hardman lunged.

Bolan squeezed off one round, which punched into the man's nose.

The warrior shoveled the rest of the stacked ruble notes into the pockets of his coat and returned to the hall. He walked swiftly down the steps, pausing at the steel door to the casino. On the other side of the barrier, he heard music, laughter and the sound of the spinning roulette ball.

The Executioner caught his breath as he planned his next step. Men like Citta, Baker and Carella were a dime a dozen. The New Brotherhood would send others to replace them and be back in business by tomorrow night.

Unless there *was* no business.

Bolan took another deep breath. The art gallery shared common walls with the buildings on both sides. Fire was out of the question. And the men and women in the casino, while they might not be entirely innocent, certainly didn't deserve the death sentence for a little illegal gambling.

The Executioner shoved the Beretta under his coat and drew the Desert Eagle. No, he had to get the gamblers out of the way before he eliminated the New Brotherhood hardmen. Besides Feo, the bartender, he had spotted two more men with bulges under their armpits.

There was only one way to find out if there were more.

Bolan cracked open the door. He kept the big .44 Magnum out of sight as he peered into the casino. From where he stood, he could see Feo jiggling a silver martini shaker at the far end of the bar. Pouring the drink into a tall stemmed glass, the bartender reached toward a dish of olives.

Bolan stepped into the room and he fired twice into the ceiling, then waited for the noise to die down and the screaming to stop. As soon as he could be heard again, he said softly, "Closing time. Everybody go home."

The people stood like statues. Three more explosions from the big Desert Eagle brought them back to reality and sent them bolting for the door.

Bolan shoved the near-empty pistol into its holster. He swung the Striker from under his coat as the bearded doorman leaped past the throng of fleeing gamblers to the center of the room. The doorman raised a Skorpion machine pistol and pointed it in Bolan's direction.

An automatic burst of 12-gauge buck cut down the man before he had time to fire.

More screams echoed throughout the subterranean casino as the crowd bottlenecked at the door. In the corner of his eye Bolan saw a man in a brown leather bomber jacket level a Soviet PPsh-41 on him.

The Executioner dived behind the blackjack table as the subgun stuttered over his head, the rounds smacking harmlessly into the wall. Rolling to one side, he rose and tapped the Striker's trigger again. Hundreds of double-aught buck sliced through the bomber jacket like a swarm of angry bees.

His back against the wall by the door, an American wearing slacks and a sport coat suddenly dropped the pistol in his hands and extended his arms over his head. "Don't shoot!" he screamed. "Don't shoot!"

Bolan swung the Striker back and forth across the room, checking for more resistance as the last of the casino patrons scrambled out the door. He turned back to the American against the wall. "Down on the floor," he ordered.

The man fell onto his face.

"Hands behind your back."

Bolan wrapped a flexible cuff strip around the man's wrists and rolled him onto his side. "I want you to watch this," he said. He let the Striker fall to the end of the sling and drew the Desert Eagle.

The New Brotherhood man mistook his intentions. "*Please* don't...."

Bolan ignored him. He dropped the near-empty magazine of hollowpoints from the Desert Eagle, then reached across his chest, pulling a full load of hot-load armor-piercing Magnums from under his arm. Shoving the spike-tipped penetrators into the Desert Eagle, he started at the front door, circling the room and squeezing off two rounds each time he passed a slot machine.

Bells, oranges and cherries danced out of control as the mighty .44 Magnums drilled through the one-armed bandits at over eighteen hundred feet per second.

The Executioner was halfway around the room when he heard the first siren in the distance. He put a pair of rounds through the wheel, another through the axis and the wheel tumbled to the floor.

The sirens were louder now, no more than a block away. Hurrying back to the man on the floor, the warrior pulled a marksman's medal from his blacksuit and pinned it to the man's lapel. "Tell Furelli and Pool I said 'hi,'" he told the man. "And tell them I'm running out of medals, but not to worry. They'll know my work when they see it."

As heavy boots sounded on the steps outside, he sprinted through the steel door and up the steps to the alley door.

Bolan closed the door behind him and stared into the darkness for any sign of the *militsya*. The alley appeared clear.

Breaking into a jog, the Executioner began planning his next move against the New Brotherhood as he headed back toward the hotel. The RI mole had mentioned a massive white-slavery prostitution ring in Odessa, on the Black Sea.

Bolan came to the end of the alley. He let a *militsya* car race past on its way to the casino before darting across the street. He'd need wheels for what he had planned on the Black Sea coast. It was time to fly the MiG back to Moscow for the ZIL.

The ground war was about to begin.

ALEXANDR SOLOMENTSEV stared through an alcoholic haze at the waiter. He lifted his glass, trying to sip slowly at the drink. It didn't work. He downed the shot in one gulp and returned the glass to the table where the waiter filled it again.

What was happening to him? Solomentsev wondered. It seemed that despite his best intentions, he craved alcohol in ever-increasing quantities. This hadn't been the case a year ago. He had been able to drink like a gentleman.

Almost, Solomentsev admitted. Never quite like a gentleman. But certainly not like this.

Briefly he wondered if Tachek had believed his story about a stomachache. It was true, in a way. Ever since Leskov had called asking him to meet him at the bar, not only his stomach but his mind and very soul had ached to do so. He had left work even earlier than he needed to in order to give himself time for a few quick ones before his former mentor arrived.

"Just a few," Solomentsev murmured. Just enough to drive away the hangover from the previous night.

The young man's mind drifted back to the argument he'd had with his wife the night before. True, he had consumed all of the Armenian brandy they had received from Leskov as a Christmas present. But that was only to get it out of the house, out of the way, so it would no longer be a temptation. If it wasn't there, he couldn't drink it.

Right?

Natalya hadn't understood when she found him on the living room floor that morning. She *never* understood.

Solomentsev heard movement to his side. He looked up from his glass to see Leskov grinning down at him. The colonel shrugged out of his hat and coat and sat down.

For a brief moment Solomentsev thought Leskov was studying him, trying to get a fix on his condition. He pushed such thoughts from his mind. He was getting paranoid.

"So, you beat me here today?" Leskov said as the waiter brought him a glass of vodka. "I don't blame you, Alexandr. The pressure of your position must be unbearable." He turned to the waiter. "Bring us a bottle and leave it. It will save us time, and you shoe leather."

The waiter hurried to the bar and returned with a bucket of ice and an unopened bottle of 110-proof vodka. He set both on the table and left.

Leskov poured them each a double. A little voice in the back of Solomentsev's foggy mind screamed, "No!" The aide ignored the warning and raised his glass. "To ushhh, Pyotr," he said, and even he could hear the slurred *s*.

Leskov nodded. They downed their drinks and the old man poured again.

Solomentsev's eyes blurred. His mind drifted. The next thing he knew, he heard himself say, "Frank Hlupnik. A Czechoslovakian colonel. Belasko has—" He stopped suddenly in midsentence. What was he doing? Had he blacked out? How had this conversation begun, and why was he spouting out state material he had been sworn to keep secret?

Through the mist in his brain, Solomentsev saw Leskov smile. A kind, fatherly smile. "Relax, Alexandr. Trust me."

Solomentsev nodded.

"What type of transportation does he have?" Leskov asked.

Again, the voice of caution screamed in the back of Solomentsev's mind. Again, he ignored it. What was the point? He had already told Leskov far more than he should have. He might as well come clean. Leskov would either report him for revealing classified material or he wouldn't. He was far past the point where it made a difference. "A car," he slurred. "ZIL. He also has a MiG-23 at his disposal."

Leskov nodded. He glanced at his watch and chuckled. "Natalya will be angry with you again? For drinking with me?"

Solomentsev nodded. "Yes," he said. "If she knows it."

Leskov chuckled. "Take my word for it, Alexandr. If she sees you, she will know it." He waved a hand across his face and scowled. "What do women know of the pressures we face?" he said bitterly. "They cannot understand that we need a release of some sort." He paused, then said, "I will call Natalya and tell her you are on special assignment. You can stay at my apartment tonight."

Alexandr Solomentsev stared across the table. Leskov. His friend. The man had helped him climb the ladder of success. Now, the colonel was making sure he did not fall back down the rungs. Leskov would help him save his marriage.

A rush of warm camaraderie flowed through Solomentsev.

Spurred on by the fraternal feelings, Solomentsev reached for the bottle. He would pour Leskov a drink. They would toast their friendship.

Misjudging the distance, the young man sent the bottle crashing to the floor. Vodka seeped from the shattered glass like blood from a ruptured heart.

SNOWFLAKES FELL on the aide's head and shoulders as Pyotr Leskov steadied him with one hand. With the other he struggled to open the car door.

Saliva dripped from Solomentsev's cherry-red lips in the subzero air. "You're my...friend, Pyotr," the man mumbled almost incoherently. "You're my...*good* friend."

"Yes, yes," Leskov said with tolerance. "We are friends, Alexandr." He folded the drunken shape into the passenger's seat. "Now sit still and be quiet or you will get sick." Circling the car, Leskov slid behind the wheel and started the engine. As the car warmed up, he watched thick clouds of exhaust shoot from the tail-pipe in the rearview mirror. He glanced to his side.

Solomentsev had passed out. Short, raspy snores scraped from his throat. His chin kept time with the snores, bouncing against his chest like the bobber on a fishing line.

Leskov turned back to the windshield as the engine continued to warm up. The spectacle made him want to vomit. He had best get the young lush home before Solomentsev had the same desire and soiled the car's upholstery. Throwing the car into gear, he pulled away from the curb and started down the slushy street.

A mile from his apartment, Leskov pulled into an alley behind the Moscow Planetarium where an old red, four-door Datsun stood against the rear wall of the building.

The colonel glanced again to his side. Solomentsev burped, then resumed snoring. The president's aide was dead to the world—for now. But he could wake up anytime, and Leskov wanted no witnesses to what he intended to do in the next hour. It would be safer to have another bottle on hand, just in case.

A young man in a black leather, metal-studded motorcycle jacket walked from the Datsun to Leskov's window. The old man rolled it down. "Stolichnaya," he said. "Give me a quart."

The young man eyed him skeptically. "You are not police?"

Leskov's patience grew thin. He pulled his credentials from his coat and watched the young man's face grow pale as he shoved them through the window. "Hardly," he barked. "But if you do not do what I instructed you to do immediately, you can be sure you will find yourself in jail just the same."

The man in the leather jacket hurried to the trunk of the Datsun. He returned a moment later with the bottle. Leskov offered no money. The young man didn't ask for any.

When they reached the high-rise apartment building, Leskov parked on the street and turned once more to Solomentsev. He had no intentions of trying to carry the man up the steps—not with his bad back. Shaking the young man by the shoulder, he received a grunt for his effort. Several slaps across the face brought a more coherent response.

"Where . . . are we?" Solomentsev mumbled.

"We are home, Alexandr. Come."

A few minutes later, Leskov steered the inebriated figure through the door of his apartment and onto the couch. He heard the drunken snores again as he crossed the room to the kitchen table. Lifting the phone, he dialed the main number of the Committee for State Security, then the extension for the Division of Investigations.

Leskov glanced at the fax machine next to the phone while he waited for the line to connect. The machine was the only modern thing in his apartment; the only item that suggested anyone more important than a factory worker lived there.

A familiar female voice answered. Good, Leskov thought. Olga Gogol—a husbandless matron, dedicated to the department and gifted intelligence analyst. And more importantly, a woman who knew how to keep her mouth shut. "Good afternoon, Olga," the colonel said. He gave his ID number and waited while Gogol compared his voiceprint to the one on file.

The woman finally came back on the line. "Go ahead, Colonel," she said. "How may I help you?"

"With a list," Leskov replied. "I must know every privately owned storage facility in the Moscow area. Eliminate all but those with rental areas large enough to store an automobile."

"Yes, Colonel. You will have it on your desk when you arrive in the—"

"No, Olga," Leskov interrupted. "I must have it immediately. Fax me the list at home as soon as you've compiled it." He hung up.

Leskov rose from the table and walked to the kitchen area against the wall. Fishing a teapot from the cabinet, he filled it at the sink and set it on the stove. As the water began to heat, he turned back to the man across the room on the couch.

Perhaps the time had come to recruit Solomentsev. When the drunken young idiot realized what he had done, he would also realize that he was now under Leskov's "hammer." Solomentsev could either join Leskov's cause or be exposed to the president.

The colonel turned back to the stove as the water began to boil. A sudden thump behind him made him glance back over his shoulder. Solomentsev had rolled off the couch to the floor. The jolt hadn't even awakened him from his stupor.

Yes. The time *had* come. When Solomentsev sobered up, Leskov would come clean. The young drunk would realize the jeopardy in which he'd put himself. He could then be forced to transmit disinformation to the president and the American, thereby doubling his usefulness.

Leskov grinned. The leak could flow both ways.

Digging through the top cabinet, the colonel found the tin of strong Azerbaijani tea behind the salt. Dropping a handful into a ceramic bowl, he was about to pour the water when the sudden chatter of the fax machine stopped him.

He hurried to the table and waited while the machine continued to click. When it stopped, he ripped away the page, pulled his reading glasses from his pocket and squinted at the list.

Leskov smiled. Moscow was a city of seven million people. In Chicago, or Munich, or any city where free enterprise had been around very long, there would have been hundreds of rental agencies to sort through. But in Moscow the decadent ways of the West had only just begun to take over.

The page contained seventeen rental facilities.

Leskov looked at the clock on the wall. He still had an hour before the businesses closed for the day. It should be no problem.

Lifting the phone, he dialed the first number on the list. The voice of a teenage girl said, "How may I help you?"

"I am sorry to disturb you," Leskov said, affecting a Czechoslovakian accent. "My name is Colonel Frank Hlupnik. I rented a space from you a few days ago and I have lost my key."

"What number space did you rent?"

Leskov sighed. "That is my problem. The number was engraved on the key, and without it I can't—"

"On the key *chain*. The numbers are on the chains."

"Yes," Leskov said, sighing again. "You see how bad my memory has become? Could you check your records and see which space is mine? I will gladly reimburse you for the key."

"One moment, Colonel." Leskov heard the girl set the phone down. A moment later, she returned. "We have no record of you renting a garage, Colonel," the voice said. "Could you have—"

Leskov interrupted her. "You will think me even more foolish than before, but while you were looking, I found the key. It was in my pocket all along. And you are correct, I have called the wrong business."

Leskov and the girl exchanged quick pleasantries and he hung up.

He continued down the list. On the eighth try the voice of an old man answered, "I remember you, Colonel Hlupnik. Number Ten, on the corner. We have an extra key here at the desk."

Leskov hung up. For a moment, he sat grinning at Solomentsev. Then he pulled a ballpoint pen from his shirt pocket and underlined the address. Frunze Nab. The rental garages were across the river from Gorky Park.

Leskov lifted the receiver and dialed once more.

"Hotel Kosmos," a voice answered.

"Room 1401."

A moment later, Ray Furelli came on the line. "Yeah?"

Leskov took a deep breath and chuckled into the receiver. "I have good news, Mr. Furelli."

"Yeah, well, we could use some."

"For a small extra fee to my retirement fund," Leskov told the Mafia enforcer, "the New Brotherhood can rid itself of Mack Bolan once and for all."

THROUGH THE LARGE PICTURE windows, Jake Pool watched the planes land and take off on the airport runways. Harsh foreign voices chattered around him in the waiting area, making the gunslinger uneasy. He shoved his back harder against the wall, reaching automatically under his coat for the reassuring grips of his pistols.

His hands fell over the empty holsters.

Pool cursed under his breath. Those bastard terrorist Arabs were to blame for that. The cowards. It was their fault the airport metal detectors had been moved just inside the front doors, meaning he had to leave his guns in the van.

He pulled the whiskey flask and Talwin bottle from his pocket. His head didn't hurt, but he stuck two of the pills in his mouth just in case, then held the flask to his lips. He'd run out of whiskey on the way back from K'achta, and the vodka Furelli had given him tasted worse than armadillo piss. But it did the trick—calmed him down. Got his mind off the fact that the headache might come back.

And that every man jack who walked down the concourse just might be Jack McCall.

Pool took another swig of the vodka, grimacing at the taste. He glared at a short, thin man in one of those jackrabbit hats everybody wore in Russia. The man stared at his own black cowboy hat as he passed.

Was it McCall? Maybe. It'd be just like the sneaky little coward to pose as a Russkie. But the bastard wouldn't dare try anything. Not now, anyway. Not until he caught Pool without his back to the wall again.

A voice over the loudspeaker announced the incoming flight from New York, first in Russian, then English. Pool's thoughts returned to the reason he had come to the airport. As the first passengers began to deplane, he thought of Bolan. That's what Furelli had called the American. But Pool knew Bolan wasn't the bastard's real name.

Could *Bolan* be Jack McCall? How could he be? Bolan was too tall—too big all over. McCall had been a shrimpy little bastard in Deadwood.

Careful now, hombre, Pool silently reminded himself. You don't look exactly the same this time around, either. Bolan might be McCall. Remember, souls like that could be cagey.

Pool continued to watch the passengers as they filed past the flight attendant at the doorway. No, Bolan might be dangerous, but he wasn't the soul of Jack McCall. Pool could feel it. He was somebody else. He might be a bastard, but he had guts. Doc Holliday? Cole Younger? Maybe. Maybe even Jesse.

A well-dressed man wearing a yellow paisley tie exited the ramp and started toward the baggage claim.

Pool let his eyes follow. A moment later, another man wearing a dark suit and sunglasses got off. His tie was a series of white-and-yellow stripes.

Pool didn't know the men's names, but he knew who they had to be—more of Esposito's troops from New York.

Two dark-skinned latinos in flashier dress disembarked. Pool recognized the first. Juan "Pistola" Martinez had worked for Hernandez off and on for the past few years. He'd been the fastest gun Hernandez had—until Pool himself had joined the ranks. Martinez wore a bright red shirt under his white Caribbean style suit. The knot of his canary tie had been pulled down, away from his throat.

The man who walked with him wore a blue shirt with an identical yellow tie.

Pool watched as six more men left the plane wearing yellow ties. Then he stood and walked to the baggage area.

As the luggage began to arrive on the conveyer belt, Pool's mind drifted again to the man known as Bolan. He just might be John Wesley Hardin. He'd pulled some pretty typical Hardin shit. Sneakin' around. Hiding behind trees, afraid to face him in the open.

The gunslinger felt the hatred rush through his veins. Hardin had gained half his reputation in the last life from the lie he told about backing Wild Bill down in Abilene.

Pool reached up and curled the ends of his handlebar mustache. Bolan had to be Hardin. Well, he'd meet the bastard soon. And if there was any possible way to pull it off, he'd stage things so the bastard would have to draw on him. That might not be possible with the ambush Furelli and the KGB asshole had planned, but he'd give it a try.

When the last of the ten men had claimed their luggage, Pool turned on his heel and led them through the airport to the parking lot. When he reached the van, the man in the gunslinger's hat pulled himself up behind the wheel. He grabbed the nickel-plated Colts from under the seat and dropped them into the hand-tooled leather cross-draw rig on his hips.

The side door slid open and the men began crowding into the back of the van. Pool took another drink from the flask. He smoothed his mustache in the rear-view mirror, then stared at his reflection.

Pool's face twisted into the well-practiced grin. His left eyebrow lowered. Jack McCall? John Wesley Hardin? It didn't matter. He'd have the bastard's scalp hanging from his gun belt by sunrise.

The last New Brotherhood hardman slid into the seat next to him as Pool started the engine. He glanced over his shoulder as he backed out of the parking space, his grin widening. Everything was falling into place.

The men in the back of the van looked like a twentieth-century version of Butch Cassidy's Wild Bunch.

## CHAPTER EIGHT

Heavy snow fell over the slush covering the Moscow streets, adding a layer of white atop the brown, like icing on a chocolate cake.

The cab stopped at a red light. Down the block in the distance, Bolan saw the sign announcing TSUM, another of the giant government-owned department stores.

The driver pulled to a halt in a yellow no-parking zone in front of the store. The Executioner, dressed again in the Czech colonel's uniform, stepped out of the cab. "I won't be long," he told the driver in his halting, accented Russian.

The driver laughed. "You have never shopped in Moscow if you believe *that,* Colonel," he said. He pointed to the meter attached to his dashboard, shrugged and added, "It's your kopek."

Bolan entered the front door and stopped just inside. The place was packed wall to wall with lines. Threading his way through the mass of people, he passed stacked tins of caviar, rows of vodka bottles, cheap furniture and household appliances. Finding himself amid several aisles featuring the wooden Russian dolls known as *matryoshkas,* he continued past groupings of clay figurines from Kymkovo and entered the music department.

The Executioner paused to get his bearings. Guitars, violins and other instruments hung from wooden pins in the walls, and like the other departments he'd already passed through, cardboard boxes, both packed and empty, littered the floor.

TSUM might be second only to GUM as Russia's leading department store. It might be the Macy's of Moscow. But it looked more like Sam's Wholesale on stocking day.

Bolan continued down the aisles, passing frenzied shoppers and surly salespeople. He found a sign reading Men's Clothing and took a place at the end of the line.

The Executioner studied the people around him as he waited. He saw a few men, but mostly women. And this wasn't their first experience with the "hurry up and wait" routine of Russian shopping. Several had brought knitting or paperback books to help pass the time.

Bolan heard the click of a loud overhead speaker. A voice came over the air: "Attention shoppers. We have just received a shipment of toilet paper. Please proceed in an orderly fashion—"

The voice was drowned out by excitement from all sides. Books slammed shut and knitting needles were shoved back into purses, as the women elbowed one another out of the way and ran toward the Household Department.

Bolan found that the line in front of him had been cut by two-thirds.

A pale, short-haired woman wearing the uniform of the store appeared suddenly at his side. The Executioner turned to see her eyeing his uniform. "Are you on official business, Colonel?" she asked.

Bolan glanced ahead of him. The line in front would still mean at least a thirty-minute wait. And that was simply to pick out the items he'd need, and receive a ticket. The next line, equally time-consuming, would be to present the ticket and pay. Then, he'd be required to submit to a third line in order to pick up his purchases. The whole process would take hours.

"Yes," Bolan said. "Official business."

The woman led the Executioner down the aisle, past hateful stares of jealousy from those still in line. Quickly he picked out a pair of typical laborer pants in heavy wool and a gray turtleneck sweater. He moved to a row of long, bulky greatcoats and found his size.

The saleswoman's eyebrows had risen higher with each decision. She wouldn't ask him, but the Executioner knew she was wondering why a Czech colonel, visiting Moscow on business, needed civilian laborer clothing.

Bolan walked to the shoe area and found a pair of sturdy knee-high boots lined with fleece. He tried them on, nodded to the saleswoman, then said, "I thank you for your kindness in this matter. My luggage has been misplaced by the airline."

The saleswoman's face broke out in mirth. She wrinkled her nose. Then happy to have her question answered without having to ask, she said, "Ah, the airlines. What we have to go through when traveling!"

In the cab once more, the Executioner tossed his sacks on top of the suitcases. He gave the driver the address of the storage garages and settled back for the long ride.

As they started toward Frunze Nab, Bolan critiqued his mission so far. Things were moving along smoothly, but it was time to change a few minor strategies. The Colonel Hlupnik cover, however well it might have worked, was growing thin. He had unavoidably left a trail in Vladivostok. Appropriating Khrushchev's uniform in K'achta was even stronger evidence that something might be amiss with the Czech colonel. The New Brotherhood and their RI informant had their own line of communication, and sooner or later they'd put two and two together. When they did, they wouldn't come up with four.

They'd come up with Czechoslovakian Colonel Frank Hlupnik.

As the driver turned onto Frunze, Bolan saw the metal pontoons of the paddleboats glistening in the water of the Moscow River.

As they neared the short row of garages, the green light in the Executioner's brain suddenly flickered an amber warning. Parked along the curb, a half block from the garages, was a Toyota sedan with an Intourist decal in the window. Exhaust fumes rose through the frigid air from the idling engine, and as they passed, the Executioner saw five latinos, two in the front, three in the back.

The yellow light flashed brighter. The New Brotherhood? Maybe.

Scanning ahead, Bolan saw two more vehicles with their engines running. Both sat on the street just the other side of the garages, and both bore the same Intourist rental stickers. Men of lighter skin coloring, but with the same carnivorous looks in their eyes, sat in the vehicles.

Bolan removed his uniform hat and leaned quickly forward as the driver's foot moved toward the brake. "Drive on by," he said. "I forgot something."

The taxi resumed speed and passed the garages.

"Is there a store nearby?" Bolan asked. "One that sells hardware?"

The driver nodded. "A new place. About one mile." He continued down the street to Frunzensky, turned away from the river and drove several blocks to Usacova Avenue.

There, on the corner, Bolan saw the new prefab metal building. A few years, maybe even months ago, they'd have had to return to TSUM for what he needed. A neighborhood store like this would have been out of the question.

The driver stopped in front of the building. Bolan caught himself chuckling at the sign in the window. A few more years and Moscow would look no different than Buffalo or L.A.

The red-and-white sign in the window read Ace Hardware.

Inside the store, Bolan found an egg timer, a roll of black electrician's tape, a two-liter bottle of lamp oil and a roll of thin nylon cord. He searched the shelves for copper wire. Not finding any, he asked the shopkeeper.

"In two weeks."

Bolan nodded. Free enterprise might be on its way, but it hadn't solved the shipping problems, yet. Picking a cheap transistor radio from a display by the counter, he paid for the items and returned to the cabs.

"To the garage now?" the driver asked when the Executioner returned.

Bolan shook his head. "Changed my mind. Take me to the metro station. The one just north of the river on Komsomolsky."

The driver nodded and threw the cab into reverse, backing away from the store.

Bolan gathered his luggage as they pulled into the metro lot. He paid the driver, added a heavy tip, entered the station and walked swiftly to a row of lockers.

The New Brotherhood men in front of the rental garages meant one thing: the Hlupnik cover was burned. And somehow, they'd even found out about the garage. How that had happened was a matter for future investigation. For the present the simple fact that it had happened, and how to work around it, was to be dealt with.

The Executioner pulled a coin from his pocket, dropped it into the slot and swung the locker door open. Grabbing the suitcase containing the detonators, the TSUM and Ace bags, he stuffed the rest of his luggage inside and closed the door.

As he walked toward the men's room, he considered the simple solution. He could call Tachek and request a new ZIL and equipment, leaving the New Brotherhood men to watch the garage until Siberia thawed. But with the leak from the president's office now flowing like a geyser, the New Brotherhood would find out.

They'd just set up on whatever location was chosen to pick up the new car.

No, he might as well get it over with now and take out a few of Esposito and Hernandez's gunners while he was at it.

In the men's room Bolan entered a toilet stall and closed the door behind him. Quickly he stripped from his uniform, donning the new gray pants and turtleneck. The Beretta's shoulder rig went over the sweater, the Striker's sling hung opposite. The Executioner wrapped the gun belt holding the Desert Eagle around his waist, then covered the weapons with the new overcoat. Grabbing the *shrapki* he'd bought in Saint Petersburg, he stepped out of the stall.

Bolan moved to the mirror and ran a comb through his hair, waiting until a teenager in a Guns 'n' Roses sweatshirt finished at the urinal. As soon as the young man had left the room, he reached into his pocket for the false mustache and spirit gum Kerensky had given him. Making sure the mustache was straight, he returned to the lockers and stored the suitcase and bags.

The snow fell harder as Bolan left the metro station and started down the street toward the river. He ran two fingers across his mustache, securing it in place as he made his way to the garages. If the diversion worked, he'd have a few seconds to slip unseen inside the garage. Then he could take his time to prepare before bursting past the New Brotherhood men. Then, the chase would be on. And while the Executioner might not know the streets of Moscow like his own backyard, he had driven them more than the New Brotherhood gunners. He knew many of the twists and turns, nooks and crannies, that might serve as hiding places.

He crossed Furenzi Street toward the paddleboats, lowering the earflaps on his hat and pulling the collar of his greatcoat around his throat as he passed within twenty feet of one of the New Brotherhood cars.

"BUT," DMITRI LERMONTOV said, "that is enough about me and my work. I have even begun to bore myself. Tell me more about yourself, Katerina Kerensky."

Kerensky heard the words as if they'd come from far away—the end of a long, hollow tunnel. "What?" she said suddenly, her head jerking back to the man across the table.

Lermontov laughed softly. "You are preoccupied tonight, Katerina. Or is it simply me? I know I can become tiresome with my rambling."

Kerensky smiled. "No, Dmitri," she said. "It's just that I have other things on my mind tonight. I'm sorry. Please, go on. What you are saying fascinates me."

A waiter in a black tuxedo appeared at their table and lifted the bottle of Crimean wine, freshening their glasses before moving on.

Lermontov shrugged, then continued. "The students are taking their annual interest and aptitude tests this week," he said.

Kerensky tried to listen, but the words faded away. It was useless. She could think of nothing but the leak to the New Brotherhood, and the humiliating polygraph to which she had been required to submit.

She had been trained in the use of the instrument herself. She understood it thoroughly. In order to interpret the subject's responses to pertinent questions, certain control questions had to be used, questions the examiner could be certain the subject *would* lie about. These questions were formulated during the preexam interview, by finding either a skeleton in the subject's closet, or some embarrassing situation the individual didn't want known.

The waiter returned, glanced at their glasses, then moved on.

"Some of the students will not be suitable for college," Dmitri said. "So we will point them toward..."

Kerensky felt herself swallow. Tachek had utilized the old standard control for female subjects, broaching a subject he knew she would be forced to lie about in shame.

She remembered the president's deadpan face as he asked, "Your husband has been dead how long?"

"Four years this October, Mr. President."

"You are still a young and vital woman, Colonel. Have you dated other men?"

"No. Perhaps someday. But not yet. My work and daughter have kept me busy."

"Of course," the president said with a fatherly smile. "But you are only human. How have you handled the physical frustration of losing your lover?"

Kerensky lifted her wineglass to her lips. She felt herself flush as the same humiliation she'd experienced during the exam rushed through her. In truth she had handled her physical desire the way all people handled it when alone. In the manner that men joked about—and women pretended to be ignorant of.

Tachek had pressed on. "Your answer, Colonel?"

"It has been no problem, Mr. President. I have kept busy," Kerensky had repeated.

And she had seen in Tachek's face that he knew he had his control.

The colonel heard a tinkling sound. She looked across the table to see Dmitri smiling in amusement as he tapped his spoon against his water glass like a speaker calling banquet guests to order. "May I have your attention, please?" he said good-naturedly.

Kerensky sighed. "I *am* sorry, Dmitri," she said. "Please believe me...it is not your company that is disturbing. It is the pressure of my work at the moment."

Dmitri nodded. "I understand."

Kerensky kicked herself mentally. What was she doing? She was blowing it, that's what. When she had met Dmitri two months ago during the parent-teacher conference at her daughter's school, she had felt an instant attraction. It had been the first such longing she had experienced since the death of her husband. She had held little hope, however, that a romance would bloom.

Katerina Kerensky was nothing if not a pragmatist; she knew what she saw when she looked in the mirror. A middle-aged woman who was neither ugly nor pretty, but very, very plain.

And Dmitri Lermontov looked more like a male model showing what the well-dressed high school principal would be wearing this year.

Kerensky glanced nervously around the restaurant. All of her adult life she had heard stories of the Aragvi restaurant, with its white tablecloths, elegant decor and eager-to-please waiters. The woman in her had secretly wanted to dine here as long as she could remember. And now, the man of her dreams had made that dream come true.

But she was too busy thinking of the New Brotherhood to enjoy it.

Kerensky rose from her chair. "Excuse me, Dmitri," she said. "I must visit the ladies' room." She moved quickly across the room, conscious of her walk, wondering if her hips were wiggling too much—or not enough—and constantly aware of their size. She had never owned a cocktail dress before today, and the only one she had been able to find at GUM for this occasion made her look like a female elephant whose skin had tightened to the point of snapping.

Kerensky found herself alone in the restroom. She stood before the mirror, collecting her thoughts. She would have to come to some kind of terms with the problems of her job if she wanted to enjoy this evening. And she had better have a good time tonight. The way she was behaving, another date with Dmitri Lermontov seemed unlikely.

She reached into her purse and found her lipstick, studying her face as she freshened her makeup. No, she had never been pretty. But with a little care, she was not hard to look at. She had always tried to take care of her appearance with the same diligent effort she threw into her job. But in her work, the results of that labor had seemed more evident.

Her work again. Was there no way to get it off her mind, even for a few hours? The leak to the New Brotherhood had to come either from her, Solomentsev or the president himself.

Well, she thought, they were down to two.

Could President Tachek have sabotaged his own plan for reasons unknown to her? Stranger things than that had happened within Russian politics.

She paused, staring at her reflection. No, it made no sense. Tachek's reforms had brought strong opposition from factions of the military and former hard-line party members. That opposition would be strengthened beyond measure if Belasko failed. It was unthinkable.

Kerensky dug through the bag for her rouge compact. Carefully she applied one tiny spot of red to each cheek and rubbed it in with her fingertips.

Solomentsev. Polygraph or not, it had to be Solomentsev. Someway, either voluntarily or through stupidity, Alexandr Solomentsev was aiding and abetting the enemy. And there was only one way to find out how and why.

Starting tomorrow, she would stick to the young aide like borscht to the stomach of a starving man.

Kerensky took a step back, studying herself in the mirror. Her cheeks now glowed a deep, healthy pink, and her lips glistened provocatively under the bright rest-room lights. She looked . . . well, still not pretty maybe, but no longer plain.

Still looking at her reflection in the mirror, Katerina Kerensky said, "I am what one would call attractive," then blushed when she realized she had spoken out loud.

Kerensky turned and walked through the door. Tomorrow she would get to the bottom of the leak. But tonight she would be Katerina Kerensky the woman, rather than Katerina Kerensky the Russian Military Intelligence colonel.

Dmitri looked up as she neared the table. His eyes widened, then softened. She saw for the first time that he felt the same attraction for her that she did for him.

"Katerina," he whispered. "My God, you look lovely."

Kerensky stifled a girlish giggle. She felt like a teenager on a date with the captain of the soccer team. Her heart pounded within her breast. It would be nice to have a man in her life again. Then suddenly, another giggle escaped her lips.

Dmitri's eyes lighted up as he responded to her new attentiveness. "What is it, Katerina?" he asked. "What is so funny?"

"Oh, nothing." She bit her lip softly, forcing the laughter to stop.

But in her heart, Kerensky continued to giggle. She knew the catalyst of her mirth could certainly not be shared with Dmitri Lermontov. At least not on the *second* date.

For what Katerina Kerensky had just thought was that had she met Dmitri Lermontov a few weeks earlier, the president of Russia might have had a much more difficult time establishing his control question.

A FRIGID GUST OF WIND swept across the Moscow River, cutting through the Executioner's overcoat. Dusk had fallen over the city, and the lights surrounding the paddleboat dock shone down on the black water of the small harbor.

Bolan descended the embankment toward the tiny boat house. At the edge of the water ten paddleboats floated on pontoons, chained to the rail. Farther out, near the center of the river, a series of bright orange floats marked the end of the safe boating area and the beginning of the shipping lanes.

The warrior stopped at the open ticket window of the shack. Leaning on the counter, he read the sign on the rear the wall: One Hour—Two Rubles. Two Hours—Three Rubles. An elderly man bundled in blankets rose from a folding chair behind the counter. He tapped a white-tipped cane in front of him as he moved forward, his eyes staring sightlessly past the Executioner. "Yes?" he asked.

"Two hours," Bolan said, pressing three rubles into the old man's outstretched hand.

The Executioner watched as the blind man expertly felt the bills. Satisfied, he exited a side door and tapped his way toward the line of paddleboats. Fishing a key from his pocket, he bent forward, unlocked the chain and looped it from around one of the pontoons.

A sudden thought hit the Executioner. "Do you own these boats yourself?" he asked.

The old man laughed. "The Motherland."

Bolan climbed on board. He settled behind the bicycle pedals as the boat rolled under his weight.

"Stay inside the floats," the blind man cautioned, then turned back to the shack.

Bolan guided the boat toward the center of the river, glad that he didn't have to devise some plan to reimburse the man for what was about to happen. Since the pontoon boats still belonged to the state, Tachek would have to put this one on his expense account.

As he reached the floats, the Executioner heard a ship's horn toot. He looked up to see a cargo vessel sail by toward Moscow's shipping area. Tying the boat to one of the floats, he twisted back toward shore in his seat.

The three New Brotherhood cars were still parked along Frunze. And from the new angle, Bolan could see something else—a flat-brimmed black gunslinger's hat sat in the back seat of the car nearest Garage Number Ten.

For a split second the Executioner considered just dropping the Beretta's sights on Pool and getting it over with. But if he did, he'd never reach the garage.

No, once again, Pool would have to be put on the back burner.

Bolan pulled the bottle of lamp oil from beneath his coat. Twisting the cap, he poured half of the flammable liquid onto the deck and watched it soak into the cracked wood. With the Mini Tanto, he pried off the plastic face of the transistor radio. Ripping out the radio's copper wires, he used them to connect the detonator to the timer.

On the other side of the floats, a tour boat cruised by. Smiling faces beamed from the decks; excited hands waved.

Bolan waved back. Then, dropping the detonator into the bottle of lamp oil, he pulled the electrician's tape from his pocket and secured the bomb to the steering column on deck.

He turned back toward the New Brotherhood troops. The gunners still stared away at the garages.

The warrior bent to the egg timer. The maximum duration was one hour. He would need all of that time, and the cheap device might be off as much as five minutes.

He glanced at his watch. If he worked off a ten-minute safety interval, he'd have fifty minutes.

The Executioner set the timer, rose from his seat and stared down at the dark, murky waters. Ice the size of silver dollars floated along the surface with the current.

Bolan still didn't know what the temperature outside might be. But whatever it was, the water would be colder.

He walked to the edge of the deck. It was time.

With a final glance toward the New Brotherhood hardmen, Bolan pulled the rabbit hat from his head, stuffed it into his coat pocket and dived over the side.

The near-frozen water of the Moscow River enveloped the Executioner, striking from all sides like thousands of merciless, simultaneous hammers. Bolan's heart skipped a beat as the water soaked quickly through his clothes, dragging him down.

Nausea, and a faint, giddy sensation threatened to overwhelm him. Then, slowly, first his arms, then his legs began to stir. He swam slowly at first, picking up speed as his mind overcame the temptation to give in, give up.

Gradually sunlight began to filter through the darkness as he rose through the water. A moment later, his head broke the surface and he gasped for air.

Training, and the instinct for survival, took over as Bolan swam diagonally from the paddleboat toward shore. Glancing toward the cars near the dock, he dived once more beneath the surface, swimming underwater until his stiff fingers finally hit the gravel surrounding the bank. Clawing his way up the bank, he fell to his stomach, gasping for breath as the icy wind swept over his back. The nausea and dizziness returned, seductively urging him to stay where he was; to go to sleep and let others worry about what still lay ahead. Then jerking himself suddenly to his feet, the Executioner staggered up the bank as the wind continued to bite through his saturated clothes.

His sight blurring, the Executioner stared back in the direction of the cars. A block away, the New Brotherhood hardmen still watched the garage. Forcing his legs to move, he crossed Frunze and hurried down a side street leading to Komsomolsky.

A new numbness crept through the Executioner's tortured frame. He recognized the symptoms. He was literally freezing as he moved. But movement was the only thing that might save him. With a sudden burst of will, he broke into a jog, turning up Komsomolsky and heading toward the metro station.

Several curious mouths gaped open as the Executioner dripped his way through the station to his locker. His frozen fingers dropped the key twice before he got it into the lock. Pulling out the suitcase that contained his gray suit, he returned to the rest room and shut himself once more inside the toilet stall.

The Executioner paused, catching his breath. He brought his wristwatch up to his face, the tightened muscles in his arms and shoulders screaming with the movement. It seemed like hours ago that he had dropped into the Moscow River.

It had been less than ten minutes.

As fast as his frozen limbs allowed, Bolan changed into the gray suit and trench coat. Wringing out his sweater and pants in the toilet, he shoved the soggy garments into the suitcase.

Bolan moved back to the mirror. He was surprised to see the false mustache still in place, and the absurdity of the fact brought a smile to his pale lips. He studied the skin on his nose and cheeks. They were still flushed red with blood. He ignored the impulse to rub his skin for warmth. Even with the rosy complexion, he might well have entered the first stage of frostbite. Permanent tissue damage would be the result.

Returning to the locker, the Executioner stowed the suitcase, walked stiffly to the snack bar at the corner of the lobby and ordered tea.

The woman behind the counter set a tall, steaming glass in front of him.

Bolan sipped the tea, gradually beginning to warm as the liquid coursed through his body. He kept one eye on his watch. With the ten-minute safety interval, he had thirty minutes left.

After four glasses of tea, the Executioner began to feel human again. The nausea had receded to a slight queasiness, and all but the last of the fuzziness had left his brain.

But he didn't try to deceive himself. He wasn't over the shock his body had experienced. His resistance had been all but used up, and he would be highly susceptible to the cold until he recovered fully.

With supreme effort of will, Bolan pushed away from the counter. The chill rushed through his body the moment he hit the outside door. His legs stiffened almost immediately, and the numbness returned to his fingers. He pushed on, cutting down an alley and coming out behind the garages.

Shuffling to the end of the row, the Executioner risked a quick look around the corner. From his position he could just see the back seat of the nearest car. Pool's black hat stood out among the other faces turned his way.

The Executioner ducked back. His eyes clouded once more. The sick, churning nausea returned tenfold. Through the haze he saw the hands of his watch. If the timer was on, he had eleven more minutes to endure the cold before the bomb ignited.

Seconds turned to minutes. Both seemed like eternities. The wind howled down the alley, causing tiny icicles to form in the Executioner's damp hair.

Reaching into his pocket, he pulled out the garage key and gripped it in unfeeling fingers. He looked back at his watch.

It had been thirteen minutes since he took up position behind the garage. The cheap egg timer was off, all right, but it was slow, rather than fast.

A disarming though suddenly hit him. The timer might not work at all.

As he returned his deadened hands to his pockets, Bolan heard the explosion. His head shot around the corner again in time to see flames burst through the night on the dark waters of the river. Immediately he sprinted from behind the garage, his eyes glued to Pool and the rest of the men in the back of the rental car.

They had turned toward the river.

Bolan forced his cold, weary legs to the front of the building. On the river beyond, the paddleboat burned like a Viking funeral pyre. He glanced quickly down the street toward the other New Brotherhood vehicles. It was too dark to make out the men inside. He'd have to hope that, like the gunman closer by, they were preoccupied with the explosion.

The Executioner jabbed the key at the lock, missing. He took a deep breath, concentrating, and tried again. The key shot inside and he twisted the latch, the steel of the apparatus screeching.

Reaching down with both hands, Bolan gripped the handle and pulled upward. The exhausted, frozen muscles in his shoulders screamed in protest. Then slowly the door started up.

When the opening was two feet high, the Executioner fell to his side and rolled under the barrier into the garage. He reached overhead and grasped the metal flange at the bottom of the door. Pulling himself to his feet, he let his weight lower the door.

Suddenly all was dark.

The unheated garage felt like the tropics compared to the biting wind outside. Bolan struggled to his feet.

The dizziness now was almost overpowering. His stomach threatened to empty, and his lungs felt as if they might burst with each new gasping breath.

Pulling the Mini-Mag from his pocket, the Executioner switched on the beam and followed it to the door of the ZIL. He slid into the passenger's side, reached over the seat for the greatcoat Kerensky had given him and wrapped it around his trembling shoulders.

Just a few minutes, Bolan told himself. He needed a few minutes to gather his strength. The gunners hadn't seen him enter the garage. If they had, they'd have already opened fire. Just a few minutes to get his body and mind working again. Then he'd smash the ZIL through the door and be on his way. A few... just a few...

WHEN THE EXECUTIONER awoke, he felt as if someone had beaten him with a baseball bat. And morning sunlight was streaming through the cracks in the overhead door.

## CHAPTER NINE

Alexandr Solomentsev's head pounded. He opened his eyes, then clamped them shut against the pain as his mind struggled to clear.

Where was he?

He forced his eyes open again. His face contorted at the soft morning light seeping through the slats of the venetian blinds. He was lying on his side. Long sticky strings of saliva hung from his open mouth, gluing his cheek to the carpet.

Where the hell was he?

Gradually his brain began to focus in woolly, painful clarity. He recognized the room. Leskov's apartment.

Solomentsev closed his eyes again. Choppy thoughts raced through his mind. Little by little, the events of the night before came back to him as disconnected, random events. He fought to organize them.

He had left work early. Why? To meet Leskov. They had gotten drunk. No, *he* had gotten drunk.

Guilt swept through him. He had done something, something he shouldn't have.

What?

Solomentsev lifted an arm. The movement sent a battalion of jackhammers pounding through his skull. He forced the other arm up and gripped the side of the coffee table. Pulling himself to his knees, he toppled to his back on the couch as the jackhammers changed to razor-edged daggers.

The ceiling whirled above him. Solomentsev caught his breath. His stomach rebelled and he felt a sick, bitter, burning sensation in his upper chest. Somewhere in the distance, he heard the sound of running water. Then the water stopped and the obscure outline of a man appeared in the doorway to the bathroom.

"Good morning, Alexandr." Leskov's voice. "You slept well, I assume?"

Solomentsev squinted at his former mentor. Leskov wore the familiar brown slacks and a white ribbed undershirt. One side of his face was covered with shaving cream. The other had already been scraped clean by the straight razor in his hand.

"What time is it?" Solomentsev mumbled.

"Almost nine."

He felt the fear rush through him. He struggled to a sitting position, the cobwebs in his head swirling as if caught in a sudden gust of wind. "I must get—"

Leskov held up a hand, silencing him. "I have taken care of everything. The president's secretary has been informed you have come down with the flu. And I called your wife again, apologizing for keeping you out all night and assuring her that your assignment would be over by late afternoon. Don't worry." Leskov turned and disappeared into the bathroom.

Solomentsev crossed a forearm over his forehead. Shame engulfed him. He had done it again. After promising both Natalya and himself it wouldn't happen. "Pyotr," he called weakly. "Pyotr..."

Leskov returned to the room, buttoning his shirt. A necktie hung over one shoulder. "Yes, Alexandr?"

"Do you have any...aspirin. Perhaps some American Alka-Seltzer?"

Leskov shook his head. "I am sorry." The colonel's eyes traveled to the kitchen table. Solomentsev's followed. In the middle of the table, next to a clean glass, sat an unopened bottle of Stolichnaya vodka. "Perhaps a little hair of the dog that bit you would help?" Leskov said. He walked toward the bottle.

"No," Solomentsev said quickly.

Leskov chuckled. He lifted the bottle and unscrewed the cap, pouring two fingers into the glass. "Suit yourself," he said. "But *I* could certainly do with a little. I have felt better myself."

Solomentsev watched him down the vodka. This was a different Pyotr Leskov then he remembered when the colonel had been his section chief. In those days drunkenness on the job, or missing work due to a hangover, would have been grounds for dismissal. Perhaps imprisonment. "Your attitudes have changed, Pyotr."

Leskov turned to him and shrugged. "I have grown older, Alexandr. And with age has come maturity. We aren't supermen." He began knotting the tie around his throat. "Your work with the president places you under unbelievable stress. And when you get home you have family problems you must deal with. Occasionally you are due a break. A little relaxation. A little fun." He finished with his tie and reached for his coat. "Are you certain you would not like a drink? One drink cannot hurt you, Alexandr. It will simply straighten you out. Make you feel better.''

The thought sent a strange combination of desire and fear through Solomentsev's soul. He wanted more than anything to help himself to the bottle; drive the pain from his skull and the nausea from his belly. But deep in his soul he knew....

"No, thank you, Pyotr."

Leskov nodded. "Then stay here and relax." He pointed toward the new Japanese tape player on the end table next to the couch. "Listen to some music while I run a few errands. If I have not returned by the end of the day, you can go home at the regular time. Natalya will be none the wiser." He walked to the small closet, opened the door and took down his overcoat and the brown fedora. Then, moving back to the kitchen cabinet, he placed his glass in the sink, pulled another from the cabinet and set it next to the bottle on the table. "In case you change your mind." Leskov smiled and disappeared through the front door.

The small apartment was suddenly silent. Solomentsev forced himself to a sitting position on the couch, feeling as lonely as he had ever felt in his life, and wondering why. He lay down once more, crossing his arm over his forehead and pressing hard against his skull. The pain refused to go away.

He opened one eye. Across the room the bottle beckoned to him like a beautiful naked woman.

*"One drink will not hurt you, Alexandr."*

Solomentsev sat up, staring across the room. One drink? When was the last time he had had just one drink? When was the last time the first drink had not sent a craving through his body for more and more? He couldn't remember. It seemed that vodka had become an all-or-nothing affair during the past few months; feast or famine.

For a moment the word *alcoholic* played around the edges of Solomentsev's mind. He shoved it away. Alcoholics were old men in ragged, stinking clothing. They drank directly from the bottle and they had no homes. They didn't hold down jobs, particularly positions of importance like chief assistant to the president of Russia.

A sudden sharp, piercing pain shot through Solomentsev's brain. He grasped the sides of his head with both hands, closing his eyes. When he reopened them, the bottle still stood smiling at him from across the room.

One drink. One drink couldn't possibly make him drunk, and it would take away this terrible pain in his head. Leskov had no aspirin. One drink would be medicine.

The decision was made suddenly. Solomentsev rose to his feet as if the couch had caught fire. Hurrying to the table, he uncapped the bottle with trembling hands, filled the glass to the brim and gulped it.

Shivering, he set the glass back on the table and stood in awe as the vodka swirled through his stomach, calming the butterflies that had flapped their wings against his abdomen all morning. A smile of intense pleasure crossed his lips. He held out his hands and saw only the slightest of tremors.

He stared at the bottle. He didn't feel drunk. This drink had certainly done nothing but what Leskov had predicted. It had driven away the pain. Steadied his nerves.

Almost.

Solomentsev filled the glass again. He sipped more slowly this time, savoring the pungent aroma that only good Russian vodka produced. This one was definitely his final drink. It would finish the recovery the first drink had begun, and he'd make it last. He'd nurse it through the rest of the morning while he listened to Tchaikovsky on Leskov's new machine, then go home to Natalya and the boys. Tomorrow he would return to work and start over.

He walked quickly across the room, silently congratulating himself on the steadiness of his pace and the fact that he would drink no more. He dug through the pile of cassette tapes next to the player. No Tchaikovsky?

A mild depression settled over Solomentsev. His heart had been set on this greatest of all Russian composers.

He came to a tape entitled 40 Russian Melodies, performed by the Moscow Art Orchestra. There would be some Tchaikovsky on it somewhere. It would have to do.

Solomentsev slipped the tape into the machine and returned to the couch, sitting comfortably back as dramatic stringed instruments began playing "Down the Volga." He sipped the vodka, marveling at its taste. So smooth. So... perfect. He had tasted an American vodka once while on assignment in Washington. It had made him want to wretch.

The song ended and the tinkling sounds of the "Little Bell" relaxed Solomentsev further. He closed his eyes, drifting in the euphoria brought on by the music and alcohol. He had been a fool to wait this long. These two drinks had brought him back to the world of the living. And he wanted no more.

The "Faded Chrysanthemums," "Kazbek," and "Meadowland" serenaded him from the tape player. Then suddenly, the music ended, and the tape player snapped off with a harsh, lonely click.

The spell suddenly broken, Solomentsev jerked in his seat. His eyes opened wide as anxiety raced through his soul. The utopia produced by the two drinks had worn off. He felt a sudden, irresistible desire to jump up and run from the apartment, which had become dreadfully lonesome once more.

Solomentsev looked at the bottle, half-empty now, on the table. If the good feeling had left him, that must mean the alcohol had worked its way through his system.

One more drink couldn't hurt.

An hour later, Alexandr Solomentsev staggered into the hall. He steadied himself on the handrail as he stumbled down the stairs through the front door.

Desperately he hurried down the street, peeking into the alleys as he raced by.

At the third alley he came to, Solomentsev saw the car. He stumbled toward the man standing by the open trunk.

"Stolichnaya," Solomentsev slurred as he reached into his pocket.

The man at the trunk grinned. He reached into a box and lifted a quart bottle of the same vodka Solomentsev remembered from Washington. "I am out of Stolichnaya," the black market man said. "But this will have the effect you seek."

Without hesitation Solomentsev grabbed the bottle and twisted the cap.

SLOWLY, HIS FROZEN muscles threatening to cramp with every move, the Executioner exited the ZIL and moved to the overhead door. The frigid weather had warped the wood, and he stared through a crack into the sun.

The New Brotherhood car was still parked on the street, a hundred feet away.

Bolan stepped back from the door. He squatted, stood, squatted, stood, repeating the process until he felt his body start to warm. He flexed his toes, then moved to his ankles and his calves, flexing then relaxing each muscle group until he'd reached his neck. The cramps began to subside.

The Executioner moved back to the ZIL. He opened the trunk, pulled out the AK-74 and took a seat behind the wheel. Setting the weapon on the seat next to him, he opened a can of tuna from the stores he'd bought earlier. As he ate the fish, two apples, and drank from a bottle of mineral water, he loaded the assault rifle's magazine. When he'd finished, he returned to the crack in the door.

Sometime during the night, Moscow's snowplows had cleared the streets. And with the rising temperature and the threat of running out of gas, Pool and his henchmen had turned off the engine.

Bolan grinned as he bit into another apple. It might have warmed up some, but the New Brotherhood gunners would still be cold. And from what he could see through the crack, they looked tired. Pool and company had been there all night—maybe all of the day before as well. Fatigue, as well as constant exposure to the frigid weather, would affect their judgment and reaction time.

At least the Executioner hoped it would. He'd be outnumbered ten to one when the shooting started.

Bolan watched Jake Pool sip from a silver flask as he finished eating. Then, back behind the wheel of the ZIL, he took a deep breath, mentally preparing himself for what was about to come.

Lifting the AK with his left hand, the Executioner jacked the first round into the chamber and felt the jar as the bolt slid forward. Then, in one swift movement, he twisted the key and threw the ZIL into gear.

A high-pitched shriek echoed in his ears as the tires peeled rubber across the concrete. The overhead door exploded, sending chunks of aged wood showering over the hood as the car burst from the garage.

As the wooden rain fell away from the windshield, Bolan stuck the rifle through the window, aimed toward the Toyota and squeezed the trigger.

A full-auto burst of rounds roared from the weapon. The frame of the Intourist vehicle sank as the tires blew. Raising his aim, Bolan fired again, and the windshield disintegrated in a storm of splintered glass and blood.

The ZIL skidded toward the Toyota on a patch of ice. Fighting the wheel with one hand, the Executioner maneuvered around the New Brotherhood car and turned onto the street. Behind him, he heard the engines of the other two cars roar to life.

Bolan dropped the AK and grasped the steering wheel with both hands, racing down Frunze along the river. Behind him, the two cars fell in behind.

At the corner of Novoluzneckij, he skidded through a right-hand turn. Beyond, he knew Frunze Nab became Luzneckaja as the river continued south. Then the road running parallel to the water turned into Savvinskaja Nab as the Moscow River looped back north, farther west. Continuing on this course, he'd encounter the river again in another few miles.

The Executioner glanced into the rearview mirror as he tore past Lenin Stadium. The New Brotherhood cars were two hundred yards behind.

Gradually Bolan let up on the gas. The lead car behind him closed the gap, and rifle barrels extended from the windows. Fire cascaded over the ZIL as the river appeared once more in the distance.

The Executioner slowed further. He had a plan for the car behind him, and that plan meant he'd have to risk their fire, hope they hit nothing vital for a few moments more.

The guardrail running along Savvinskaja loomed dead ahead. Suddenly Bolan hit the gas pedal. The ZIL shot forward in a burst of speed. The chase car behind followed suit.

At the last possible second the Executioner stomped the brake. The ZIL skidded across the road into the oncoming lane, narrowly missing a tractor-trailer before striking the guardrail and fishtailing back into control on Savvinskaja.

Behind him, the Executioner heard the screech of tires. He looked into the mirror as the Toyota burst through the rail and disappeared down the embankment into the river.

Two down. One to go.

Hitting the pedal again, he picked up speed as the second car continued pursuit. He'd have to take another sharp turn soon, when the river bent west again. The Executioner considered the same strategy, then quickly brushed the idea from his mind. The hardmen weren't stupid. They'd just seen one of their cars taken out by that approach. It wouldn't work a second time.

They'd be expecting the same thing, so the Executioner would do the opposite.

Car horns honked, and angry drivers raised their fists in protest as Bolan led his pursuers through a red light at Borodino bridge. He allowed the gunmen behind him to close the gap again, noting that this time they moved up more slowly; more cautiously. He increased speed as he neared the intersection of Savvinskaja and Kalinin.

Ahead, a fork appeared in the road. Savvinskaja continued to follow the river, and Kalinin angled back toward downtown Moscow. The Executioner bore down on the pedal, gunning the ZIL to top speed as he neared the intersection. A few shots rained over his head, but for the most part it appeared that the hardmen were waiting to see which way he'd turn.

Bolan stayed on Stravvinskaja, starting into the curve as he came abreast of the side street. Then suddenly, he cut the wheel to the right, skidding into a complete one-eighty before wrestling the car across the oncoming lane onto Kalinin.

He looked up in time to see the Toyota hit the brakes. The driver twisted the wheel too fast, and the vehicle spun in circles, threatening to tip before coming to a halt in the center of the river road.

The warrior picked up speed again, squealing off Kalinin at the first corner and down a side street to Tchaikovsky Ul. He slowed to the speed limit when he saw no more signs of pursuit, then cut back to Kalinin and began threading his way back across town to the metro where he'd left his luggage.

The ZIL was now a marked vehicle, and therefore useless. It didn't matter—it was time to change not only identities but tactics as well. He'd abandon the car at the metro, take the train to Kiev Station and head south by rail.

THE TRAIN FROM MOSCOW slowed as it neared the city. Bolan looked through the window of the compartment to see the lights of Kiev. Split down the center by the Dnieper River, the political, industrial and cultural center of Ukraine consisted of two distinct geographical sections.

To the west of the river stood high, rolling hills. The east consisted of a seemingly endless plain, the monotonous tableland broken only by the machinery and chemical plants of the Darnitsa—Kiev's industrial area.

The Executioner felt the sharp, shooting pains of muscles not fully recovered from the Moscow River's icy waters as he lifted his luggage and stepped down from the train. Still dressed in the rumpled gray business suit, his shabby appearance had brought on three passport inspections during the trip.

The Dwight McNeil identification had passed scrutiny each time, but he'd drawn a polite suggestion from railroad security officers: shave and clean up if he wished to avoid such further inconveniences.

An unlicensed wildcat taxi driver stood next to the door of his Datsun as Bolan exited the depot. With a slight wave, he beckoned the Executioner forward.

Bolan gave the man the address of the Hotel Dnieper, the top Intourist lodging. It was the logical place for Dwight McNeil to stay while he went about his agricultural research.

Traffic on Kreshchatik, Kiev's main boulevard, was light, and ten minutes later they entered Lenkomsomol Square and pulled to a halt in front of the hotel. The Executioner paid the driver, entered the lobby and walked inside.

A tourist shop was located just inside the front door. Bolan showed his passport and entered. Bypassing the usual souvenirs, he found a section with travel needs and purchased a small box of washing detergent.

The clothes he'd bought in Moscow would be needed again that night. But an American agriculture expert sending Russian peasant attire out from the hotel to be cleaned would draw attention. And the concept of neighborhood self-service laundries was still light-years away.

Bolan walked to the front desk and presented his passport. A few minutes later, he pushed through door number 211.

The room was small, even by Eastern European standards, and dried paper curled down from the walls near the ceiling. A wooden chair rested against the wall to one side of the single bed. Gray-brown stains fell from ceiling to floor in the corner next to the bathroom, marking the path of plumbing problems on the floor above.

Bolan opened his luggage. The sweater and heavy wool pants still dripped with water from the Moscow River, and mildew had begun within the confines of the suitcase.

Filling the bathtub with water, he added detergent and began to scrub as he considered the developments of the night before and their relevance to the overall operation.

The leak from the president's office to the New Brotherhood had widened to a flood. Pool and Furelli seemed to be getting word of his movements before he himself knew what they'd be.

The Executioner had appraised the situation during the long ride from Moscow to Kiev. He had come up with only one conceivable answer.

The leak somehow stemmed from Solomentsev.

Pouring more soap into the tub, he continued scrubbing. Solomentsev had passed the polygraph. So what? Even trained examiners who were honest admitted the exams weren't perfect. The results were a matter of human interpretation, and where that was involved, mistakes could be made. Tachek seemed like an honest, decent man, intent on improving conditions in his country. But he was human, and a politician to boot. His natural instinct would be to cover potential mistakes, not admit them.

Pulling the plug from the tub, Bolan stared at the wet clothing as the water circled around the drain and gurgled into the pipe. The events of the previous night and that morning proved another important item.

The relationship between Russian Intelligence and the New Brotherhood was more than a passing acquaintance. Whomever Hernandez and Esposito had on the inside was high up in the intelligence organization. High enough to use the agency's resources without drawing suspicion his way.

The New Brotherhood had learned of the Hlupnik ID. That could have been done through the leak. But not even Tachek, Kerensky and Solomentsev had known of the garage across from Gorky Park. That information had come through diligent investigation, and it had come quickly, implying the use of organized information and cross-filing.

That meant a computer network, and a computer network meant government.

Bolan started the water again, rinsing the suds from his clothes under the tap. He wrung the garments out, then hung them over the shower rod to dry.

After a quick bath and shave, the Executioner dressed in the Czech uniform. He'd be taking a chance walking the streets of Kiev as Frank Hlupnik. But the Czech colonel had gotten him through security checks where nonmilitary ID wouldn't have, and he needed it one final time.

The Executioner exited the hotel by a side door to Kirov Street, walking south past the Ukrainian Academy of Sciences. He followed the sidewalk up the steep slope above the river and saw a line of cabs in front of a park to his left. Walking to the door of the nearest vehicle, he climbed in back and gave the driver the address of the Arsenal Workers monument on Sichneve Povstannya Street.

As they passed a bookstore, an idea struck the Executioner. Directing the driver into the parking lot, he said simply, "Wait."

Bolan was met at the door by a stocky woman who politely inquired how she could help him.

"I am looking for a dictionary," the Executioner said, making sure his halting, broken, Czech-accented speech was even worse than usual. "Czech-Russian, Russian-Czech."

The woman's smile brightened. She pointed him down an aisle.

The Executioner found a section containing Langenscheidt translations, paid, and returned to the cab. A few minutes later, the driver let him out in front of the Arsenal Workers Monument.

The Executioner worked the dictionary's spine between his hands as he walked past the monument, folding a few of the pages and dog-earing others to give the book a look of use. A quarter mile from the monument, he saw the iron gates surrounding the Trotsky Soviet Officers Hospital.

The grounds surrounding the building might have been those of any V.A. hospital in the United States. Old men sat in rocking chairs on the porch. Nurses pushed others along the sidewalks in wheelchairs. A few patients, slippers and pajama legs visible beneath the tails of their brown overcoats, walked among the gardens. Mental rather than physical casualties, these patients stared at the flowers and grass, their minds trapped in a world of retreat that would never again know the strain of combat.

Bolan stopped at the gate. Two men dressed in immaculately tailored, double-breasted honor guard uniforms goose-stepped forward to meet him, their Great Patriotic War rifles supported upright in their left hands.

The Executioner returned the salute, then opened the dictionary. Stumbling, he finally got out that he had come to visit a friend.

The ranking guard passed him through. Bolan walked down the sidewalk between rows of evergreens and up the steps to the main entrance.

The only difference between the matron in the lobby and the one who had stopped the Executioner in the bookstore was their attire. Short and mousy, the female lieutenant wore a shapeless brown tunic and skirt. An unadorned Sam Brown belt girded her ample waist. The name Pilnyak beamed in polished bronze from the tag on her left breast.

From behind the folding card table that served as the information desk, Lieutenant Pilnyak stared at Bolan with suspicious eyes. "State your business," she ordered.

The Executioner began rummaging through the dictionary. "I...am...here...for...to..." he said slowly, flipping through the pages.

Lieutenant Pilnyak tapped her pencil on the desk impatiently as she waited.

"From . . . before . . . friend . . ." Bolan went on.

The tapping grew louder.

"When . . . young . . . no, *younger* . . ."

In exasperation the woman rose from behind her desk. "You are here to visit a friend? Is that what you are attempting to say?"

Bolan nodded vigorously.

"From where do you know this friend?"

Bolan returned to the dictionary, silently staring at the pages, turning, staring, turning, staring.

Pilnyak drew in another agitated breath, then framed her question differently. "Where did you meet him . . . your friend?"

Again, the Executioner's head bobbed up and down.

The lieutenant blew air between her teeth. "Where did you meet your friend?"

"Ah," Bolan said. "Intelligence school. In Minsk."

The lieutenant seemed encouraged. "And what is his name?"

Bolan turned his hands palm up, then tapped his forehead with his fingertips. "I remember only the first name," he said. "But if I hear the last, I will know it."

The lieutenant's impatience faded and the suspicion returned. "If you do not remember his name, how did you know he was here?" she spit sharply.

Bolan thumbed through the dictionary. When he saw the impatience return to Pilnyak's face, he said. "Another friend told me."

Pilnyak eyed the colonel's bars on his shoulders, obviously trying to decide what type of officer could be so stupid. Czechoslovakian, of course. Bolan watched her expression change again, this time to uneasiness, as she considered the situation.

The Executioner had said the magic word. "Intelligence." If he had met his friend at intelligence school, the natural conclusion to be drawn was that he had been allied with the KGB. And the next conclusion that could be drawn was that being uncooperative might get Pilnyak in trouble.

"What is the first name?" the woman asked.

Bolan smiled good-naturedly. "Boris."

It was like saying "Joe" in America.

Closing her eyes, ready to begin a task that held no hope of success, Lieutenant Pilnyak opened the large hospital registry book in front of her. "Akhmatova?" she said. "Boris V. Infantry?"

The Executioner shook his head.

"Aksyonov, Boris, tank crewman. Arbatrov, Boris, Spetsnaz. Astoravitch—"

"Yes," Bolan said quickly, "that is him."

Pilnyak's head jerked up from the book. "Arbatrov?"

Bolan nodded.

Pilnyak sighed in relief and slammed the book shut. "Third floor. Room 315." She motioned to a uniformed man across the room who came hurrying over. "Corporal Chukovsky will escort you."

Bolan followed the corporal onto the elevator and down the hall to the room. Chukovsky stood outside as the Executioner entered, noting the nurse's instructions clipped on the door.

Sergeant Boris Arbatrov had undergone gall bladder surgery that very morning.

The Executioner closed the door behind him and glanced at the sleeping form in the bed. Once in a great while, luck was with you, he reminded himself. Arbatrov was big. At least the Executioner's height, maybe even a little taller. His uniform should fit.

A short, halting snort exited the Spetsnaz sergeant's nose. Arbatrov would be out for several more hours, and he'd have no need of his credentials or uniform while he remained in the hospital. The Executioner should have several days before they were even missed.

Quickly Bolan slid open the drawer in the table next to the bed. He pocketed the black leather case he found inside.

In the closet next to the rest room, he saw the uniform. The gall bladder attack must have hit Arbatrov during training—he had entered the hospital in camouflage fatigues and the blue-and-white hooped T-shirt worn by all Commonwealth special forces. Unlike other top units, Spetsnaz had no beret of its own, and the standard light blue beret of the airborne units sat on the shelf behind the uniform.

The Executioner folded the uniform and slipped it with the beret under his coat.

Chukovsky ushered the Executioner back down on the elevator, then down the sidewalk to the gate. The guards gave him another sharp salute as he exited the grounds and walked away.

Colonel Frank Hlupnik had served the Executioner well. But now it was time for the colonel to retire, and let Spetsnaz Sergeant Boris Arbatrov take his place.

## CHAPTER TEN

Katerina Kerensky guided the unmarked RMI vehicle into the parking space in front of the Workers' Café on Kalinin Prospekt. She killed the engine and stuffed the key ring in her purse.

The colonel glanced down at her lap. The black skirt had ridden high over her knees again. It was shorter than most she wore and made her feel self-conscious. She looked briefly at the top of her black hose. For a woman who'd seen the better side of thirty, she had to admit that her legs didn't look too bad.

Grabbing the hem of the skirt, Kerensky raised her hips and wiggled it back down. She adjusted the rearview mirror, scowling at her reflection in the glass. The blond wig and sunglasses made her feel ridiculous. Part of the time she felt like the Mata Hari character in one of the B-grade Russian films made during the Stalin era. The rest of the time, she thought she looked like a hooker plying her wares around Arbat Square.

The thought brought a giggle from deep in her throat. The way she'd been behaving the past two nights, the second identity seemed more fitting.

Kerensky looked at her watch. It was almost time for the government offices to close. Solomentsev would leave the president's office in a few minutes and head across Red Square to this street.

She sighed out loud. Yesterday's attempt at surveillance had been a disaster. Assuming Solomentsev drove a car to work, she had waited a block from the entrance to the Kremlin parking lot, sitting patiently behind the wheel in the same blond wig and glasses. She knew the thin disguise would never fool anyone who knew her well, so she had been determined to stay well away from close scrutiny by the president's aide.

Solomentsev had surprised her. He had exited the building on the other side. She had caught a glimpse of him as he crossed the square toward this street, but by the time she'd driven around the block he had vanished.

Kerensky unfolded the newspaper in her lap and raised the pages, making sure they could be seen through the window if anyone cared to look. All she had learned yesterday was that her mark rode the metro rather than driving. But at least that was something, and she knew where to begin her tail tonight.

The colonel angled her head toward the newspaper, but behind the dark lenses of her glasses, her eyes stared at Red Square. Her mind drifted back to her lovemaking with Dmitri after she'd lost Solomentsev the night before. She felt a warm rush through her body.

She smiled. This time, she let the warm feeling engulf her. She and Dmitri had made love for the first time after leaving the restaurant two nights earlier. At first it had been awkward—for both of them.

The loud bell from Red Square rang shrilly, signaling the end of the working day and jerking Kerensky's attention back to the street. But she continued to smile, thinking of how awkward that first time had been for both of them. Afterward, they had lain naked under the covers, both silently wondering what the other was thinking. Then, without warning, they had both broken into boisterous, simultaneous laughter.

The laughter broke the ice. They had talked, made love, talked and made love the rest of the night. They had told each other their most intimate personal secrets. She had even confided to Dmitri the humiliation of the polygraph control question.

"You will never need to resort to that again," her lover had promised.

In those few hours Kerensky had grown closer to her daughter's school principal than anyone she had ever known, even the man who had been her daughter's father.

She dropped the newspaper into her lap as the realization of that fact brought on a sudden burst of nostalgia. She and her late husband had been close, but never in the way she and Dmitri already were. A tear formed in the corner of her eye, and as she whisked it away with her handkerchief, she saw Solomentsev pass the car and continue down the street.

The colonel gave him a hundred-foot head start, then exited the vehicle and fell in behind. Workers on their way home crowded the sidewalks, and she made sure several always shielded her from Solomentsev. She needn't have bothered. The man didn't turn around. He hurried on like a man on a mission ordered by demons.

All thoughts of Dmitri pushed to the back of her mind, Kerensky dodged slow-moving strollers and baby carriages, threading her way through small gatherings of men who blocked her way as they stopped to chat. Six blocks from Red Square, Solomentsev turned down an alley. Kerensky hurried to the corner and cautiously peeked around the edge of the bricks.

Without looking back Solomentsev turned another corner into an alley.

Kerensky paused. Should she risk following further? She had no idea where the alley eventually led. It might be a dead end. And if Solomentsev suddenly doubled back...

Making her decision, Kerensky hurried down the alley. She stopped at the corner where Solomentsev had disappeared, then inched her head around the edge.

She jerked back around the corner as if a coiled snake had greeted her. In the brief glance she had seen Alexandr Solomentsev, not three feet away, standing with another man at the rear of a car.

Kerensky hurried back to the street. The alley *had* dead-ended. Any second, Solomentsev would return the way he'd come.

She ducked in front of a store window, then casually looked down the alley once more. What was Solomentsev up to? Was the man next to the car his New Brotherhood contact? She hadn't had time to discern what their business might be.

A moment later, Solomentsev appeared again. He looked up and down the alley, then pulled a bottle from under his overcoat, twisted the cap and held it to his lips.

Katerina Kerensky leaned back against the glass of the window, covering her mouth with both hands to keep from laughing out loud. The clandestine meeting she had suspected to be with the New Brotherhood was nothing more than the purchase of bootleg vodka.

The colonel glanced back around the corner. The president's aide was still guzzling. He stopped and shuddered, his eyes red and wet.

Kerensky moved two stores down, staring into another window, the laughter gone suddenly from her soul. These weren't the actions of a man who'd stopped for a quick one on the way home from work. Solomentsev was trying to get as much vodka into his system as he could, as fast as possible.

His behavior was that of the chronic alcoholic.

Kerensky waited, a new world of possibilities opening up in her brain. She knew well the president's stand on alcohol abuse. What would happen if he learned his right-hand man had succumbed to the disease?

The cold hard facts were clear. Solomentsev was vulnerable to blackmail by anyone who knew his secret.

A few minutes later, the man came out of the alley, the bottle hidden somewhere under his coat. He turned away from Kerensky and continued down the street.

Kerensky fell in behind again, watching the slight weave to his step. It would not be noticeable if she hadn't been looking for it. So far, Solomentsev still had some control of his disease.

She felt her pulse quicken as they neared the metro station. Then her heart dropped as Solomentsev passed by.

Where was he leading her?

Two blocks later, Solomentsev turned into a parking garage. He stopped briefly at the window, took a key ring from the attendant, then disappeared up a ramp to the lot.

Kerensky kicked herself mentally. He had done it to her again. Solomentsev did drive, after all. But he left his car at this lot, a common practice for bureaucrats who got little exercise. The government even encouraged it, providing free parking spaces to those who took part in the program.

Turning sideways toward the street, Kerensky saw the ZIL roll down the ramp. There was no point in hurrying back to her own car. Solomentsev would be long gone when she returned.

As the ZIL turned away, Kerensky started slowly back up the street. Today had been like yesterday. A complete bust.

As the colonel passed a sign announcing the Ukrainian Café, she saw a familiar face enter. The man wore a frayed brown suit and matching fedora. Kerensky frowned. She knew him from somewhere. But disguised as she was in her blond wig and glasses, he didn't give her a second look.

Moving down the street, her dark mood lifted. The surveillance hadn't gone as well as she'd planned, but at least she'd learned two valuable things. First, Solomentsev had a drinking problem, and her instincts told her it played some role in the leak. And second, she had a new starting place for tomorrow's tail. This time she'd be ready and waiting at the parking garage.

Kerensky opened the car door and slid behind the wheel. Her depression vanished as she changed from

RMI officer back to woman and mother. Ivanna would be starving when she got home.

Her remembered pleasure of the previous evening returned as she thought of Dmitri. She'd have to cook something special tonight. She and her daughter were having company.

THE DANK ODOR of the river filled the Executioner's nostrils as he crossed the bridge to the east bank of the Dnieper. Although nearly ten in the evening, many of the lights in the windows of the Darnitsa area factories still shone. Against the backdrop of the moon, thick smoke drifted toward the sky.

Bolan hadn't been able to rinse all of the detergent from the sweater, and the coarse material irritated his skin beneath the shoulder holster. Likewise, the gray woolen work pants had scoured angry red blotches on his hip beneath the Desert Eagle.

The discomfort was a small price to pay, Bolan thought as he continued under the dock lights. A small amount of pain to trade for the security afforded by the Beretta and Desert Eagle. While he stood little chance of encountering the New Brotherhood this evening, the mission he had undertaken—a necessary prelude to what he had planned later for Esposito and Hernandez—held its own dangers.

It required he go places where a soldier could die as quickly as he might on the battlefield.

Dockside bars.

In every town bordering a large body of water in every country in the world, there lay a section of the city devoted to sailors. But sailors were hardly the only patrons who frequented these establishments. Thieves, prostitutes and penny-ante drug dealers were among the *less* menacing. Terrorists, mercenaries without morals, and killers-for-hire were among the *more*.

The Executioner came to a lone shabby building that sat less than a hundred feet from the harbor. Tar shingles that had once covered both the roof and outer walls lay scattered around the shack. A few still hung stubbornly to the dirty plywood.

The hand-scrawled sign nailed to the door read simply Gib's.

As he mounted the steps to the porch, Bolan heard loud Russian folk music scratching its way from a well-used phonograph inside. He pushed through the door. The music continued, but all laughter, all speech, all noise of any other kind stopped abruptly. Twenty heads turned toward the unfamiliar face, sized him up, then gradually returned to their conversations.

Bolan moved to the bar, taking in the room with one quick glance: the usual mixture of locals and sailors from surrounding areas, women in soiled, revealing clothes, a few grubby children, their eyelids faltering as evening grew into night.

The walls were devoid of all decoration except a crude painting behind the bar. A woman, nude and perhaps a hundred pounds overweight, stood next to a stream, holding a flower in her chubby fingers.

A man wearing a frazzled shawl sweater looked up from behind the bar. "What'll it be?"

"Beer," Bolan replied.

The bartender grabbed a lukewarm bottle from beneath the bar and set it in front of him.

The atmosphere was wrong. While there was no doubt in the Executioner's mind that all sorts of petty crime took place in and around Gib's, this was a closed group; a clique. It would take days, maybe weeks, to gain the confidence of anyone in this bar. Time he didn't have.

Bolan gave Gib's one beer and ten minutes before leaving. He moved on along the docks, entering, then leaving each establishment as soon as he'd checked it out.

Close to midnight he came to a building that had once been a private home. Built in the architectural style of the czar-era, sections of the house had crumbled with time. They had been restored with whatever material was at hand, in whatever style was most effortless.

Three of the six ornately carved columns that had once supported the second-story porch had been replaced with four-by-five posts of rough cedar. One of the four front windows was of ancient, expensively cut concave glass. Two had been replaced with ordinary flat panes, and cardboard had been taped over the fourth. The frame around the front door had been intricately carved, but the door itself was of stark, unpainted plywood.

The entire building looked like the home of some landed gentry who had retained its property but lost all cash flow.

In Russian the sign read Riverside Inn.

Unlike Gib's, none of the patrons seemed to notice the Executioner as he entered the front room and took a seat at an empty table. A waiter strolled over, took his order and returned a moment later with a beer.

Bolan had raised the glass to his lips when a buxom young woman in a low-cut dress slid into the seat across from him. She smiled seductively, opening her mouth to reveal a row of brownish-yellow teeth. Then, as if remembering what her smile revealed from practice in front of a mirror, the woman's lips clamped tightly. The result was a forced, phony smirk.

"You are new," she said in a low, suggestive voice. "You will buy me a drink?"

The waiter had already returned with a glass of pinkish wine. He set it before the woman and turned to Bolan.

The Executioner peeled a bill off his roll, noticing the woman's flicker of interest when she saw the money.

"My name is Rana." The woman leaned forward, letting her breasts swell over the neckline of her thin dress. "And you are..."

"Frank," Bolan replied. "From Prague."

"Ah! A Czech! My uncle came from Moravia."

Bolan listened as the woman rattled on, leaning forward and back, each time letting her enormous breasts work their way farther out of the dress. From the corner of his eye he saw a thin, seedy man in a brown suit eyeing him from the bar.

The Executioner recognized their game immediately. It was a variation of an international con used the world over.

As the woman's left breast threatened to free itself from her dress, the man at the bar rose and strolled drunkenly across the room.

"You are big, Frank," Rana purred, staring into the Executioner's eyes. "I like big men." She leaned farther forward.

Bolan played along, letting his eyes fall to her cleavage.

"It makes me wonder if you are big all over...." As if having a life of its own, Rana's breast finally toppled out of her dress, exposing a large, pink nipple.

At the same time the man from the bar lost his balance and fell against the Executioner. "Excuse me," he muttered drunkenly. He straightened and started away from the table.

The Executioner's hand shot out. Grasping the man's wrist, he jerked him back to the booth. Scooting closer to the wall, he pulled the man down into the seat next to him. "What's your hurry, friend?" he asked. "I was just getting ready to ask you to join us."

The thin man stared at him like a fox caught in the chicken house.

Bolan snapped his fingers over the table. "Let's have it," he ordered.

The pickpocket paused, then reluctantly reached into his coat and pulled out Bolan's roll of bills.

The Executioner stuffed the money back in his pocket. He drew the Mini Tanto and pressed the point into the man's ribs beneath the table. "Let's talk," he said.

Rana let out a burst of angry Russian about her partner's clumsiness.

"Give him a break," Bolan said. "I never felt a thing." He turned to the pickpocket, jabbing the knife harder into the trembling side. "What's your name?"

The man grimaced. "Gregor."

"You and I are going for a walk, Gregor."

Gregor's eyes flickered anxiously around the room.

Bolan read their meaning. "Don't even think about trying to signal your friends." He moved the lapel of his coat, showing the pickpocket the straps of his shoulder rig. "You'll be dead before they figure out what's going on." He turned back to Rana. "Take off," he ordered. "Business is over for the night."

The warrior rose and pushed Gregor through the door. They circled to the side of the building where the Executioner shoved the little man against the wall.

"You will kill me now," Gregor said matter-of-factly. He seemed resigned.

"No, not now." Bolan sheathed the Tanto. "In fact I'm going to give you a chance to make more money tonight than you would picking pockets." He shoved bills into the front pocket of the little man's coat.

Gregor's eyes widened in curiosity. Then they closed into knowing little slits, his head nodding slowly as Bolan explained what he needed. "You have come to the right man. I know exactly where to take you."

"Good. But let's get something straight up front. You tried to fool me once tonight already. It didn't work. You *are* good, and there's always the chance you might be able to fool me later. Maybe take me to the police, or hustle me down some dark alley where your friends are. Like I said, it might even work."

Suddenly drawing the Desert Eagle from his hip, Bolan rested the muzzle against Gregor's chin. "But consider the consequences in case it doesn't."

Gregor nodded. "I will not try anything."

The pickpocket led the way from the docks to the industrial section of town. They took a winding route of streets and alleys away from the river, occasionally encountering groups of men sharing bottles of vodka.

They all seemed to know Gregor. Some greeted him like a long-lost brother. Others looked like they'd strangle him if they caught him alone.

Entering an alley behind a chemical warehouse, they descended a cracked concrete staircase to a door one flight down. Gregor rapped on the wood. A moment later, the door cracked open and a nose poked through the opening.

"I have brought you business, Herr Schneider," Gregor said.

Tiny round spectacles appeared above the nose and behind them Bolan saw the eyes squint suspiciously.

"He is okay," Gregor said. "Let us in."

Schneider stood back from the door, and Gregor led the Executioner into the subterranean apartment.

Bolan glanced around the tiny room. This was the den of a forger, all right. A slanted work desk, much like that of an architect, sat in the corner beneath an overhead light. Cameras of all shapes and descriptions lined a shelf along the wall. Passports, some Russian, had been stacked on a table. Next to the passports, the Executioner saw a stack of interior travel visas.

Schneider wore a brown apron and green eyeshade. "Before you tell me what you have come for," he said. "Let *me* tell you something. I am the best at what I do. And I charge accordingly."

Bolan nodded. "I am willing to pay." He told the little German what he wanted.

Both Schneider and Gregor gasped. "Please leave," the German said. "You cannot afford what I would charge to take such a risk."

Bolan pulled the roll of bills from his pocket. "Let's see if I can."

Schneider shook his head. "If we are discovered, we will all be executed."

The Executioner peeled three thousand rubles from the roll. Schneider stared greedily for a moment, then resumed his posture of indifference. "A great German once said 'He that is of the opinion that money will do everything may well be suspected of doing everything for money.'"

The Executioner didn't respond. He counted out two thousand more and pressed the bills into Schneider's hand. The little man stared back blankly.

Bolan gave him another thousand. Schneider hesitated, then walked to the shelf and pulled down one of the cameras. Adjusting the lens, he motioned Bolan against a pale gray backdrop. The shutter clicked.

Moving to the table against the far wall, Schneider scooted it to the side, rolled back a throw rug and pulled two loose planks from the floor. He grunted as he lugged a steel firebox from the hole, pulled a key from his apron and opened the lid.

Bolan watched the forger dig through his files. A moment later, he pulled out two sheets of stationery and an official's seal.

Schneider moved to the work desk. "Please take a seat while I work," he said, "and do not speak." He paused and drew a deep breath. "The consequences of discovery are considerably worse than forged ballet tickets. I do not wish to make mistakes."

Bolan dropped into a frayed armchair as the German straightened his glasses, took a seat at the work desk and switched on the light.

The Executioner leaned back, taking advantage of the rare opportunity to rest. His mind drifted back to the words Schneider had quoted: "He that is of the opinion that money will do everything may well be suspected of doing everything for money."

Good words, for most circumstances. But Schneider had been wrong about two things. First, Bolan wasn't risking his life for money. He was doing it to ensure that organized crime never got a foothold in the Commonwealth.

And the second mistake Schneider had made was attributing his quotation to a "famous German." That was unless Benjamin Franklin had been German.

THE LONG BLACK LINCOLN town car passed under the flashing neon lights, and pulled to a halt in the yellow no-parking zone in front of the theater.

Don Joseph Esposito stared out the back-seat window as The Phantom of the Opera blinked on and off overhead. "Keep an eye out for him, Carl," Esposito told the driver.

The driver coughed. "Excuse me, sir. How, uh, how will I know him?"

Esposito snorted. "Oh, you'll know him, Carl. He'll be the obnoxious little spic dressed up like Elvis who looks like he hit the lottery the minute after he swam the Rio Grande.''

Carl laughed. "Yes, sir. New money, no class?"

"You hit the nail on the head, Carl."

Don Joseph leaned forward, lifted the wine bottle from the bar set into the back of the seat and poured Vitiano Classico into his glass. He sipped the smooth red Chianti as he watched people pass by. Broadway hadn't changed in fifty years. Men and women in evening dress still hurried to the theaters, doing their best to ignore the outstretched hands of the men and women in rags.

Esposito saw an angry face in a blue uniform cross the street toward the Lincoln.

"You fuckin' blind?" The cop pulled a ticket book from under his long blue coat with one hand as he pointed to the no-parking sign with the other. "You can't read, or what?" He began to write.

Esposito hit the window button and the glass rolled down. "Officer," he said softly.

The cop continued to write.

The don spoke again, this time more loudly. "Officer."

The cop looked up angrily from the ticket book. He frowned into the window, then his face suddenly drained of blood. "Uh, oh, Mr. Esposito," he said. "Gee, I'm sorry. I didn't see it was you." He laughed nervously. "Like, uh, how am I supposed to see through the dark window? The department hasn't issued those new Superman X-ray goggles yet, right?" He waited anxiously for the mafioso's reaction to his feeble joke.

Esposito smiled pleasantly. "Well, we'll have to see about that, Officer—" he squinted at the name tag above the cop's breast pocket "—Wilkins. I'm having lunch with the commissioner next week. I'll find out what's caused the delay."

The cop laughed uneasily. "You take care now, Mr. Esposito," he said and shoved the ticket book back in his pocket.

Esposito hit the button and the window rolled up. He settled back into the leather seat and watched the cop hurry off down the street, no doubt congratulating himself on getting out of a potentially sticky situation.

The Mafia don frowned. This was the world he had lived in for years. A world where he parked where he wanted, did what he wanted, and had lunch with men like the police commissioner. He was a respected citizen. A pillar of the community.

What had possessed him? What had made him let a no-class dope-dealing spic like Hernandez talk him into risking it all with some hare-brained scheme to take over Russia?

Esposito sipped his wine, feeling his stomach sour and the burn begin in his esophagus. The ulcer. The fucking ulcer. Hernandez had brought it back, which meant instead of his beloved Chianti and tagliarini, he could look forward to several weeks of Maalox and bland pasta. He set his glass on the tray next to the bottle.

Hernandez suddenly appeared on the sidewalk, flanked by the man he called Erich. Esposito eyed him through the window. The little spic wore a tasteless white tux and matching bow tie beneath a new white wide-brimmed hat. The don snorted. The brown camel-hair overcoat might as well have had the price tag still hanging from it à la Minnie Pearl.

"May I assume that's him, sir?" Carl asked.

Esposito nodded.

The chauffeur straightened his cap and exited the vehicle, hurrying toward Hernandez as Erich lighted the cigarette in his boss's mouth. The German's free hand shot under his coat when he saw the chauffeur.

Esposito rolled down his window. "Get in," he growled.

Hernandez frowned, crushed out the fresh cigarette and led his bodyguard to the Lincoln. He slid into the back as Erich crawled into the front next to Carl.

"Let's go, Carl," Esposito said. The driver twisted the key, and the Lincoln started down Broadway.

"Where are we going, Don Joseph?" Hernandez asked.

Esposito ignored him. "We've got trouble. Trouble that keeps pushing my retirement farther and farther away."

"Oh?" Hernandez smiled. "Then we will deal with it."

Esposito resisted the temptation to slap the young fool. "Our buddy Bolan's still running wild through Russia. He completely demolished the Saint Petersburg casino. Not to mention the loan-sharking business upstairs."

Hernandez frowned. "He must have gone there directly from K'achta. It is lucky we sent the new men, Don Joseph. As soon as he returns to the garage—"

"He's already been to the garage," Esposito snapped impatiently. "He took out two of your men with a rifle. All five of mine went over some bridge into the Volga, or whatever river they've got in Moscow. The cops are still trying to fish them out of the water."

Hernandez didn't answer. He turned to the window as the car continued down the street under the flashing lights. "Then he knew of the setup in advance?" he finally asked.

"That's what I like about you, Hernandez," Esposito said. "You catch on *so* quick." He leaned forward, tapping Carl on the shoulder. The driver pushed a button on the dash, and a thick glass privacy shield shot up between the two seats.

"Then there really is another informer besides the Bahamian cop," Hernandez said.

Esposito shook his head in disgust. "Like I said, Hernandez, you're *brilliant*. I've had my men checking. Pinder wasn't a snitch at all. He was a retired cop trying to make ends meet so his daughter could go to college. You run a hell of a loose ship down there, my young friend. If I'd have known that when—"

Hernandez stiffened. "With all due respect, Don Joseph, have you checked into your own men. Is it possible that the rat is from your own nest?"

Esposito snorted. He felt the burn in his chest intensify as he fought the temptation to just drop Hernandez off at his hotel and send a couple of men with machine guns to visit him later that night. "Nobody in my organization knew what we'd decided except me. I called in each of the men separately and told them to pack for cold weather. That's all they knew until they got on the plane."

Hernandez frowned. "I had no choice but to send word back to the Bahamas in my absence, Don Esposito. Which of course means—"

"Exactly my point. You don't run a business in the Bahamas by staying at the Mayfair in New York and eating at the Pierre every night. If you want things done right, you keep your eyes on them."

Hernandez nodded. "I will take care of this, Don Joseph. I'll call Pool and—"

"You'll do no such thing. You stay off the phone to that lunatic. For all I know he may be our problem."

"But Don Joseph—"

"Shut up, Hernandez." Esposito watched the confidence drain from the Colombian's face. Hernandez had mistaken the caution he'd exhibited so far for weakness. Well, it was time to show the young punk who the real don was—where the real power lay. "You've got a lot to learn, you little prick," he went on. "But don't you worry. I've got a vested interest here, and I'm going to teach you myself."

The Lincoln pulled onto an access ramp to the interstate.

"Where are we going, Don Joseph?" Hernandez asked, a new nervousness creeping into his voice.

Esposito chuckled. "Don't worry. You're not being hit. At least not yet."

There was a long, silent pause, then Hernandez asked again. "Then where are we going?"

Esposito leaned forward, finding his wineglass and holding it to his lips. Fuck the ulcer. He had other things to worry about right now. "JFK," he told the man next to him. "And then to Russia."

## CHAPTER ELEVEN

With the Spetsnaz uniform underneath, the gray pin-striped "Dwight McNeil" suit clung to the Executioner. From behind the wheel of the rented Hyundai, Bolan glanced down at his thighs. He wouldn't be asked to model for *Gentlemen's Quarterly* with this fit, but with the trench coat over it, the men he was about to see wouldn't notice.

Until it was too late.

Bolan returned his attention to the main gate to Sukhoi air base on the outskirts of the village of Umah. Several military vehicles had entered the grounds during the past half hour. They had been passed through the gate with a halfhearted salute from the guard.

As he continued to watch, an unmarked Datsun turned into the drive. The guard stepped down from the shack and held up his hand. He examined an ID stuck through the window, wrote on the clipboard in his hand and stuck a pass under the windshield wipers before allowing the car to advance.

The answer to gaining access to the base was obvious. Get a base-marked vehicle.

The Executioner settled back against the seat. Two military installations had been within driving distance of Kiev, and both would presumably stock what he needed. But the closer, an inland naval outpost along the river, was where Boris Arbatrov's papers listed him on temporary duty as an unarmed combat instructor. Arbatrov's face was likely to be well-known; in fact, as a member of Russia's most elite corps, he was likely to be a celebrity.

Which was why the Executioner had instructed Herr Schneider to direct his orders to Sukhoi.

Bolan watched a jeep hurry through the gate. Sukhoi air base existed primarily for pilot training. The surrounding terrain of both hills and plains provided a variety of education for the helicopters, interceptors, and all-weather attack-recon planes housed on base.

But the installation provided a second function as well, maintaining a storage area for army ground forces in southern Ukraine.

On the other side of the guard shack, the Executioner saw a supply truck exit the gate. Two men, both wearing the Russian equivalent of airman first-class uniforms, sat in the cab. The truck turned from the drive onto the road leading into the village. Throwing the Hyundai into drive, Bolan pulled in behind.

He eyed the vehicle as it neared the city limits. The cab was long, which meant it contained a bunk to the rear of the seats. Like American semitrailer rigs, one man could sleep while the other drove, relieving each other behind the wheel without interruption during long hauls.

The truck pulled to a halt in front of a grocery store across the street from a small tavern. Bolan followed.

The driver dropped to the ground and entered the store.

Bolan lifted the Russian-Czech dictionary from the seat next to him and exited his vehicle. Inside the store he saw the driver talking to a man in a butcher's apron while two other men loaded boxes onto a dolly.

The Executioner bought a box of gauze bandages and a roll of adhesive tape, and walked back to the sidewalk. Opening the dictionary arbitrarily, he stared down at the pages as he strolled toward the truck, watching in his peripheral vision for curious eyes. When he reached the passenger's window, he frowned, then looked up and tapped on the glass.

An irritated enlisted man rolled down the window as if it might be the hardest task he'd been asked to perform in years.

"Excuse me," Bolan said, holding the dictionary to the window and pointing halfway down the page. "Can you tell me—" The Executioner's left fist shot suddenly through the window, erasing the irritation from the airman's face as he knocked him out.

Two seconds later, Bolan had swung up into the truck. Working quickly, he undid the airman's tie, fashioned it into a gag, then secured the man's wrists and ankles with plastic handcuffs. Lifting the unconscious man over the seat, he dropped him into the bunk and pulled the curtain.

The warrior drew the Beretta and squatted on the floor beneath the window. A few moments later, he heard the door to the store open. Several sets of feet shuffled forward.

"Yuri?"

The sound of the truck's rear doors opening echoed into the cab. Then the Executioner heard the boxes being dropped into the storage area.

"It appears that your friend has deserted you," said another voice.

Bolan rose over the edge of the window. The other airman stood next to the man wearing the butcher's apron. He pointed across the street toward the tavern. "Yes. No doubt he thinks I will come and find him. We will see how he enjoys the walk back to the base—and explaining his absence to the sergeant."

The butcher laughed. Bolan dropped back below the window as the airman circled the truck and opened the door. He was already halfway inside when the warrior shoved the suppressed Beretta into his ribs. "Make a sound and you're dead. Get in, start the engine and wave goodbye to your friends."

The airman did as he was told, a sick, chalky half smile on his face.

"Now drive," Bolan ordered.

The airman started slowly down the street, the big gears grinding as he shifted. "Where are we going?"

"Find a nice, quiet, out-of-the-way place," the Executioner said. "As soon as we get there, I'm going to pop up and take a quick look around. If you've tried anything, or if anybody spots me, you'll be the first to die."

"But what if you are seen and it is not my fault?" the airman asked.

"Then it'll be tough luck."

The traffic and other noises of the village began to fade. A few moments later, the airman turned off the road, parked and hit the emergency brake. Keeping the Beretta aimed at the frightened man behind the wheel, Bolan rose and took a seat next to him.

They were on a dirt road next to a windmill. He could see the village half a mile away.

The airman turned to him, his eyes fixed on the extended suppressor. "Is this what you wanted?"

"It'll do." Bolan brought the Beretta around in an arc against the airman's temple.

Securing the man as he'd done his partner, Bolan shoved the airman over the seat on top of the other man. He reached into his coat pocket, found the gauze pads and tape and set them on the seat next to him. Then he stripped off his "Dwight McNeil" suit, leaving the Spetsnaz uniform.

Ten minutes later, the Executioner turned the supply truck onto the drive to the base. He propped his left elbow on the window, then rested his cheek casually on his hand to distort his features.

The guard glanced up briefly, then waved him through.

Bolan pulled into the first parking lot he came to and threw the truck into neutral. Quickly he pressed the gauze against his cheek and wrapped the tape around his head. Then returning to the street, he kept well below the speed limit as he cruised the base, looking for anything that might lead him to the land-support armory. He passed a fitness park where several men in sweat suits jogged around a cinder track while others played soccer on a field in the center.

Just past an officer's housing area, the Executioner came to a small business area with a bowling alley and

NCO club. The ten-foot chain-link perimeter fence appeared two hundred yards on, but halfway there he saw a one-story block building with two armed guards out front. Their uniforms weren't Russian air force. Even in the distance, the Executioner could see the shoulder patches—an open parachute flanked on both sides by aircraft, surmounted by the familiar red star. Shoulder slings held the guard's folding stock AK-74s in assault position at their waists, and both men wore the same blue beret as Bolan's.

Vozdushov Desantiye Voyska. Russian airborne forces, first-class soldiers second only to Spetsnaz in terms of training and efficiency.

Bolan frowned as he guided the truck forward. Boris Arbatrov's uniform could work for him or against him at this point. Peacetime soldiers had a way of creating their own internal wars to keep things interesting. And competition between Russian special forces was no different than in America. Get an Army Green Beret, a Navy SEAL, and a Marine Corp LRRP together in the same room and you could take bets on how long it would be before the fight broke out.

The Executioner pulled to a halt in front of the building and shoved the beret on top of his head. One of the paratroopers, a tall rangy man, elbowed the other in the ribs and pointed his way. The shorter man, older and with the build of an Olympic lifter, smiled.

Unlike their counterparts in the West, Spetsnaz troops wore no distinctive badges or patches. Boris Arbatrov's uniform was the same as that of the airborne and air-assault forces.

The paratroopers continued to smile as Bolan stepped down, saluted and walked forward.

The smiles faded quickly when he showed them his Spetsnaz credentials.

"You have orders, Sergeant?" the weight lifter said stiffly.

Bolan handed him the papers Herr Schneider had prepared, then stared boredly away as he waited.

The weight lifter's eyebrows rose. "We have received no advance notification of this transfer, Sergeant."

Bolan shrugged with indifference. He adjusted the bandage on his face. "That is no concern of mine. And I am in a hurry."

The rangy man frowned. "You have a curious accent, Sergeant. I do not recognize it, and accents are a hobby of mine. Would you mind telling me your place of birth?"

The Executioner stared holes back through the man's eye sockets. "I was born and grew up in Moscow, *Corporal*," he said, stressing the lower rank. "And I suspect you would have a curious sound to your speech if you, too, had been shot in a training accident." He patted the bandage again for effect, then added, "By a careless member of the 103rd Air Guards."

The corporal broke eye contact and looked away.

The muscular trooper in charge was no fool. He hesitated.

"Do I need to remind you again that I am in a hurry?" Bolan said, keeping him off balance. "Perhaps this matter should be taken up with the base commander." He turned and started back toward the truck.

The corporal hurried forward, catching his arm. "I am sorry, Sergeant. But as you know, we must be careful. Particularly with orders such as these. Please, follow me."

The paratrooper led the way into the building and down the hall to a steel door. Fishing through his uniform for a key ring, he opened the door and ushered the Executioner inside.

A few minutes later, he helped Bolan load the RPG-7 antitank rocket launcher into the back of the truck next to the grocery boxes.

As he boarded the truck and reached for the key, the Executioner heard the corporal mutter under his breath. "Spetsnaz. Shit."

Bolan grinned as he drove back toward the gate.

HIS COAT over his shoulder, the sweater bunched under his arm, Bolan looked no different than dozens of other people who had just left the train and headed immediately to the beach. But the Executioner hadn't ridden the train to Odessa, the resort town known as the Pearl of the Black Sea.

An RPG-7 would have been a little hard to explain to the conductor.

Bolan locked the door of the Hyundai and walked toward a concession stand. Sunbathers, swimmers and volleyball players laughed and shouted along the edge of the water as he passed. A quarter mile from shore a crowded fishing boat had dropped anchor, and at least fifty rods extended over the rail. Excited voices carried across the water as someone reeled in a catch.

The Executioner's heavy work boots sank into the damp sand as he neared the concession stand. Through the open window, he saw a young man wearing a floral Hawaiian-style shirt unbuttoned to the waist. A Chicago White Sox baseball cap sat atop his head. The kid grinned at a bikini-clad teenaged girl as he lifted a dripping bottle of Pepsi from the cooler behind the counter, took the girl's money and handed it to her.

"Thanks," the girl said.

"Ciao, baby," said the boy.

Bolan smiled as he walked to the phone booth at the side of the building. He could have been at Coney Island or Laguna Beach.    Dropping a coin into the slot, the Executioner dialed the number of the Skyline Resort. The line clicked several times as it made the connection, then started to ring.

From the intelligence file provided by Tachek, Bolan had learned of the curious operation in Odessa. Before *perestroika,* several state-funded apartment complexes had been started along the shore. It was to be a socialist version of the Western "time-sharing" concept for vacation homes. Russian factories in Moscow and Leningrad would operate the various complexes. Individual workers from these companies would receive two weeks' vacation in one of the condos each year.

Halfway through construction, however, the slipping Soviet economy had given the state cause to reconsider the project. And when an Azerbaijani businessman named Zaid Muradi stepped forward with an offer on the partly completed buildings, the bureaucrats had jumped at the chance.

Construction had resumed. When the various complexes were completed, many were sold to foreigners as condos. But the mysterious investors backing Muradi had retained one group of buildings and designated it the Skyline Resort.

The former KGB agent who had conducted the investigation claimed that Zaid Muradi still functioned as the resort manager, as well as a high-class New Brotherhood pimp who provided flesh to the Skyline's guests.

The phone still to his ear, Bolan heard another click. Then a low, throaty female voice said, "Good day."

"Good day back to you," Bolan said, his voice as American as he could make it. "I'm on my way down to your little town, and I'd like to make a reservation."

The woman switched to impeccable English, her voice losing none of the sexy quality in the transition. "We'd be happy to accommodate you, sir. Will the reservation be for one?"

"Yes. Just me. Business."

The woman clicked her tongue in pity. "Business travel can be *so* lonely," she purred. "But perhaps you might meet some new...friends during your stay with us."

Bolan laughed. "Yeah, well, I'm sorta counting on it. Had a friend who stayed with you a few weeks ago. He highly recommended I give you a try."

"We'll have a condo ready for you when you arrive. It has a view of the sea, kitchenette, and—" she paused dramatically "—a king-size bed. Now, if I could just get your name and a little information—"

"Dwight McNeil," the Executioner said. He gave her the number of McNeil's American Express card, said goodbye and hung up.

Back at the Hyundai Bolan opened a suitcase and pulled out a blue knit pullover shirt and pair of khaki slacks. He changed in the car, getting into character for the role he was about to play.

Dwight McNeil needed once again to come off as a successful, semicrude American businessman with plenty of money on hand.

But this time, gambling wouldn't be the way McNeil planned to spend it.

The Skyline Resort faced the sea. It consisted of five redbrick buildings marked A through E over the front doors. A valet wearing black slacks and a red vest met Bolan as he pulled up in front, the warrior noticing a bulge under the vest as he stepped out of the car and handed the man his keys.

The valet pointed him toward a sidewalk that led between buildings C and D.

Bolan followed the path, passing a man wearing green gardener slacks and a matching shirt. The man seemed more interested in the cigarette he was smoking than the rake that rested against the bricks. He adjusted his belt as the Executioner passed, tucking the rubber grips of a revolver out of sight beneath his shirttail.

Bolan rounded the corner and saw the swimming pool in the middle of a courtyard. Men and women lounged in chairs and lay on towels at poolside. Gray hair curled from the flapping abdomens of most of the men, but the women accompanying them looked like they'd be right at home leading a television aerobic class, and they seemed to represent most of the ethnic groups found in the Commonwealth

But as different as they might appear, the women had two things in common: any one of them would have done justice to a *Playboy* centerfold, and they all looked frightened out of their wits.

A lifeguard sat at the top of his perch. He eyed Bolan as the warrior walked by, his hand drifting casually into an open sports bag that hung from the arm of his chair. Then, apparently deciding the new arrival was no threat, he turned back to the pool.

Bolan stopped at a sliding door to the one-story office building. Through the glass, he saw two more men dressed in street clothes, reading magazines on a couch.

The atmosphere was low-key and relaxed around the Skyline Resort. But the gunners were here. They just weren't advertising the fact.

The Executioner slid the door open and stepped inside. A ginger-skinned woman sat behind the reception desk, and she smiled as Bolan entered.

"Hello," she breathed in the same voice he'd heard on the phone. But the lusty demeanor was more transparent in person—far more forced—and beneath the facade of sexuality, the Executioner smelled fear.

"Hi." Bolan smiled.

"My name is Nadenka. You must be Mr. McNeil."

"That's right, Nadenka. Got my room ready?"

"Certainly." She lifted a key from the desktop. "You look tired. Are you ready for bed?"

Bolan laughed. "Almost. But that driving takes it out of you, you know? I need a shower first. Maybe a drink or two—"

Nadenka lifted the phone. "And what will you be drinking, Mr. McNeil? I'll have it sent up."

Bolan hesitated. "I know you probably don't have it here," he finally said. "But I usually drink bourbon."

Nadenka batted her eyes. "We do our best. Wild Turkey? Jack Daniel's? Or if you prefer, we have Jim Beam or—"

"Hey, you guys are all right," Bolan said. "Make it Jack. And, uh, any chance you can deliver it yourself?"

As soon as the words left Bolan's lips, a short, dark-skinned man in the middle of a hair transplant walked through a nearby office door. The smile on his face affected only his mouth, never reaching the cold black eyes that stared through the warrior with a shrewd, ferretlike quality.

Zaid Muradi.

Muradi hurried forward, grasping the Executioner's hand and pumping it up and down as if he'd just found his long-lost brother. "Welcome to the Skyline Resort, Mr. McNeil. I am sorry, but Nadenka is perhaps your *only* request that we cannot satisfy." The little man's chest puffed out in pride. "She and I are engaged to be married. But please—" he indicated the door "—let me show you around the grounds. And then I'm certain we can find companionship that will suit you."

Bolan followed the swarthy little man outside. They passed the pool again, where Muradi greeted each guest by name. When they reached the edge of the court-yard, the little man dropped onto a white concrete bench next to a statue of the goddess Aphrodite. "Please, Mr. McNeil." He patted the seat next to him. "Sit."

Bolan took the seat next to him and stared at the pool.

"I am sorry if I misled you about the grounds," Muradi said. "What you see . . . is it." He laid a hand on the Executioner's shoulder. "But you will not be disappointed. The recreation here at the resort takes place inside. Whatever you like, it will be provided for you."

Bolan resisted the impulse to pull his shoulder away. "And just what's available?"

The smirk stayed on Muradi's lips as he went on to list a menu of sexual perversions that would have made the Marquis de Sade blush with embarrassment.

Bolan shrugged. "Like I told Nadenka, I'm tired right now. Why don't you have some cute little thing bring me my bourbon in about an hour. Make sure she speaks English. Somebody who hasn't been here long, know what I mean?"

Muradi's lecherous grin returned. "I know *exactly* what you mean. And I have just the right girl in mind for you, Mr. McNeil. Now..." He stood. "I will show you to your rooms."

Five minutes later, the Executioner stood alone in condo number seven on the second floor of building C. Huge conversation-pit sofas ringed the off-white walls, which had been decorated with cheap nudes. French doors opened onto a balcony facing the rolling waves of the Black Sea.

A smaller screened porch sat just off the small kitchen and looked down onto the pool. A back staircase led from the porch down into the courtyard.

The king-size bed Nadenka had promised was the focal point in the bedroom, and to the side sat a Jacuzzi large enough to accommodate half-a-dozen bodies.

Bolan hung his shirt and slacks in the closet and stepped into the shower. As the hot spray hit his face, burning off the grime from the past two days, he considered his planned course of action. He had requested an inexperienced girl for a specific reason. Russian Intelligence suspected that the prostitutes at the Skyline Resort had been kidnapped and were kept there against their will. But "will" could be broken over a matter of time. Most people gave up quickly, resigning themselves to whatever fate presented itself. In short they abandoned hope.

The Executioner wanted someone who was new, fresh—a woman in whom the hatred of her predicament hadn't yet been vanquished. A woman who still clung to the hope of being saved, and wouldn't be afraid to assist in that rescue herself.

The knock on the door came as the Executioner stepped out of the shower. Wrapping a towel around his waist, he hid the Desert Eagle under another towel and walked to the back balcony.

The young woman holding the bottle of Jack Daniel's in her hand could have been no more than twenty. Long, milk-white hair cascaded down her neck like a waterfall, broke, then fell again over the swell of her breasts. Through this blond wall, the Executioner could see a tiny wisp of transparent red material that pretended to be the top of a swimsuit.

The girl forced a smile as the Executioner opened the door. He stepped back and let her walk by. The woman set the bottle on the kitchen table, then turned back. Her mouth opened to speak, then clamped back shut.

Bolan smiled at her. "Relax. What's your name?"

"Anna," came the soft reply.

"Okay, Anna."

The woman stared him in the eyes, and behind them Bolan saw the current of terror that charged through her.

Anna was new to this game, all right.

"You want a drink, Anna?" Bolan asked.

The beautiful young woman shrugged, her tanned shoulders trembling. "Do... do you want me to have a drink?" she asked.

Bolan felt his eyebrows lower. "Yes. I think I do." He hadn't caught the accent when she'd said her name, but now he placed it. Swedish.

The Executioner walked to the cabinet and pulled down a highball glass. In the refrigerator he found ice cubes and a bottle of mineral water, mixed a light drink and handed it to her. "Go on in the living room and sit down," he said. "I'll be back in a minute." He followed her down the hall, then turned into the bedroom.

The Executioner hurried into his sport shirt and slacks. When he came back out a moment later, Anna had taken a seat on one of the couches. Her glass was empty on the coffee table, and next to it was the dental-floss bikini she'd worn.

Naked, Anna stared down at the carpet. Then almost inaudibly, she said, "Please, you seem nice. And this is my first time. Could we . . . could we just get this done?"

Bolan didn't answer. He turned back into the bedroom and returned a second later carrying a white dress shirt. Tossing it to Anna he sat on the couch across from her and said, "Put it on. I'm not going to hurt you."

The girl's eyes shot up. "You . . . you do not wish to have sex with me?"

"No."

"I do not please you?"

"You're a good-looking girl, Anna," he said. "And I like good-looking women as much as the next guy. But I'm not in the habit of forcing myself on them."

Anna's eyes filled with relief. She slid her arms into the shirt and began buttoning the front. Then suddenly she stopped. The horror returned to her eyes, and Bolan remembered the menu of kinky sex Muradi had mentioned earlier.

Once again the Executioner barely heard her when she said, "Then, what is it you *do* want to do?"

"I want to talk, Anna. That's all."

Anna was still suspicious. "Just talk?"

"Well, no," Bolan said. "I'd like to help you get out of here. You and all the rest of the women who want to leave."

Anna stared back at him, her face a mixture of hope and disbelief.

The Executioner stood, walked to the table and poured her another drink. "Sit back, get comfy and listen to me, Anna," he said. "I'll tell you exactly why I'm here, and how this place is going to be different after we're gone." He handed her the glass. "Relax. The peasant uprising that's about to take place is going to make the revolution 1917 look like a Sunday-afternoon round of golf."

IT WAS AN ENRAGED Alexandr Solomentsev who burst through the door of the Ukrainian Café, his eyes sweeping the room for Leskov. The colonel had called the president's office less than ten minutes earlier, demanding, not asking, that Solomentsev meet him here immediately.

Solomentsev removed his gloves as he fought to keep from screaming for the man. In order to leave the office he'd been forced to invent another tale of personal emergency. And his lies were beginning to raise Tachek's suspicions.

The president's aide spotted Leskov. The colonel grinned to him from a corner booth. Solomentsev started forward. Had the old man's sanity left him? Perhaps *he* could get away with these absences from work—he had less than six months before retirement. But Solomentsev was in the middle of his career.

Reaching the booth, Solomentsev removed his coat and hat, and sat down. Leskov had helped him in the past, and that would always be appreciated. But loyalty had a point after which it became foolishness. He had already missed work two days this week just to keep the lonely old man company. He wasn't only risking his job, but his marriage as well.

All that was about to stop.

"Pyotr," Solomentsev said, trying to keep the emotion out of his voice. "I cannot continue to—"

Leskov held up a hand as the waiter approached and set two glasses of iced vodka on the table.

Solomentsev looked at the waiter and shook his head. "No," he said. "I cannot drink today. Take mine away."

The waiter reached for his glass.

Leskov's hand shot forward, gripping the man's wrist. "Leave them," he said in a low, threatening voice.

"No. Take mine," Solomentsev repeated. "I cannot drink with you today, Pyotr. I have come only to tell you that—"

"Leave the drinks," Leskov snarled. "If my friend does not drink his, I will drink it for him." He released the waiter's arm, and the man hurried away.

"I must return to the office. I have work to do. You know that."

"Can't you indulge an old man one more time?"

"I do not understand all of this, Pyotr. What has become of you? All that seems to please you lately is to get me as drunk as possible."

"That has pleased me very much, Alexandr," Leskov said.

Solomentsev stared at him in wonder.

"I must explain a few things, old friend," Leskov said. "I will be brief. But you must listen very carefully. Your beloved career, and perhaps even your life, depend on it.''

Solomentsev sat numbly and waited.

Leskov cleared his throat before going on. ''Our country is on the verge of destruction, Alexandr. Destruction at our own hands. Or at least at the hands of men who claim to be of us, but are not. Men like Tachek.''

Solomentsev sat in astonishment as Leskov went on to describe his relationship with the New Brotherhood, and how he and several other hard-liners of the former KGB planned to use the wave of organized crime to unseat President Tachek.

The young aide sat back against the seat. He felt like someone had poked him in the sternum with the end of a hockey stick. ''*You*, Pyotr?'' he said.

Leskov nodded.

''Then I have been your unwilling informant,'' Solomentsev said. His eyes rose to the ceiling as the magnitude of what he'd done sank in. ''It is I who have been the leak.''

Leskov added a chuckle to his nodding. ''You have served your country well. Until now, you have not been aware of it. But from this time forward, you will join me. You and I, and the others who feel the same as we do, we will save Mother Russia together.''

Solomentsev shook his head. ''No.'' His voice rose gradually in pitch as he said, ''No. No. *No. No!* I will not be part of it, Pyotr!'' He jerked to his feet. ''I will inform the president immediately. You will be removed from duty. You will be tried. You will be . . . hanged, Pyotr. You will be *hanged!* And damn well you should be!''

Leskov shrugged. "Perhaps. But if I am hanged, Alexandr, you will be next to me on the gallows."

Solomentsev felt the blood rush from his head through his chest, down his legs and out his feet. His head felt suddenly light, and for a moment he feared he'd pass out.

How could he tell Tachek the truth without revealing that he had violated his own sacred oath of secrecy?

"Sit back down, Alexandr," Leskov said quietly. He lifted his glass with one hand and pushed the other drink toward Solomentsev with the other. "Drink your vodka. Like a good boy."

Alexandr Solomentsev lifted his glass and stared at the clear liquid.

"We will drink to the new Soviet Union," Leskov said. "The new Soviet Union that will be like the old one we knew and loved." He threw back his head and drained his glass.

So did Solomentsev. And ordered more.

## CHAPTER TWELVE

Pyotr Leskov's holiday home looked like a cross between the military briefing room of some third-world
country and a medieval torture chamber.

Three dozen metal folding chairs ringed the walls. A
map of Moscow hung taped to the mantel over the
fireplace. Another large map—the former Soviet
Union—covered the window facing the river.

The second map blocked out what little light would
have filtered into the room through the snow clouds
outside. An eerie, dusty twilight bathed the room.
Ominous shadows danced along the walls as the flames
leaped in the fireplace.

A brief glance at the fifty-odd New Brotherhood
members packed into the living room was enough to
divide them into the four subgroups they represented.
The men from Esposito's New York Mafia were
dressed in expensive, conservative suits and wool
overcoats. Hernandez's cartel gunners wore flashier
garb—bright pastel shirts and slacks—and favored soft
leather trench coats with gleaming buckles at the waist.
The ties around both the Americans' and Colombi-
ans' necks cost more than the entire ensembles worn by
Leskov's circle of hard-line former KGB agents, and
the locally recruited Moscow toughs could be distin-

guished by their mixture of Russian peasant clothing and black-market goods from the U.S.

Don Joseph Esposito sat in an armchair by the fireplace, watching through a crack between the window and map as cars continued to arrive, parking a hundred yards down the river in the gravel lot. He felt the heat of the roaring flames against his left arm and leg, but his entire right side might as well have been in a deep freeze. He glanced overhead at the rough beams running along the ceiling, then let his eyes trickle down over the cracked wallpaper on the walls.

*This* was the country home Leskov had bragged about? The one he worried he wouldn't be able to keep after he retired? *This* was why he'd sold out his country?

Esposito shook his head. Russia. No central heating, and you could fit this whole shack into his garage at home. And still have room for the servants' quarters.

One of Hernandez's gunmen approached the fireplace. He extended a bottle of the Armenian wine that had left Esposito's belly aflame when he tried it a few minutes before. A flicker of kindling ignited in his belly at the memory.

"A drink, Don Joseph?" the man asked.

Esposito shook his head. His eyes traced across the room to where Hernandez stood talking to one of the Intelligence agents. The stupid little bastard was waving his hands around, trying to get some worthless point across in a combination of pidgin English and broken Russian.

The mafioso scratched his head. How in the hell did he ever get mixed up in this? How did he let this little fool from Bogotá talk him into the joint operation he called the New Brotherhood? The name had *Hollywood* written all over it, which of course was the glamorous image the South Americans had convinced themselves they had.

Esposito watched Hernandez pull a gold case from his pocket and remove a hand-rolled cigarette. His ever present bodyguard, Erich, stepped in with the lighter.

The Mafia leader squinted. The Colombian still hadn't seen the writing on the wall. But Don Joseph Esposito hadn't run the largest organized crime Family in the world for forty years without developing a few instincts. Of course instincts weren't facts. Instincts were sometimes wrong.

But this time he didn't think so.

Esposito watched Erich return the lighter to his pants and stand back like Hernandez's faithful dog. The burn in his stomach intensified. Before the day was out, he'd know whether his instincts were correct.

The don rose slowly to his feet. He stood in front of the window and cleared his throat.

Immediately all conversation halted.

Esposito let his eyes roam the room as the men hurried to find seats. Hernandez took the armchair he'd occupied by the fire, trying to show the room that he was still at least *second* in command.

"Let's get started," Esposito said, pulling a silver Cross retractable pencil from his shirt pocket. He used it as a pointer and tapped the large map in the southeast corner. "Bolan started here. He's been moving progressively west ever since." Esposito's gaze shifted to his own men. He had imported twenty more to replace those who'd been found floating in the river. Ray Furelli sat in the middle of the group. At the sound of Bolan's name, the enforcer's face took on the look of a four-year-old who'd just come out of an amusement-park spook house.

"But this is a big country," Esposito went on. "We've got a lot of operations up and running. Since the bastard cut off contact with the president's office, there's no way to know where he'll strike next." His eyes fell on Jake Pool. Arms crossed, the crazy son of a bitch was leaning against the back wall of the room as if it were the door of the Long Branch Saloon. Next to him was another of Hernandez's cartoons they called Pistola.

Esposito paused and took a deep breath. Pool had been vaguely amusing when they'd met in the Bahamas, spouting a warped theory of reincarnation that made him sound like he was one taco short of a combo plate. But his eccentricities had become a liability now. As soon as his guns were no longer needed . . .

Leskov spoke up suddenly, breaking into the mafioso's reverie. "We must set a trap," he said. "As you people like to say, give Bolan an offer he can't refuse."

Esposito turned to the old man. Leskov sat smiling ignorantly in an armchair across from Hernandez. Was it any wonder that Russia was going down the tubes? Here was a high-ranking Russian Intelligence officer spouting lines from *The Godfather* like it was real life, for God's sake.

The mafioso forced a smile. They still needed the pompous old fool. "Exactly, Colonel," he said, turning toward the new man at Leskov's side. Tachek's right hand, the colonel had said. "You're Solomentsev, right?"

The young man nodded nervously. He was young, around thirty. Scared. He held a glass of wine in his hand, close to his lips like it might try to get away. The kid's eyes were red and bloodshot.

Esposito tapped the map. "Okay, Solo. Somebody's leakin' shit from us back to your president. Who?"

A silence fell over the room as the men looked quickly at one another.

Solomentsev took a gulp from his glass. "I don't know. Whoever it is reports directly to the president. I get the information I pass on to Colonel Leskov from Tachek himself."

"But you do talk to Bolan, right?"

"On occasion. But he is aware of the leak. His calls are infrequent."

"But he *does* call."

"Yes."

"Where is he now?"

Solomentsev shrugged and took another gulp. "He never gives that information."

Esposito blew air between his teeth in disgust. "Jesus Christ, Solo, can't you trace the call?"

Solomentsev finished his drink in another gulp. "The president will not allow it. He has given his word. And before you ask, the answer is 'no,' there is no way to do it without Tachek's knowledge."

Esposito nodded. "Okay, okay. Then here's what we do. I haven't worked out the details yet, but the colonel's right. We're gonna set a trap." The silver pencil moved to the smaller map of Moscow over the fireplace. "The colonel's got an abandoned warehouse near the Arbat district. What we do is set up a phony dope deal, then Solo, you make sure Bolan gets wind of it. Then it's a simple matter of setting up on the place and blowin' Bolan's ass to kingdom come when he shows up."

Murmurs of consent filled the room. Esposito turned to his side. "Hernandez," he said. "You, me and Leskov need to go check out the place."

Hernandez nodded. "Erich, bring the car around."

The German rose and left the room.

As soon as Erich was gone, Leskov spoke again. "This man, Bolan. We have dealt with him in the past. He is not stupid. He will not fall for such a simple plan."

Esposito sighed inwardly. He forced another smile. "No, he's not stupid and he won't fall for it. But he doesn't have to." Amid the confused expressions in front of him, Esposito saw Jake Pool nod toward Hernandez and disappear from the room. A second later, the back door closed quietly.

"Furelli," Esposito went on, "pick thirty men and set up in the warehouse. Bolan will know it's a trap, but I'm betting he won't be able to resist the challenge to take us all out at once. We'll position the rest of the men and Leskov's people a few miles away with radios. Once he's taken the bait, they can move in and we'll catch him in a cross fire." He paused and cleared his throat. "I've dealt with this bastard in the past. He'll recon something this big before he strikes. If you see him, Furelli, hit the radio. Do not, I repeat *do not* try to take him out by yourselves."

Murmurs of understanding now replaced the confused frowns.

Hernandez nodded. "I have only one question, Don Esposito," he said. "If the men in the warehouse see Bolan, why should they not kill him then? The odds will be thirty to one."

Esposito smiled, and this time his amusement was genuine. There was a certain humor in Hernandez's refusal to recognize just what they were up against. "I'll admit the odds will be stacked," he said, his eyes boring into the Colombian's. "But you don't know Mack Bolan like I do. They'll still be stacked in his favor."

ROTISLAV PUGACHEV left the house and walked swiftly along the river toward the parking lot. "Not too fast," he warned himself under his breath. He recalled a line from one of the textbooks on deep-cover investigation. *You must always behave as if the enemy is watching. He is.*

Pugachev watched the snow fall onto the water, and suddenly a tense longing hit him in the gut. The sight reminded him of his birthplace.

Which birthplace? Pugachev thought, and the notion brought a sardonic smile to his face. Rotislav Pugachev had been born in the village of Balakova, on the Volga.

"Erich" had been born in Bad Schwalbach, on the Rhine in Germany.

Pugachev continued to force his legs to move casually toward the cars. There was no point in hurrying anyway, he told himself. They were going to the warehouse. It would be hours before an opportunity arose to slip away to call the president.

The Russian Intelligence mole considered the dilemma as he watched the water run lazily down the river. Both Tachek and the American needed the news of the phony drug deal as soon as possible. And Tachek should learn of Solomentsev's and Leskov's traitorous behavior immediately.

But was the information worth risking his cover?

Pugachev pulled the keys from his pocket as he reached the cars. The tinkling noise somehow added to his loneliness. As he stuck the key into the door, he made a solemn oath to himself. When the assignment was over, he'd never work deep cover again.

A broad smile suddenly spread across the agent's face. For months he had vacillated, trying to decide whether it was time to retire to a desk job. Now, with the decision finally made, he felt as if a hundred-pound pack had been lifted from his chest.

Pugachev slid behind the wheel, visions of evenings and weekends with his wife and daughter floating pleasantly through his head. He stuck the key in the ignition, his good mood vanishing at the knowledge that Leskov had provided Esposito with this vehicle. The colonel was a special insult to all the good, honest agents who served their homeland.

As he started to twist the key, Pugachev's eyes fell suddenly to the seat next to him. Leskov had also furnished the top New Brotherhood men with cellular phones.

And Hernandez had left his here, in the car.

Pugachev glanced quickly back to the house. Should he chance it? The house stood less than two hundred feet away, with no obstructions. Anyone watching through the windows had a clear view of the cars.

But the map covered the window. And the men of the New Brotherhood had shown no indication that they didn't trust him. The open area could work to his advantage, as well. If he kept the phone below window level, they couldn't see what he was doing, and he'd have ample time to react if anyone came out of the house.

Pugachev made his decision in a heartbeat. He had information that couldn't wait. The American's life, and the future Russia, rested on his shoulders.

Reaching across the car, Pugachev opened the glove compartment and spread a city map of Moscow across the seat. The map would give him a reason for bending over if anyone did come this way. Then, making sure the phone was still out of sight, he squinted down in the direction of the map and tapped the president's private number into the instrument.

Tachek answered on the third ring.

At the same instant he heard the president's voice, Pugachev saw a dark black shape appear in the rearview mirror. His head jerked to the back of the car.

Jake Pool stood behind the car, grinning through the rear window. The gunslinger's lips moved. "Get out of the car, Adolph," they mouthed.

Pugachev buried the phone under the map and stepped out of the car. Pool walked to the side of the vehicle and stopped. The man in the flat black hat threw the tails of his coat back over his gun belt, the grin staying on his face as he spoke.

"I know who you are," he said, nodding slowly. "Didn't think I recognized you from last time around, did you? Thought you'd pulled the wool right down over old Bill's eyes, didn't you... Mr. Bob Ford."

Pugachev stared at him, confused. "Who is this... Bob Ford?"

Pool threw back his head and cackled. "Can't say as I blame you. I wouldn't admit shooting a man in the back either—even if it was a no-good second-rate thief like Jesse James."

Pugachev looked toward the house. Esposito and Hernandez, followed by Leskov and several other men, had come out onto the porch to watch.

"You've got iron on your hip," Pool said. "Go for it."

"What? You want a gunfight? Like a cowboy?"

Pool's grin finally faded. He spit to his side, then reached into his pocket and came out with a kopek coin. "When it hits the ground," he said and flipped the coin into the air.

Rotislav Pugachev watched the coin turn against the cloudy sky, reach its peak and begin its descent. His mind flashed back to Harmon Pinder.

When the coin hit the gravel parking lot, he went for his weapon.

The flash of silver in the mole's eyes became a burst of red in his brain.

Then, everything went black.

FOR THE FIRST TIME IN DAYS, Anna Gustaffsson Ballard relaxed as she sipped her second bourbon and water. But the sadness, the hopelessness, remained in her soul.

Although she hadn't yet been forced to perform any of the perverse sexual acts the other girls spoke of, Anna had heard the bizarre stories of what some of the Skyline Resort's clientele demanded. This man sitting across from her—was he for real? Did he really plan to get her out of here, or was this talk of escape just some elaborate prelude to some outlandish fantasy? And if he was serious, could he really pull it off?

Suddenly the image of her sister crossed Anna's mind. No. He couldn't help her. She shouldn't even talk to this man.

If she did, Greta would die.

Anna eyed the man across the room. He radiated such a quiet confidence. She had seen the scars on his chest and back when he'd worn only the towel. Some of them were bullet wounds, like the one her Uncle Sture had brought back from Cyprus while serving with the NATO forces. Others looked like they'd been done with a knife, and yet others...well, she had no idea what had caused some of the scars. But the bottom line was that while this man seemed good, even gentle in many ways, he had seen great violence.

If anyone could help her and Greta, Anna realized, it would be him.

A glimmer of hope shot through the young Swedish girl. Even if he failed, and she and Greta both died in the attempt, would that be any worse than the future that now lay before them?

Maybe it wouldn't hurt to talk to him.

"Tell me about yourself," the man said suddenly, as if following her thoughts.

Anna started to speak, then stopped.

The man urged her on. "Tell me how you got here, Anna. Trust me."

The bourbon cruised through Anna's body and suddenly made her bold. "Is your name really McNeil?" she asked with a abruptness that surprised her.

The man smiled. "No, but that's what your friend Muradi thinks. So under the circumstances, I think we'd better stick with it."

"Muradi is *not* my friend."

Bolan nodded. "Poor choice of words. Talk to me, Anna."

"It's a long story."

The warrior looked at his watch. "We've got to kill enough time to make Muradi think you've done your job," he said, "so go ahead. It'll give me an idea of how the operation works."

Anna held her glass in her lap as she began. "Do you know Oland?"

McNeil nodded. "Baltic island just off the Swedish coast. Bridge leads over from—"

"Kalmar."

"Right. It's a resort island, mainly."

Anna nodded. "My husband is an American musician," she said. "Guitar player. He was playing at the Pizzeria, a nightclub in the city of Borgholm. One night last week, my sister and I were sitting at a table, listening to Donnie—that's my husband—sing. Two men came in." She felt herself shudder. "They asked us to dance. That, in itself, is not so unusual." Anna realized how it had sounded and felt herself blush.

"I can imagine it isn't," Bolan said.

Anna searched his face for some hint of licentiousness. She found none. "We said no. They were rough-looking men, and older." She saw a smile play at the corners of Bolan's mouth, and realized once more that her words could have been misinterpreted. "I did not mean anything about older men—"

"Go on, Anna. Just tell me how you ended up here."

"So the men left and we forgot them. Later, Greta got a headache—beer does that to her—and she wanted to go home. Donnie still had another set, so I walked her to her car." She felt her breasts rise as she drew in a deep breath. "The men were waiting for us in the parking lot. They kidnapped us."

There was a long silence, then Anna went on. "They forced us into a van with guns, then gave us..." She frowned, searching for the word, then raised her hand and moved her thumb down to her first two fingers.

"Shots. Some kind of sedative."

"Yes." Anna nodded. "Greta and I woke up on a ship at sea. Then another shot, and I was here... without my sister."

"You don't know where Greta is now?"

Anna felt tears begin in the corners of her eyes. She shook her head. "No. But I have my suspicions."

Bolan waited for her to go on.

"One of the other girls, Katra is her name, came here after working on a ship. She says it's a cruise ship that sails the Black Sea and provides girls for the guests. The same people run it that own this place."

"Do you know anything more about it?"

"No. Perhaps Katra will."

"How long have you been here, Anna?"

"I arrived yesterday. You were to be my first...how do they say it in America? I heard Donnie use the word once—trip?"

"I think you mean 'trick.'"

"Yes, trick. You were to be the first trick. Yesterday I did indoter...indotra...." She looked again to Bolan for help.

"Indoctrination?"

"Yes. It was threats, mainly. What would happen, both to me and my sister, if I tried to escape. They have guards here, Mr. McNeil. You cannot see them. But the gardeners, the valets, they all have guns."

"I've seen them."

"Muradi has sworn that if I escape, Greta will die. And if Greta escapes, they will kill me. The other women's families have been threatened as well. That's how Muradi maintains control. Escape seems impossible."

Behind Bolan's frown of concentration, Anna saw the wheels of his brain begin to turn. Could he come up with something? Some way to get her, her sister and the rest of the women away from these monsters who keep them as slaves?

Anna finished her drink and set it on the coffee table. She didn't know whether it was reality or the bourbon, but her anguish was beginning to turn to hope.

"Tell me about the setup," Bolan said. "Where do they have you living?"

"Scattered throughout the complex," Anna told him. "We each share an apartment with three other girls when we are not with the customers. I am in building C, apartment 2."

"The customers apartments are scattered, too?"

"Yes."

Suddenly a knock sounded at the back door. Bolan rose quickly, holding a finger to his lips. He stripped off his shirt and unbuttoned his slacks.

He held the shirt against his side, hiding the butt of the Desert Eagle as he walked through the kitchen to the back door. At the top of the steps, just outside the glass door, he saw Zaid Muradi. The pimp's hand scratched nervously at the rows of hair transplants on his scalp.

The Executioner pushed the door open.

"I am sorry to bother you, Mr. McNeil, but the girl I sent you is new. I wanted to make sure she was satisfactory. If not, I can replace her with—"

Bolan went into his crude American businessman act. "Got no complaints at all, Zaid," he said. "You just *try* to replace little Anna in there and I'll wring your neck."

Muradi laughed dutifully.

"But I tell you what you *can* do, Zaid," Bolan said. "If two's company, three ought to be a real party. There's a girl Anna was telling me about, Katra I think she said her name was."

Muradi nodded. "I will send her to you immediately," he said. He turned to descend the steps, then twisted back and coughed. "Uh, should I add the new charge to your American Express card?"

Bolan nodded. "Never leave home without it."

The Executioner resnapped his pants and slipped the shirt over his head as he walked back to the living room.

Muradi was good to his word. Two minutes later, another knock came at the door.

Katra seemed the antithesis of Anna in every way. Short, sturdy, and with a bosom that threatened to burst through her tight tube top, she strutted into the living room with a faked air of sophistication. Seeing Anna in Bolan's shirt, she pulled her top above her head.

Bolan reached out and caught her wrists. "You can put it back on."

Katra looked quizzically at Anna, who nodded.

Briefly, with the Executioner's help, Anna explained the situation. As she spoke, both the hardness and sophistication began to fade from Katra's face. Tears streaked silently down her cheeks. When she spoke, the Executioner noted a hint of Israel in her enunciation. "But they will kill my mother," she said. "They know where she lives...."

Bolan shook his head. "We'll take care of that. Which apartment have they got you in, Katra?"

"A-6."

Bolan glanced at his watch, then smiled at the two frightened women. "Okay," he said. "I want both of you to go back. Get your stories together about what happened up here, and whatever it is, make it sound real. I still need to look like just another customer. Don't tell the other women what's going down yet— Muradi may have spies." He stared into the two sets of frightened eyes. With any luck, the terror would be gone in a few hours.

"Stay ready," the Executioner said. "When I come for you, we'll have to move out fast."

NIGHT FELL over the Black Sea coast, turning the deep-blue waves gliding up onto the sands an inky black.

From the back porch of his condo, Bolan watched the cellular yard lights switch on. He stared down at the deserted swimming pool. The last of the swimmers and sunbathers had left thirty minutes ago, retiring to their own quarters to rest from the afternoon's debauchery and gather strength for the perversions of the night.

A lone sparrow chirped from a treetop on the other side of the office building. The only other sounds came from the "gardeners" and other plain clothes New Brotherhood guards who prowled the grounds.

Bolan walked back into the bedroom. He slid quickly into the nylon gear that carried the Beretta and Desert Eagle and hung the Striker over his shoulder. The London Fog trench coat cloaked the weapons and extra ammo magazines from view.

Slowly the Executioner descended the back staircase to the courtyard. Dressed as he was, he looked like a resort guest on his way to dinner in Odessa before returning to satisfy another appetite. He reviewed his battle plan as he neared the pool. The New Brotherhood's threats to kill their captives' families were probably just that—threats. It seemed unlikely that they'd go to that extent, when kidnapping more women would be easier. It simply wasn't good business.

And as he'd seen in Anna, the fear alone was strong enough to make her think twice about escape—even with his help.

On the other hand Anna's sister was accessible. She might be an exception to the rule. The New Brotherhood could easily decide to make an example of Greta to reinforce the other women's fears and prevent future problems.

Bolan turned toward the parking garage as a guard passed the pool, then cut back to the office as soon as the man had disappeared around a corner. The front windows of the one-story building were dark, but a soft glow glimmered from Muradi's office in back.

The Executioner pulled gently on the handle of the sliding door. Locked. Slipping the Mini Tanto blade between the door and frame, he flipped the latch upward and stepped inside.

The glow he'd seen outside now appeared from Muradi's private office. Crude, hoggish snorts accompanied the light, both drifting through the open door.

Bolan traded the Tanto for the Beretta, moved to the opening and looked inside.

His stealth had been unnecessary. Zaid Muradi's attentions were staunchly planted on the task in which he was engaged.

Nadenka's dress lay draped over a chair. Naked, save a white garter belt and high heels, she had been tied over the desk. Behind her, Muradi thrust forward, sweat streaming down his face.

Nadenka's hollow eyes were fixed absently on the wall, her expression telling Bolan that the scene had been played out too many times in the past, and that withdrawal from reality had become her only avenue of escape.

He stepped into the room and flipped on the overhead light. "Party's over."

Muradi's eyelids jerked up. He stumbled quickly away from Nadenka, his passion quickly ebbing.

Bolan kept the Beretta aimed at his chest as he moved to Nadenka. Drawing the Tanto with his left hand, he sliced her ropes. "Get dressed," he said softly.

The woman stood frozen for a moment. Then she burst into sobs as her mind suddenly returned to reality. She reached for her dress.

Muradi's hands had fallen to cover his shriveled crotch. "You are the police," he said. "We can work this out."

"You bet we can," Bolan said. "But not the way you think." He cocked the hammer of the Beretta, the sound echoing tinnily off the walls in the small office. "I want you to tell me about the ship."

Muradi was no hero. "It is in port right now."

"Where?"

"Here in Odessa. It sails for Yalta at midnight."

"More," Bolan commanded.

"There are two types of tickets," the frightened pimp went on. "Singles, or swingers. Singles, mostly men, go to enjoy the women we provide. The swingers can engage in orgies."

"I'll take a couple of swinger tickets," Bolan said.

A foolish glimmer of hope flickered in the pimp's beady eyes. "If that is all you want—" Without warning Muradi dived for the desk drawer.

A soft *pfffft* choked from the Beretta. Muradi fell to the floor screaming, his hands clasped over his left thigh.

"How many gunmen are on the grounds?" the Executioner demanded.

Muradi closed his eyes again. "Help me," he begged.

"How many?" Bolan repeated.

"Twenty-four."

"Where do they stay?"

Muradi gasped for air. "Three of the apartments are used."

"Numbers?"

"C-4, D-7 and 8."

At a slight sound the Executioner turned to face Nadenka. The woman held a 9 mm pistol, and the tension in her face relaxed as she squeezed the trigger. The hollowpoint smashed through Zaid Muradi's eyebrows and out the back of his head.

Nadenka continued to weep softly. If anyone deserved to die, it was Zaid Muradi.

Bolan walked over to her and gently took the gun from her hand. "How does the Brotherhood check on this place?'' he asked. ''Do they call in, or did Muradi call out?''

''Both,'' Nadenka said in a dead voice. ''If they do not hear from him tonight, they will call to find out what is wrong.''

The warrior nodded. Somehow, he had to delay their suspicions. His gaze fell on the answering machine on the desk. He hurried to the phone book next to it. Handing the book to Nadenka, he said, ''Look through here. Find me the number of a business that's folded recently.''

Nadenka's eyebrows rose.

''Just do it,'' the Executioner said. ''I don't have time to explain.'' He glanced at his watch. It was still business hours in Washington. Lifting the phone, he got an overseas operator, gave her Hal Brognola's office number and waited on the call to go through.

All hell was about to break loose at the Skyline Resort. When it was over, he'd have about three dozen women on his hands. Women who'd need someplace to go.

Under better circumstances, he could call Tachek's office and inform him of the situation. But the leak to the New Brotherhood ruled out that idea. They might get the word before the Executioner had a chance to reach Anna's sister.

Brognola was likely to have connections in the area. If not, he could go through Stony Man Farm. The Cold War might be over, but the CIA wouldn't have abandoned the country. The spooks could take care of the women until other arrangements were made, and by the time the New Brotherhood learned of what had happened, the Executioner should have located Greta and the other women.

Unless the New Brotherhood honchos called the resort and got no answer.

As the warrior continued to wait on the line to connect, he heard the door slide open in the outer office. A voice called out in Russian, "Mr. Muradi? Is everything okay?"

Bolan covered the mouthpiece. "One of the guards?" he whispered to Nadenka.

The secretary nodded.

"Mr. Muradi? I saw the light...."

"Tell him to come in," Bolan said.

"Come in, Ivan. Zaid is on the phone. But he needs to talk to you."

The door slid closed and footsteps shuffled toward the back office. The man dressed as a gardener entered the room just as Brognola came on the line. "Hello?"

As the gardener stared in shock at Bolan, a 3-round burst of suppressed hollowpoints flew across the room. The intuder slumped to a sitting position against the wall.

"It's Striker," Bolan said into the mouthpiece.

"Yeah, I recognized your voice."

"I'm in the middle of something, and I don't have time to explain."

"What else is new?"

"Hal, I'm about to have two, maybe three dozen female hostages on my hands in Odessa. I've got to move quick or others will die."

"I'll handle it. Odessa's the last Russian port before Turkey. CIA's bound to still have people in the area. The trick will be getting to them."

"Pull out of your hat whatever you have to, Hal. This is going to go down hard and fast." He gave Brognola the address of the resort.

"Okay. How soon do you need them?"

"Now," Bolan answered and hung up.

Nadenka pointed to a number she'd underlined in the phone book—Big Buck's Barbecue. "A man from Montana put it in a few months ago," she said. "It lasted two weeks."

Bolan nodded. He lifted the receiver again and dialed the number. When the connection clicked, he punched the Record button on the answering machine.

"The number you have reached is either out of service or undergoing repair at this time," a woman's voice said in crisp Russian. "Please check to ensure you have dialed correctly, then..."

When the message had been recorded onto the outgoing tape, Bolan replaced the receiver and switched the machine to Answer. He didn't know how much time the ploy would give him, but he'd have to hope it was enough.

Turning to Nadenka, he said, "Lock yourself in and wait until I get back."

Then, slipping through the glass door, the Executioner started toward the buildings.

## CHAPTER THIRTEEN

The resort guards had been trained to prevent the escape of helpless young women, not defend against a soldier's attack.

They went down easy.

As Bolan stole through the shadows of the apartment complex, taking out the opposition, the hushed whir of suppressed 9 mm rounds was scarcely audible. One by one, eleven Brotherhood men fell.

When the last body had been deposited in a trash Dumpster behind the parking garage, the Executioner made a final tour of the grounds. All clear. Taking Muradi and the gardener into account, he had taken out a baker's dozen savages threatening the new democracy.

According to Muradi, there were two dozen guards on the grounds. That meant the rest would be off-duty in buildings C and D.

Thirteen down. Twelve to go.

Shoving a fresh magazine into the Beretta, the Executioner entered the hallway of building C. The structure was identical to the one he had inhabited, which meant apartment 4 would be at the west end, downstairs. He kept the 93-R hidden under his coat as he passed the staircase and paused at the door. Pressing his ear against the wood, the warrior listened.

Silence.

Bolan slipped the American Express card from his passport case and wedged it into the crack just below the knob. He heard a soft click as the spring lock flipped open. Quietly he twisted the knob and pushed open the door.

More silence. And darkness.

The Executioner slipped into the room, closing the door softly behind him. His warrior ears had been trained in countless jungle missions where the smallest sound might mean impending death.

All he heard now was the faint reverberation of snoring from the bedroom. Silently he moved toward the short hallway that led to the sound.

Suddenly bed springs creaked, then footsteps padded toward the hall. A switch flipped, and the hallway was illuminated with bright, blinding light.

Bolan squinted, and saw a New Brotherhood man in striped pajamas standing before him. When the man spotted the Executioner, his eyes opened wide in spite of the blaze of light.

He whirled toward the bedroom, but a 3-round burst of 9 mm rounds stitched him from tailbone to neck.

Bolan charged down the hall, still squinting as his pupils tried to adjust to the light. Fuzzy images jumped from three sets of bunk beds as he rounded the corner into the room.

Tapping the trigger, the Executioner fired another burst of hushed hollowpoints into a blur reaching for a rifle against the wall, following through with another burst of suppressed fire that took out a man on an upper bunk. As the Executioner groped the wall for the light switch, the dark specter toppled toward the floor. The gunner's foot hooked into the bed frame as he fell, bringing the top bunk tumbling down over him in the darkness.

Bolan's fingers found the switch and flooded the room with light as the three remaining men fumbled blindly for weapons. He flipped the Beretta to semi-auto and loosed a sustained burst, lessening the odds even further. When the last New Brotherhood man had fallen, he dropped the near-empty magazine from the Beretta and reloaded.

The grounds of the Skyline Resort were still silent as the Executioner made his way through the shadows to building D. He paused just inside the entry door. The tricky part was about to begin. Apartments 7 and 8 would be directly across the hall from each other, upstairs. If he was lucky, he might be able to take out the gunners in one without alerting the men across the hall.

Voices drifted through the door of apartment 7 as the Executioner listened.

"Hit me," a Russian said in English.

The near-imperceptible sound of a card being slapped on a table followed the request. A chorus of laughter followed.

"Twenty-two ain't the game," an American cackled.

As the hilarity died down, the Executioner slipped out the American Express card.

Cracking the door, he looked in to see four men seated around a card table. Two wore cheap Russian suits. Another was dressed in Western-cut slacks and a pearl-snapped sports shirt. The fourth, wearing only dingy gray boxer shorts, was dealing the cards.

The Executioner saw no reason to wait on the next hand.

Throwing the door wide, Bolan sprayed the table, tapping the trigger of the 93-R and sending 3-round eruptions showering across the room in a thunderburst of death. The two Russians fell first, their hands clamped against their chests as blood drizzled between their fingers.

The American in the cowboy shirt joined them a split second later. His fingers clawed spastically for the revolver in his belt as three more rounds tore through his throat. A Colt King Cobra .357 toppled to the floor as a fire-hose blast of crimson shot from under his chin.

The man in the boxer shorts bolted to his feet. He broke from the group and lunged toward an Uzi propped against the wall in the corner.

Three more 9 mm Parabellums cut him down halfway there.

The Beretta locked open. In a heartbeat the empty mag had fallen to the floor and been replaced with a full load. Bolan glanced quickly over his shoulder. So far, no reaction from apartment 8.

The Executioner moved cautiously toward the bedroom. Somewhere in the apartment, he'd find two more New Brotherhood gunners. And while the men across the hall might not have heard the suppressed rounds, anyone in the bedroom would now be on alert.

Stopping at the door, he peered around the corner, then jerked back, flattening against the wall as a gunner appeared and fired off a quick round.

Dropping to his knees, the Executioner rolled into the doorway. He came to a halt on his side as more gunfire streaked overhead. He squeezed the Beretta's trigger, drilling more hollowpoints into the chest of a New Brotherhood hardman against the far wall.

The man died on his feet, his lifeless fingers freezing on the trigger of the Uzi in his hands. The barrel of the subgun shot upward, emptying the rest of the magazine into the ceiling as the body slammed back against the wall and slid to the floor.

Suddenly the apartment was silent.

Deadly quiet.

A soft, near-inaudible cough came from the closet. Bolan holstered the Beretta and drew the Desert Eagle.

The ear-piercing burst from the Uzi would have sounded the alarm in apartment 8. The 93-R's suppressor was now useless. In a few seconds more gunners would race across the hall.

From here on in, speed and power would be the Executioner's only ally.

Bolan moved cautiously to the half-open closet door. Short, choppy, frightened breaths emanated from behind a closet rod of dangling shirts.

Ripping the hangers to the side, the Executioner looked down to see a terrified gunner huddled on the floor, both of his hands hidden under a fallen shirt. "Please," he pleaded, "I don't want to—" His hand suddenly shot from under the shirt clutching a Bumblebee Pocket Partner .22.

The Desert Eagle roared.

The smell of burned cordite permeated the room as the big Magnum's boom died down. Movement flickered in the corner of the Executioner's eye. He turned to see a New Brotherhood gunner in the hallway. A 12-gauge explosion roared past his ear as a four-inch hole appeared in the closet door an inch from his head.

EVEN THE PILLOW STUFFED under Katerina Kerensky's new overcoat didn't keep out the bitter Moscow wind. The RMI colonel stared at her reflection in the shop window. The coat and pillow had been today's additions to her disguise. She didn't think Solomentsev would recall the sunglasses and wig, but if he did, her new "pregnant" look should be enough to convince him that the blond woman on the street across from Red Square was not the one he'd seen the day before.

As she pulled her collar tighter around her throat, a vulgar American catchall term crossed her mind. While she would never consider uttering the word out loud, it didn't hurt to think it. And it seemed the only word to accurately describe her ongoing attempts to tail Solomentsev.

Yes, Kerensky thought to herself, she was fucked.

Solomentsev had done it to her again.

Yesterday she had seen the president's aide leave the Kremlin, then driven quickly to the parking garage to wait, which was exactly what she had done. Wait.

Solomentsev had finally arrived two hours later, weaving even worse than the day before. Where had he been? To the alley again? No, that couldn't account for such a delay. He had met someone along the way—undoubtedly his New Brotherhood contact.

As her anger mounted, Kerensky focused on the reflection of the ridiculous blond wig. The frustration made her want to rip it off. Her eyes fell to the pillow.

"Solomentsev, you are driving me to the costumes of a clown," she muttered under her breath.

In the window Kerensky suddenly saw the familiar gray overcoat and rabbit *shrapki* approach the curb.

She continued to watch as Alexandr Solomentsev hurried across the street and passed behind her, his face a mask of anger.

She gave him a hundred feet, then fell in behind. The colonel wouldn't lose her prey today, even if that meant sticking to the man like glue. She'd find out where Solomentsev went, what he did and with whom. And if he spotted her and saw through the asinine disguise, then so be it.

Solomentsev's pace quickened, and Kerensky struggled to keep up. Wherever he was headed, the president's fair-haired boy was determined.

She was less than twenty feet behind when Solomentsev ducked into the doorway of the Ukrainian Café.

Kerensky slowed. Should she follow him inside? Yes. She had to. She couldn't risk losing the man again. Each day that passed increased the risk—to Belasko, Tachek and the entire Commonwealth.

Solomentsev opened the door. Kerensky caught it before it swung shut again.

The young aide ignored her as he walked quickly toward a table in the corner. Kerensky took a seat in the booth nearest the window. She started to unbutton her coat, remembered the pillow and left it on.

As her eyes adjusted to the semidarkness, Katerina Kerensky saw Solomentsev remove his own coat and drop into the chair across from a man in a brown suit and hat.

Facts, memories and suspicions raced through Kerensky's mind, vying to gel into one tangible thought that made sense. The man in brown was the same man she had noticed here two days earlier. The man she had vaguely recognized. But from where?

The waiter appeared at her side. Kerensky ordered a soft drink. Furtively she watched the two men as the waiter moved to them and set glasses on the table. Solomentsev pushed his away. The man in the brown hat pushed it back.

Kerensky felt her heart beat furiously in her chest. Solomentsev was angry. She couldn't hear his words, or see his face, but the animated gestures that accompanied his speech told her so.

The man in the hat listened patiently, then began to speak.

Suddenly Solomentsev's arms fell to his sides.

Kerensky sipped her soda as the two men continued to talk in hushed voices. Then suddenly Solomentsev lifted his glass and quaffed it down.

The men continued to drink, the young man's shoulders slumping further each time the older man opened his mouth.

Without warning the two men rose, donned their coats and walked toward the door. Kerensky stared at the wall as they passed, then stood and hurried to their table.

She glanced covertly around the room. The rest of the bar was empty, and the waiter had disappeared through the swing doors that led to the kitchen.

Kerensky grabbed the glass from which the mysterious man in the hat had drunk and dropped it into the pocket of her coat. Her memory might refuse to recall the man's identity, but the fingerprints on the glass would refresh it.

Through the window Kerensky saw Solomentsev and the other man pause briefly on the street. Then the president's aide turned unsteadily toward the parking lot, and the man in the hat started back in the direction of Red Square.

Kerensky shot out of the door, crossed the street and raced toward the parking garage. Two teenaged boys laughed as she hurried past them, pillow-abdomen bobbing furiously with every step. A child pointed to her stomach, then looked up at his mother for explanation.

The colonel glanced across the street as she came abreast of Solomentsev. He stared at his feet as he staggered toward the garage, the only person on the block not interested in the crazy pregnant woman.

When she reached her car, Kerensky slid behind the wheel and started the engine. Her heart continued to beat like a jackhammer against her chest, not so much from the run but from excitement. She no longer had any doubt that Solomentsev was the source of the leak. The pieces of the puzzle fit too neatly. And now she was about to follow that leak and discover where it emptied.

Kerensky caught her breath, forcing herself to relax as Solomentsev reached the garage window, took his keys from the attendant and wobbled out of sight up the steps. His black ZIL drove down the ramp a moment later and turned the same way it had the day before.

The unmarked RMI car fell in behind, staying close. Traffic was heavy, and Kerensky prayed that in his drunken state, Solomentsev wouldn't notice her. She couldn't lose him this time. She had come too far for that.

The ZIL crept through the downtown Moscow traffic, crossed the river, then headed southeast on Lenin Prospekt, finally entering a suburb and pulling into the driveway of a modest, single-family home.

Kerensky drove on by, made a U-turn at the corner and parked in time to see Solomentsev stagger up the steps and into the house. She reached for the pillow under her coat and her hand brushed the lump in her outer pocket. Yes, the glass. But it would have to wait. She couldn't possibly break surveillance until she was certain Solomentsev wouldn't be leaving again tonight.

Sliding the pillow behind her back, the RMI colonel positioned it just above the tailbone and settled back for the long wait. For the first time since she'd spotted Solomentsev, she thought of her new lover. She and Dmitri had planned another intimate evening.

Well, those plans would not only have to be put on hold, she'd have no way of getting a message to him for the next several hours.

Katerina Kerensky sighed. "I'm sorry," she said out loud. "I love you as much as I love my country, Dmitri." She paused, then added, "But I have loved my country longer."

THE RECOIL of the big .44 Magnum drove the Executioner's wrist back. He dived face-first to the carpet as the man with the shotgun fell back into the living room.

A triburst of rounds shredded the walls above Bolan as he rolled to his side, snaking back toward the open doorway. Down the short hall, he saw more men from apartment 8 cross the hall and join a gunner with an AK-47 in the living room.

The man with the assault rifle suddenly sprinted toward the bedroom. Bolan rolled back, shoved the Desert Eagle into his holster and swung the Striker into play. As the man with the AK burst into the room, he squeezed the trigger.

The Striker's autorounds angled up, splattering through the New Brotherhood gunner's ribs and slapping him against the side wall as the heavy double-aught pellets scrapped his torso. The AK fell to the carpet as the gunner's mouth opened wide in a silent scream. He spun across the wall to the closet before pirouetting to the floor.

Bolan rose to his knees and scooted along the carpet back to the door. On the other side he heard the muted sounds of laboriously controlled breathing.

Rising to his feet, he aimed the Striker chest-level, then backed two feet from the wall. The autoshotgun jerked against his wrists as the wall exploded in a flurry of Sheetrock and two-by-four studs.

The Executioner heard the scream. As the white storm in front of him settled, he saw the half-foot hole in the wall, and through it, the body sliding to the floor.

Bolan dropped prone again as a sudden volley of rifle fire stitched more holes along the wall from the living room. His cheek against the carpet, he edged one eye around the corner into the hall.

In the center of the living room stood two hardmen, their AK-47s still aimed at the common wall to the bedroom. The gunner closer to the Executioner wore red sweatpants and soft leather slippers. The other, barely out of his teens, still fought a losing battle with acne.

Both men's faces showed their indecision. They stared at the wall, wondering if they should try to enter the bedroom.

Bolan dropped the near-empty Striker and unleathered the Desert Eagle. He had started to raise the weapon when he saw a flicker of movement outside the front door. A third man, more careful than the others, peeked around the corner into the living room.

The Executioner took him out first. Dropping the sights on a spot in the wallboard a foot from the door frame, Bolan sent a screaming .44 Magnum round drilling through the wall with over nine hundred foot-pounds of energy.

Adjusting his aim, he swung the big Magnum to the gunner with the acne. The crater face took on a whole new look as a .44 round punched through it.

The man in the red sweatpants spotted Bolan's position on the floor a second late. As the front sights of his assault moved into target acquisition, the Executioner pumped two raging hollowpoints into his chest and abdomen.

Bolan was on his feet and moving before the last body landed on the carpet. He leaped over the dead man in the hall and quickly checked the kitchen on his way out of the apartment. Rushing past the body in the common hall, the Executioner burst through the door of apartment 8 to see a skinny New Brotherhood gunner wearing only white Jockey underwear and dialing the phone.

The man knew death when he stared it in the face.

Dropping the receiver, he feebly raised a nickel-plated Browning Hi-Power, his face resigned to his fate.

The Executioner provided it for him.

Rushing back to the hall, Bolan saw the door to apartment 6 inch open. Ducking his head, he shouldered past a Japanese man and spoke to a nude Oriental girl on the couch. "Get dressed and get down to the office. Tell the rest of the girls to do the same on your way out of the building."

The girl reached for a pair of panties next to her. "What is happening?" she asked.

"You're getting out of here," Bolan said. "Now move!"

The girl grabbed a dress from the arm of a nearby chair and hurried out of the condo.

The gray-haired man snatched her arm as she started to leave.

Bolan brought the heavy barrel of the Desert Eagle down on the man's wrist. He jerked his hand back in pain. "You're through touching her," the Executioner growled. He brought the heavy barrel down again, this time crashing into the Japanese's temple.

The man slumped to the floor as the girl raced from the apartment. She was knocking on the door to unit 5 as Bolan descended the stairs and headed back to the building next door.

The Executioner kicked the door to apartment 2. Anna, wearing only a bra and panties, sat on the couch fighting off the hands of a young man in a business suit.

The man rose from the couch as Bolan neared. "How dare you!" he yelled, angered at the intrusion.

"I beg your pardon," the Executioner said as he launched a right cross that sent the man reeling back across the couch.

Bolan pulled Anna to her feet. "You have a phone in here?"

Anna nodded toward the kitchen.

"Call Katra first. Tell her to get all the girls out of her building and send them to the office. You do the same, then cover building B. I'll get the others." The beautiful young Swede nodded as he turned and sprinted back toward the door.

Bolan raced through buildings A and E, notifying the captive women. The Desert Eagle in his hand was enough to dissuade interference from most of the timid resort patrons he encountered. Two more men fell to the right cross, but most wanted only to escape the madness and return to their wives before their whereabouts became public.

Even if they knew how to contact the resort owners, they weren't about to take time.

Racing back to the office, the Executioner found twenty-seven partially dressed women huddled in the outer office. Anna had thrown on a pair of jeans and a T-shirt.

"Everybody here?" the Executioner asked her.

Anna nodded.

Bolan lifted the phone. A moment later, Brognola answered. "They're on their way, Striker. I can't tell you over the air where they left from, but they should show up any minute."

"Okay, Hal. Thanks." Bolan hung up.

The receiver had barely hit the cradle when a soft knock sounded on the rear door of the office building. Bolan made his way through the throng of frightened women and swung the Striker from under his coat. Jerking open the door, he shoved it into the belly of a man with a Vandyke beard and wearing a Greek fisherman's cap.

The man looked down at the barrel. "I was warned you weren't the most gracious host," he said. "My name's Owensby. Orders came down through the pipes. But I was told they originated from somebody named Brognola. That ring any bells for you?"

Bolan nodded and tucked the shotgun back under his trench coat.

Owensby let out a sigh of relief. "Then you just give me your code name, and we're on our way out of here."

The Executioner tapped the Striker through his coat. "Same as the gun."

Owensby shrugged. "Good enough for me. Shall we load 'em up?"

Bolan and Owensby escorted the girls through the door to the parking lot. Four Dodge vans, all bearing the words Black Sea Florists, sat idling, their lights off.

The women sniffled and sighed as they boarded the vehicles. Katra and Anna stood next to the Executioner, then embraced before the dark-skinned woman got into the final van.

Owensby walked over. "We better get going, miss," he said to Anna.

Bolan shook his head. "She stays with me."

Owensby's eyebrows rose. "Can't say as I blame you."

"Get the women safe," Bolan said, ignoring the innuendo. "And keep somebody next to the phone. I'm not finished this evening, and Brognola will be getting word to you again.''

Owensby nodded, then turned, stepped up after Katra and slid the door shut behind him.

Bolan and Anna watched the vans drive away. "Where will they take them?" Anna asked.

The Executioner shrugged. "I don't know But someplace safe. And from there, home." He turned, looking down at the beautiful woman in the moonlight. "Owensby was right, you know. We better get out of here before police or other Brotherhood men show up."

Anna nodded. Then shyly she said, "Er, could we just take a second? Could I call my husband and tell him I'm all right?"

Bolan smiled down into the innocent face that had seen so much horror. And yet, Anna had been lucky. He had arrived before she'd had more than a taste of the perversions the Skyline Resort offered. The Executioner couldn't help wondering if the other women would ever recover, ever be able to return to their husbands or boyfriends and lead a normal life.

Anna stared up at him, her face revealing her complete trust. "Do we have time to call Donnie, Mr. McNeil?" she asked.

The Executioner didn't deceive himself. The worst might still lie ahead in their quest to locate Anna's sister.

"We'll make time, Anna," he said and led her back toward the door.

THE BLACK ZIL CRUISED slowly down the street, stopping and starting in the heavy traffic. Mario Hernandez stared out the side window, watching the passing buildings. He thought of Esposito and felt like a fool. Thank God, the Mafia man had been too tired to come along to see the warehouse. The old fart had suddenly grown fangs, and he...well, he just flat scared the piss out of Mario Hernandez.

And learning that his trusted bodyguard Erich was really a Russian Intelligence spy hadn't helped Hernandez's confidence any, either.

Ahead of the ZIL, a red Toyota suddenly cut into the traffic from a side street. Leskov stomped the brakes.

The Colombian watched the heads in the Toyota's back seat. The car was packed with laborers returning home after work. They all wore funny little Russian workmen's caps and passed a bottle back and forth.

Leskov began humming some classic Russian song. Hernandez vaguely recognized the off-key version. He gripped the dashboard as traffic slowed once more and they skidded to a halt behind the Toyota.

Turning in his seat, Hernandez saw Jake Pool behind him. The gunfighter was playing with his revolvers again, breaking open the loading gates, checking the loads, then spinning the cylinders flamboyantly.

Pool must have sensed that he was being watched. He looked up, and the tails of his bushy handlebar mustache curled up in the familiar, lopsided grin. The nickel-plated Colts flashed like mirrors as he twirled the weapons, then slammed them back into the holsters on his sides.

Hernandez returned the smile and turned back to the front. Knowing Pool was along made him feel better. Yes, Esposito was right. Pool *was* crazy. The cowboy clothes. The reincarnation. The man's whole persona—it was more than just an act. The outrageous bastard actually believed he was Wild Bill Hickok.

But so what? Hernandez thought as the ZIL began to move again. He did his job, and he did it oh, so well.

As the ZIL picked up speed, Hernandez glanced over his shoulder again. Furelli sat opposite Pool, staring out the window at oncoming traffic. Esposito's heavy hitter looked, well, *terrified* was the only word that seemed to fit. He might be the top gun back in New York, but he was out of his element riding through Moscow with a Russian Intelligence agent and a psychopath cowboy who considered death little more than a costume change.

The Colombian returned his eyes to the road as they neared the Arbat—Moscow's version of Greenwich Village. What was really bothering Furelli, Hernandez knew, was the same thing that had made Esposito decide to personally come to Moscow and take over the operation. A name.

Mack Bolan.

"Shit," Hernandez said out loud. He felt Leskov's eyes turn toward him. He ignored them. How tough could one man be? Okay, Bolan had done some damage to the Mafia in the past. Big deal. So had Elliot Ness, and business had gone on as usual. And sure, Hernandez himself had heard about a lone-wolf killer who'd cut into the Medellín cartel and other organizations on occasion, and now he suspected Bolan was that man. But they were still delivering their dope, weren't they?

The career of this man they called the Executioner had to have been blown out of proportion. Like a movie.

An idea suddenly hit Hernandez, and he caught himself chuckling. He had wanted to get into the film business for years—snort some coke with the big names and wake up each morning with a new little bitch who thought he'd make her a star. Yes, that's exactly what he'd do when this was all over. He'd fly to Hollywood, set up a film company and start production on a movie about this bastard.

Hernandez stared down the pedestrian street into the Arbat. Street musicians and artists roamed the area, and less than twenty feet away stood a long-haired young man wearing a black zippered motorcycle jacket. Eyes closed, he strummed the strings of the guitar in his hands as a handful of admirers looked on.

"*Shtatniki,*" Leskov grumbled. "Stateniks, we call them. They try to pretend they are American. They like to have the latest clothes and decadent pop music." He grunted and turned back to the windshield.

Hernandez saw the contradiction of emotions on the old man's face. It amused him. In many ways Leskov reminded him of the policemen he dealt with at home. But there was one major difference—the Colombian cops rationalized their graft with low police pay. The RI colonel had convinced himself that he was on the take in order to save Russia.

Hernandez laughed out loud at his thoughts as the ZIL turned into a light-industrial area. Leskov's rationalization made sense, of course, only in his own twisted mind.

How could you save your country by supporting those who intended to destroy it?

Hernandez's laugh faded as the ZIL passed an ancient Russian Orthodox church that stood out like a sore thumb in the crumbling neighborhood. They pulled to a halt in front of a storage building across the street from a burned-out apartment house.

The drug lord surveyed the warehouse as they left the car and walked up the sidewalk. Grass grew in the cracks along the concrete, and the windows had been broken out and boarded over. "We have used this warehouse in the past for interrogations," Leskov said, a sudden gleam in his eyes. The gleam faded just as suddenly. "Since the current president came to office," he went on, "it has been deserted." The colonel pulled a key from his pocket, unlocked the door and ushered the men inside.

The front room of the warehouse was empty except for a straight-backed wooden chair in the middle of the room. A bare light bulb hung suspended from the ceiling. Scattered throughout the room were discarded strips of adhesive tape, yellowing with age. The floor area had stained a deep, black-red around the chair.

Hernandez didn't have to ask what had caused the stains.

"It will do?" Leskov asked.

Hernandez nodded. "It will do. Have some other chairs brought in. Does the building have electricity?"

Leskov stared back at him as if he'd ask if the walls were made of gold.

"Then we'll need space heaters," Hernandez said. "I don't want the men stiff and cold when Bolan arrives."

Hernandez crossed the room to a door in the rear wall. He stuck his head through the opening and saw another room, identical to the front. Another chair, more tape, more stains.

The drug lord walked back to the other men. He pointed to the bloodstains on the floor. "Soon, Mack Bolan will make his contribution to the design."

Leskov laughed, Pool cackled and Furelli let a feeble, nervous smile play at the corner of his lips.

Hernandez looked back to the chair. If he got the chance, he'd tie Mack Bolan to the seat himself. Then he'd kill the bastard slowly.

The Colombian visualized the picture in his mind. It would make a terrific climax scene.

Both in reality, and in the movie.

## CHAPTER FOURTEEN

The man at the microphone belted out a Russian-accented, heartfelt rendition of an Elvis Presley song.

Anna's perfume wafted up into the Executioner's nostrils as they swayed to the rhythm of the stage band. He glanced down at the young woman in his arms. Luckily the Skyline Resort provided their captives with evening dress. In the sparkling sequined gown, Anna looked stunning—and out of place with the man in the rumpled gray suit. But no one on the ship seemed to care about the Executioner's haggard appearance. At least if they did, they were too busy to pay attention.

No, Bolan thought as he scanned the ballroom, noting the hungry, anxious looks on the faces of the dancers. The guests on board the *Aphrodite* cruise liner had other things on their minds.

Bolan and Anna continued to dance. They had boarded the ship an hour before, checked into their cabin, dressed and gone to the voyage's "get acquainted" party.

So far, they had seen no sign of Greta.

As he continued to scan the room, the Executioner's eyes fell on various passengers. Many were the swingers Muradi had mentioned—couples who now danced with their partners but searched constantly over the crowd for other potential bed mates, their eyes filled with unbridled lust.

Single men—and a few women—lined the walls, checking out one another and waiting for the arrival of the prostitutes.

As the song ended, a man mounted the steps to the stage, wearing more gold braid then Bolan would have guessed his skinny shoulders could have supported. He waited for the final chords to die down, then stepped up to the mike.

"Ladies and gentlemen," he said in English, "I am Captain Bishop, and I'd like to welcome you to the *Aphrodite*—the realist's version of the Love Boat." He waited as a few chuckles rippled through the crowd. Quickly he introduced the band, then said, "And now, I would like to present some very special employees of Aphrodite International." With a dramatic sweep of his arm, Bishop indicated a closed door at the right side of the stage.

As the band broke into a quiet rendition of "Love is a Many Splendored Thing," the door opened. A beautiful young redhead stepped out. Her ample bosom stretched tightly against the low-cut black gown as she walked seductively toward center stage.

"May I introduce Lesley, from Los Angeles," Captain Bishop said, "followed by Anne, from London...."

A ravishing woman entered next, with coal-black tresses that fell to her waist.

Bishop continued to introduce the women as they paraded onto the stage and lined up like cattle at an auction. Just like their counterparts at the Skyline Resort, they represented every ethnic group imaginable and shared only one common trait: fear.

"Greta, of Sweden," Bishop said, and an older version of Anna walked through the door in a white dress.

Bolan glanced down. Tears formed in the corners of Anna's eyes. Without looking up, she nodded.

"We will sail shortly," Bishop said after the last girl had entered and taken her place in line. "And I will bore you with my presence no longer. You did not come for me." He waited in an obviously practiced pause. "Or perhaps some of you *did*." When the laughter had died down, he said, "Get to know the girls. Have fun with them—that is why they are here."

The captain walked to the edge of the stage amid the applause of the audience, then turned back to the band and said, "Maestro, if you will."

The band began playing the love theme from *Romeo and Juliet* as Bishop descended the steps to the dance floor and disappeared through a side door.

Bolan took Anna in his arms. Holding her close, he whispered in her ear, "Get over to Greta as soon as you can without drawing attention. Tell her to stand by—be ready for anything. And have her pass the word along to the other girls. Tell them as soon as they're back onshore to stay together. Then *you* look around for Owensby and the vans. Got it?"

Anna pushed him to arm's length. "What are you going to do?"

"What I do best," he said, and turned to leave.

Anna jerked him back by the arm. "Will I see you again?" she asked.

"Probably not."

Both happiness and melancholy tried to crowd onto the woman's face. She stood on her toes and kissed the Executioner on the cheek. "Thank you."

The warrior turned and hurried across the floor.

The ship's horn announcing departure brought more applause from the passengers as Bolan hurried from the room. He caught up with Bishop on the main deck just as the captain started up the ladder to the flying bridge. "Need to talk to you, Captain."

Bishop looked down, his beady eyes shining under the deck lights. "No time right now, sir. We're sailing." He held the rail as he climbed the steps. "Just find one of the stewards—"

"Fine," Bolan said curtly. "I'll tell Esposito you didn't have time for him."

The captain stopped halfway up the steps. "You from the company? Why didn't you say so?" he asked nervously. "What's the prob—"

"Let's go on up," Bolan said, following the man up the ladder to the bridge.

The ship began to move as they reached the communications room. A smartly uniformed radioman was the only occupant. "This'll need to be confidential, Captain," Bolan said.

"Out," Bishop ordered briskly, and the radioman disappeared.

The captain dropped into the radioman's place. "What do you need?"

"Stop the boat."

"What? Are you crazy?"

The Executioner drew the Desert Eagle from under his jacket. "A lot of people seem to think so," he said. "Just do it. You'll live longer."

The captain stared down the bore of the large Magnum, then reached for the intercom. Hitting a button, he said, "Cancel orders to sail."

A second later, a voice came back, "Return to dock, Captain?"

Bishop looked to Bolan.

The Executioner shook his head. "Drop anchor."

The captain gave the strange orders. "What now?" he asked, still staring at the Desert Eagle an inch from his face.

Bolan lifted a pen from the table in front of him. Using a yellow pad next to the microphone, he wrote quickly, then ripped the top page away and handed it to Bishop. "I assume you've got simultaneous contact with all deck areas and cabins. Get the band quieted down, then read this." He tapped the Eagle's barrel on Bishop's nose. "Word for word."

Bishop glanced down at the page. "You're crazy," he said. "*I'd* be crazy to read—"

The warrior jammed the .44 between the captain's eyes. "Then I'll give you a choice," he said. "Crazy or dead?"

Bishop turned back to the mike. The blood drained from his face. "Attention, all passengers and crew," he read. "There is no reason to panic. I repeat, no reason to panic. But we will be forced to evacuate the ship immediately. All passengers are to return to the docks by lifeboat and await further instructions. All crew are to assist in the evacuation, then return immediately to their posts for further orders."

Bolan reached forward, took the mike from Bishop's hand and set it on the desk. "Very good."

A second later a steward appeared at the door. "Captain, what—"

The Executioner hid the Desert Eagle behind his back and said, "Bomb threat. Probably nothing. But we have to check it out."

The steward looked to Bishop for confirmation. Bishop nodded. "Get on with the evacuation," he ordered.

The young man left. A moment later, the Executioner heard the first whines as the lifeboats dropped into the water. He picked up the pad and began to write more instructions.

Thirty minutes later, a voice broke the silence in the radio room. "All passengers ashore, Captain. All hands at post."

The Executioner handed Bishop the new page of orders. The captain read it silently, all surprise now faded from his eyes. He turned to the mike. "Attention all crew. Commence searching assigned areas for anything resembling an explosive device. Report any suspicious objects immediately. Do not, I repeat, do not attempt to disassemble yourself."

Bolan nodded. "Now call your radioman back." He shoved the Desert Eagle into the holster under his coat and said, "Don't let out-of-sight be out-of-mind, Bishop. I can have the gun out and drill one through your head before you can sound an alarm. And I will."

The captain nodded. He had started to speak when the radioman suddenly returned.

"Captain Bishop and I will be overseeing the search," Bolan told him. "Stay at the mike." He nodded toward the yellow pad. "Record all reports. We'll be back shortly."

Bolan nudged Bishop down the steps to the main deck and toward the captain's gig.

"Take us down, Laslo," Bishop ordered a crewman as they stepped over the rail into the smaller craft. A moment later, they were speeding away from the *Aphrodite* back to shore.

The confused passengers mingled near the water as Bolan tied off the gig at the dock. He shoved Bishop over the rail and stepped up after him.

"Was it a bomb?" a woman wearing inch-thick makeup asked the captain as Bolan pushed him through the crowd. Bishop didn't answer.

"Was it a bomb?" another voice asked. Then others heard the word, and their cries went quickly from "Was it a bomb?" to "It might have been a bomb," to "It *was* a bomb."

The word "bomb" continued to float through the anxious mass of people as Bolan pushed Bishop through their midst.

Anna and Greta had already ushered the captive women away from the confusion up the steps to the parking area. The two sisters, hand in hand, stood in the center of the group near the edge of the lot.

As Bolan prodded Bishop toward the waiting Hyundai, he saw the familiar Black Sea Florist vans pull into the lot. Owensby dropped down from the vehicle in the lead and began loading the women.

The Executioner opened the door of the Hyundai and guided Bishop into the passenger's seat. He bent quickly and wrapped Flex-Cuffs around the captain's wrists.

A small grove of sea pines grew on a ridge a hundred yards down the road paralleling the sea. The Executioner had spotted the trees when he and Anna had arrived. Far enough away to avoid the curious eyes of spectators, yet still within the five-hundred-meter range of the RPG-7, he had mentally marked the spot as the most likely point of attack.

Throwing the Hyundai in reverse, Bolan backed out of the parking space, then headed toward the road.

"Where are you taking me?" Bishop asked anxiously. "Are you going to kill me?"

"Not if you behave yourself. But don't get me wrong. I should. But I've got a message for you to deliver after I'm gone. For now, just keep quiet."

The frightened captain took him at his word. Bishop's jaws clamped shut, and he stared straight ahead into the night.

The Executioner stopped the car ten feet from the trees and got out. Opening the trunk, he flipped the hinges on the black hard case.

Attaching the two-piece launcher tube to the RPG-7, Bolan pulled out one of the rockets and inspected the oversize hollow-charge warhead. Sliding the range finder on top of the weapon, he moved to the edge of the ridge.

The Executioner took a firm stance, pointed the tube toward the *Aphrodite,* and checked the range through the optical—375 meters, well under maximum.

Locking his left hand around the foregrip, Bolan dropped the sights on the New Brotherhood boat and squeezed the trigger.

The rocket sizzled from the launching tube, the tail fins flaring out for stability as it flashed toward the cruise ship. A moment later, the 85 mm warhead struck the thin hull, penetrated to the engine room below and exploded.

A second eruption sounded from across the water as the ship's diesel engines went up in a fireball of death. Flames leaped from the bowels of the ship, rising past the main deck and climbing to the captain's bridge.

Far below in the parking lot, the jaded passengers of the former "Lust Boat" oohed and aahed like children at a fireworks display.

Bolan broke the RPG down and returned it to the case.

Captain Bishop remained silent as the Executioner drove back down the hill toward the dock. As they neared the parking area, he finally said, "I'll do whatever you want. Just tell me."

Bolan didn't answer. He guided the Hyundai around the cars as the last of Owensby's rescue vans pulled away, taking the captive women to safety.

The Executioner frowned. He had now exhausted all the intel on the New Brotherhood from the RI file. Which meant he no longer had any choice. He would have to call Solomentsev and get another lead.

It also meant that, sooner or later, the New Brotherhood would know where he was going.

"You said you wouldn't kill me...you had something for me to do," Bishop said in a weak voice. "You haven't changed your mind?"

Bolan slowed the Hyundai to a stop near the crowd. He drew the Mini Tanto from under his arm and turned toward Bishop. The captain opened his mouth to scream but nothing came out.

The Executioner cut through the plastic restraints around the man's wrists and pointed toward the door with the tip of the blade. "You go contact Esposito and Hernandez."

The flesh under Bishop's chin quivered as he asked, "What do I tell him?"

"What you saw. Now get out."

Bishop didn't have to be told twice. As he opened the door, Bolan grabbed him by the arm. "Oh, yeah," he said. "And tell them I'm just getting started." He threw the car back in gear and cruised slowly past the fascinated onlookers.

KATERINA KERENSKY was no longer embarrassed by the blond wig, sunglasses and pillow stuffed under her overcoat. It was not that she'd grown accustomed to the disguise.

The fear in her heart had pushed all other emotion to the side.

Kerensky found a parking space half a block from the Ukrainian Café, pulled in and got out. She walked casually down the street, checking her watch.

She had thirty minutes before Solomentsev left the president's office for the day. *If* he didn't take off early as he'd been doing.

Kerensky fingered the small transmitter in her side pocket as she walked, the movement somehow steadying her nerves. What she was about to do would result in one of two things: she'd be regarded as a hero of Russia, the woman who had discovered the leak from the president's office, or she'd find herself in prison.

It depended on who wound up on top when the whole mess was over.

Through the dirty glass of the outside window, Kerensky could see that the bar was still empty. Twisting the knob, she inched open the door and crept inside.

Through the swing door to the kitchen, the RMI colonel heard the clank of pots and pans, and the tinkle of glasses and bottles as the waiters prepared for the after-work trade. She moved quickly toward the booth where Solomentsev and Leskov had sat the day before, peeling the paper backing off the transmitter as she walked. With a final glance around the room, she reached under the table and pressed the adhesive side of the transmitter firmly in place.

Kerensky had turned to leave when the waiter suddenly burst through the doors. "Good evening," the man said, setting a tray of glasses on the bar next to the door. "Would you like a table?"

"Good evening," Kerensky returned. "No, thank you. I am in a hurry. A Pepsi to go, please."

Kerensky waited anxiously while the waiter disappeared into the kitchen. She glanced compulsively to her watch every few seconds, praying that Solomentsev wouldn't appear early.

After what seemed like an eternity, the waiter returned and handed her a plastic cup filled with watered-down cola. She paid and left the café.

Back in the car, Kerensky opened the glove compartment. She pulled out the receiver and a micro-cassette recorder, connected the wires and switched on the instruments. A soft scratching sounded from inside the bar, then she heard the ring of glassware as the waiter began putting the glasses on the shelf behind the bar.

The colonel leaned back against the seat. Her heart raced as she recalled the phone call she'd gotten from the forensic lab only hours before.

The prints on the vodka glass belonged to Colonel Pyotr Leskov, a high-ranking Russian Intelligence hard-liner scheduled to retire soon.

A shiver of fright rippled through Kerensky. She was playing with fire. Leskov was not only high-ranking, he was one of the most influential officers in RI. He had powerful friends in all spheres of the Russian government, men who supported his right-wing approach. Unless she obtained undisputable evidence that he had sold out, even the president wasn't likely to believe her.

Kerensky watched a woman wearing an expensive sable coat push her way through the door to the café. A moment later, the sounds of the waiter seating her echoed clearly over the transmitter. Kerensky frowned. The clarity of the noise meant the woman was close to the booth where Solomentsev and Leskov sat. She hoped the proximity wouldn't restrain the men's conversation.

The colonel froze as the familiar brown suit and hat appeared in her peripheral vision. She slumped slightly in her seat as Leskov passed the front bumper and entered the bar. She saw the brown shadow fade into the darkness through the window, then heard the waiter seat him as well.

Kerensky listened closely. The transmitter was top of the line. She should even be able to hear the man's breathing in the otherwise still room. She adjusted the volume and pressed her ear close to the speaker on the reciever. Nothing. Then suddenly she heard the old man's voice as clearly as if she'd been in the room.

"Vodka," Leskov said. "Stolichnaya. And bring one for my friend. He should be here soon."

Kerensky let out a sigh of relief. The transmitter was working. It was simply not as sensitive as she had thought.

A well-dressed man wearing a matching muskrat greatcoat and hat entered the bar. Kerensky listened to him take a seat. A moment later, the woman's voice sounded over the airwaves.

"I am sorry, Jerzy. We must see each other no more. I think Danilushka knows."

The man's voice whispered back. "He cannot know. We will be careful. I love you, Karolina."

As the man and woman continued, Kerensky heard Leskov's muffled voice in the background. "Bring some caviar."

Kerensky slammed her fist down on the steering wheel. She had been wrong. The woman hadn't taken a seat *near* Leskov and Solomentsev's booth. She was *in* it. Instead of the clandestine overthrow of the Russian government, Kerensky was listening to a clandestine love affair.

The RMI colonel watched Solomentsev walk quickly passed the front of the car and push through the door. A moment later, she heard him greet Leskov and then the voices of the illicit lovers broke in to drown out the rest of their dialogue.

Kerensky made her decision in a heartbeat. She turned the volume off and dropped the receiver with the recorder into her purse. Ripping open the glove compartment, she pulled out the wireless earpiece, shoved it into her ear and glanced into the rearview mirror. It looked like a small hearing aid.

Kerensky found the directional microphone, jammed it between her abdomen and the pillow, and exited the vehicle.

She had come too far to back out now.

Entering the bar, Kerensky didn't wait to be seated. She walked quickly to the table behind the two men, took a seat and stared at the back of Solomentsev's head.

Then, covering the directional mike with a wad of crumpled tissues from her purse, she set it on the table and aimed at the booth.

"He called this morning," the RMI colonel heard Solomentsev say. "I gave him the address of the warehouse. He knows the transaction is to take place tonight."

Leskov's deep raspy chuckle echoed in Kerensky's ear. "Then this man you call Belasko will be dead before morning. Our problems will be over."

THE RI MOLE HAD DONE good work so far. But Bolan found it hard to believe that he had not only learned the exact location of the New Brotherhood's biggest drug transaction to date, but the time as well. No, there had been a little too much detail in what Alexandr Solomentsev told the Executioner over the phone.

Rap music blasted through the open doorway on the corner as the big man in the white overalls walked along the pedestrian street. Paint can in one hand, a one-gallon bucket dangling from the other, Bolan crossed the street and walked two blocks before heading toward the address Solomentsev had given him. He passed a variety of light-industrial sites before entering a seedier, run-down area of vacant commercial businesses and multifamily dwellings. As if in defiance, a tall, ancient stone Russian Orthodox church stood on the corner. A half block beyond, the Executioner saw the warehouse.

As he passed the church, Bolan spotted the half-burned apartment house directly across the street. He frowned. It was close. Dangerously close. But if he was right, and the drug deal was nothing more than a setup to draw him in, he wouldn't find a more strategic site to launch his counterattack.

The Executioner crossed the street and walked purposefully to the front door.

Like every other structure in the neighborhood—except the church—the windows in the building had been broken out. Some had been boarded over, others left to gape vacantly at the unkempt lawn facing the street. The front door had been removed.

Bolan entered the hallway, pulled a paintbrush from his overalls and dipped it into his bucket. Starting at the top of the door frame, he swept the bristles smoothly down the wood as he watched the warehouse across the street. Painting a building that should have been condemned and torn down long ago might raise a few eyebrows in America. It didn't make a lot of sense. But in a fledgling democracy, where the average worker was used to doing what he or she was told, such eccentricities went ignored.

The Executioner studied the warehouse across the street as he painted. At first glance the building looked as if it hadn't been used in years. Weeds grew from cracks in the sidewalk, and the last coat of paint might have been ordered by the czar. But as his trained eyes explored further, they picked up small discrepancies.

The weeds in the sidewalk had been recently trampled. Several of the stalks lay broken on the concrete.

Someone had been there recently.

But more importantly, a gleaming silver chain lay unrusted at the side of the door. Next to it was an open padlock.

Which meant someone was inside the warehouse now. Finishing the doorway, Bolan moved to a front window. He ripped a small scrap of wood from the bottom corner and knelt next to it. Through the gap, he could see the warehouse. Setting the paint can on the floor, he settled in.

His patience was soon rewarded. A black ZIL cruised down the street. The tinted windows blocked the Executioner's view of the occupants, but the presence of such a vehicle in the neglected vicinity stood out like a yuppie at a Hell's Angel beer bash. The car slowed, then stopped.

A few seconds later, the warehouse door opened.

Ray Furelli walked down the sidewalk to the car. His head and shoulders disappeared behind the ZIL hood as he bent to the rear window.

Preparations for the drug deal? The Executioner's gut instincts said no.

The window on the Executioner's side suddenly rolled down and a pudgy arm in a brown suit coat flicked a cigarette butt out onto the street. Bolan leaned forward, wishing he'd brought binoculars. He circled his index finger tightly down to his thumb and covered one eye, blocking out excess light and focusing on the open window. Peering through the tiny aperature, he saw two other men in the back seat of the car.

One was Mario Hernandez.

The other, Don Joseph Esposito.

The Executioner dropped his hand as the ZIL pulled away, watching as Furelli walk hurriedly back to the warehouse and closed the door.

Bolan stood and gathered his painting equipment. Taking a rear exit, he cut through the backyard of the apartment house to another deserted building in the next block, then hurried back toward the Arbat.

It was a setup, all right. No matter how big the dope deal might have been, it didn't warrant the presence of the two top New Brotherhood men. Bolan could think of only one reason they would even be in Moscow right now.

Him.

When he reached the pay phone in front of the record store, the Executioner dropped a coin into the slot and dialed the president's office.

Solomentsev answered on the second ring. "Yes?"

"Belasko," Bolan said. "I got away without writing down the address of the warehouse. What was it again?"

Solometsev read it back to him.

"Okay. I'll need a cover of some type. Tell me about the surrounding area."

"A slum, you would call it in America, I think. Most of the buildings are deserted. Scheduled to be torn down. But there is a church that still operates nearby."

Bolan no longer had doubts as to the source of the leak—Solomentsev had to be involved. But before he exposed the traitor to Tachek, he intended to use him to set a counter trap.

"The church is good," the Executioner said. "That means priests. They come and go?"

"Certainly. The church services several surrounding residential neighborhoods."

"Good enough," Bolan said and hung up.

The Executioner returned to his car. The knowledge that he'd be scoping out the warehouse soon should bring the bulk of the New Brotherhood gunners running. Esposito and Hernandez might even decide to be there themselves.

The Executioner unlocked the Hyundai and slid behind the wheel. It was time to organize. Prepare for battle. Slip back into the apartment house.

Then, when the New Brotherhood had gathered inside the building, while they waited for him to show up disguised as a priest, the Executioner would take them out.

## CHAPTER FIFTEEN

The two perimeter guards at the edge of the Arbat district might as well have had Russian Intelligence stenciled across their foreheads. They sat smoking cigarettes, their hat brims snapped low over their eyes, in yet another seemingly endless line of black government ZILs.

The two agents didn't give the painter carrying the big cardboard box a second glance as he crossed the street and headed toward the warehouse.

They were looking for a priest.

The Executioner stopped abruptly when he reached the backyard of the apartment house. Through the burned-out rear entrance he heard whispers. Setting the box on the grass, he withdrew a brush, a paint can and a bucket. He stuffed the brush into the bib pocket of his overalls and gripped the can in his left hand. Then drawing the Beretta, he covered it with the empty bucket and moved toward the building.

Making no attempt to conceal his approach, Bolan whistled happily as he crossed the door into the common hall, then headed toward the apartment he'd used to recon the area.

The voices suddenly halted.

The Executioner stopped in the hall and dropped the can of paint to the floor. "Night work," he muttered loud enough to be heard. Then sarcastically he mimicked, "It has be done tonight, Vasily, if you want to keep your job." He set the paint can on the floor, keeping the bucket-covered Beretta at the ready. "And all this for a building that will be torn—"

A dark shape appeared in the doorway. Suddenly the beam of a flashlight hit the Executioner in the eyes. He jerked toward the light, feigning surprise.

"Who are you?" the man with the flashlight demanded in Russian. "What are you doing here?"

Bolan shielded his eyes with his free hand. A second shadow appeared behind the first. Looking to the side, he let his vision clear.

"I said what you are doing here?" the man repeated, the dark outline of a pistol hanging at arm's length at his side.

"Trying to see," the warrior replied. "The manager sent me. Could you move the light?"

As the beam shifted, the Executioner squeezed the trigger.

The hushed 9 mm round made the bucket sound as if it had been hit with a hammer. It punched through the metal bottom and into the New Brotherhood gunner's head. The flashlight tumbled from his hand, clattering across the floor, as he fell.

Bolan saw the second hardman step into the hall and raise a pistol. He triggered the Beretta again, and another round stabbed through the bucket into the dark shadow's chest, taking him out of play.

The Executioner scouted quickly through the apartment building, assuring himself there were no more guards stationed in the other units. He returned to the backyard for the cardboard box.

The box was the only change in the "painter" disguise he had worn that afternoon. Neither the Russian Intelligence nor the other people along the streets had given it a second glance. In addition to the tools of a painter's trade, it contained an RPG-7 rocket launcher.

Bolan stepped over the bodies in the hallway and set the box on the floor. Fatigue threatened to overtake him as he pried more of the plywood off the front window. He had gotten little rest during this mission in Russia, and regardless of a man's physical stamina, overwork eventually caught up. He paused, taking a deep breath as he gazed through the window at the warehouse across the street. With a little luck, he might be able to rest later tonight.

But the Executioner had never depended on luck. Fortune was too fickle a lady to rely upon, favoring first good, then evil, with no loyalty to either side. Bolan preferred to put his faith in more predictable, down-to-earth entities like strategy, firepower and planning. But those had their limitations, and whether the warrior trusted in luck or not, he knew she often entered the game and changed the stakes.

Tonight, she had been on the Executioner's side, putting the top New Brotherhood men together under one roof, a roof that stood far enough away from the inhabited buildings to enable it to go up in flames without endangering innocents.

And with Esposito, Furelli, Hernandez and Pool out of the picture, the Executioner's Russian campaign could end.

Armies fizzled quickly without generals.

He would rest then.

Bolan's eyes roamed up and down the street. Three light poles stood between the curb and sidewalk, but the lights on top of two had been smashed by vandals. The third sat just to the right of the warehouse and illuminated a small vacant lot adjacent to the building. Combined with the moon, it gave him good visibility, and he saw several cars in the lot. Now that it was set up, the New Brotherhood was taking no pains to conceal its presence.

Bolan's eyes moved to the sides of the warehouse. In the shadows he saw slight movement. He looked farther down the street. Lights blazed in the windows of the church. The rest of the run-down buildings were dark.

But while he couldn't see them, the Executioner knew more hardmen lurked somewhere in the other abandoned buildings. Esposito and Hernandez's strategy was simple. Lure the "priest" to the warehouse. Then, when he appeared, the rearguard would move in.

Of course, they hadn't counted on a priest having a rocket launcher at his disposal.

Bolan opened the cardboard box and removed the black plastic case. He assembled the weapon, then stripped off the overalls to reveal his blacksuit. Kneeling once more by the window, he waited.

A group of teenaged boys came walking down the deserted street throwing rocks. They took four shots at the streetlight, gave up and moved on.

Fifteen minutes later, the same ZIL Bolan had seen that afternoon rolled to a stop next to the warehouse. Four men left the vehicle and went inside—Esposito, Hernandez, Pool and the man in the brown suit.

The Executioner waited another fifteen minutes to make sure no more New Brotherhood men would arrive, then inserted the rocket and extended the RPG tube through the window. As he took aim, he heard footsteps on the sidewalk outside.

Bolan turned toward the noise. A tall cloaked figure carrying a walking staff sauntered toward the light pole.

The Executioner felt a chill race down his spine as the man passed under the light. In a microsecond, the warrior knew what was about to happen.

Suddenly New Brotherhood gunners moved in from all sides.

Bolan watched as the front door of the warehouse opened and more men streamed out. He saw Hernandez walk forward, say something to the man with the staff, then slap him across the face.

The cloaked man's head snapped back, and the staff fell to the ground. Gunners grabbed the man's arms and dragged him inside the warehouse.

As the front door closed again, the Executioner looked back to where the staff had fallen. Shining at the top was a bright silver Christian cross.

The mark of a Russian Orthodox priest.

Without hesitation Bolan dropped the rocket launcher to the floor and rose to his feet. Lady Luck had arrived again, this time dealing the pat hand to the New Brotherhood. He couldn't use the RPG now without killing the priest, and if he didn't act quickly, the man would be as dead as if he had.

Hurrying out the back door, Bolan sprinted around the block, then cut down an alley behind the warehouse. He had a few minutes, he reasoned, before Esposito and Hernandez perceived their mistake. Until then, their guard would be down. But as soon as they realized they had the wrong man, they'd be on the alert again.

And they'd kill the priest to make sure he didn't talk.

Bolan slowed as he drew abreast of the warehouse, dropping to all fours and crawling behind a row of trash bins. The outside light fixtures had gone the same route as those in the front, but in the moon's bright glow, he saw that three men guarded the rear entrance.

Two of the men stood carelessly in front of the door, while the third sat on a rotting wooden chair in front of a grimy window that led into the rear room.

There was no time to plan.

Bolan drew the suppressed Beretta as he rose from cover. One of the guards turned and spotted the warrior, and clawed for his own weapon. The Beretta spit three hushed rounds, and the hardman was down and out.

As the Executioner swung the pistol toward the door, the other gunners went into action, hauling out their hardware and looking for a target.

The Executioner's next burst of gunfire caught the closer man in the throat, a spray of blood splashing blackly to the ground. His partner reached for him as he collapsed, but another trio of subsonic hollowpoints sent the last man tumbling over his friend.

The Executioner circled the trash bins and raced to the window. He dropped to one knee and stared through the soiled glass to see the priest already tied to a chair in the center of the room. Hernandez, Pool and

Furelli, flanked by two other hardmen, stood around the man in the cloak. Esposito was nowhere to be seen.

Bolan smiled grimly as Furelli slipped into a pair of black leather gloves. Fate had again shuffled the deck. He had a clear aim through the window. He could still take out three of the top men, rescue the priest and come back for Esposito.

As the Executioner slipped a fresh magazine up the butt of the Beretta, he saw Esposito appear suddenly in the doorway that led to the front room. The Mafia don barked a sharp order, and Hernandez and Pool disappeared into the front room. The door closed after them.

So much for luck.

Bolan saw Furelli draw back his right hand. The Mafia hitter launched a haymaker that sent the priest's head snapping back. The chair rocked, then the man in the black cloak tumbled to the floor.

The Executioner stood and took three steps back from the window. He held the Beretta at arm's length in both hands as his feet shifted into a Weaver's stance.

Ray Furelli never knew what hit him.

A 3-round burst splintered through the window into the mafioso's face, obliterating his nose and both eyes. The two other men stared in disbelief for a second.

A deadly second.

That was all the time it took for Bolan to sprint the short distance back to the window, cross his arms over his face and crash through the glass. The Executioner fell into a shoulder roll, springing back to his feet a foot from a surprised gunman holding an Uzi.

Bolan jammed the Beretta into the man's cheek and fired point-blank. The first blast of the 3-round burst propelled the gunner's head back from the barrel. The second two hollowpoints drilled through the charred flesh of the contact wound and sent the man spinning back across the room.

The Executioner turned to the third man who was trying to get a Remington 870 into play. The Executioner tapped the trigger once more. The first two rounds hit the shotgun itself, ricocheting off the receiver as the Brotherhood gunner screamed in pain and dropped the weapon as if it were made of fire.

The third raging 9 mm slug sailed past the falling weapon and lodged in the shrieking gunner's heart.

Bolan pivoted toward the door as it banged open. Two flashily dressed latinos burst into the rear room to try their luck with pistols. The Executioner stitched a neat line of holes over each man's heart, then knelt next to the priest as the pair fell facedown in the doorway.

The warrior holstered the empty Beretta and drew the mammoth .44 Magnum. He laid down a steady line of cover fire through the door with one hand as the other jerked the Mini Tanto from his shoulder harness and sliced the ropes that bound the priest.

Dozens of return rounds blew back through the doorway to the rear room of the warehouse, digging ragged holes along the walls and taking out the shards of broken glass that clung to the edges of the window. But the New Brotherhood hardmen stayed clear of the opening.

A luckless hardman in a striped pullover stuck his head around the corner as the priest rolled free. A 240-grain jacketed hollowpoint popped the man between the eyes, expanded and took the top half of his head with it as it sailed on into the front room.

A stray round ricocheted off the Remington 870 on the floor. Its soft nose flattened and deformed on impact, then changed course and sailed up and into the Executioner's abdomen.

Bolan continued firing through the door, keeping the New Brotherhood hardmen at bay. His left hand fell automatically to the wound, his fingers scraping across the jagged edge of the bullet. The round had lost most of its velocity by the time it reached him.

Lots of blood. But little damage. Bolan pulled it free.

From the corner of his eye, the Executioner saw the priest dive for the Uzi on the floor. The man fumbled with the subgun, then found the safety and a steady stream of autofire blew through the doorway as the Uzi jumped in his unskilled hands.

Bolan shook his head. "Get outside," he ordered. "I'll cover the door." He finished the mag of the Desert Eagle and swung the Striker into play, carpeting the doorway with automatic pellets as the priest crawled out through the window. The man's heart was in the right place, but he was an amateur. As much as he'd like to nail Esposito and Hernandez, here, tonight, the Executioner wouldn't risk the man's life. Luck had dealt her final hand for the evening. And Hernandez and Esposito had won at least one more sunrise.

With a final burst from the automatic scattergun, Bolan turned and dived after the priest. He hit the ground, rolled back to his feet and grabbed the man by the arm. "Let's go," he said and took off down the alley.

THE ATMOSPHERE in President Tachek's office was one of impending doom.

"I cannot believe it," Tachek said flatly. "Alexandr?"

"Yes," Kerensky stated calmly.

The president looked at Bolan who nodded in agreement.

Kerensky stood and walked to the desk, taking a microrecorder from her purse and placing it in front of the president. She pressed a button, and a voice Bolan assumed must be the man in the brown suit came from the machine. "Then this man you call Belasko will be dead by morning. Our problems will be over."

Solomentsev's voice answered. "Sooner or later, Pyotr, Tachek will figure this out. He is not as foolish as you think."

The other man laughed. "Perhaps not. But he will be foolish enough to trust you until it is too late—for the American, *and* himself."

Tachek's face turned scarlet. His features twisted into a grotesque mask of rage as the tape played on, and the man in the brown suit threatened to expose Solomentsev's alcoholism if the young man didn't continue to cooperate.

When the tape had finished, the machine clicked off and the room fell once more into an uneasy silence. Finally Tachek took a deep breath to compose himself and turned to Kerensky. "Colonel, please accept my apology." He looked across the desk at Bolan. "I do not understand this. How did Solomentsev deceive me so well on the polygraph?"

Bolan shrugged. "There are a number of ways," he said. "But my guess is—"

The door opened suddenly and Alexandr Solomentsev entered the office. "You sent for me, Mr. President?" The aide's gaze fell on Bolan and he drew in his breath, suddenly realizing without being told what was going on.

Tachek stood up behind his desk and walked to his aide. The president was a good six inches shorter than Solomentsev as he stared up into the young man's frightened eyes. "I know the answer to why," he said. "My only question is how, Alexandr," he said. "How were you able to pass the polygraph exam?"

Tears formed in the corners of Solomentsev's eyes. "It was administered before Leskov began talking to me, Mr. President. I never intended to—"

Tachek nodded. "Yes, Leskov is no fool. He would have known that I would test you. So he waited." The president's face fell. He looked suddenly ten years older. Tired. "The best deception is always innocence," he said softly.

The tears overflowed and began dripping down Solomentsev's cheeks. "Mr. President," he said. "Please believe me . . ."

Slowly the anger returned to Tachek's face. He drew his hand back suddenly and slapped his aide across the face. "You have disgraced me, your country and yourself," he ground out through clenched teeth. "This is the only moment since democracy came to this great land that I regret it. The torture chambers of the czars would have been too good for you, Alexandr."

Tachek turned on his heel and strode back to the phone on his desk. Picking up the receiver, he said, "Send me three guards immediately," then slammed the instrument back into its cradle.

The young aide began to weep openly. He fell to his knees on the carpet. "Mr. President, please. I can explain...."

Tachek turned the other way.

Bolan cleared his throat. "Mr. President," he said, "I'd like to make a suggestion." When Tachek turned, the Executioner went on. "First, cancel the guards. The last thing we need is Solomentsev in prison."

The president and Kerensky turned to him, staring as if Bolan had lost his mind.

"At least for now," the warrior went on. "When I'm finished here, what you do with him's up to you."

Tachek crossed his arms and leaned forward on his desk. "Go on."

"Let's look at the whole picture. As far as Leskov and the New Brotherhood know, Solomentsev's cover is still intact. Which means we can use him, Mr. President. We can use Solomentsev to set a trap that they have no chance of escaping." He tapped the bandage under his shirt. "Esposito and Hernandez know I got shot last night. There was a lot of blood, and they have no way of knowing the wound was superficial and just happened to be in a bloody area of the body. That's the bait we'll use to reel them in."

The president's eyes flickered with interest. Bolan turned to Kerensky. "I'll need some help," he said. "Spetsnaz is under RMI command, right?"

Kerensky nodded.

"Then get me a hundred crackerjack troops—men and women. And find a small hospital that can be evacuated before nightfall."

Bolan turned back to the president, who stared at him, waiting. As the Executioner explained the rest of his plan, Niklai Tachek began to smile again.

DON JOSEPH ESPOSITO looked out the rear window of the ZIL. In an identical vehicle next to him he saw Leskov and Solomentsev.

Esposito turned to the front. A block down the street, just past the Central Palace of Pioneers, he saw the lights outside the emergency room of the Gavilova Trauma Clinic.

Two shadowy figures passed through the doors into the hospital.

"That makes thirty-eight inside so far," Jake Pool commented.

"Another ten minutes, they'll all be inside," Hernandez added.

Esposito ignored their small talk. Conflicting emotions rushed through the old man's heart, making him wonder how he really felt at this moment. Ray Furelli had not only been his top gun, the man had been his son-in-law—his daughter's husband, and the father of three of his grandchildren. Furelli's body was now on ice in some Russian funeral home. The emotion that death produced was simple to understand—sorrow.

But what confused Esposito was the other emotion that coursed through his veins. Joy. Pure, unadulterated joy. He was about to do something hundreds of men had failed to do over the years.

Kill Mack Bolan.

Careful, Esposito admonished himself. It wouldn't be smart to be too confident yet. Other men thought they had Bolan trapped. Those men were dead.

In spite of the warning, Esposito felt the joy surge through his heart. Yes, many men had tried to kill the Executioner. And they had died. But finally, the reign of the man known among the Families as Mack the Bastard was about to come to an end.

Bolan was wounded. In the hospital. Helpless.

That information had come straight from the Russian president's office, from the president's top aide.

As he continued to watch the hospital, Esposito felt Hernandez lean forward. The Colombian lifted the bottle of Chianti from the floorboard and unwrapped the plastic covering from a package of paper cups. He poured wine into one of the cups and handed it to Esposito. "It is almost over, Don Joseph," he said, beaming. "Let us drink to it."

A sudden fury overtook the mobster. He turned, took the wine, then threw it in Hernandez's face. He saw Pool's hand drop to his side, but before the gunfighter could draw, Hernandez said, "No, Jake. Furelli was family."

Pool shrugged and turned back to the front.

"That's right," Esposito said. "You want to be the one who explains that to my daughter? Ray Furelli was a better man than you'll ever be, Hernandez. And he's dead because of your incompetence."

Hernandez opened his mouth to speak, then turned away, the wine still dripping down his cheeks.

Esposito's ulcer flared. He rolled down the window for fresh air, and the wet odor of the river just to the north flooded the car. He watched three more men enter the hospital through a side entrance. The sight calmed him.

Yes, soon it would be over.

The old man's mind drifted back over the years to old friends who had fallen to the Executioner's guns. Friends he wished could be with him tonight to see Bolan finally go down. Men like Sergio Frenchi and Julian DiGeorge, the Talifero brothers and Arnesto "Arnie Farmer" Castiglione. Unlike Hernandez, these were men who had fought the Executioner, men who could appreciate the magnitude of what Joseph Esposito was about to accomplish.

Esposito heard the first drops of rain hit the roof of the car, then a soft spray blew in on the cold wind. Reluctantly he rolled the window back up. The rain came down harder, but he could still see the outlines of the men as they continued to enter the hospital every few minutes, alone or in pairs.

The mafioso welcomed the rain. With any luck it would wash the blood of the Executioner from the streets, and the memory of the man from his brain.

THE FACE OF THE MAN who pushed the meal cart into room 433 looked like it had seen a boxing ring or two. It had. Spetsnaz Corporal Pavel Smelyakov had been the middleweight champion of the 2nd Military Directorate of Russian Military Intelligence. What Smelyakov hadn't seen until now, at least through the eyes of an orderly, was a hospital.

From his bed against the wall, Bolan watched the stocky man throw the cover off the tray and lift the AK-74. "There are close to seventy men inside the building already," Smelyakov said. "They are covering the doors, windows—all exits to prevent your escape." He grinned. "Are you planning to escape, Mr. Belasko?"

"Hadn't planned on it."

"*They* are the ones who will be trying to escape," Kerensky said, rising from her chair at the edge of the bed. She smoothed the wrinkles from the front of her white nurse's skirt with her hands, then lifted the blood-pressure cup from the table and wrapped it around Bolan's arm. Pumping the bulb, she read the gauge and shook her head. "My heart is ready to leap from my chest," she said. "Does *nothing* disturb you?"

"I guess familiarity breeds contempt."

The walkie-talkie on the table suddenly blared. "Colonel, approximately forty men are moving toward the elevators and stairways."

Kerensky keyed the mike. "Affirmative. Keep us posted." She reached under her skirt, yanked a Makarov from a thigh holster and covered it with a towel.

Smelyakov primed the bolt on the AK-74, stepped into the washroom and closed the door.

The Executioner heard footsteps in the hall. A man dressed in a smartly cut American business suit appeared suddenly in the doorway. He held a bulky potted plant in his hands. "Belasko?" he asked as he walked through the door.

Bolan nodded.

Another man appeared next to him. The two walked toward the bed, smiling as three more men entered behind them.

The smiles faded as they reached Bolan's side. "From the New Brotherhood," the man with the plant said, his hand suddenly shooting into the thick leaves.

The sheet rose slightly next to the Executioner as the New Brotherhood hardman's hand came out of the plant gripping a compact Smith & Wesson 669. Then the sheet began to jump as the deafening roar of automatic 12-gauge explosions filled the room.

The Striker's stubby barrel poked through the singed cloth as the men next to the bed fell to the floor.

Bolan threw the sheet to the side. He saw Kerensky take out one of the backup gunners with a double-tap from her Makarov as the man groped for the MAC-10 under his coat.

The bathroom door flew open. The other two backup gunners fell under a deadly cross fire as Smelyakov's AK-74 jumped in his hands.

The Executioner leaped to his feet and tore the hospital gown away, revealing the combat blacksuit. As the clamor in the room died down, he heard the gunfire in the hall.

Racing into the corridor, Bolan saw Spetsnaz personnel dressed as doctors, nurses, transcribers and orderlies wielding rifles and submachine guns. New Brotherhood hardmen—Mafia, cartel, RI and Russian hoods-for-hire—returned the fire and scrambled for cover behind whatever hospital equipment was available.

As he sprinted toward the nurses' station at the end of the hall, Bolan saw a patient on a gurney suddenly rise. The man sent a full-auto burst of fire from his Stechkin APS into a renegade Russian Intelligence agent. A mafioso toting an Uzi stepped from the doorway of a waiting room as the Stechkin ran dry and took aim.

Bolan dropped the subgunner with a continuous line of buckshot.

The Executioner raced on.

As he came to the staircase just past the nurses' station, the door suddenly opened and two Russian street punks carrying sawed-off shotguns dropped to their knees, firing. Bolan's weapon proved superior, as did his aim. The Striker drove the gunners back into the stairwell and sent them tumbling down the steps in a flurry of blood.

As the autoshotgun locked open empty, a sudden volley of rounds flew over the Executioner's head. Drawing the Desert Eagle, he dived back over the counter of the nurses' station and dropped to his knees to reload. Shoving more 12-gauge shells into the Striker, he saw a Spetsnaz soldier in surgeon's greens take two rounds in the chest.

Leaning around the counter, Bolan traced the angle of trajectory and saw a New Brotherhood gunner brandishing an Uzi at the end of a side corridor. A stroke of the Striker's refreshened trigger sent the gunner sprawling onto his back, dead.

The Executioner sprinted back to the stairs. He leaped over the two street punks, down one landing, and heard the same sounds of fire on the third floor as he passed. As he reached the entrance to the second floor, an RI agent firing a Kalashnikov burst through the door.

Bolan tapped a round into his abdomen. The man fell to the floor screaming.

As the sounds of automatic fire thudded dully through the steel fire door to the second floor, Bolan walked slowly forward. The man continued to shriek in agony. Gut wounds meant a slow, painful death, but the traitorous agent wouldn't suffer long. As soon as he'd told Bolan where the New Brotherhood's top dogs were hiding, the Executioner would give him a mercy round.

Kneeling over the dying man, Bolan said, "Make it easy on yourself. Where are Esposito and Hernandez and Pool?"

"In the car," the man gasped out. "Behind the emergency room."

Bolan leaned back. He started to reach for the Desert Eagle, then stopped as the man suddenly stiffened, then closed his eyes.

As he started to rise, the Executioner heard heavy boots on the landing behind him.

THROUGH THE POURING RAIN, Mario Hernandez watched the strange flashes of light that kept appearing in the hospital windows.

"What do you suppose that is, Don Joseph?" he asked.

The mafioso shrugged. "Who the hell knows? Maybe some kind a treatment or something. You know, X rays."

"Yeah, maybe," Hernandez said. "But you'd think it would just be in one part of the building, wouldn't you?" He looked out the window to the other ZIL parked next to them. Leskov and Solomentsev sat watching the lights.

"Who knows? Relax. We got almost a hundred gunners in there and Bolan's wounded bad. You saw the blood."

The emergency-room door suddenly opened and a ragged figure staggered out into the rain. Hernandez watched in horror as the man drew closer. Blood streamed from his mutilated face. The man's hands gripped his stomach as he moved toward the ZILs like something out of a horror movie.

"Son of a bitch," Pool said suddenly. "It's Pistola."

Juan Martinez fell against the rear window on Hernandez's side of the car. His fingers clawed down the glass leaving trails of blood as he slid to his knees, then slithered out of sight beneath the car.

"Let's get the hell out of here, Hernandez," Esposito said suddenly. "Something's gone wrong."

"I agree," Hernandez said. "Jake, let's..."

Hernandez's voice trailed off as he realized he was talking to an empty front seat.

Through the rain, he saw Pool swaggering toward the hospital.

Esposito leaned forward over the seat. "Shit. The asshole took the keys with him." He flopped back.

"It's all right," Hernandez said. "If anything happens, Leskov's car is here. Besides, like you said, Don Joseph. We've got Bolan almost a hundred to one."

"Yeah. Maybe."

BOLAN HEARD THE HAMMERS notch back as his hand fell toward the Desert Eagle.

"Make another move and it'll be your last," the voice behind him said. "Raise your hands, stand up and turn around. Slow."

The warrior did as he was told. He turned to see Jake Pool and the gaping bores of the twin Colt Single Action Army revolvers.

Pool's grin seemed to cover his face. "Who are you?" he asked.

"I think you know the answer to that," Bolan told him. "I left some calling cards along the way."

Pool threw back his head and laughed. "You did indeed, didn't you? I wondered at first. You sneakin' around in the bushes and disguisin' yourself. Those were *some* calling cards, all right."

Bolan frowned. He had meant the marksman's medals.

"Thought for a while you might be Jack McCall," Pool went on. "But you showed a little too much sand for that weasel. Then, after that gambling thing in Saint Pete's, I knew it was you." The smile began to fade. "You was gambling when old John Selman finally blew your brains out down El Paso way, wasn't you, Wes?"

Bolan stood staring at the man. Wes? El Paso? What was Pool talking about?

Pool's eyes suddenly narrowed. "Let's get one thing clear before I kill you, Wes," he went on. "You *never* faced me down in Abilene like you told folks. *You* know it. *I* know it. But I want to hear you say it. Wild Bill never backed down from nobody."

Sudden comprehension dawned. Wes—John Wesley Hardin. Pool thought he was the Texas gunman legend who claimed he got the drop on Wild Bill Hickok, then let him go. Hardin had been a gambler, and if the Executioner wasn't mistaken, he had been killed in El Paso by the local constable.

"Go on," Pool prodded. "Say it, Wes."

"Oh, I backed you down all right," Bolan said. "But that's because you were always smarter than you looked, Bill. You knew I was faster than you, and you weren't too crazy about dying."

Hatred flooded Pool's eyes as the mustache drooped below his chin. "You're a lyin' son of a bitch, Hardin," he snarled.

"Prove it," Bolan said. "Prove you're faster than me."

Slowly Pool's thumbs rose to the hammers of the Colts and eased them down over the firing pins. He holstered the weapons and reached into his pocket, his eyes never leaving the Executioner's. "When it hits, Wes," he said. "When it hits." He flipped the coin into the air.

As the coin struck the stairwell's concrete floor, Bolan's hand streaked to his hip. His fingers curled around the grips of the Desert Eagle.

In front of him he saw Pool slap leather on both sides.

The .44 Magnum floated from the nylon speed rig like a feather in the Executioner's fist. His thumb found the safety.

Twin blurs of silver flashed before Bolan's eyes as his index finger entered the trigger guard and pulled.

Three mighty roars split the silence in the stairwell. The Executioner heard rounds hit the concrete walls, then ricochet around the tiny area.

Then Jake Pool toppled to his knees, blood pouring from the corners of his mouth. His eyes stared up wildly at the Executioner. "McCall?" he said, and fell forward onto his face.

THE RAIN FELL on Bolan's head and shoulders as he left the hospital by the emergency-room exit. He reached into the pockets of his blacksuit, reloading the Striker as he walked down the street toward the ZILs in the parking lot. As he neared, one of the engines started. The car spun its wheels over the wet pavement as it tore off toward the exit to the lot.

A dull thud came from inside the vehicle, and a moment later the ZIL crashed head-on into a streetlight.

Bolan stopped beside the other car and opened the door. "Get out," he ordered the men inside.

Esposito stepped out of the vehicle and leaned against the fender, followed by Hernandez.

The Colombian drug dealer forced a grin. "We can do business, Bolan. We can make you rich."

The mafioso shook his head. "Don't waste your breath. You don't have much left."

"Sure I do," Hernandez retorted, but the quaver in his voice betrayed him. "Bolan's a reasonable man. He'll give us a chance. Won't you?"

The Executioner stared at the man. "What kind of chance do you want, Hernandez? You want a chance like the one the people who buy your dope have? One like the girls had at the Skyline Resort? On the ship?"

"Any chance, Bolan. Any chance at all." As soon as the words left his mouth, Hernandez clawed inside his jacket, hoping to unleather his pistol. No way.

The Striker roared in a long, continuous burst, the muzzle-flash lighting up the night. Hernandez died with his hand still inside his jacket. Esposito's body slid against the car and stopped in a sitting position. Lifeless eyes remained open, staring accusingly at the Executioner.

Bolan walked to the street light and pried open the front door of the other ZIL. The front of the car had caved into the front seat, and in the wreckage, he saw Solomentsev unconscious on the floor. The president's former right-hand man had a six-inch gash in his forehead where he'd hit the windshield on impact. A Makarov 7.62 mm pistol was still gripped in the young man's hand.

Pyotr Leskov lay over the steering wheel, blood seeping from the bullet hole in the side of his head.

Solomentsev was still breathing.

Leskov wasn't.

Bolan rested the Striker over his shoulder as he hurried back to the hospital. Kerensky walked forward to meet him.

"It's over," he said softly.

WELCOME TO

# JAMES AXLER

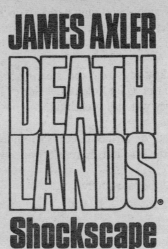

## DEATH LANDS®

### Shockscape

**A shockscape with a view—
and the danger is free.**

Ryan and his band of warrior survivalists chart a perilous journey
across the desolate Rocky Mountains. Their mission: Deliver the hired
killers of a small boy to his avenging father.

**In the Deathlands, survival is a gamble. Death is the only sure bet.**

Omega Force is caught dead center in a brutal Middle East war in the next episode of

# OMEGA

## by PATRICK F. ROGERS

In Book 2: **ZERO HOUR**, the Omega Force is dispatched on a search-and-destroy mission to eliminate enemies of the U.S. seeking revenge for Iraq's defeat in the Gulf—enemies who will use any means necessary to trigger a full-scale war.

With capabilities unmatched by any other paramilitary organization in the world, Omega Force is a special ready-reaction anti-terrorist strike force composed of the best commandos and equipment the military has to offer.

# THE FREEDOM TRILOGY

## Join Mack Bolan's fight for freedom in the freedom trilogy...

Beginning in June 1993, Gold Eagle presents a special three-book in-line continuity featuring Mack Bolan, the Executioner, along with ABLE TEAM and PHOENIX FORCE, as they face off against a communist dictator. A dictator with far-reaching plans to gain control of the troubled Baltic state area and whose ultimate goal is world supremacy. The fight for freedom starts in June with THE EXECUTIONER #174: Battle Plan, continues in THE EXECUTIONER #175: Battle Ground, and concludes in August with the longer 352-page Mack Bolan novel Battle Force.

Available at your favorite retail outlets in
June through to August.

FT93-1